CW01459793

THE IMPERATIVE OF DESIRE

The Imperative of Desire

ELENA GRAF

PURPLE HAND PRESS

Purple Hand Press,
www.purplehandpress.com

© 2021 by Elena Graf
All rights reserved. No part of this book may be reproduced, scanned, or distributed in
any printed or electronic form without permission.

This is a work of fiction. Names, characters, places and incidents are the product of the
author's imagination or used fictitiously, and any resemblance to actual persons, living or
dead, businesses, institutions, companies, events, or locales is entirely coincidental.

Trade Paperback Edition
ISBN-13 978-1-953195-00-5
Kindle Edition
ISBN-13 978-1-953195-01-2
ePub Edition
ISBN-13 978-1-953195-02-9

Cover design by Corrie Kuipers
Cover painting by Leon Kamir Kaufmann (1872-1933) This work is in the public domain
in its country of origin and other countries and areas where the copyright term is the
author's life plus 70 years or fewer.
Editor: Elaine Mattern

10.29.2023

THE GERMAN EMPIRE - 1910

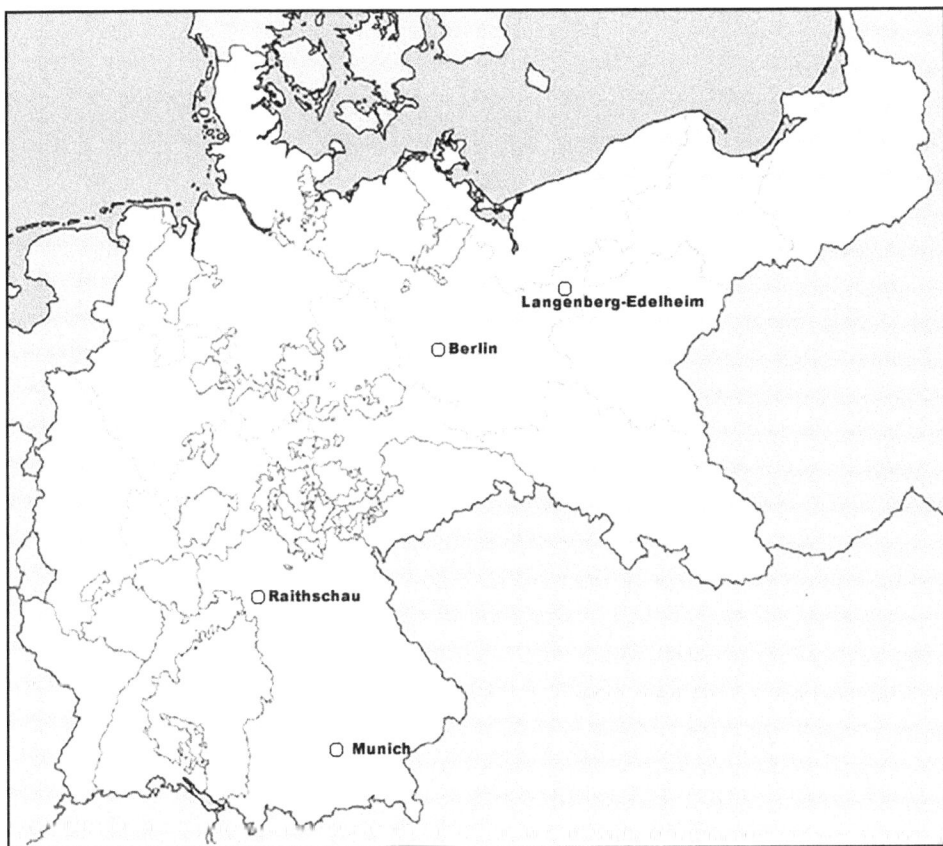

Langenberg-Edelheim

Berlin

Raithschau

Munich

To my parents, who taught me there is always a story in history.

1

Yellow finches were dancing over the meadow when the old driver's attention faltered. The carriage lurched as it pitched into a rut. In an instant, Grandmother flung her arm across the seat, slamming me against the leather backboard so hard that my ribs ached.

"Are you all right, my darling?" Grandmother asked anxiously. "I feared you would fall." I nodded to assure her, while secretly rubbing the spot where her arm had squeezed my chest. She laid a soft hand that smelled of rosewater on my cheek. "That's my good girl." Her hand fluttered up to her hat, as big around as a wagon wheel, but a silk scarf along with a multitude of hat pins had kept it secure.

"My, that gave me a start." She called to the driver, "Zimmel! Mind the road, will you!"

"Yes, *Gnädige*. My apologies," the old man called over his shoulder.

My eyes sought the yellow finches, but they'd had their fill of thistle seeds and had moved on, replaced by sparrows picking out the centers of the dried daisies and coreopsis. Grandmother let the wildflowers grow along the road because they were pretty. At home, the mowers cut them down, leaving only pointed stubble that I could feel through the thin soles of my shoes. At that time of year, they would be cutting the second hay, but I wouldn't be there to watch.

The baby had died within a week of his birth. Afterwards, the halls of Schloss Edelheim were silent except for the sound of muffled weeping from my mother's rooms. Father asked me not to sing so loudly and to play elsewhere. Fortunately, Grandmother had rescued me from the gloom.

The nuns opened the convent gate as our carriage approached. The towering stone walls of Obberoth blocked the sun, creating a chill as their shadow crept over our carriage.

"Do you remember coming here?" asked Grandmother as we entered the courtyard.

I shook my head dramatically, swinging my blond braids. In fact,

I vaguely remembered the towers and the bumpy ride through the cobblestone courtyard. My father had brought me to this place when I was very young.

"The headmistress here is my sister. She is your godmother," Grandmother explained.

"Tante Veronika is my godmother," I corrected. I was fond of my beautiful, red-haired cousin, who always let me sit on her lap.

"Yes, Veronika is also your godmother…at your father's insistence." Grandmother's tone indicated she did not entirely approve, but then she smiled. "What a lucky girl you are to have two godmothers! The bishop had to give permission because your grandaunt is a nun."

"What's a nun?" I asked.

Grandmother looked momentarily perplexed. "A nun is a woman who devotes her life to God," Grandmother finally said. "Nuns never marry and live with other women in order to pray and be of service."

I struggled to make sense of this. I knew that mother and father were married. They often had loud arguments that sent me scurrying into my hiding places. The cavernous space under the dining table in the great hall was my favorite. Perhaps foregoing marriage was a good thing.

A young nun greeted us as we alighted from the carriage. She bowed to Grandmother, and we followed her heels through the corridors of the convent school until we arrived at a door. After only one knock, the iron hinges squealed, and the door opened. The woman standing in the doorway was even taller than Grandmother, who was taller than any woman I knew, even Mother. Clad all in black, she made a severe impression. Yet her eyes, the blue of Alpine ice, were merry and kind.

"Welcome back, Katje," the woman said, kissing Grandmother on each cheek. "And here is little Margarethe!" She knelt so that she could speak directly to my face. As a small person, I appreciated this gesture toward equality, but also found it curious. "Welcome to Obberoth, my dear girl," she said and reached to embrace me. Her enthusiasm frightened me. I hid in Grandmother's skirts. Her crinoline petticoat made a crinkling sound as I pressed closer to her thigh. "Go on, Grethe. Stand up straight."

Grandmother reached down to stroke my hair, while I suspiciously regarded the woman in black. "This is your grandaunt, Sister Scholastica, my sister. Say 'good day,' to your *Tante* like a big girl."

The woman rose from her knees in one smooth motion like a giant raven taking flight. "She's shy, of course," she said, giving me a little smile of affection. "She has no idea who I am. We must become better acquainted."

The indulgent smile and the warmth in her voice encouraged me to leave the protection of my grandmother's skirts and have a look at my grandaunt. She was so tall my neck ached from looking up.

"She's a clever child. Go on, Grethe," said Grandmother, nudging me forward, "show my sister what you've learned."

I understood the time to perform had arrived, yet try as I might, I was unable to recite the text I'd been encouraged to prepare. My mind went completely blank.

"Give her something to read, Klärchen," urged Grandmother, realizing I was flummoxed.

My grandaunt turned to a bookshelf and took down a leather-clad volume. It was not, as I had hoped, something simple, like the Bible or the *Tales of the Brothers Grimm.* No, she had chosen Schlegel's translation of Shakespeare's *As You Like It.*

Tante turned her pale eyes on me, which caused me to squirm. "Read, child," she ordered in a firm voice.

Once the trembling ceased and my voice was steady, I opened the book and read where my eyes fell: "I met the duke yesterday and had much question with him. He asked me of what parentage I was; I told him as good as he, so he laughed and let me go."

A smile of satisfaction spread across my grandaunt's face. Evidently, my performance had pleased her. "How old did you say?" she asked Grandmother, but her eyes never left mine.

"Five years, this September. She's very tall for her age." Grandmother took a piece of licorice out of her purse. Besides the taste, I liked that licorice turned my tongue black. When I stuck it out to demonstrate, the maids' cries of false horror delighted me.

"She adores mathematics," my grandmother continued, finally removing her hat. She placed the hat pins in the brim and laid the hat aside. "When she became bored with arithmetic, Karl began teaching her geometry."

"Indeed," said my grandaunt, peering at me. She removed a piece of foolscap from a box on her desk, dipped her pen into the inkwell, and drew a figure on the paper. "What is this, my little Margarethe?"

"A circle."

"Very good, my pet. Now can you tell me how big the circle is?"

"May I have a ruler and a pencil?" Nodding, she took these items from her desk and handed them to me. I drew a chord in the circle. "I also need a compass," I murmured, wishing I had thought of this sooner. *Tante* studied me for a moment, but she opened her desk again and found a compass. I drew overlapping circles from the chord's points of intersection. "This is the diameter," I explained.

"And why is that useful, Margarethe?" asked *Tante*, leaning closer.

"The outside of the circle is this measure multiplied by Pi." I recited the number to twenty positions after the decimal. I could have gone on. Grandfather had explained that this unusual number went on forever, which I understood but did not find useful. Tante nodded, evidently pleased. After measuring the diameter and calculating the circumference, I announced, "The circle is 4.3472 centimeters."

"Very good," said *Tante*, handing me a sugar biscuit. I wolfed it down like an animal. She gave me another and poured me a glass of milk from a large earthenware pitcher.

Meanwhile, I could see my grandmother was trying to conceal a smile of triumph. "She also reads Latin," she revealed, "and a little Greek."

"Does she now?" *Tante* turned in my direction and caught me licking the sugar crystals off the biscuit.

I could tell she was curious about the Latin. She took a book down from the shelf. "Eat your biscuit, Margarethe. I would like to hear you read something." I crammed the biscuit into my mouth, and she handed the book to me. Fortunately, she had chosen something basic—Julius Caesar's account of the Gallic Wars, the primer of every budding Latinist. With a long, elegant finger, she indicated where I should commence reading. Of course, anyone who knows the sound of the characters can moronically reproduce them.

"What does it mean?" asked *Tante*, her hands vanishing under the front flap of her uniform.

I translated the passage into German as best I could: "When informed of these matters, Caesar, fearing the fickle disposition of the Gauls, who easily take positions, yet are much inclined to change, decided that nothing was to be entrusted to them."

My grandmother and my grandaunt regarded one another in wordless communication. I was given another sugar biscuit. While I ate it, I reflected that my father trained his dogs in this manner, with bits of dried meat so they would sit and heel at their master's will. Indeed, my grandmother stroked my head as if I were a puppy.

"She is much more than clever," said my grandaunt in an excited voice. "You must allow me to teach her."

I liked that idea. I looked expectantly at my grandmother, but she shook her head. "Not yet, Klara. Her father wants to keep her at home and has decided she will have a tutor." Grandmother continued to pet me as if I were her Affenpinscher. "Fritz has already selected a school in England… when the time comes."

"Why not here with us?" my grandaunt asked indignantly.

My grandmother sighed. "Let him do as he wishes. You know how stubborn he is."

"But she will be bored in an ordinary school."

"Perhaps, but she will also learn to be like other girls…unlike you."

My grandaunt compressed her lips into a straight line, which is how I realized how much this remark had wounded her.

"You will have her soon enough." Grandmother patted her arm. "Be patient, dear."

Before we left, my grandaunt knelt so that her eyes were level with mine to say her farewells. As I studied her pale eyes, I realized that I had finally met someone who understood me.

~

"She stinks," said my mother, wrinkling her nose as I came near. My father chuckled and pulled me closer. I realized it was his boots that stank, fresh from the muck in the stall. Despite a ride and a tramp through the field, they still shone like black mirrors. Before we had gone out for our ride, he had demonstrated the proper way to polish boots with a bit of spittle in the shoe wax. I took great pleasure in spitting into the tin. My father commended me on my enthusiasm for this part of the task.

"Send for her nurse to bathe her," added my mother, never looking up from her needlework.

My father winked at me. "Come, Grethe. Let's go outside. Your mother doesn't appreciate the scents of the stable." I found it difficult to imagine anything better. My father had put me in a saddle as soon as I could sit erect. My pony was my prize possession.

Although my mother was an expert rider, she seldom accompanied us on our jaunts, whereas Father would look for occasions to be with me, whether for a ride or to play with the new puppies from his prize Weimaraners. He often stole me from the nursery and would sit me on his lap while he cut up an orange or an apple with his little gold-handled folding knife. He gave me his beer to sip and make mustaches with the foam. Sometimes he let me sit on his shoulders and comb his hair with a tortoise-shell comb while he read to me. He never protested when I used a little saliva to make the combing easier, although it made his hair as stiff as my starched pinafore.

A footman brought Father his shoes. He took off his smelly boots, and we went out to the terrace that overlooked the south garden. Father sat me on the wicker couch. When he took a seat beside me, the wicker creaked a bit in protest. He was very tall, but graceful for someone of his height. His hair was still nearly as blond as mine. Like the Kaiser, he waxed his mustache so that it turned up at the ends. Once, I filched the pot of wax from his dressing room and used it to stick paper butterflies on the windows of the nursery. Father was stern when he discovered my thievery, but on that occasion, he only patted my behind.

He searched inside his tweed hunting coat, found a butterscotch, and handed it to me. While I happily sucked on the sweet, he filled his pipe from his tobacco pouch. I liked that scent even better than horses. It was aromatic of leather, bay rum, and whiskey. I only knew how whiskey smelled because I had once taken the crystal stopper out of the decanter and had a sniff.

Father took his time lighting his pipe. The ritual intrigued me. It began with filling the pipe with tobacco, carefully tamping it down with little silver tools, and then lighting it with a match struck on the sole of his shoe. The tobacco glowed bright orange for a moment. When my father left off drawing air, it began to smoke.

"How marvelous to be at home," he said with a sigh. "I wish I could remain longer."

"Why must you go?" I asked.

He put his arm around my shoulder and gave me a little squeeze. "Because it is my duty."

"What is duty?" I asked, sitting up straight because I sensed this was important.

"It is something that one must do because it is the right thing. Mostly, it is something you would not want to do, given the choice."

My father was a soldier. He had once explained that soldiers obeyed orders, whether they wished to or not. I reasoned that duty was like an order, but if so, whence did it come? My father laughed when I spoke my deduction aloud. "Duty is something one learns so well that there is never a question. It is inside you," he said, poking my tummy until I giggled.

I badgered my father on this subject. He said that when I was old enough, he would give me Kant to read.

"Read it to me, Papa. Then you can explain."

"I would rather break my leg than read Kant again," he said, making a face. Fortunately, he laughed, or I would have thought he was serious.

"Why must you be in the army?

"Because we all must be of service. It wouldn't do to sit about all day. A career is important."

"For girls too?"

He frowned. "Well, yes. I suppose it's important for girls too."

"I shall be a soldier like you when I grow up," I proclaimed.

My father was kind enough not to laugh. "No, my dear. Girls cannot be soldiers."

I considered this with a frown. It was the first time I had perceived the limits of my sex.

~

With great ceremony, my mother bequeathed her dolls with fancy dresses to me. They remained untouched, sitting on the tuffet in the nursery. When I passed by, their vacant stares and painted, rosebud mouths unnerved me. I glared in return. When I lay down to sleep, I turned my back to them to block the light from the window reflected in their lifeless glass eyes.

One day, out of pure curiosity, I pulled off their pretty heads and found they were completely hollow inside. My nurse was horrified when she found the decapitated dolls lying on the nursery floor and ran to fetch my mother.

"Margarethe! What have you done!" Mother shrieked at the sight of the headless dolls. "These were the greatest treasure of my girlhood." She sat down on the tuffet and began to cry. I pitied her, weeping over such useless things.

"I'm sorry, Mother," I murmured, tugging at her skirts. I was only sorry to have caused her pain but not to discover the dolls' terrible secret. I wondered if she knew it too.

Eventually, Mother mopped her face with her lace handkerchief and trained her eyes on me. I glanced down at my dress and soiled pinafore. No doubt, my hair was a tangle. Nurse often had to yank the brush through it to get out the knots, sometimes burrs from running through the fields with the servants' boys. Mother gazed at me, clearly telegraphing her disapproval. I'd long known that I was a disappointment to her, despite resembling her in every way. I had her tall, lanky build, her blond hair, and her dark blue eyes. Everyone else in the family had eyes as pale as ice.

I waited for Mother to say something, but she merely sighed and left. She sent the miserable dolls to be repaired. When they returned, looking no worse for their decapitation, I pointedly ignored them. I preferred to play with Father's jack-in-a-box and his multicolored wooden blocks, which I used to build forts and castles. Grandfather gave me a miniature stable complete with miniature animals. My mother was appalled to find the bull posed to rut a cow, a scene I had frequently observed in the barnyard. After that, she unsuccessfully tried to confine me to the house, but I always managed to get away and return with burrs in my hair.

Fortunately, there was one area in which my interests and Mother's intersected. She was an accomplished pianist and widely known for her amateur recitals. For my fourth birthday, she gave me a miniature piano, brought at great expense from Vienna. I was not a prodigy at music, composing symphonies in the cradle like the divine Mozart, but I had a good ear and could reproduce melodies after a single hearing. Mother said that my long fingers were ideal in a budding pianist.

Reading music was even more interesting than reading words. In my imagination, the little black notes on the score danced as I played.

"*Mutti*, why can we only hear music while it is being played?" I asked one day.

"Oh, Margarethe, what nonsense you say sometimes. Why do you ask such questions?"

"Because I want to know. I can always see a flower or a dog. But music disappears when the notes fade away."

Mother shook her head in disapproval. "You are a most peculiar child."

My godmother, Lady Veronika, who often came to walk with my father in the garden and then afterwards disappeared with him into the little boathouse on the lake, often needed to soothe my injured feelings. When she found me weeping in a corner after my mother had offered her opinion about my oddness, she allowed me to climb into her lap. She stroked my hair and kissed me. "You are not peculiar, my darling. You are *exceptional*."

Exceptional.

I liked the sound of that.

∼

Mother's remedy for my peculiarity was Mlle. Celine de Courcelles, who had descended from an old French noble family and had been educated in the best convent schools. My new governess' duties were to teach me French and how to behave like a lady, a goal I did not share, but Mademoiselle had several advantages in pursuing her agenda. She was quite handsome, and I adored the sound of her voice when she spoke her own tongue. The first French words I learned were her pet name for me: "*Petite Sauvage.*" I melted into a puddle of cooperation whenever she said it.

I expressed my devotion by composing doggerel in which I extolled her "tiny teeth" and "limpid, pale hair." Mlle. Celine took no offense at these unwitting insults and seemed quite charmed.

"You are a poet, my darling," she would say and kiss me.

Thus encouraged, I composed more bad verse. She always listened intently and with a completely serious face.

She wore a delicious scent that compelled me to follow her everywhere. I sniffed the air like a dog when she passed. At night, I would slip out of the nursery and into her bed. Although she clucked her tongue, she never sent me away. I snuggled against her soft breasts and inhaled her intoxicating cologne. She had little need to discipline her "little savage," having conquered me with love.

About this time, Grandfather had begun to bend Papa's ear concerning my education. While it amused him to teach me mathematics, Latin, and Greek, he knew there should be a more disciplined approach.

Father assigned his adjutant, Lieutenant von Scheppel, to the special duty of instructing me in German, history, and geography. Every day, for two hours, he sat very straight in his chair and held forth on such mind-numbing topics as the mountain ranges in China. While he did, I entertained myself by inventing heroic stories in my head. That is not to say that I didn't learn anything from Scheppel. He taught me how to stand at attention, march and crisply salute. Despite my father's discouraging words, I was still determined to become a soldier.

While I was learning to march, Mlle. Celine noticed Lieutenant von Scheppel's handsome looks. Eventually, there was a change in her figure. Shortly after that, both Scheppel and Mlle. Celine vanished.

~

After Mlle. Celine left, Father decided I knew enough French, and it was time for me to learn English. He expected me to go up to Oxford as he had. Oxford provided me with my next tutor, a young woman, who had read natural science at Somerville College.

Father introduced me to Miss Westerfield on the terrace. I instantly liked her strong face and intelligent gray eyes, but I felt nervous when she surveyed my soiled pinafore, stained purple from the blackberries I'd been picking with the gardener's sons. Nurse had tried to get me to tidy myself before meeting my new tutor, but I'd run away and hid from her in the hall of portraits. Naturally, I expected a reprimand, but Miss Westerfield simply led me away to the nursery without a word. After she unpinned her bonnet and set it down, she took a seat in the rocking chair and regarded me with a calm, steady gaze.

"I see you have been picking berries," she said in English.

"*Ja, Fräulein. Ich habe Beeren gepflückt.*"

She nodded "Let's try to speak English. Say, 'Yes, Miss Westerfield, I have been picking berries.'" I tried to repeat this, but, of course the W came out wrong. "Very good. You learn quickly, and even though you don't speak my language, you understood me." She smiled. She had a broad mouth, so her smile seemed to take up her entire face. "Let's put on a fresh pinafore, shall we? And then, if you like, I shall read you a story."

At that moment, I knew that we would get on splendidly. She was even able to convince me to take a bath.

English came easily to me. My father had spoken it to me even before Miss Westerfield's arrival so that I might accustom my ear to the sounds. So much of the language was like German, but it was simpler because there were no case endings. What I found difficult was that syntax was so important.

Miss Westerfield had me practice English by reading Oscar Wilde's fairy tales aloud. She was intrigued that I remembered everything I read and could later recite it by heart. Before bedtime, we would lie on my bed in the dark, and I would tell her the story of the "The Selfish Giant" or "The Nightingale and the Rose." I loved these sessions, but I missed Mlle. Celine's scent. Miss Westerfield wore none, but she always smelled of Castile soap. When she held me close, I could feel her soft breasts. Unlike my governess, she always returned me to my own bed when I tried to creep into hers. If I'd been frightened by a bad dream or hearing a noise in the dark, she would sit with me, holding my hand until I fell asleep.

Miss Westerfield was pleased to learn that she was not solely responsible for my education. Grandfather continued to teach me Latin and Greek as well as mathematics. He was amazed that I could grasp the rudiments of calculus, although he found it difficult to convey the concept of infinity to a child. After a long and laborious effort to explain it, he threw up his hands in exasperation.

"I understand," I said.

"You do?" marveled Grandfather.

"Yes, of course, infinity is the space between the stars."

His pale eyes glowed with pleasure. "Well, yes, but of course, it is."

I liked the symbols of mathematics. They were so square and certain, even the Greek letters, which I knew from reading Homer. Grandfather explained that the Arabs had invented algebra, and then read to me from the *Tales of the Arabian Nights*. Father had brought home a multi-colored carpet from Persia when he was posted there with the foreign service and explained that the colorful stitches had been hand-knotted by children no older than I. On clear nights, I would imagine riding on my magic carpet into the space between the stars.

Miss Westerfield began my scientific education with a butterfly collection. I preferred beetles, but my tutor liked butterflies, and I liked her, so I went along with the scheme. After we chloroformed the poor creatures, we pinned them to a velvet-covered board in a shadow box. We progressed from butterflies to botany. We collected every plant found on Edelheim's lands, and there were many. We roamed the forests, tramped through the meadows, and got soaking wet feet in the marshes. The specimens were meticulously dried in a press, using newspaper to absorb the moisture.

We arranged everything carefully in a leather-bound volume and annotated all the entries with the common and Latin names as well as my impressions of the habitat. Miss Westerfield held my hand as I formed the letters. Grandmother had tried in vain to help me learn to write, but I simply couldn't. Meanwhile, I had developed my own shorthand. Unfortunately, no one else could read it. Although I could write all the mathematical symbols quite well and even print the Greek letters, it took some time before my penmanship was legible.

After the scrapbook was complete, Miss Westerfield and I reviewed it together. "You can see how much your handwriting has improved," my tutor said in an encouraging voice as we turned the pages. "Shall we write to your grandmother and invite her to come and see it?"

I nodded eagerly. Miss Westerfield gave me a piece of stationery and a pen. It required several tries to produce a letter without inkblots and cross-outs, but Grandmother was so charmed by the invitation, she kept it in a wooden box along with other relics from my childhood.

As a reward for my achievement, Grandmother induced my grandaunt to lend me a copy of the famous herbal that my ancestor, Margarethe von Raithschau, had written in 1242. It was a fairly recent copy, but hand-lettered, nonetheless. The illustrations were exquisitely drawn, but it was the Latin text that intrigued me. It detailed the medicinal qualities of each plant and how it might be used either to heal or to poison. Miss Westerfield explained that, in those days, poisons were employed quite often.

On her return to Raithschau, Grandmother took me with her. Miss Westerfield had gone home to England to visit her family, and Grandfather thought it best to get me out from under foot. My parents had lost another child. This son had also died within a week of birth. I had been spared the first funeral, being too young, but this time, I was outfitted with a little black dress and miniature veil and walked behind the casket on the way to the village church.

My father firmly held my hand. Mother was unable to attend. She had not yet gotten over the loss of her first son. Sometimes, she would take me to the church crypt to lay little nosegays of pink, miniature roses. There were piles of little dried nosegays on the tiny coffin. No one ever dared to remove them. Now, another tiny coffin was placed beside it and more nosegays were laid.

After the funeral, Mother took to her bed. The drapes were drawn. It was always dark in her room and airless. The place smelled of old lavender. When she allowed me to visit, I sang to her. Sometimes, she would manage a weak smile in response. She drank too much from little, brown bottles. I heard the word, "laudanum" whispered among the maids. The doctor was unaware of Mother's habit until the night she vomited so violently she nearly died from a stomach hemorrhage. I watched them take the bloody towels out of her room. My father confiscated the brown bottles, and after that, Mother gradually got better.

∽

By the time I returned to Edelheim in October, my mother had emerged from her rooms, and Miss Westerfield was back from England. Things were looking up.

Unfortunately, Father hadn't given up the idea that I should become a history scholar. He had studied history at Balliol after a stint at Sandhurst arranged by one of Grandfather's friends in the foreign office. Lieutenant Albrecht had studied at university and actually knew something. Unlike Scheppel, he didn't force me to memorize the names of mountain ranges.

It was Lieutenant Albrecht who taught me that there is always a story in history, and he told them vividly. After the lesson about Attila the Hun, I was afraid of every shadow for a week. For months afterwards, I was too terrified to walk alone through the armory hall, where empty suits of armor stood at attention.

Albrecht was useful as well as fanciful. He taught me how to build kites from newspaper and thin strips of wood and complex bridges made of matchsticks. At his suggestion, my father donated the tin soldiers of his youth so that I might learn military strategy. Albrecht and I recreated famous battles of the past on the library floor until our toy war annoyed the maids trying to dust. At that point, Father demanded we relocate our campaigns to the nursery.

My tutor also taught me to fence with a miniature sabre minus a point or sharpened edge. My father came to watch and said that I had the makings of a fencer.

"Would you like to see my dueling scar?" Father asked in a tantalizing voice.

"Yes, please!"

He pulled up his sleeve to show me the fine white line running down his forearm.

"Were you defending the honor of a woman?" I asked. Miss Westerfield had me reading Malory's *Morte d'Arthur*, and my head was filled with romantic tales of noble knights and damsels in distress.

Father chuckled. "No, little mouse. There were no women involved." I was disappointed to learn that he'd belonged to a student fencing club, and the wound came from sparring with live blades rather than a real duel. He explained that a fencing wound, or *Schmiss*, was a badge of honor, and I instantly decided I must have one.

That year, Lieutenant Albrecht stuffed my head with magical things. I rode my pony and built tiny sailboats of leaves and twigs. In the winter, I rode in a sleigh behind two quick-stepping, white Trakehners, the Prussian warmbloods my father raised at stud.

Then, something terrible happened. At the end of the school term, Miss Westerfield announced that she was going to Dublin to finish her education. She explained that, although women were allowed to attend Oxford lectures and sit for examinations, they could not matriculate, not even in the women's colleges. Ambitious women went to the more liberal University of Dublin to receive their credentials.

"But who will teach me now?" I asked in a sad voice.

"I'm sure your father will find another tutor soon. Maybe someone who can teach you more than I can. I'm sure you would like that."

I pouted. I still missed Mlle. Celine and often dreamt of her. Despite Miss Westerfield's attempts to explain why she must leave and her optimism for the future, I felt betrayed, furious, and frightened. I retreated to my new favorite hiding spot in the hayloft of the cow barn. The *Schloss* had one hundred eighty-six rooms, so there was no lack of places to hide, but the cow barn with its scents of hay, rich manure, and spilt milk always made me feel especially safe. Below, I heard people moving about—the stable hands, the gardener's son, and my nurse calling my name. I watched the activity through a knot hole in the floorboards.

Eventually, Miss Westerfield came into the barn. In a fit of confidence, I had revealed my secret place in the loft. She gazed upwards, knowing exactly where to look. For a long moment, we eyed one another through the hole in the floor. Then she lifted her skirts to avoid the dust of the hay and approached the ladder. As she was about to step on the second rung, she cried out in pain.

I waited in my hiding place to see what would happen next. Miss Westerfield got down and gripped her foot. When I saw the blood flowing through her fingers, I realized she was injured and scrambled down the ladder to help her. I offered my handkerchief, which was still clean, as a bandage. Her face was contorted in pain and ghostly white. "Please get help," she managed to say.

I ran for the cow master, who enlisted two of the cowhands to help Miss Westerfield into the house. Meanwhile, I ran ahead to tell Wolff, the majordomo, what had happened. Wolff knelt beside me. He asked me to slow down as I spewed out my version of the events. I was telling him about the rusty nail and the blood gushing out of the wound when the cow master arrived with Miss Westerfield. Wolff patted my shoulder. "You did well today, Lady Margarethe. You showed you have a clear head in an emergency. Your father would be proud."

Hearing his praise, I felt important and grown-up, but evidently I was not grown-up enough to watch while the doctor examined Miss Westerfield's foot. Wolff told me to wait outside in the hall. Instead, I watched from above. I had found a place in the attic where a small hole in the ceiling above my tutor's room allowed me to see and hear all that went on below. I sometimes used it to spy on Miss Westerfield while she was dressing. I had never seen an adult woman naked before. Miss Westerfield's breasts were white and soft, her nipples, the palest rose. Her beauty was so heart stopping that sometimes, I couldn't bear the sight of it.

Through the hole in the ceiling, I listened to the doctor's concerns. The nail had gone straight through from the sole of the foot to the instep. The doctor doubted the wound could be cleaned effectively, so he dug in it with a crude probe. Then he poured antiseptic directly into it. I watched wide-eyed and incredulous, knowing it was barbaric. Miss Westerfield's face twisted in pain, but she clenched her teeth and never cried out.

The doctor who attended Miss Westerfield was not the regular physician. The town doctor had gone on an extended holiday to visit his family in Cologne. Instead, the majordomo had summoned an elderly doctor who had retired from the regiment. He was dirty. His fingernails were encrusted with filth, and he stank of stale beer. Day after day, I watched him examine his patient, not even washing his hands before he unwound the bandage to inspect the injury.

They would not allow me to see Miss Westerfield, who had become feverish and was talking gibberish. I, meanwhile, lay on my belly in the attic overhead to keep an eye on things.

By the fifth day, the injured foot had begun to darken. I understood from the conversation below, this was not a good sign. I began to daydream about inventing a powerful potion that would miraculously turn the foot back to its normal pink color and restore my tutor to health. In my imagination, I would carefully tend the wound, rubbing in a healing ointment, and soothing Miss Westerfield's feverish brow with cool cloths.

Despite my rich fantasies, the foot only continued to darken. Finally, it turned completely black.

By then, I could no longer bear the separation. When no one was looking, I let myself into Miss Westerfield's room and crept into bed beside her. She was in no position to protest. Her face was pale as death. Her forehead was covered with beads of sweat, and the blackened foot was fetid. The scent remained in my nostrils for days.

Miss Westerfield's feverish delusions passed momentarily, and she recognized me.

"Oh, little Margarethe, how kind of you to come."

I clung to her.

"Please forgive me," I begged. "I am so sorry."

"It was an accident." She kissed me and stroked my hair.

"But if I hadn't hidden in the barn…."

"Sh, my darling child," she said, laying a finger on my lips. "It's no one's fault, just bad luck."

Then she lost consciousness again.

The next day the doctor came. I heard him speaking to my mother. She was in charge now. Father had been sent abroad again with one of our foreign delegations.

"The foot must be amputated, or she will die," the doctor announced bluntly.

Mother looked perfectly aghast. "But she's so young, barely twenty."

The regimental doctor shrugged. "I'm sorry, *Gnädige*, but it cannot be helped. She will die otherwise."

My mother nodded gravely and left the doctor to his awful work. This time, at least, he washed his hands, and put on an apron. He set an iron poker in the fire to heat, stoking the coals until they glowed red. He asked one of the footmen and a maid to assist.

The limb was now black to mid-calf. He drew a line just above the darkened flesh with his fountain pen to indicate where he would cut. Then he traced around the circumference with a scalpel cutting through the flesh. As he did, I felt a strange and intense pain deep within my bowels as if I were being probed with something sharp. I suddenly remembered how animals released their bowels when they were threatened, especially when they were slaughtered or shot during the hunt. There must be a connection, I reasoned. Perhaps in watching what the doctor was doing to Miss Westerfield, I'd been creating a physical mirror of her pain in my body. I could turn away or try to stop the sympathetic response. I willed my mind to block all physical sensations. I willed it with all my strength. Miraculously, my pain stopped.

To my horror, the doctor took a great saw from his kit. The rhythmic sound of cutting through the bone was like that of a woodsman felling a tree. The blackened foot separated from the limb in minutes. The doctor threw it into a basin. The maid turned aside to retch into a chamber pot while the doctor took the glowing iron from the fire and seared the edge of the stump. I could smell the distinctive scent of burning meat, even in the attic.

"That was quick work, *Herr Doktor*," said the footman, looking a bit queasy, although he avoided vomiting like the maid.

The doctor laughed. "In the old days, before ether, and the wounded came in from battle, we had no time to be fancy. Someone held them down, and we cut off the shattered limbs just like that!" He snapped his fingers. "I could do a dozen in an hour!"

We were not at war. There was no great hurry. He could have taken some time to do right by Miss Westerfield.

The maid wrapped the amputated foot in a towel and took it away while the old doctor bandaged the wound.

"Now there's nothing to do but wait and see," said the doctor, scratching the unshaven whiskers at his throat.

I wish I could report that Miss Westerfield recovered and, despite her infirmity, went to Dublin to matriculate for her degree, but her fever continued. The blackness that had claimed her foot and lower extremity moved into her knee, then her thigh, and eventually, it ran through her entire leg. Fortunately, she never awoke from her misery. She died a week later.

Father returned, not because of these minor readjustments in the household, but because he had leave. He sent a wire to Miss Westerfield's family in England and inquired as to what should be done with her remains. They gratefully accepted Father's offer to inter her in the churchyard in the village.

Again, I was required to walk behind a casket. I had grown a bit since I had last performed this duty, so my black dress was shorter but still fit. We stood in for Miss Westerfield's kin during the funeral. We followed the Roman rite, but father had asked the Lutheran pastor of the village to do the honors because Miss Westerfield was Anglican.

I began to cry when they lowered the coffin into the grave, but Father gave my arm a sharp yank and then pressed it hard with his fingers. The pain stopped the tears at once. Afterwards, he explained, "One must always put on a good face, Margarethe, even when you are in great pain. One must hold oneself with dignity, especially for the sake of those who depend on us."

I nodded, swallowing the great lump in my throat, for I had loved Miss Westerfield and would miss her.

"How am I to learn now, Father?" I asked, feeling lost and bewildered without her.

"You are going to England," he explained. "As soon as summer ends."

2

The landscape passing by the train window was so unlike the dark forests of Edelheim or the rolling hills of Raithschau. The terrain was flat, dotted with tidy farms, pretty villages, and occasionally, smoke-blackened cities. I marveled at the open sky because there was so much of it. Everywhere I looked, I could see the horizon. Father smiled at my wide-eyed fascination. "Yes, England looks quite different."

Not only was the landscape strange, so was the food. Our afternoon tea arrived on a little cart covered with white linen. The tiny sandwiches were made of soft, white bread with the crusts removed. They were filled with deviled ham or egg salad with sliced gherkins. I liked the shortbread biscuits, although not as much as the sugar cookies at Obberoth. The tea was nearly as dark and strong as that our Russian maid brewed. When I made a face, Father added extra sugar and splashed some milk into my cup.

While we ate, I was glad for a lull in the conversation. Father had used the ride from London to offer advice on how to "get on" at school. He had enrolled me at Chilton Hall under the anglicized name of Margaret Stahle, the E swallowed rather than pronounced. While in England, I must speak only English. Most importantly, I must avoid any reference to my noble titles. "There is a place for titles, Grethe, but school is not one of them," Father had explained.

From a young age, I knew that Grandmother's title passes through the female line. One day, I would be Countess Raithschau in my own right. The house rules of Edelheim and Leichthal included a writ of remainder. Sons were given precedence as usual, but, in the absence of a male heir, a female child could inherit the titles.

Lieutenant Albrecht had made my heritage the subject of many lessons. He taught me how to read the entries in the *Almanach de Gotha*, the great book of the German nobility. As we traced the twisted and intertwining branches of my family tree, I learned a few interesting facts: I was descended from the *Uradel*, the old aristocracy. Grandfather was a *Reichsgraf*, which meant the title went back to the Holy Roman Empire. Both of my parents had a member of the "tall fellows" regiment in their bloodlines, hence the great height in my family. Apart from these curious tidbits, reading the *Almanach* was as boring as memorizing the names of mountain ranges in China.

"Reserving information about oneself can often spare you from envy, and that's good," Father continued after we ate. I tried to look attentive, but my patience for this topic had worn thin. "In school, you must try to be like the others. Esprit de corps and conformity are the goals. Blend in, and your life will be so much easier." His voice had the sure ring of experience. When I gazed out the window, Father finally realized he had lost his audience. He lit his pipe and opened a book.

We arrived at Chilton Hall in time for Evensong. The afternoon sun streaming through the stained-glass windows dappled the dark wood of the pews with brilliant colors. The chapel smelled of furniture polish and long-extinguished candles. We were early for the service and had to wait for some time before the students entered in age and size order, primary school first, then the grammar school, followed by the faculty, wearing their academic robes. Led by the student choir, the assembly began to sing Tallis's divine hymn, "If ye love me." I was transfixed by its simplicity and beauty. Long after the singing ended, the melody replayed in my mind. I silently sang it for days afterwards.

When the chapel service ended, the other students headed to the dining room for supper, while we went to our interview with the headmistress of the primary school. Miss Burke was a tall woman, whose stern expression reminded me of my grandaunt, the nun. Height and severity are apparently essential to the role of headmistress. Miss Burke inspected me through her pince-nez, while I cautiously returned the inspection.

"Well, well, Miss Stahle," she said with a pronounced Scottish brogue. "You look older than seven, but we shall put you in the first form nevertheless."

"I had my seventh birthday only last week."

"You speak English quite well," she observed, sounding surprised.

"Thank you, Miss."

"Don't you curtsy to your elders?" She tilted her head and regarded me as if I were a strange insect.

I blushed and glanced at my father for guidance. I had been taught to curtsy to none but senior nobility and the Kaiser. Father nodded his encouragement, and I made an abbreviated curtsy.

The headmistress rang a little bell on her desk. A young woman came in. "Please escort Miss Stahle to the first form dormitory, while I speak to her father."

Father and I exchanged a look, and that was the last I saw of him until Christmas.

~

Although I followed Father's advice to the letter, my education in England got off to a rough start. My classmates were learning to read from a primer that detailed the exploits of Norma and Jonathan and their dog, Rex. Bored, I occupied myself with more stimulating reading. When the mistress called upon me, I never knew the place. Finally, she wondered aloud if I were mentally deficient. The other students tittered. From that day forward, she ignored me. At least, the stalemate meant she would leave me alone. I happily went back to the copy of *Robinson Crusoe* I'd secreted behind a dust cover with the school crest.

The other mistresses were somewhat kinder and speculated that I simply lacked facility with English. Fortunately, for my future as a student, one of the mistresses had the curiosity and patience to investigate. Miss Stafford took me aside. She handed me the primer and asked me to read aloud.

I shook my head. "I don't like that book."

"All right, then," said Miss Stafford with a frustrated sigh. "What would you prefer to read?"

I removed my copy of *Robinson Crusoe* from my satchel and began to read aloud. I had gotten to that part in the novel when Crusoe saves Friday from the savages. It was very exciting.

I looked up to see Miss Stafford frowning. "Thank you. That will do. What else have you read?"

"Miss Westerfield gave me a list," I said proudly, searching in my satchel for the paper.

"And who is Miss Westerfield?" she asked, looking curious.

"My tutor, but she died. First, they cut off her foot because it was all black. I watched them do it."

She gave me a skeptical look.

"I swear it is true."

"You don't need to swear. I believe you." She reached out her hand. "Show me your list." I handed over the paper on which Miss Westerfield had written the book titles. Miss Stafford read the list aloud: "*Wuthering Heights, Pride and Prejudice, Little Women, David Copperfield.*" She stared at me. "Which of these have you read?"

"Only *Little Women*. I prefer adventure stories."

"Such as?"

I was reluctant to reveal I had ignored Miss Westerfield's instructions, but Miss Stafford seemed kind, so I told her the truth. "*Gulliver's Travels, Ivanhoe, Two Years Before the Mast*, and *The Last of the Mohicans.*"

The mistress stared at me. "And where do you find these books, Miss?"

"In our library at home."

"How long have you been reading?"

"I don't know," I replied truthfully.

"What do you mean, 'you don't know'?"

I compressed my lips as I thought about this. "I can't remember when I couldn't read," I admitted.

She nodded and reached out for my book. Reluctantly, I handed it over. "Come with me."

She led me directly to the headmistress's office. Punishment now seemed likely, yet I couldn't understand what I had done wrong. I had carefully followed all of Father's instructions. I'd allowed everyone at the school to mispronounce my name as "stale," and I had told no one that I would one day be a countess.

Before I was allowed into Miss Burke's office, Miss Stafford took a moment alone with her. While I sat on the hard bench outside the door, I wondered if I would be caned. I had seen the red marks on the back of the legs of other students after meeting with the headmistress.

Eventually, the door opened, and Miss Stafford gestured for me to enter.

"So, Miss Stahle, I understand that contrary to the opinion of some of your mistresses, you are quite able," said Miss Burke, looking down at me through her pince-nez. "Stafford tells me that you are surprisingly well read. Please, do us the honor of reading to us."

Miss Stafford returned my copy of *Robinson Crusoe*. The two women sat in rapt attention while I read the description of Crusoe's kindness to Friday after the rescue. I had to agree that it was an engaging part of the story.

After a few minutes, Miss Burke rang the little bell on her desk. "That will do," she said sharply.

I took a deep breath and looked up. Now, I would certainly hear my punishment, I thought, but Miss Burke did not address her remarks to me. Instead, she glanced at Miss Stafford and said, "Well, Stafford, where does this child belong?"

"I have no idea, Miss Burke. She's only seven."

Miss Burke turned to me. "Can you read Latin?"

"Yes, Miss."

"And Greek, I suppose."

"Yes, Miss."

"Can you do your numbers?"

"Yes, Miss. My grandfather has been teaching me geometry and explaining about functions that go to infinity."

"Good heavens!" exclaimed Miss Stafford, "calculus?"

"This is highly irregular," complained Miss Burke. "Why weren't we informed?" I realized the question was rhetorical, which was fortunate because I had no idea why my father had not been candid about my prior education. Miss Burke handed my book to me. "Very well, Stafford, test the girl to see where she belongs." She waved us out.

Miss Stafford tested me in every subject imaginable. She brought in the

Latin and Greek mistresses as well as Mlle. Richard, the French mistress. They were intrigued to learn that I had picked up some Russian from the kitchen maids. They also discovered that my handwriting was illegible, and I was completely deficient in geography, despite having a well-developed ability to read maps. It was determined that for most subjects I would sit with the eleven-year-olds in the grammar school, even though my knowledge was far beyond theirs in most subjects, especially classics and mathematics. As for the rest, Miss Stafford volunteered to tutor me privately.

As we sat shoulder-to-shoulder during my lessons, I began to notice Miss Stafford's looks. She was not an especially pretty woman, but she had porcelain skin and auburn hair. She was the sort of redhead whose eyebrows and lashes are nearly invisible. She had a trim figure and a tiny waist, courtesy of the corset all adult women wore in those days. Her clear, hazel eyes moved me most of all. They were full of intelligence and always calm and purposeful.

At first, I was afraid to notice Miss Stafford's attractive features or begin to like her because I felt it would be a betrayal of Miss Westerfield. Eventually, I realized my former tutor would have encouraged me to find a new teacher who could foster my talents.

⌣

As I learned the Anglican hymns, I felt more comfortable singing in assembly. One day, while we were singing a familiar anthem, the music mistress left her usual position with the choir and headed down the aisle. To my horror, she stopped at the end of my pew and pointed to me. She waved to indicate I should come out. I pushed my way past the others in the row. One pinched me on the way because I stepped on her foot.

"Come with me," said the music mistress, and I followed her to the front of the chapel. She pointed to an empty place in the soprano section. "Go on," she ordered in a whisper, and I took a seat in the booth next to a senior girl. The others in the choir stared at me curiously. I was curious myself, but I needed to wait until the assembly ended to learn more.

After the students filed out, the mistress dismissed the choir and led me to the music room in the chapel basement.

"Do you know why I singled you out this morning?" she asked, closing the door.

"No, Miss," I responded anxiously. Up to now, I'd feared the possibility of punishment, but there was the hint of a smile in her eyes, so that seemed less likely.

"You were singing so loudly I could hear you from the front of the chapel," she explained.

Was this wrong? I wondered. I liked the song, which is why I sang it so loudly.

"Your voice rings out like a clarion call above all the others', but when you sing in a group, you must modulate and blend your voice. It's for the greater good. Do you understand?"

Father had explained the concept of the greater good during his lecture on the train, so I understood...a bit. I nodded. With a sigh, she sat down on the piano bench and smoothed her dress. She asked my name, and I told her my English name. "Margaret Stahle."

"I am Miss Chadwick." She smiled. "Who taught you to sing?"

"No one. I learned from listening."

"Can you read music?"

I nodded and she handed me a sheet of music, the soprano part of a Gilbert and Sullivan chorus. "Sing this, please."

I cleared my throat and eagerly launched into it. After I finished the first stanza, she stopped me.

"You have a strong voice and good breath control, but there's no need to sing so loudly."

She uncovered the piano keys. "Now, sing the notes that should follow the ones I play." I followed her directions. "You have a good ear." Then she hit an out-of-tune key, and I grimaced. "That bothers you?" She asked. She continued hitting the key until I was nearly writhing in pain. Mercifully, she stopped. "Tell me the name for these notes," she said, playing them.

"Middle C, G, B."

"And these."

Again, I answered correctly. She asked me to sing notes without any musical cue, only their names.

"You have perfect pitch," she concluded. She turned around and gave me a careful inspection. "Would you like to learn the correct way to sing?"

"Oh, yes!" I declared.

"Can you play the piano?"

"Yes, Mother taught me."

"Play something for me." She vacated the piano bench, and we exchanged places. I smiled, feeling the heat from where she'd sat. Although I was tall, my feet dangled from the bench. It was impossible to reach the pedals, but I made do as best I could. While I played, I could see from her eyes that my performance had impressed her.

"Would you like to continue learning the piano?"

"Yes, Miss."

"Very well. I shall write to your father regarding lessons," she said with a smile. "Now, run along to your mistress. Tell her that I kept you after the assembly. She can speak to me if there's any question."

"Thank you, Miss," I said and happily ran off to class.

When I returned to Edelheim that summer, I found a surprise. At the end of the line of servants assembled to welcome me was a boy. He was exactly my height and like me, a towhead. As I looked him over, I realized that I had seen his face before. Even more intriguing was where I had seen it—in the mirror. As if to confirm this thought, my mother said, "Good Lord in heaven, they could be twins!"

He was too well dressed to be a servant's child, and the uncanny resemblance suggested he could be related. "Who is that?" I asked cautiously.

"He is my nephew," Mother explained, guiding him forward by the shoulders. "Margarethe, meet Konrad von Holdenberg, your cousin."

The boy and I eyed one another. He raised his right brow. I raised the left. He was left-handed. I was right-handed. This served to tell me that as identical as we appeared, we were somehow opposite. We were not twins, but mirror images.

We spent the day getting acquainted. I showed my cousin some of my favorite hiding places, swearing him to secrecy. I introduced him to the servants' sons, my usual playmates. They looked him over with suspicion and afterwards, shunned me for reasons I didn't understand. Privately, they explained that Konrad was a sissy and a tag-along, so they weren't interested in his company. I didn't care what they thought. I was delighted to have a new friend, especially one who looked just like me.

Konrad was assigned to the room adjoining mine. At bedtime, I curled under my eiderdown and was about to drift off to sleep when I felt movement on the bed. The coverlet lifted and cold air rushed in. I rolled over and came face to face with my mirror image.

"What are you doing here?" I asked, surprised and annoyed.

"Protecting you."

"Protecting me? From what?"

"The trolls under the bed!"

I sometimes strained to listen to the sounds I heard during the night, but trolls under the bed were not something I had considered.

"Don't be silly. There's nothing to fear. Nurse is right next door." I nudged him, hoping he would get out of my bed, but he didn't.

"I'm afraid of the dark," he confided in a whisper. In those days, I found the dark frightening myself, so I was somewhat sympathetic. Sometimes, the light reflecting in the dolls' glass eyes made me think they were possessed, and I kept watch over them until my eyes burned.

"If I tell you a story, will you go to sleep?" I asked.

He nodded eagerly. I recited one of the fairy tales I had memorized. Eventually, I heard him snoring softly. He was taking up most of the bed. I gave him a nudge, but he never stirred. Finally, I jabbed him sharply with my elbow. He woke, sputtered, and finally moved over to give me some room.

On the succeeding nights, he reprised the ploy of slipping into my bed. Finally, Nurse ordered the footmen to move another bed into my bedchamber.

Now that Konrad knew I could recite fairy tales, he demanded one every night or he refused to sleep.

"How can you do that?" he asked when I'd finished reciting Wilde's "Selfish Giant."

"I don't know."

"Do you remember everything you read?"

"Only if I enjoy it."

∾

By eavesdropping on my parents' conversation, I was able to learn the reason for Konrad's visit. Father had recently been appointed rector of the Prussian military academy at Groß-Lichterfelde. He had initiated a summer program of military exercises for cadets identified as having officer potential. My uncle considered his son "soft" and wanted such tendencies beaten out of him as soon as possible. He thought training with the cadets would be just the thing to toughen him up.

Unaware that I was hiding behind the drapes in the drawing room, Father confessed in hushed tones that he had his own reasons for taking in my cousin.

"Grethe needs companions of her own class," Father said. "The company of the servants' children isn't doing her any good."

"I agree," said Mother, violently yanking the needle through her embroidery. "She's turning into a ruffian playing with those awful boys. She's always unkempt and filthy." It went unsaid that I never played with the girls, only the boys.

"She'll grow out of it," my father said in my defense. "Don't worry."

Father lit his pipe and puffed thoughtfully. "Your brother is too hard on Konrad. He's a good boy, really."

"Richard doesn't want him to become a nancy."

In my hiding place, I wondered what a "nancy" was.

"Oh, what rubbish!" scoffed my father. "He's just a boy, after all. What he needs is guidance and attention. A few weeks in the cadet camp will do him good."

But Konrad refused to participate in the military exercises unless I joined him. Father hadn't planned for this, but he said he didn't see any harm in it. Side by side, my cousin and I learned to shoot, use a sword and lance, build a fire under any conditions, and swagger. The cadets would laugh whenever they caught us at swaggering practice.

While it was fun and games for us, the exercises were deadly serious for the cadets. Someday, they would lead men into battle and live or die by their training. I paid close attention, for I was still determined to become a soldier like Father, even if girls weren't allowed. Everything about soldiering appealed to me—the cadence of the march, the crispness of the drill orders, the flinty smell in the air after firing a gun. Father had miniature rifles and small revolvers specially made for Konrad and me so that we could learn to shoot, as well as strip down, clean, and reassemble our weapons against the clock.

A cadet officer was assigned to look after us while father was busy with training or business around the manor. At night, we slept in Father's well-appointed field tent, which lacked for nothing in terms of convenience. It had a wooden floor, furniture, including a dining table and cots with thick wool blankets that smelled of moth balls. The only real difference between sleeping in the house and the tent was the sound of the animals at night. We could hear them creeping outside the tent, crushing twigs and leaves underfoot. Sometimes we heard them growl at one another or the plaintive cries of their prey as they pounced. On such occasions, Konrad would slip into my cot and pull the camphor-smelling blankets over his head.

"You must learn to be brave or you will never become a soldier," I lectured sternly.

"I shall never be a soldier," he replied with conviction. "Never."

Along with the cadets, we learned how to cook over an open fire and make coffee with the grounds at the bottom of the pot. We weren't allowed to drink the coffee, but we knew how to make it. It always smelled good, and I wouldn't have minded a taste, but Father said that coffee was for grown-ups, and I would have to wait.

Part of the cadets' survival training was learning to live off the land. We foraged for edible plants and wild mushrooms. Using our miniature rifles, we had to hunt for our dinner. My first kill was a rabbit. The bullet propelled the poor creature far from where it had once stood, happily munching some clover. I stared in horror at the sight of it writhing and the blood spurting from its tiny body.

"Put it out of its misery," ordered Lieutenant Braun, the cadet officer in charge. "One shot in the head." After that, the sad twitching finally stopped, and the rabbit lay still.

Braun explained how to prepare my kill for the stew pot. When I cut open the rabbit's still warm body and peeled away its skin, I felt nothing but regret for ending its life. Braun deftly cut it up and made a tasty stew with wild onions, mushrooms, and greens collected from the fields and forest, but I had to force myself to chew the tender meat. Every bite stuck in my throat.

"You mustn't be squeamish about such things," my father said, watching my face. "It's no different from eating the meat from the farm, the chickens and pigs we slaughter for food. But you must never kill a creature unless you intend to eat it. Killing for sport alone is wrong."

Konrad was more squeamish. He would not even taste the savory stew. My father's aide-de-camp offered to get Konrad some supper from the house. Father would have none of it.

"Let him eat what we all eat," he ordered.

Our meals were often game, so Konrad sometimes went hungry. As I ate, he stared at me with round eyes designed to make me feel guilty. We both found eating the trout and salmon from the stream or the lake less difficult. The eyes of the fish weren't dark and soft like the rabbit's, and the fish bodies were always cold to the touch. At first, I disliked opening the belly of the fish to remove the guts. Then Father explained the purpose of the parts inside, and I was fascinated.

The perch in the lake were easy to catch, but this type of fish liked to swallow the hook. Father showed us how to disgorge it. "A fishing hook can mean the difference between a good meal or starvation for a soldier, so the hook must always be retrieved when possible," said my father, twisting the bloody thing out of the fish's throat.

Eventually, I learned to enjoy foraging for food. It reminded me of the heroic Robinson Crusoe marooned on his island, and I invented my own adventure stories, which I told Konrad at night instead of fairy tales.

Sometimes, the soldiering lessons were boring and repetitive. Konrad and I would run off to get into mischief more appropriate to our age. Where mischief was concerned, I was the mastermind, and Konrad, my willing accomplice. We stole lumber from the sawmill and built ourselves a fort in a tree. From that vantage point, we could see all the goings-on in the camp, including the two cadets who liked to slip away to kiss and fondle one another.

"Why do you think he is putting his hand down the other man's pants?" I wondered aloud.

"It must feel good," observed Konrad. "Look at his face."

I was aware of the "slugs and puppy dogs' tails" aspect of boys, for I had seen the gardener's son whip out his small organ to relieve himself. Whenever an adult male did this, I averted my eyes because it seemed so important to my father that I do so. I envied males their ability to urinate while standing. I diligently practiced but only succeeded in soaking my stockings in the process.

Konrad and I liked to play "doctor," so I got an eyeful of how differently we were made. This aspect seemed especially odd to me because otherwise, we were completely alike. My hair was longer and tied in braids, but I was still flat-chested, so our private parts seemed the only real difference.

The summer days grew shorter. The cadets went home for their holidays. In August, I would go with my father to visit his parents at Raithschau, and Konrad would return to his family in Cologne.

The last night of his stay, Konrad and I remained awake to watch a meteor shower. We sat together on the window seat in my bedchamber and wished upon the falling stars.

"I must have a profession to earn a living," said Konrad with a sigh after we spoke of our dreams for the future. "If I can earn enough money, things will be better for us." His family, despite holding a baronial title, had no wealth. Father sent them money to keep them from destitution.

"I shall also have a profession," I declared proudly.

"No, you can't! Girls get married and their husbands have a profession."

"I can have a profession, if I wish," I replied and showed him my tongue. "Papa says that we of the nobility must be of service."

"Yes, we must. But what kind of profession would you have?"

"I shall become a soldier," I declared.

Konrad suddenly couldn't resist roaring with laughter. He laughed until he fell on the floor. "Girls can't be soldiers, you goose!"

"They can't?"

"No, of course not."

Although Father had said exactly the same, I still refused to believe it. I knew I would make a good soldier given the chance. With my little rifle and revolver, I had become a deadly accurate marksman. I could swagger with the best of them, and my father always complimented me on my camp coffee. The thought that I could never put these skills to practical use was extremely disappointing.

"Maybe I'll become a priest," Konrad announced.

"Oh, I wouldn't like that. Not at all."

"Why not?"

"Well, then you would have to go where they tell you, and we couldn't play together."

"When we're grown-ups, we won't be playing."

"Grown-ups play too. Papa plays billiards and cards. He wagers on the horses. Mother makes useless things with her needlework."

"Yes," he said, looking reflective. "I suppose that's how grown-ups play."

After that, we were each alone with our thoughts of our imagined futures. I began to see my hope of following in my father's footsteps dissolve. It was vaguely replaced by the idea of becoming a teacher like my grandaunt, Sister Scholastica. But I certainly couldn't become a nun. Someone needed to provide an heir to Raithschau, and now it looked like I might need to provide an heir to Edelheim as well. The idea that I was something of a brood mare was troubling, but I pushed the thought far out of my mind. In that summer of 1903, adulthood and its dreaded responsibilities seemed very far away.

~

As much as I enjoyed my adventures with Konrad, I missed school. Specifically, I missed Miss Stafford. During the term break, she had been travelling through the great cities of Europe with some of her university friends to take in the artistic masterpieces. She sent me a postcard from wherever they landed. I fantasized that she and her companions might find their way to Edelheim, where we had an impressive collection of valuable art, but despite being considered one of the great houses of Prussia, Schloss Edelheim was certainly out of the way.

I anticipated our reunion with great excitement. Once again, Father escorted me to school, and we ate tiny sandwiches on the train. Those made with thinly sliced cucumbers instantly became my favorite.

"I'm sure you'll be happy to see your friends," Father opined, lighting his pipe.

After his earnest advice about how to "get on," I didn't know how to explain to him that I had no friends. My age peers found me odd, and our interests rarely overlapped, so they ignored me. The older girls, whose classes I shared, dismissed me as a child.

Miss Stafford was surrounded by students when we arrived. I was so excited that all I wanted was to throw my arms around her, but as I approached, she showed her palm to warn me away. I was crushed. Only my father's lessons in putting on a good face kept me from bursting into tears.

The other girls went off to play hoops in the garden. Not a single one came to greet me or ask me about my summer. I headed to my dormitory and opened the book I'd been reading on the train, a Karl May western Father had passed on to me after reading it.

Not long after, Miss Stafford came to look for me, but I ignored her. She sat down beside me on my bed.

"How was your summer?" she asked.

I shrugged.

"Did you get my postcards?"

"Yes," I murmured.

"Did you like them?"

"Yes, thank you," I said with icy politeness.

She began to talk about the sights she had seen during her travels.

Eventually, she realized I wasn't listening and studied me carefully with her calm, hazel eyes. "I'm sorry, Meg," she said, using the pet name she reserved for private use. Otherwise, she called me, "Miss," or by my Anglicized surname. "I can't show favoritism to you in front of the others, but I was very happy to see you."

I eyed her cautiously. "I missed you so much!" I finally admitted.

She smiled. "I missed you too."

She reached for my hand. Hers was warm and soft. Her eyes glowed as she described the amazing art in the Louvre and looking up at the Sistine Chapel until her neck ached. I told her about Konrad and the cadets, and how I'd learned to make coffee in a tin pot over a fire.

When we'd finished sharing our adventures, she said, "Why don't you come outside and play with the others?"

I shook my head. "They don't like me."

Her eyes softened with sympathy, and I wondered what long-ago hurt she had remembered. "They don't understand you, Meg."

"Why not?"

"Because you're different. But try to be patient. Intelligence is a gift that should be shared, but first you must get them to listen."

"How?"

"I'll explain that part. Now, let's go outside and enjoy the sunshine."

We sat on a bench near where the other girls were playing. "Now, Meg," said Miss Stafford, "I've missed hearing you recite fairy tales. Why don't you tell me one?"

I launched into Andersen's "The Little Match Girl." Some of the other students noticed us sitting under the tree and approached. One girl sat down on the grass, heedless of the dampness from that morning's rain. More girls came and sat beside her. Soon, I had a sizable audience of eager, young faces turned to me.

"Tell us another," begged a girl when I'd finished the tale. I looked to Miss Stafford for direction.

"Go on," she encouraged with a smile. "Tell them another." I began to recite "Rapunzel."

Once the story was done, the girls drifted back into their usual groups, leaving me alone once more.

"Don't worry," said Miss Stafford, putting her arm around me and giving me a little squeeze. "Popularity is overrated."

~

A new student arrived, and I finally made a friend. To be sure, the reason for our connection was necessity. She spoke Russian and a little German, but almost no English. By default, I became her interpreter. Kristina was the daughter of a Russian diplomat, who was a member of the high nobility. She often laughed at what she called my "kitchen Russian." A few double entendres had slipped into my vocabulary. "Yes, Meg, the word 'arse' can be an endearment," Kristina explained, "but not in polite company."

After that I used the word as often as I could. I would taunt her with it until she stuck out her tongue.

"Now, *that* is vulgar." It became a little game between us.

In exchange for my services as a translator, Kristina offered to teach me to read Russian. Unfortunately, there was precious little material in Russian at Chilton Hall, but on a visit to London, Miss Stafford found a book of Russian fairy tales in an antique bookstore, along with a Russian-English dictionary with phonetic pronunciation.

Because I could read classical Greek, learning a language with a different alphabet was not as difficult as one might expect. Soon I was reading the stories of Baba Yaga, the witch, to Kristina's satisfaction. She wrote to her father and asked him to send more books in their language, as well as a Russian Bible.

I was grateful to learn as much as I did because Kristina's father was recalled from his post before the end of the term. Tearfully, Kristina bequeathed the books her father had sent. I wrote to her in St. Petersburg, sometimes in Russian for the practice, sometimes in German. I anxiously awaited her letters in return. Then, one day, a letter came from Kristina's father. Written in carefully lettered English, it explained that my friend had died from a fever. I cried myself to sleep that night and for many nights thereafter. The housemother reported my inconsolable grief to the headmistress, who sent Miss Stafford to look in on me.

"Why don't you read the Russian Bible Kristina gave you?" Miss Stafford gently suggested. "Perhaps it will comfort you."

The books of the Bible were set off by icons of the Byzantine saints decorated with pure gold. St. Helena bore her true cross; St. George's horse trod a dragon underfoot. St. Nicholas wore a brilliant scarlet cloak. As I studied the golden pictures, I imagined the august company my friend was keeping in heaven.

But the golden icons proved too rich for my blood, so I exchanged the Russian Bible for the *Book of Common Prayer* that was used in our services. Chilton Hall was decidedly "low-church." Our chaplain usually wore academic robes, never ornate vestments. Eucharist was reserved for high feasts, and civic responsibility was a common theme in his sermons. Listening to him preach on the duties of the king's subjects, I found many congruences with what I'd been taught. The virtues of loyalty, duty, and keeping a stiff upper lip meshed perfectly with my Prussian sensibilities. Unwittingly, I was becoming an Anglo-German, an odd chimera like my father.

∽

By the time I returned home, I'd lost interest in religion. The cadets were back…and Konrad. My uncle, Richard von Holdenberg, had accompanied my cousin to Edelheim. We were having lemonade on the terrace with my parents when he suddenly snapped at me. "What are you staring at?" His face was red, and he was scowling. In fact, I can't remember ever seeing him smile.

After Uncle Richard barked at me, Father encouraged me to play elsewhere.

"Why is your father always so angry?" I asked Konrad as we headed to the garden.

"He's ashamed because he has to take money from your father."

I knew the basic elements of Uncle Richard's story from eavesdropping on my parents' conversations. I remembered the day the ancestral estate of the Holdenbergs had been sold to pay my uncle's debts. A wealthy merchant bought it as a summer house moments before foreclosure. Father had been paying the mortgage, while his brother-in-law secretly took another. "Let this be a lesson to him," father had growled when he heard about the sale of the house.

Since then, Father had been sending money so that his brother-in-law's family could live in a decent house in Cologne. He also purchased a trading company, hoping my uncle could earn a living as a merchant. The trading firm went bankrupt within the year. After that, Father provided the man with an income and paid for the education of his sons.

"It's cheaper that way," I'd heard Father explaining to Mother, who responded with a withering look. She put on airs to hide her humiliation at her family's ill fortunes, but knowing the truth, I smarted with embarrassment on her behalf.

The visit with Uncle Richard did not improve. He snarled at Mother for some ridiculous slight so subtle I didn't even notice, or if I did, understand. Father ordered him into his study. Through the door, I could hear the roar of my father's voice: "How dare you speak that way to a woman? Any woman!"

"She's my sister," replied a male voice in a petulant tone.

"She's my wife. Use those words or that tone again, and you will be forced to defend your honor."

The thought of Richard von Holdenberg facing Father in a duel was comical, but after that episode, I never heard my uncle speak harshly to my mother again.

Red-faced and frowning, my uncle departed the next day. Konrad looked greatly relieved. Later, my cousin confessed that his father often flew into rages and beat him until his arms and legs were black and blue. Although my father sometimes switched me, he never left marks.

"What do you say to going into town for some licorice?" Konrad suggested.

Now that we were older, we could roam the estate freely, but we were forbidden to ride into town without an adult. I wondered if we could coax one of the stable hands into coming along and saw an opportunity for Konrad to use his silver tongue.

"Do you have any money?" I asked.

Father gave Konrad exactly the same allowance he gave me—a few coins per week, just enough to buy some candy or a small toy. The allowance was more than sufficient to meet my needs, but my cousin had causes.

The Holdenbergs were fervent Catholics. Konrad's devout grandmother encouraged him to support an order of missionary priests in Africa. Some of the coins Konrad extracted from me headed to the order's headquarters in Africa. As for the others, I had no idea where they went, only that I found myself paying for Konrad's sweets more often than not.

My sweet tooth had limits, and I reasoned that if I spent less on candy, the more I would have for things that really mattered, such as toy soldiers, kites, and adventure magazines. I too had dreams of Africa, but not of saving children. I imagined myself becoming an explorer tramping through the jungles and grassy plains in search of exotic plants and animals.

I sent Konrad to negotiate with the stable boy while I went into the house to fetch my stash of coins. The stable boy agreed to accompany us into town as long as I promised to buy him sweets. Whenever Konrad was involved, there was always a transaction.

3

"Stance!" Father shouted, "Grethe! Keep that foot behind you!" His own feet were moving as if to show mine where to go.

"Stance" had been my watchword that summer—whether leaning away from a fencing lunge or ducking a boxing punch. During pistol practice, the drill master went down the line of cadets and adjusted our posture until we crouched and stuck out our bums to his satisfaction. Eventually, I understood that all defensive stances have the same purpose: staying on one's feet.

Father was trying to cram as much training as possible into this summer. After three years as the rector of the military academy, he had resigned his post and asked for combat duty in order to advance his career. He'd seen some action in the Boer War, but now the Empire's military adventures were mostly putting down rebellions in our African colonies. Part of me hoped Father would take us along, so that I could see the wild places I had read about in my adventure magazines, but we had never accompanied Father on a deployment, and Mother was pregnant again.

The fencing master and I resumed the en garde position. I could feel Father's critical eyes on me as we circled before crossing swords. I looked forward to the daily matches. As soon as I heard a fencing champion had been hired to train the cadets, I signed up for instruction. My first request was refused, so I went directly to Father, waiting until I found him enjoying a glass of Raithschau wine on the veranda. We spoke of horses before I put forth my reasons for wishing to be trained in the art of the blade.

"Fencing trains the mind and the body in agility. It requires great mental discipline. It is good exercise. It teaches one to size up an opponent and make quick adjustments to strategy."

Father gave me a long, measuring look. "I see you are benefitting from your grandfather's lessons in logic," he said with a smile. "Very well, Grethe. You may take up Captain Lichtenfels' time, but only if you are serious about learning."

I assured him that I was.

"Good. When you complete your training, I shall challenge you to a match."

The next day, Father presented me with a French-fitted box, which contained three-quarter-scale versions of the standard fencing swords: a foil, an epee, and a sabre. At ten, I was the tallest in my form at school, but I was not quite tall enough for full-size swords. "These were mine when I was a boy," Father explained. "They're yours now. When the time comes, pass them along to the next in line."

I tried to focus on my stance, but it didn't take long for Captain Lichtenfels to knock me on my bum. More humiliated than hurt, I dusted off the seat of my dress and unhooked the tabs to let the skirt down.

"You must pay attention, Grethe!" said my father. I could see the disappointment in his pale eyes. "Maybe you should fence with Konrad. He's more your size." He glanced at Konrad, who made himself small. Although my love of soldierly things had only grown with my training, my cousin now loathed them all the more.

"All right," said my father, glancing at his watch. "That's enough for today." He patted my shoulder. "Margarethe, you have the makings of a fencer. Watch your footing."

After lunch, we had demolitions class. Father had enlisted the finest expert in the Imperial Army to lecture on the deployment of explosives. Today, I was especially eager for our lesson because Sergeant Müller would explain how to make black powder.

With a piece of chalk, he scratched the formula on a slate board. The cadets eagerly copied it into their notebooks along with the recipes for special-purpose applications. The practical part of the lesson was compounding black powder from commonly available raw materials. We ground the bright-yellow, elemental sulfur to a fine powder in a mortar with a pestle. We pulverized the charcoal between two rough stones, and added a shovelful of saltpeter from a burlap sack. Once we'd mixed our powder, each of us created a crude stick of dynamite in a waxed tube outfitted with a fuse.

Müller took us to a rock ledge near the quarry. He reviewed our previous lessons on how to set a charge and take cover before detonating the blast. When it stopped raining rocks and earth and the dust cleared, he stood and addressed the cadets. "As you can see, old-fashioned powder is quite good for removing rock and can still be used in war for construction. However, high explosives based on nitrogen compounds are far more efficient and easier to control."

He allowed each of us to set our homemade charge and detonate it. When my turn came, the explosion was simply thrilling. Proudly, I walked over to inspect the gaping hole it had left in the rock.

Father had arranged for us to eat in the house that night. Mother was close to the end of her pregnancy. As usual, she was miserable, so Father had decided that we should join her at dinner to cheer her up. I think he also wanted a respite from eating game and wild greens, which I didn't mind. It was healthy fare but tedious.

"Grethe, I heard your detonation was spectacular. Well done," said Father as he snapped open his napkin and arranged it in his lap. He turned his eyes on my cousin. "But you, Konrad. You weren't interested in the lesson?"

My cousin shook his head. "No, sir. It hurts my ears."

"The battlefield is noisier. Get used to it."

At the other end of the table, my mother was pushing her food around her plate. For weeks, she'd been eating little. Despite her enormous belly, she was thin and birdlike. Her arms and legs looked like they could be snapped as easily as twigs. Her dark eyes gazed sadly into her plate.

After dinner, I played the violin and sang. For the first time in days, I saw my mother smile.

"Your singing has improved, *Schatzi*."

I told her about my lessons with Miss Chadwick, and the exercises I'd been taught to do every day. Mother nodded in response, but I don't think she heard a word I said.

She looked so worried. She had already buried three sons. I'd been away at school when my last brother had died, so I had been spared my mother's heartrending weeping and the ceremonies that followed. There were already three little coffins behind the brass grill in the crypt. The pile of dried nosegays continued to grow.

∾

Mother gave birth to another son at the end of August. The delivery was long and difficult. My mother remained in bed, too weak to rise. It was clear from the first that the child would not survive. His delicate skin turned a vivid yellow. Within a day, even the whites of his eyes yellowed. The poor creature couldn't muster the strength to cry properly. Instead, he mewed softly like a newborn kitten.

Father sent for the priest, and we gathered in the nursery. I was elected the impromptu godmother; Wolff, the majordomo, stood as godfather. The priest mumbled his Latin prayers. Around his neck, he wore a purple silk band like the one he wore in the confessional, but there was no confession to be heard. He had come to baptize the tiny, mewling thing.

"What name do you give this child?" he asked.

Wolff glanced at his master for instruction.

"Richard Johannes," replied Father, in a soft voice. Richard was my hated uncle's name, and I wondered if it had been chosen as a consolation to my mother. At least, one child would bear a name from her family.

Father was a bit slumped on that occasion, highly unusual for a Prussian officer, but this was the fourth son he had baptized in haste. As the priest performed the rite, I recited the Latin responses.

The soft, white hands of the priest placed a pinch of salt on the infant's tongue, anointed him with oil. Finally, he sprinkled a few drops of water on his head. When it was finished, Father dismissed Wolff and headed out with the priest. I remained behind with the doctor. I noted that the administration of the sacred rite had produced no divine intervention, no miracle of recovery. The tiny thing's cries became even fainter than before. I'd once watched a baby bird that had fallen from its nest die, chirping until it couldn't.

"How long will it be this time?" I asked, raising my eyes to the doctor.

He gazed at me with curiosity and fondness. After Konrad and the cadets had departed, I was bored and began spending my afternoons at the doctor's office. He allowed me to read his medical books, and peer through his microscope. The dear man patiently answered my hundreds of questions.

"How long?" I repeated impatiently. I was accustomed to prompt attention to my questions. He gave me a quick, anxious look. I realized he was trying to find a kind way to answer my question.

"Tonight, for certain."

"Why do they all turn yellow?"

"The liver is failing. As it dies it gives off a compound that turns the skin and eyes yellow."

"Bilirubin," I said, nodding. I had read about it in his medical books. "But why does this happen? Why have all of my brothers died?"

His gray eyebrows were wild bushy things. When they came together in a frown, they seemed like tiny animals with a life of their own. "It's a problem of the blood. The blood of the mother and the blood of the child are incompatible."

I puzzled over this. How could this be? Were they not of the same blood? Even more puzzling was why I had been spared the yellowing disease while all of my brothers had succumbed. In fact, I had been unusually hale since birth.

Father returned after seeing the priest out.

The doctor cleared his throat. "*Euer Liebden*, we must speak." He glanced at me. Evidently, he wanted Father to send me from the room so that they could talk privately.

"Lady Margarethe may remain," said Father firmly. I wasn't surprised. He always insisted that I be present when difficult matters were raised, such as the time a mill hand got caught in the wheel and was crushed to death. Father said that I needed to learn everything, especially how to take bad news with grace and never avert my eyes from a grizzly sight.

"Go on, *Herr Doktor*, say your piece."

"*Gnädiger*, I know that I needn't spell it out for you. The countess cannot survive another birth. You will not have an heir."

"I have an heir," said my father, training his eyes in my direction, "the house rules allow for a female to inherit. There has been a writ of remainder since the time of the Great Elector."

"I understand, but it's hard for a man not to have a son."

But he had a daughter. Wasn't I enough? I stared at the doctor, whom I had considered a friend, shocked by his betrayal. Father nodded, and I realized that he agreed. As much as he loved me, he still wanted a son.

"Will you stay for some brandy, *Herr Doktor*?" my father asked.

"That would be most welcome," the doctor said with a little bow.

They went off. I remained with the mewling, yellow thing on the bed. I could have called my nurse to look after him, but I sat, watching him, wondering that he could be alive now, yet would be dead in a few hours.

It seemed a most curious thing.

I waited until the tiny creature's labored breathing finally stopped. I told one of the footmen to find the nurse. She arrived with a sheet of linen.

She looked at the still form on the bed and shook her head. "Poor, little thing. Gone before your time like all the others." She glanced at me. "You should leave now, Lady Margarethe."

I shook my head. "I shall stay."

She sighed. "Very well, but don't tell your father I allowed it." She washed the tiny corpse and wrapped it carefully. When she took it away, she held it tenderly in her arms as if it were a living child.

Father retreated to his study. I saw him sitting behind his desk and watched from the doorway. The crystal decanter that held his whiskey was nearly empty. The house was silent except for the loud ticking of the clock in the hall. When it chimed, I nearly jumped.

I went upstairs and listened outside Mother's door. I heard no sounds from within, so I opened it cautiously. All the drapes were drawn, and it was pitch black inside. I went through her sitting room to her bedchamber.

"*Mutti*?" I asked, opening the door.

No answer, only the sound of sniffling, punctuated by an occasional sob. I climbed on the bed and laid my cheek against her shoulder.

"Don't cry, *Mutti*." I stroked her arm. "Please don't." I tugged at her shoulder, hoping she would turn around, but she didn't. The sobs only grew louder. I moved closer, curling my body around hers. I lay there until I fell asleep.

◠

My grandparents came to Edelheim for the funeral. It was now evident to everyone that I would be the heir. The servants suddenly looked at me with new respect. They began calling me, somewhat prematurely, "*Eure Liebdenin.*" Although I was an intelligent child, I could not begin to imagine the implications of this salutation.

Mother's weeping continued. Father was distracted and drank too much. Grandfather perceived the need to get me out from underfoot. We rode up to the high bluff, where the view of Edelheim is best. From there, one could see the *Schloss* on its knoll in the center of the plain and all the fields, meadows, and forests surrounding it in a colorful patchwork.

The wind was blowing strongly that day. My hat nearly blew away, so my grandfather put it into his saddle bag for safekeeping. He was taller even than my father. He stood so insistently erect that the cadets used to say, "The old man has a pike up his arse." With the literal mind of a child, I imagined a large spear protruding from the poor man's rectum.

I never saw Grandfather stoop, not even in relaxed moments—never until that day when he stood beside me with his great shoulders slumped, pressed by regret that the burden would now pass to me.

My grandfather could be gruff, as soldiers are wont to be. He pulled me close to him, clamping my head so tightly against his shoulder that my ear hurt. He sometimes forgot his own strength and that more delicately made creatures need a lighter touch. He stroked my head and said, "Oh, my little Grethe, now you must learn the importance of duty." Despite the wind, I could hear his booming voice, capable of reaching the rear battalions when he had commanded a regiment. "You must always do your duty, my girl, no matter how hard it might seem. At the time when it is most onerous, then you must do it best."

"And what is my duty?"

"Do you see this land?" he said, gesturing to the fields below. "One day it will be yours. But don't ever think that you own it. The land owns you. Don't ever think that the people who serve you are yours to command. They command you. You are here to serve. You are the steward of the land and the people. You must preserve this sacred trust and pass it on to your children. Only then will you have done your duty."

It seemed rather simple. And it was, in fact. The day would come when I must return to Edelheim to be a cheerful prisoner of my duty.

⁓

Despite my mother's dark mood, or perhaps because of it, my father sought more attention from his glamorous, red-headed cousin. When she was visiting from her nearby estate, they disappeared more frequently into the boathouse on the lake.

Veronika was a famous beauty, who had been raised in Vienna. Her upbringing in that worldly city gave her a social ease and charm that we Prussians never mastered. Despite her well-known ability to seduce anyone with her charm, Veronika was always perfectly natural in my presence.

Not long after my brother died, Veronika found me moping in the garden.

"My, my Grethe. How tall you are! Why, you're nearly as tall as your handsome father." I basked in the comparison to my father and craved compliments because in my mind, I had become quite ugly. I had suddenly shot up. I was a willowy stick, awkward in my new height, and bumping into everything because my limbs were suddenly like ropes. My face was rearranging itself by the minute.

Veronika took my arm as we walked through the boxwood maze. "Oh, my darling, I wish there were something I could do for you. Poor girl, now you will bear the entire burden." Everyone kept telling me this. If I hadn't been frightened before, I now realized there might be cause for alarm.

"Mother cannot have another child, so there seems to be no alternative."

"You know about that?"

"Yes, *Tante*. I was there when the doctor told Father."

"Oh, Fritz! What can you be thinking?" she exclaimed, shaking her head. "That's not fit conversation for a child's ears!" She turned her green eyes on me and regarded me with a pensive look. "Despite your age, you are no child. You understand everything, don't you?"

"Not everything," I admitted in a rare moment of modesty. "But many things."

"Your poor mother. I cannot even begin to imagine her pain," Veronika, herself, was childless, so this was more than a sympathetic remark.

"She likes to hear me sing, but she won't admit me to her chambers."

"I shall speak to your father about it. He will make certain you are admitted. We must do everything we can to cheer her."

Veronika's plan worked. Mother allowed me into her room, where I sang for her. I asked her if she would accompany me on the piano that evening, and she got up from bed and came to dinner. Afterwards, she played the accompaniment for a little recital.

∾

After Father headed to his new assignment in Africa, my grandparents brought me back to Raithschau with them. Everyone was quiet on the train. We read in our opulent compartment, richly decorated with polished woods, dark velvet, and gilt. Like the chapel at Chilton Hall, it smelled of furniture polish. The generous space was appointed with every amenity: comfortable plush seats, a table for dining or playing cards, even a window that could be opened for fresh air.

No one spoke. My grandmother was reading a German translation of the first novel in Baroness Orczy's series on the French Revolution, *The Scarlet Pimpernel*. Grandmother could read English quite well, having learned the language for my grandfather's London posting, but given the choice, she preferred to read for pleasure in her first tongue.

Grandfather read the newspaper and smoked his pipe. When he got up to get coffee in the dining car, Grandmother looked over her pince-nez glasses at me. "Nothing for amusement, Grethe? Not even a book to read?" I shook my head. Grandmother reached out and patted my knee. "It will be all right, darling. Your grandfather and I will always be here to help you."

At first, I stared at her, knowing this kindly intended sentiment expressed something impossible, but I smiled to let her think it comforted me.

~

A letter awaited me at Raithschau. When I saw it was from Miss Stafford, I tore it open with a finger under the flap rather than wait for a letter opener. I managed to cut myself in the process. I sucked on the wound while I read Miss Stafford's flowing, perfect penmanship.

> My Dear Meg,
>   I am writing to you at Raithschau because I know you spend the end of summer with your grandparents. I hope this letter arrives in a timely manner.
>   I have some news. I have been appointed to the post of headmistress of another school. This has been a long-time dream of mine—to create a school for girls that encourages their individual talents. Many of my ideas for this project are the result of our collaboration.
>   I have written to your father to explain why I can no longer oversee your education at Chilton Hall. I have suggested that you might benefit from tutors rather than formal schooling. You have a fine mind and deserve the very best teachers.
>   With deep affection and all best wishes,
>   Clarissa Stafford

The postscript included the address of the new school in the event I wished to write to her.

My grandmother had been watching my face as I read. "Is something the matter?"

"My favorite mistress has left the school."

"Oh dear," said Grandmother and exchanged a look with Grandfather. She patted my arm. "Don't worry, darling. See this as an opportunity and not a setback."

~

"Oh! Bloody Hell!" Grandfather exclaimed as the rigging of the ship in the bottle collapsed again. Grandmother raised her eyes from her book but didn't chastise him. I suspect she'd long ago given up trying to correct him when he swore in my presence, using English as if he thought I couldn't understand.

I watched, fascinated as he inserted the tiny hook and once more tried to catch the center mast of the miniature frigate. I'd often wondered why a man raised so far from the ocean would be drawn to such a hobby. He'd explained that it was a challenge and taught patience. The frequent expletives proved the exercise hadn't worked thus far.

Grandmother finally put down her book. She nodded to her husband, who reluctantly set aside his tools. As usual, he would have a supporting role while she handled business.

"Grethe," Grandmother began, folding one hand over the other. I'd noticed that she did this to still them when she was anxious. "While your father is in Africa, we are empowered to act *in loco parentis*. That means–"

"I know what it means!" I snapped.

Grandmother understandably looked surprised, but lately, I had been moody and impatient with everyone. Of course, I understood the Latin words, but I wondered why they, and not my mother, had been left in charge. Since the funeral, she'd been under a doctor's care for her mental state, so I surmised they considered her unable to make decisions about my welfare.

"You will not be returning to your school in England," Grandmother said. The air crackled with energy as I waited to hear what she would say next. From my grandparents' worried faces, I was sure I wouldn't like it.

Finally, I couldn't stand the suspense a moment longer. "I'm to have a tutor, then? As Miss Stafford suggests?"

"No, dear," Grandmother said in a kind voice. "We are sending you to Obberoth."

"No!" I protested, leaping to my feet. "No, I won't go. I won't be a prisoner in a convent!"

Grandmother reached for my hand. "Darling, you have the most peculiar ideas. You will be a student at the school. Not a prisoner!"

I ripped my hand away from her grasp and ran off to my room. This was a horror I hadn't considered. Although I was often bored in my English school, I'd been relatively content. I liked the predictable rhythm of my life. Now, it would be completely upended.

"Why not a tutor?" I asked Grandmother, trying to bargain with her.

Grandmother's pale eyes softened with sympathy. "Because you are already so alone. You need the company of others your age."

"Why? They're nothing but silly, ignorant girls who care for nothing but dresses and hair ribbons!"

Grandmother nodded. "Silly though they are, you will learn something from their company. You cannot remain solitary your entire life, lost in your books. Besides, there is a more important reason for being schooled at Obberoth." She reminded me that as her only female heir, I would one day inherit the title of Countess of Raithschau and with it, responsibility for the order. "Understanding the nuns, their customs, and their Holy Rule is essential to performing your future duties."

"Please don't send me to that awful place," I begged. "Please!"

Grandmother sighed. "I'm sorry, Grethe, but it's already been decided, and your father agrees."

The temper tantrum that followed was not simply a fit of pique, but a spectacular eruption involving shrieking and hot, plentiful tears. My grandparents were shocked. I had always been a fairly reasonable child, and everyone assumed that, because of my intellectual abilities, I was more mature. In fact, I was not quite eleven. I ran to my room and locked the door. I refused to come out, even for dinner, although my stomach growled, and I was famished.

In the morning, hunger finally forced me out of my room. For the next few days, I stormed around the castle like a threatening cloud. My grandparents ignored me until I could speak civilly. I tried to enlist Grandfather in a campaign to hire a tutor, but it was pointless. Once Grandmother decided something, she almost never changed her mind.

Eventually, reason prevailed. I reread Miss Stafford's letter and realized she had been correct in her assessment. My English school mistresses, as well meaning as they were, really had no more to teach me. I was too young to go to university. And my grandparents were correct. I needed to be with children my own age.

None of us spoke about it again until the final night. Grandmother came to my room to oversee my packing. My belongings had been laid out in my sitting room, including the wool uniform I was to wear. I'd worn a uniform at my English school, but it was quite fashionable. The long, smooth skirt and crisp, white blouse evoked the Gibson Girl. The Obberoth school uniform was a gray, formless dress with a loose belt, almost like a nun's habit minus the veil.

"It's so ugly," I muttered.

"I cannot argue that point," replied Grandmother. "It was ugly in my day and has improved little since."

"I liked my English school."

"Yes, I know, pet, but they can't teach you there any longer, and my dear sister, Klara, has been waiting for you for a very long time."

"Klara? I thought her name was Scholastica."

"That is her religious name. To me, she will always be my dear little Klara."

"A religious name? What does that mean?"

My grandmother laughed merrily. "You don't understand the least thing about nuns, do you?"

"No, and I have no desire to learn."

"But you must learn, my darling. One day, it will be part of your duties to look after the good sisters' fortunes, so it is imperative that you learn how they think."

"I refuse to be changed by them!" I declared.

My grandmother laughed outright, which I found insulting. "Oh, I doubt that's possible!" she declared.

After breakfast, we drove to Obberoth in Grandfather's carriage, but this was no ordinary visit between two sisters. The nuns treated the arrival of the future Countess of Raithschau at their school as a significant event and had planned some pomp to accompany it. The mother general of the order, Reverend Mother Wilhelmina, and my grandaunt, Sister Scholastica, were waiting for us at the main gate, which had been opened to welcome us.

Grandmother, balancing carefully because she was wearing one of her grand hats, descended from the carriage. She placed her hands in Mother Wilhelmina's in the ancient gesture of fealty. Then they reversed the gesture, which signified they were each pledged to one another, but neither was the vassal of the other.

Grandmother and her sister embraced, offering one another almost girlish smiles of pleasure. Eventually, they turned their pale eyes on me. I'd had a growth spurt since I'd last seen my grandaunt during a visit the previous summer. She and I now stood at nearly the same height, but I gazed anywhere rather than meet her eyes.

"Dear child, welcome to Obberoth," she said in a warm voice and kissed me. "I have so looked forward to this day." She took my arm and Grandmother's and led us into the convent.

Two novices served us tea and sugar biscuits in the visitor's parlor. I'd long since decided the biscuits were the one good thing about the place. While my elders were distracted, I demolished the plateful. Afterwards, my stomach felt queasy, and for a time thereafter, I couldn't bear to look at another sugar biscuit.

Watching from the window of my grandaunt's office as my grandparents drove away in their carriage, I felt abandoned.

Sister Scholastica gestured to a chair. "Have a seat, Margarethe. Let's talk." I slouched into the seat. *Tante* pointed to a thick file folder on her desk. "I have been reviewing the reports of your mistresses in the English school. It seems they were often at a loss as to how to manage your education."

I shrugged, regarding her sidelong rather than look at her directly.

"Evidently, you have developed some interesting literary tastes. What did you think of Tolstoy? I understand that you read *War and Peace* in Russian."

I rolled my eyes. "Of course, I did. After all, it was written in Russian. There is also some French in it."

"And how is your French, dear? Your mistresses say you are fluent."

Another shrug.

"I'm not surprised. Your father also absorbed languages like a sponge.

What else interests you, Margarethe?" Her hands vanished into her voluminous sleeves.

"Does it really matter?" I asked in a sullen tone.

"To me, it matters."

I emitted a bored sigh. "Natural science, chemistry, mathematics… music, especially music."

"The choir mistress at your English school says you have a good voice. Once you are settled here, I shall introduce you to Sister Elfriede." She smiled warmly. "Oh, my dear girl, I have anticipated your arrival with such great pleasure!"

I slouched more deeply in my chair and glowered at her.

She shook her head. "I see we must make it difficult. A pity. I had so hoped we might become friends. But so be it. Come, let me show you to the dormitory."

The dormitory was a large hall with a dozen beds separated by curtains that could be drawn to provide privacy. Each sleeping berth had an armoire for clothing and uniforms. My trunk was already stationed at the foot of the bed. I gazed out the window, pleased to see that the dormitory was on the second story, which meant that escape, if necessary, could be accomplished without great danger to my limbs. Naturally, I was already planning my escape.

~

My education had already progressed to the point where there were few classes suitable for me. One of these was an art class, but as it turned out, drawing was not one of my talents. For my other studies, the headmistress, who had no regular teaching responsibilities, would personally instruct me. This was a high honor, but I perceived it as unimaginably annoying attention.

Sister Scholastica was unimpressed with the haphazard way in which my English schoolmistresses had dealt with me. I had so bedazzled them with my intellectual prowess they had allowed me to take the lead in what I wished to learn. *Tante* would have none of it. She sorted out my classical education and found some yawning gaps. She required me to go back and read Horace and Cicero and ignored my elaborate demonstrations of boredom.

One morning, she gave me the text of a Schiller play. She allowed me a brief moment to read aloud, then removed the book from my hands and asked me to repeat what I had read. She listened carefully while I recited the same pages word-for-word. This was nothing new to me, of course. I'd often used this parlor trick to amuse my schoolmates in England.

"You have a photographic memory. I thought so! That's why you learn so quickly. Oh, what wonderful luck!"

"Doesn't everyone remember what they read?"

"No, it is a very special and rare gift. However, it is not enough simply to remember. You must also understand the meaning behind the words. *That* is where we will focus our work."

The music lessons *Tante* had promised on my arrival were postponed until winter. She had wisely intuited that my passion for music would spoil me for more mundane lessons, so she held it back until I had demonstrated mental discipline elsewhere. Music became a treat to reward me, an intellectual sugar biscuit, as it were.

Until the day we were introduced, I had only seen Sister Elfriede from afar, but I knew she had once been a famous opera star. When she intoned the antiphons during the chant, her voice still had stunning power and clarity. She was beautiful and glamorous, even in a nun's habit, and retained an alluring worldliness. She was aware of me, of course, because of my important future role regarding the order. When we met, Sister Elfriede knew exactly who I was and everything there was to be known about me.

She gave me a long inspection with impassive eyes. "Well, well, Lady Margarethe, so we finally meet. Your music teacher in England writes that you have a good voice. Perhaps you will favor us with a song?"

I sang one of those ringing Anglican hymns that are so English. When I finished, Sister Elfriede stared at me with a frown. Had I offended these fine Catholic women by singing something so obviously Protestant?

Sister Elfriede turned to my grandaunt. "She sings with an adult voice."

Was this wrong? I was mildly alarmed.

Sister Elfriede rose from the organ bench and gently felt my neck and throat. "She has a fully formed adult larynx. One can begin serious training at this point. How old did you say?"

My grandaunt reminded her that I had recently turned eleven.

"She's exceptionally tall for her age." She glanced at my chest. "But no sign of puberty yet."

My grandaunt's brows rose at this remark, and she sighed deeply. Perhaps the thought of adding that subject to our lessons burdened her.

I flinched when Sister Elfriede put one hand on my belly, the other, on my back. It seemed oddly intimate, but I was intrigued. She asked me to sing octaves while she gave me the opening notes. She listened intently as I sang, nodding now and then. Finally, she pronounced: "She has a great deal of native talent and perfect pitch, but she has poor breath control, and terrible posture for a singer." With her hands, she rearranged how I stood. "That's better. Now, let us hear your octaves again."

When I finished, she nodded. "That will do." She sat down on the organ bench and studied me. "Do you know why posture is so important?"

"No, Sister."

"When we stand correctly it enables the diaphragm to work as it should."

"Yes, Sister."

"Have you any idea what the diaphragm is?" she asked, her hands disappearing in her habit.

"Yes, Sister." I recited the definition from the town doctor's medical texts, visualizing as I did, the cutaway diagram of the body showing its location. "It is a large muscular sheet separating the chest from the abdomen. When it contracts, it causes the thoracic cavity to expand and the lungs to fill with air."

"Very good. In short, it enables you to breathe. And breathing is essential to singing. Controlled breathing is essential to good singing. Stand up straight! We shall break you of these bad habits."

I obeyed at once. I very much wanted music lessons, so I was being uncharacteristically polite and cooperative.

"So, you will teach her?" asked Sister Scholastica hopefully.

Sister Elfriede looked me over from top to bottom. "Most certainly I shall teach her." For the first time, she smiled. "And it will be my pleasure."

~

Sister Scholastica's time could be taken up at a moment's notice by other duties, so I often had long spells when I was unsupervised. During this time, I was supposed to be reading my assignments, but sometimes I just daydreamed or read for pleasure. During one of those lazy afternoons, I was watching the laundry sisters collect the sheets from the line and suddenly had an idea.

While no one was looking, I slipped into the laundry and helped myself to a sack of washing powder, simple soap used for delicate fabrics and quite harmless. I waited until the sisters were in the chapel, singing the evening office, and let myself into the kitchen, where I spooned some washing powder into each of the nuns' sugar bowls.

The shared wall in the refectory had large openings, so the nuns could keep an eye on us during meals. The next morning, I positioned myself strategically in order to watch my prank unfold. At first, nothing happened. I was disappointed. But as more sisters stirred their tea, foam and bubbles formed. A nun I particularly disliked got as far as drinking the foul stuff. She made a face when she swallowed it rather than spit it out.

I tried to control myself, screwing up my mouth to stifle my laughter. Meanwhile, the other students were beginning to notice the foaming tea and giggled. With their laughter for cover, I finally allowed myself to laugh outright.

Then I felt Sister Scholastica's eyes on me and looked up.

"Margarethe, come with me," she said in a frosty voice.

She led me to her office and ordered me to kneel while she considered how to deal with me. Kneeling on the bare stones was brutally hard on my knees, damaged too many times from running after the dogs or falling off horses, but I refused to show my discomfort.

"I am so disappointed, Margarethe," *Tante* said, pacing. "I thought we were finally getting on."

No response seemed required, so I remained silent and stared straight ahead.

"Look at me when I speak to you!" she demanded.

I looked up. Her stern face indicated that she had not a feather's weight of patience to spare.

"Margarethe, you have so much potential, yet you frustrate the good will of everyone who cares for you. Do you suppose Sister Elfriede liked the taste of her tea this morning?"

"Perhaps she found it a change of pace," I suggested sarcastically.

From the twitch under Sister Scholastica's scapular, I guessed that she was squeezing her hands together to prevent herself from slapping me.

"You will remain here on your knees for an hour. When I return, I shall tell you your punishment."

She decided that I would have no music lessons of any kind for a week. Instead, the time usually occupied by music would be devoted to assisting the kitchen sisters in preparing meals and washing dishes.

Of course, I had no intention of performing this penance. I perceived that the time had come to put my escape plan into action. Instead of reporting for my first spell of kitchen duty, I went to my dormitory and ripped the sheet off my bed. Unfortunately, it wasn't quite long enough, so I "borrowed" the sheets from three of the neighboring beds. I tied the sheets together with knots I'd learned while training with the cadets.

I secured my "rope" around an iron sconce near the window and lowered myself to the ground. I had to drop the last meter and twisted my ankle. Fortunately, it wasn't broken.

I had landed outside the convent wall, but now, I had a dilemma. Where could I go? I couldn't hide in the woods like an animal, and I had to find shelter for the night. The only logical destination was Schloss Raithschau.

I limped in that direction. Because of my injury, the walk took nearly an hour. The old majordomo was summoned when I rang the gate bell. He took one look at me—hair full of leaves and sticks, filthy from landing in the dirt—and escorted me directly to my grandmother's sitting room.

Grandmother was alarmed at my physical state. Once she had assured herself that I was sound, she sent a servant to fetch my grandfather. They both looked stern while I recounted what had transpired. When I finished my tale, Grandfather took me outside and cut a hazel branch. He switched me hard enough to leave red marks, but not enough to draw blood. I could not be damaged goods when it came to the marriage lottery.

My grandparents allowed me to stay the night, but in the morning, Grandfather and I rode in his carriage to Obberoth. He made elaborate apologies to Reverend Mother and Sister Scholastica and assured them that it would never happen again.

My grandaunt said not a word as I accompanied her to her office. After she closed the door, she took me in her arms and squeezed me with all her might. "Thank God, you're safe!"

I was so disarmed by this dramatic reconciliation that I could do nothing except return her embrace. The greetings done, she directed me to kneel while she settled on my punishment. Eventually, she decided to allow the first punishment to stand and to be doubled. It was during this spell of kitchen duty that I learned to peel potatoes very efficiently.

∾

The remainder of the term passed more or less uneventfully with one exception. *Tante* decided it was time to have the talk about puberty. She was remarkably composed as she explained how my body would change as I became a woman, and how I would bleed. She never used metaphors and described everything in perfectly correct clinical language. Nothing about the process flustered nor embarrassed her, not even when she explained the process by which children are conceived.

"Margarethe, your little smirk suggests that you already know exactly what I am attempting to explain."

Her recognizing this disappointed me. I thought I was hiding my thoughts rather well. Plus, I was very curious to hear what she would say.

"I've watched my father's horses and dogs breed. Humans are animals, so their methods must be similar." It made a perfect syllogism. I smiled, looking for confirmation.

My grandaunt pursed her lips. "Margarethe, you are entirely too smart for your own good. But, well enough. We can skip the mechanics and go on to the spiritual component."

"You mean to speak about erotic love?"

"There are many forms of love, my dear. Eros is but one of them."

I already knew this from reading the Greek philosophers and the early Church fathers, but Sister Scholastica held forth on the subject of sexual attraction. The only word that could describe her approach was "reverential." And she had most interesting ideas about the Creator's motives for designing us to reproduce in this way.

"The desire for a lover is but a reflection of God's desire for all of creation. It was this desire to have something to love and to be loved in return that brought forth the universe. God's desire animates the universe and creates all life. It is why your body will become lush and fertile, just as when the earth becomes green and fruitful in summer. Although we have laws and rules governing its expression, ultimately, desire cannot be denied. It has its own imperative."

As I listened, I thought about her words, although I didn't really understand them. Even more, I wondered why these secrets of womanhood had been conveyed by someone vowed to chastity, and not my mother, or even my grandmother.

4

As my grandaunt had predicted, my body began to change, and it happened that very summer. The first sign was coarse hair growing in places where it had never grown before. My breasts began to bud, forming annoying pellets under my nipples. My hair grew sleeker and darkened a little, although it was still blonde, nearly white. The texture of my skin coarsened. Suddenly, my face was abloom with pimples. When I looked in the mirror, I was plainly horrified.

My response to these changes was to ride my horse through the meadows of Edelheim like a savage. The poor beast foamed at the mouth and had a terrified look in her eye, yet I pushed her ever harder. Then I would strip and swim naked in the lake to cool my feverish body. I floated around on my back, feeling the tickle of the fish spines and getting duckweed tangled in my hair.

My father's return on leave put an end to the wild rides and naked swims. Finally, Konrad arrived. Despite the absence of the cadet training, Father had invited him to spend a few weeks with us during his leave. Konrad's presence provided me with an excuse to behave in a somewhat more civilized manner. Simply having someone my own age for conversation was calming. All adults, even my father, were suddenly baffling to me.

Konrad still looked his old self. Being a boy, he would change later. Our difference in height was stunning. I'd gone through a growth spurt. My legs ached, the muscles and ligaments being pulled too fast to keep up with the bones. Konrad sat by, while my old nurse massaged my legs with liniment so that I could sleep. Konrad took it all in, curious, it seemed, but cool. His lack of sympathy angered me out of proportion to anything he did or said.

"Just you wait until it's your turn, you little beast!"

"You needn't emphasize the fact that I'm little. But it's temporary. One day I'll be taller."

"What makes you think so?"

"Because I'm a boy. And someday I'll be a man. Everyone knows men are bigger and better."

I stuck out my tongue at him.

We had other minor rows of this type, mainly because I was so irritable. I didn't understand why, but everyone annoyed me.

After Konrad left, I filled my afternoons with visits to the doctor's surgery. I managed to curb my surliness in his presence because I knew he had something to teach me. He showed me how to sample tissue from my body, scrape the inside of my cheek and prick my finger to draw blood. He taught me how to capture the samples between sheets of glass, a thicker one below and a fragile square above to flatten it. "The more transparent, the better," he explained, and showed me how to focus the mirror so the reflected light passed through the sample from below. The oil immersion lens was fussy, and I got grease stains on my dresses. I'm sure the doctor breathed a sigh of relief when I learned to focus the lens without cracking the slides and damaging it.

The mysterious, unseen world of my own flesh fascinated me. When I dutifully wrote my weekly letter to my grandaunt, I described it with great reverence. She wrote back glowing words of encouragement.

~

In July, Grandfather came to Edelheim. He and Father liked to sit on the verandah to enjoy the golden light of the fading sun. They leisurely smoked their pipes and discussed politics in hushed tones, complaining about the Kaiser's stranglehold on the government and the resultant unrest.

"He's so arrogant and self-absorbed. He won't listen to anyone," Father grumbled. "But he's too ignorant and short-sighted not to make a botch of things! What an idiot!" They spoke in English, which, of course, I understood. Fortunately, the servants didn't. Speaking disrespectfully of the Kaiser was considered treason. From time to time, Father or Grandfather looked my way to see if I'd been listening. Although I was engrossed in a new adventure novel by Jack London, I'd kept one ear alert.

Finally, the topic changed, and Father spoke of Africa. "I wish I could resign this barbaric assignment," he complained, which made me look up from my book, my ears recognizing important information.

"Fritz, that's impossible," replied Grandfather flatly. "It would destroy your career. You must finish the term of your posting. After that, you can leave with honor."

"Honor? There is no honor in this filthy campaign." Father startled me by spitting to show his disgust. He glanced in my direction, and I quickly returned my eyes to my book.

The next morning, after breakfast, Father invited me to ride out with him to visit some of the tenant farms. Although he had a farm manager to collect the rents and deal with the concerns of the tenants, Father liked to look in on them himself.

As we rode through the thick forest to the other side of the manor, I enjoyed the rich smell of oak moss and damp earth. My eyes were sharp for the tiniest movement of creatures on the forest floor, burrowing and climbing animals with sleek coats and shining eyes. The ravens flew overhead watching our progress suspiciously. Sometimes, they croaked to remind us that we were crossing their domain.

On the other side of the woods, the peasant houses, built of timber and stone, covered with stucco and whitewash, had a consistent design. Nearly every house was connected to the barn. Often the cow manger was beneath, and the scent of manure crept inside the living quarters. It didn't help that the peasants caught the effluvia from both human and beast in a common cesspool to use as fertilizer on the fields. By that time of year, the ammonia content was high enough to make one's eyes water.

I followed father's lead in declining the offer of food and drink. He'd explained beforehand that he didn't want to deprive the tenants, but when I saw the hygiene in some of the kitchens, I suspected another reason. A cat, in search of prey, prowled lazily among unwashed dishes. A pail of the chopped turnips the farmers fed their cows sat side-by-side with a pot of cut-up vegetables for the evening's stew.

As we rode back to the house, Father said, "Remember, Grethe, when visiting our people, it is more important to listen than speak. Say little but encourage conversation. Ask questions that show interest."

Other than offering these words of advice, Father was silent as we rode back to the house.

"I heard you tell Grandfather you wished to leave Africa."

"Your sharp ears hear everything, don't they?"

"That's how I learn," I said in my defense.

He stopped his horse for a moment. "Yes, I'd like to leave Africa. It's not what I expected."

I found that hard to believe. I still imagined Africa from the illustrations in my childhood adventure magazines as a magical place where snakes grew as big around as my waist, and chattering monkeys hung from every tree. I described the scenes in my head to my father, and he laughed.

"Yes, it's a wild and beautiful place, but much of Africa is grassy plains or desert. Many people struggle to eke out an existence."

"If it's so poor, why do we care about it?"

He gave me a tolerant look. "All the countries of Europe have colonies there. The empire came late to the party, so now we have only the dregs, but there are still riches to be had. Minerals. Fertile ground and a warm climate all year. The natives provide cheap labor."

"That's good, isn't it?"

"It would be if the natives did it willingly, but they don't. We treat them like dogs who need to be brought to heel by beating them." I instantly knew this wouldn't sit well with Father. He trained his dogs by offering treats of dried meat, encouraging words, and affectionate petting. "We've taken their land to use as our own, and now we treat them harshly when they protest."

"What do you do?"

He eyed me cautiously, obviously weighing how much to say. "You're old enough now to learn how the world works," he finally said. "If they don't cooperate, we burn their huts. We round them up into camps. We withhold rations until they're nearly starving, even the women and children."

I tried to comprehend this cruelty. "Why?"

"Greed," said Father. "Like other countries, we want to extract what natural wealth exists in those unspoiled lands. And if we don't take it, someone else will."

It sounded from his regretful tone that he thought this was wrong, so I asked him to elaborate.

"Stealing is wrong," he simply said. "Killing is wrong. Doesn't it say so in the Bible?"

I wanted to ask more questions, but he gave me a stern look, so I considered the lesson over.

～

Surprisingly, I was glad when summer finally came to a close because it meant a new school term would begin. I returned to Obberoth in September and found a special gift awaiting me—the sort of high-quality Zeiss microscope that one gives a new medical student. Evidently, Sister Scholastica had been paying close attention while I'd rhapsodized over my adventures in the town doctor's surgery.

There were other exciting developments. My grandaunt had talked Grandmother into funding a science laboratory, and for the first time in the school's long history, a laywoman had been engaged to teach. Charlotte von Backenstoss came to us with a newly minted doctorate in chemistry from the Ludwig-Maximilians University in Munich, one of the first women to be so honored. We proudly addressed her as "*Fräulein Doktor.*"

Dr. von Backenstoss was stern when she addressed us on the first day. She was not much older than the senior girls in the class. Perhaps she mustered a forbidding persona in the hopes of getting our respect, but her sternness was undercut by her small stature. She barely came to my shoulder. Her hair was the color of newly shucked chestnuts. She wore it in a tidy bun to keep it away from the flame of the alcohol lamp as she subsequently explained in her lecture on laboratory safety. We wore sleeve guards and tied back our hair for the same reason.

At first, I was put off by her steely demeanor, but when I allowed myself to see past it, I saw a resemblance to Miss Stafford as well as to someone from my distant past, someone I had dearly loved: Miss Westerfield.

Fräulein Doktor brought with her the newest methods of science education and laboratory technique. That semester, we engaged in many practical experiments: fractional distillation of chlorophyll from spinach, the extraction of cholesterol from gallstones provided by the local hospital, as well as finding unknown elements in a solution. For the space of that term, I wanted to be a chemist more than anything.

Dr. von Backenstoss easily wooed me away from chemistry by teaching me how to exploit the features of my new microscope, which was a step up from the one in the town doctor's surgery. I grew a bacteria farm in the girl's lavatory, where I raised interesting varieties spawned from fingernail clippings, scrapings from my teeth, and other odd sources.

Fräulein Doktor was enormously patient with my questions. She had a rich, low voice. In her presence, I practiced lowering mine to her pitch. Sometimes, I neglected to hear what she was saying because I was so busy listening to her, or I became lost in her blue-green eyes, and she needed to repeat a question to get my attention.

Apart from *Fräulein Doktor*'s classes and music instruction with Sister Elfriede, all my studies that autumn were incredibly boring. Instead of reading the assignments *Tante* had given me, I entertained myself with elaborate tales of my own invention in which I was a heroic knight rescuing beautiful damsels in distress.

I was musing about nothing in particular when my eyes fell on a section of the convent wall that had always bothered me. Sometime in the past, the ancient mortar had worked loose. It had been replaced, along with some missing stones, but the workmen had failed to match the new stones and mortar with the rest of the wall. It was a small thing, but someone should have taken the trouble to provide the eye with a smooth, unbroken impression. The more I looked at the wall, the more it offended me.

A recent chemistry experiment involving elemental sulphur had brought to mind the black powder lesson from the cadet camp. I'd almost forgotten about it, but now that it had entered my mind, it tantalized me. I secured a chunk of sulphur for my project. The remaining ingredients were easy enough to procure. The kitchen sisters used saltpeter to cure meat. There was an abundant supply of charcoal left from the fires when the laundry sisters heated the large kettles to wash the bed linens.

During one of my leisurely periods, I found the science laboratory unoccupied and set about refining the reagents. I fashioned a tube from cardboard and made a fuse from cotton twine stiffened with wax and impregnated with black powder. Essentially, I had constructed a crude stick of dynamite like the one we had made in the cadet camp. Now, all I needed was an opportunity.

I waited until everyone was in the chapel for a procession to honor Mary the Virgin. I slipped away from the assembly and scaled the wall high enough for optimal placement of the charge. Carefully, I descended, reeling out my fuse as I went. I lit it with a cigarette I'd stolen from Grandmother's handbag. As soon as the fuse began to spark, I ran and took cover. Crouching under a heavy wooden bench, I covered my ears against the expected noise and waited. Time seemed to crawl. Then, when I least expected it, a powerful blast reverberated against my body, nearly knocking me flat. The bench above me rattled, dancing around on the cobblestones.

When the noise stopped, I dared to look. Not only had the explosion taken down the mismatched section of wall, but all the rest of it as well. In the distance, I heard girls screaming in terror. One of the kitchen sisters, who'd come out to look, fainted. The billows of abundant smoke were completely satisfying...until I looked up into Sister Scholastica's face.

She hauled me out of my hiding place by the armpit. I had no idea she was so strong. "You idiot!" she said with a stinging slap on my cheek. "You could have killed yourself or someone else! What in God's name were you doing?" She had never spoken to me in that manner, so I was understandably shocked.

She dragged me by the arm into her office, where she ordered me to kneel while a messenger was dispatched to Raithschau. A short time later, my grandparents arrived. Grandmother made profuse apologies to the mother general and assured her that the wall would be rebuilt at once.

Meanwhile, grandfather cut a hazel branch. He asked Reverend Mother to assemble the students and sisters in the courtyard, where he switched me in front of everyone, but not enough to draw blood or damage my valuable skin. I must remain unblemished for the marriage lottery. I kept my face rigid and held back my tears, but the humiliation of the public beating hurt far worse than the blows. I could feel his anger and embarrassment in every stroke.

Eventually, Grandmother said, "Stop, Heinrich. That is enough!"

He threw the hazel branch away as if he loathed the thing. I knew it was not the switch he hated, nor me, his miserable excuse for a granddaughter. He despised feeling obligated to beat me.

The assembly was dismissed. My grandparents departed, and I returned to the headmistress's office with Sister Scholastica. She shut the door, but instead of asking me to kneel as I expected, she took me in her arms. "I am so sorry, Margarethe. I never meant to strike you or for your grandfather to beat you." Then she released me and sank down in the chair behind her desk. Without warning, she began to weep. "Why?" she pleaded, bright tears streaming down her cheeks. "Why do you do such things? Do you hate us? Do you hate *everyone* who loves you?" I had no idea what to say, so I merely stood there like a fool. "Get out," she finally said. "Go to your dormitory and stay there until I call for you."

Fräulein Doktor came to fetch me to dinner. She found me lying on my belly on my iron cot. When I saw her, I set aside my book and sat up.

"Let me see your back," she said.

I unbuttoned my dress and pulled up my under-blouse. Her fingers cautiously touching my skin made it smart, but I tried not to flinch.

"A cold compress will ease the pain. No real harm done. Just red marks that will undoubtedly bruise."

She left and returned with a basin and a damp cloth wrung tight. "That was quite an explosion," she said, gingerly dabbing my back. "You evidently knew what you were doing. Where did you learn to make explosives?" I told her about the munitions training during the cadets' summer camp. She chuckled softly. "Maybe now your father will think twice about including you in such instruction. Is he trying to make a soldier of you?"

If only, I thought. "He'll be furious when he hears about this. He'll switch me again."

"Oh, maybe not. He might take pride in how well you learned your lessons." She pulled down my shirt, and I buttoned my dress. "You refined the ingredients in the laboratory. I found the crucible you used. It's still encrusted, and I expect you to clean it properly. You must learn to be tidier in a common laboratory." She smiled. "But the formula was a success. Did you keep notes?"

"No. I should have thought of that! But I remember."

"Write it down for me before you forget. I want to see *every* step." She patted my arm. "Come now. Sister Scholastica wishes to speak to you before dinner."

For my punishment, I was required to read Kant's *Metaphysics of Morals* and write a detailed exposition of the central argument. I finally understood why my father had said he would rather break his leg than read Kant again.

～

After the gun powder incident, Sister Scholastica decided that I needed closer supervision. She also wanted to turn my attention to studies that would be critical to my future as the patroness of the order. My first assignment was to learn the nuns' Holy Rule, which seemed to prohibit everything except breathing. Soon, I could explain whether a conversation during the Great Silence was "necessary" or not. I understood why a sister must never walk with "precipitous step" and why banishing one's hands into the wide sleeves of the habit or beneath the odd piece of clothing, called a "scapular," was essential. Modesty was also the rationale behind the "custody of the eyes."

My next assignment was to read the correspondence between my ancestor, Margarethe von Raithschau and Mathilde von Obberoth, the medieval women who had roped my family into looking after the convent. The medieval Latin wasn't easy to read, but I understood all the words. What I couldn't understand was why friends would use such passionate language.

After a hiatus as punishment, my lessons with Sister Elfriede resumed. "Your voice has a heroic quality, perfect for the great Bach alto solos." She wasn't satisfied that I was naturally an alto because I had such a substantial upper range. "I suspect that when your voice fully matures, you may be a mezzo-soprano. Until we know, I would like you to learn a wide range of compositions." That suited me fine. My attention span was short, so variety appealed to me.

Before I headed to Raithschau for the summer recess, *Tante* called me to her study. "This has been an important year for you, Margarethe. You began it as a bombardier and end it being able to make a compelling argument for why good is 'an end in itself.' Pride may be a sin, but I am proud of your progress, and you should be as well." She studied me carefully to gauge my reaction. "I am glad we have finally become friends. Sometimes, I forget how young you are. I am tempted to speak to you as a peer, but despite your precocity, you are not. I look forward to the day when you mature, and we can look one another in the eye."

I knew she meant this figuratively, for I was now substantially taller than she. Then she gave me such an affectionate look that I melted. I wanted to blurt out how much I loved her, but I drew on the reserve I had been taught and held back.

∽

Father's term of duty would not end until autumn, so my grandparents kept me at Raithschau that summer. I was beginning to feel more at home in the old castle than at Edelheim. When I shared this sentiment with Grandmother, she looked pleased.

"This is your home, darling, as much as Edelheim. You belong to both of them, and they belong to you." She had, perhaps unwittingly, turned a simple statement into something profound, and I wondered about it for days.

Grandmother used the portraits of my forebears scattered around the house to reinforce my connection to Raithschau. Although the skills of the painters varied widely, I was able to see my resemblance to my long-dead ancestors. Through centuries of intermarriage—required because nobles must marry within their rank to retain their titles—I was related to most of the nobility of the *Reich*, which meant that my grandparents were more than my grandparents; my parents more than my parents, and Konrad was much more than my cousin. In fact, his blood was closer to mine than a brother's. Small wonder we looked so alike.

Grandmother always ended our study of the portraits in the great hall of the *Schloss*, where her life-size, standing portrait hung over the ancient open fireplace. "One day, you will stand there, Grethe. One day, when you are Countess Raithschau."

Her words chilled me, for my portrait would only hang in the great hall when my grandmother lay in her grave. Whenever the thought of that terrible eventuality flickered into my mind, I instantly snuffed it out.

⁓

"Would you like a ride into town, Grethe?" Grandfather asked as he slathered his breakfast roll with butter. Grandmother raised her eyes to him, obviously wise to his motives for an outing. He'd acquired a motorcar and now looked for any chance to drive it. I was equally happy for any opportunity to accompany him, for I too was fascinated by the contraption.

While Grandfather dealt with his supposed business at the bank, I wandered around town. Everywhere, I saw posters announcing the annual, end-of-summer steeplechase. I'd asked if I might enter the previous summer, but Grandfather had said, "No, Grethe, it's too dangerous. If something happened to you, I'll never hear the end of it." He was right about that.

Riding back to Raithschau, I casually mentioned the race. Grandfather gave me a sidelong look. Naturally, he knew what was coming next. "But Grandfather, you know I'm a good rider. I can jump with the best of them."

"No, Grethe, and that's final," he said, but where I was concerned, nothing was ever final. I pleaded and carried on until he relented.

Through Grandmother, Sister Scholastica heard that I had entered the race. She telephoned to chastise her brother-in-law for allowing me to enter. After he ended the call, Grandfather muttered, "Your sister needs to mind her own business."

Fortunately, I had learned to ride astride with the cadets. Father said that sidesaddle riding was "a ridiculous affectation" and had never encouraged it. Sidesaddle riders were banned from competition, which conveniently eliminated most women.

The race was fast approaching, so I chose one of Grandfather's Arabian mares and practiced every day, becoming deliciously dirty in the process. After a wild ride, I came home in my muddy riding clothes, stomping dirt over the polished floors of Raithschau. Grandmother scolded me, but I secretly took delight in my filth.

The day of the race finally arrived. The course was extremely challenging with a dozen high jumps and a winding ride over rough terrain. The last jump was over a high fence with a stream on the other side. My horse and I had practiced it many times, but she'd never liked it. As we approached the jump, I could feel her getting skittish. I squeezed my knees tighter to secure my seat. That only caused the horse to veer away at the worst possible moment. She stumbled, and I felt myself forcibly ejected from the saddle.

Time seemed to stop after I became airborne. With an odd detachment, I observed the serene beauty of the tree canopy and the unclouded sky passing slowly above me. Then my boot caught on the fence, and I came down hard. I actually felt the bone snap. The intense pain made me nauseous, but I was compelled to see the extent of my injury. The broken bone poked through my bloodstained breeches. In a sudden moment of stunning clarity, I marveled that the marrow looked like pink foam.

The race officials dispatched a stretcher at once. Grandfather, who had witnessed the accident from the reviewing stand, struggled to keep up with them. He was out of breath when he arrived. He tried to keep his expression neutral, but I could read his concerns in his pale face.

Dr. Schulte, the new town physician, had been called to attend me. He looked ashen as he surveyed the injury. He cut open the leg of my breeches with shears, soaked a cloth in phenol, and covered the broken ends of the bone. Even the light pressure as he secured the splint was excruciatingly painful.

"Quickly!" ordered the doctor. "We must take her to a place where I can perform surgery."

The nearest hospital was in Würzburg, an hour's journey by motorcar. The doctor's surgery was small and hardly an ideal setting. The only logical place for an operation was the infirmary at Obberoth, which was as well-equipped as a small hospital

"Can you save the leg?" my grandfather asked anxiously as they transported me in his motorcar to the convent.

"Yes, we can save the leg. It's a clean break and looks uglier than it is, but we must act at once to avoid infection."

My grandaunt looked faint when she saw me. "Dear God!" she

exclaimed and crossed herself. Fortunately, the infirmarian, an experienced nurse, took charge. She set up sterile drapes and laid out a surgical tray. "Think of something pleasant," she said as she placed the ether mask over my nose. Her face was the last thing I remember.

When I awoke, I was lying in bed in the convent infirmary. My leg was suspended in the air by a rope over a pulley. On the other side was a lead weight. The leg was in traction, the infirmarian's assistant explained, to help the bone heal in the correct position. I still felt groggy from the ether, but the pain was intense. They gave me a bitter draught, and mercifully, I fell asleep.

The doctor came to inspect the wound. He'd cleverly created a little window in the cast for changing the bandage. Dr. Schulte had a kind, earnest face, but otherwise, he wasn't much to look at, being very tall, gangly, and round-shouldered from stooping. His hair was already thinning although he was barely twenty-five.

Now that I'd gotten over the shock of the accident, my curiosity returned. I asked the doctor to describe my injuries. He patiently answered all my questions.

"Why must I be tied to the ceiling?"

"It keeps the bones in place and stretches the muscles, which prevents painful spasms."

When the doctor came again, he brought x-rays from his surgery. I could clearly see the outlines of the bones, but otherwise the gray tones meant little. He taught me how to interpret one light area from another; how to see the ghostly outline of the soft tissue, and how to navigate my way around the structures. He quizzed me and took great delight in my getting the answers right. When Sister Scholastica visited that afternoon, I recounted my conversation with the doctor. Her pale eyes, watching me as I spoke, were shrewd.

The infirmary sisters waited on me hand and foot. Being the future patroness of the order and the grandniece of the headmistress guaranteed me first-class care. I loathed having to relieve myself in a bedpan in their presence and having them bathe me, but I was tied to a chain suspended from the ceiling and their prisoner.

A novice, who'd already trained as a nurse, was assigned to look after me. After attending to my dressing, Sister Monica often remained to read to me.

"Sister, you know I am quite capable of reading that book on my own."

"Yes, I know, but it isn't easy to hold a book when lying in that position, and don't you take pleasure in hearing someone read to you? I always find it a great comfort."

She smiled. She had calm, gray eyes and a kind face. When she changed my dressing, her hands were warm and gentle. She read with great expression in a low, musical voice. I was quite taken with her. In fact, all the sisters were nothing but kind. I had many hours to consider the harm my pranks might have done to the nuns. When *Tante* came that afternoon, I offered an apology.

"Well, well, Margarethe, that is a big step in the right direction. I accept your apology. We all want the best for you. You needn't fight us every step of the way."

Finally, Dr. Schulte cut off the cast and unstrung me from the hateful contraption. My leg was tender at first. I walked with crutches for a week, then with a cane for another. I had a jagged scar on the side of my thigh, where the bone had poked through the flesh. It remained red and ugly for some time, but fortunately, I could walk as well as ever. As far as I was concerned, the matter was concluded, but I don't think Grandmother ever forgave my grandfather.

∼

Sister Elfriede examined my throat in the light from the window and carefully felt my larynx. "Your vocal cords have stopped growing. We can now determine your *Fach*."

To aid in this, she had me learn a variety of operatic roles from Gluck to Wagner. She encouraged me to learn some Italian roles: Princess Eboli and Amneris. She began teaching me Italian, which she had picked up during her career as an opera singer. "A singer must always learn the languages she sings, or it is mere mimicry. A native speaker can always hear when the singer doesn't know the real meaning of the words. Learn as many languages as you can, Margarethe."

When I learned a role, she insisted that I learn the entire opera, not merely the famous arias. "Train your memory and your mind to embrace the whole of the opera, not merely a few favorite parts."

She seemed pleased with my progress, but one afternoon, after a vigorous practice, she sat me down in her little office off the music library.

"Margarethe, there is something I must tell you," she said in a solemn tone that instantly put me on edge. I feared bad news from home or worse. "You have a powerful and beautiful voice, one of the finest voices I have ever heard. With the right training and the will to realize your potential, you could have a spectacular operatic career."

While she was delivering this compliment, her expression remained grave. "But something's wrong," I observed cautiously. Perhaps there was some flaw in my voice or my singing that she had been too kind to reveal.

"Margarethe, I am trying to explain that you are a truly gifted singer, but you cannot have an operatic career."

"Why not?"

"Because you are highborn."

"Why does that matter?"

She looked frustrated. "It would be a scandal for a lady of your station to sing on a public stage. Your grandmother would never allow it. Nor your parents."

"Then why would they allow you to teach me?"

Sister Elfriede looked directly into my eyes. "Your parents love music. They knew, just as I knew from the moment I first heard you sing, that you have real talent."

"But they can't stop me from singing."

"No, you can provide polite entertainment after dinner, but you can never sing as a professional."

In fact, I had never gotten as far as imagining myself on the stage. I only knew that the pleasure of making music gave me joy.

"It breaks my heart to tell you this, but I must tell you the truth because I am so very fond of you." A maelstrom of emotions churned within me.

Finally, I burst into tears. Sister Elfriede took me in her arms and let me weep into her wimple. "Dear girl, I am so sorry. I am even more sorry to be the one to tell you."

After this remarkable conversation, I was so upset I couldn't sing for days. I shunned Sister Elfriede and skipped my voice lessons. I hardly spoke to anyone. My grandaunt noticed my stormy expression and pulled me aside after chapel. "What's troubling you, child?"

"You've broken my heart!" I said dramatically.

"How? What have I done?"

"I can never be a singer, yet you allowed Sister Elfriede to train me! That was nothing but cruel!"

My grandaunt, attempted to embrace me, but I fended her off. She stood there with an imploring look. "I knew how you love to sing. To deprive you would have been an even greater cruelty."

"But you tempted me, and now I discover that a career in music is impossible!"

"But no one can stop you from singing. That is your God-given talent," she said in an encouraging tone. Her optimistic expression faded as I continued to glare at her. "Sister Elfriede is beside herself thinking she has hurt you. Go, reassure her. I'm sure she only told you the truth out of kindness."

I rolled my eyes, amazed that the adults around me thought I should comfort them after they had crushed me with their "kindness." But I loved Sister Elfriede, so when I knew the nuns' choir practice was nearly finished, I looked for her in the chapel.

"Thank God, you've come back!" she exclaimed, flinging her arms around me. "Let's sing together. It will make us both feel better." We sang a Bach alto-soprano duet. It was extremely difficult for me because I was nearly choking with tears, but I pulled myself together to assure Sister Elfriede that I had forgiven her.

~

Shortly before the end of term, Sister Scholastica summoned me to her study. When I arrived for the appointment, *Fräulein Doktor* was already seated in one of the visitors' chairs. My grandmother, wearing one of her grand hats, sat beside her. Such a distinguished gathering worried me, but they were all smiling, which somewhat allayed my fears.

Sister Scholastica gestured to a chair that had been brought in from the anteroom, and I sat down. "Thank you for joining us, Margarethe," said *Tante* after a long inspection to assess my mood. "We are here to discuss your future. You will be pleased to learn that Miss Penrose, the principal of Somerville College has agreed to review your application."

Fräulein Doktor reached over and patted my arm. Grandmother gave me a radiant smile.

"Now, we all know what your primary duties are," my grandaunt continued, "but you also have a choice regarding how you will serve, which is why we have put so much effort into your education." She gave me a penetrating look. "Margarethe, what is your heart's fondest desire? If you could do or be anything in this life, what would it be?"

I blurted out the truth: "If I could be anything, I would be a singer."

"Now, that simply won't do!" said my grandmother, turning to me. "No lady of the *Uradel* can sing on a public stage! It's unthinkable!"

My grandaunt's little wave, a gesture obviously meant to advise her sister, was poorly concealed. Grandmother rolled her eyes. *Fräulein Doktor* raised a brow. However, *Tante*'s message was clear: Let me handle this. She rose and asked her secretary to find Sister Elfriede. Another chair was brought.

Sister Elfriede gave me a quick smile as she entered the room, but when she saw all the dour faces, it instantly faded.

"Sister Elfriede, we are discussing Margarethe's education," Sister Scholastica began. "Will you give us a frank evaluation of her vocal abilities. I know you are fond of your pupil but do try to be objective."

Sister Elfriede focused her gaze on the headmistress. "Lady Margarethe has an extraordinary voice, extremely powerful and her range exceeds that of a dramatic mezzo-soprano. She has a resonant chest voice that goes down to the F below the staff. Her upper range is nearly that of a soprano. She is very young, and her voice may darken as she matures, but it is bright and can carry above any accompaniment."

This detailed analysis apparently tried *Tante's* patience. There was a slight pucker between her brows. "And what does all that mean in layman's terms? Could Margarethe have a career as a professional singer?"

"Without doubt," said Sister Elfriede with great conviction. "Properly trained, she could be one of the great mezzos of her generation."

"If we asked, would you be willing to contact your friends in the music world to secure a spot in a conservatory?" asked *Tante*, regarding me carefully as she spoke.

"But of course. It would be my pleasure."

"Thank you, Sister," said my grandaunt, giving her a nod. "That will do." As Sister Elfriede headed to the door, she shot me a quick, anxious smile. Obviously, she was in my camp.

Beside me, my grandmother could barely contain herself. "What do you think you're doing, Klara? I mean *really*?"

Again, my grandaunt offered a little, dismissive gesture advising her sister to stay out of the conversation.

"So, Margarethe," *Tante* began, clasping her hands on the desk and leaning forward. "Shall we ask Sister Elfriede to look into conservatories for you?"

I glanced at *Fräulein Doktor*. "I am also interested in science."

"From what I understand, Somerville College has excellent tutors in the sciences," said *Fräulein Doktor*, looking flattered. "Are you interested in scientific research or teaching?"

"Neither. I think I'd like to become a physician."

"What!" exclaimed my grandmother. She glared at her sister. "Klara, you said that you had this in hand!"

Tante patted the air, obviously to urge patience on her sister. "And when did this idea occur to you, Margarethe?" my grandaunt asked, peering at me intently.

The fact is, the idea had come to me while we'd been talking. I needed time to think, so I focused on *Fräulein Doktor*, who looked as curious as the others. I mentally retraced the path that had brought me to that point. Clearly, it had begun with Miss Westerfield's brutal amputation. Reading the town doctor's medical books and learning how to use his microscope had been more than a way to pass an idle summer day. But the event that had sealed my fate was Dr. Schulte's patient explanation of how he'd repaired my shattered leg.

"Dr. Schulte inspired me, I think."

I looked around at their faces. *Fräulein Doktor* looked pleased. *Tante*'s pale-eyed gaze was intense but thoughtful. Grandmother was frowning.

"Medicine is not an easy path for a woman," Sister Scholastica finally said.

"Must I do something easy?" I asked, perplexed.

Fräulein Doktor stifled a laugh. *Tante* gave her a sharp look, but then her lips curved into a smile.

"Well then, Dr. von Backenstoss," she said, "how can we best prepare my grandniece to study medicine?"

5

Fräulein Doktor had trained as a chemist. Biology wasn't her strong suit, but she dutifully integrated more botany and zoology into her lectures. She anesthetized a bull frog with chloroform. While we gawked in horror, she delicately clipped open the creature's chest so that we could observe its beating heart. While I watched in fascination, the other students squealed with disgust. Beside me, a girl melted into a dead faint. Fortunately, our teacher was prepared with smelling salts.

"Give us some room!" she ordered, snapping open the cotton-wrapped, glass capsule. The stricken girl's head abruptly jerked up, and she opened her eyes. Two of my classmates helped her to her feet.

"Anyone who finds the lesson too difficult may have a study recess," said *Fräulein Doktor*, sounding annoyed.

Everyone left the room except one other student. "All right, then. Let's get back to the lesson." Dr. von Backenstoss mercifully ended the frog's life with an overdose of chloroform. Leaning in to see the details, I nearly bumped heads with her as she continued the dissection. Finally, she removed the frog's legs with quick work of her scalpel. She set up a battery and wire leads to demonstrate how the frog legs responded to electrical stimulation. At that, the other student who'd remained left the laboratory.

Fräulein Doktor studied me. "It doesn't disgust you, does it, Margarethe?"

I shook my head. "No, *Fräulein Doktor*. I've seen an amputation." I described how I'd watched the doctor cut off Miss Westerfield's foot.

"Good. You'll need a strong stomach to study medicine."

When a calf at Raithschau was still born, *Fräulein Doktor* asked if we might have it for study. The cow barn was not an ideal location for a science lesson, especially because we could hear the mother's plaintive lowing for her lost calf. I blocked it out of my mind and focused on the organs *Fräulein Doktor* had laid bare with her scalpel.

"Although humans are built differently, there are correspondences to our organ systems. You'll see when you dissect a human corpse."

The Imperative of Desire

Intrepid though she was in designing appropriate lessons, *Fräulein Doktor* knew her limitations. She arranged for me to spend one afternoon a week in Dr. Schulte's surgery. He gave me a clinical coat and allowed me to attend his pediatric consultations. I stood by to take notes for him to review later.

The *Bürgermeister's* wife eyed me suspiciously as the doctor examined her daughter's throat. Given my grandmother's important role in the town, the woman would never dare complain outright, but Dr. Schulte noticed her disapproval and nodded in my direction. "Lady Margarethe, why don't you peruse my library while I see this patient?"

On my way out, I heard the woman ask in a loud whisper, "What is *she* doing here?"

Dr. Schulte tactfully diverted her with questions about her daughter's symptoms. After that, he weighed which patients he allowed me to observe. He never let me into the examination room with adult patients for obvious reasons.

Most of his cases were fairly pedestrian: wounds from farm equipment, broken digits, sometimes fractured limbs. Infections were common. He allowed me to prepare the samples and inspect them under his microscope. Dr. Schulte demonstrated how to stain the specimens swabbed from a patient's throat or scraped with a thin spatula from a skin eruption. The color improved the definition, he explained, and the cells' reactions helped define them. The dyes had magical names like crystal violet, malachite green, methylene blue, rose Bengal.

By the term's end, I'd absorbed enough practical medicine that the doctor began discussing his cases with me. I learned that diagnosis was a complex art rather than a science, a curious mixture of empirical observation, accumulated knowledge, and intuition.

I was smitten.

Konrad didn't come to Edelheim that summer. His mother had died in the spring from a mysterious female cancer, and the family crisis that ensued kept my cousin close to home. Until Father had leave and came to Edelheim, I found amusement in riding into town or visiting the tenants.

A girl my age, who had seemed friendly when I'd visited with Father, now wouldn't even look at me. I heard her mother mumble something about "knowing her place." It was the same with the servants' children, who'd been my playmates when I'd been a child. They tipped their hats and scurried off when I approached. The maids, who'd often chatted with me, were now silent except to acknowledge my requests. They kept their eyes downcast and curtsied when I passed them in the hall. The town doctor was somewhat friendlier but professed to be too busy for more than a brief conversation. I didn't understand what had changed until I looked in the mirror and realized that I was no longer a girl.

Mother didn't seem to care how I occupied my time. She was a late riser, so I seldom saw her until lunch. After dinner, she played the piano. Sometimes, she would invite me to sing to her accompaniment. Our conversation was minimal. By the end of the second week at Edelheim, I'd nearly lost my mind with boredom. I rang Veronika and asked if I might pay her a visit.

Veronika could always be counted upon for sparkling conversation, one of the reasons my father found her so attractive. She had a gentle sarcasm that was always amusing rather than biting. Although I was intellectually precocious, much of her humor went over my head.

"I hear from your father you intend to study medicine," Veronika said one evening after I'd played the piano for her entertainment.

Her husband, who'd fallen asleep during the recital, awoke with a series of snorts and coughs. "My apologies," he said, rising. "I think I shall retire for the night."

Veronika's green eyes followed him as he left the room. Clearly, it was no love match. He had his horses and dogs like any country gentleman and spoke about little else. I couldn't understand what a chatterbox like Veronika saw in him.

"People tell me that young people of our class are entering the professions more and more," continued Veronika after the baron had departed. "It's become quite fashionable. How modern and forward-looking of you!"

"I'm not doing it because it's fashionable, modern, or forward looking," I said indignantly. "I'm doing it because it interests me."

"What about parties and pretty dresses? No interest there?"

I shook my head.

Veronika sighed. "You have always been exceptional, Grethe." She smiled. "But I promised your father I would help you get on. Let's go to Paris in the spring. I'll show you all the sights."

"Maybe. If *Tante* allows it."

"Oh, she will," said Veronika with a mysterious smile.

~

That night, I awoke with stunning pains in my abdomen and terrible pressure below. When I rose to relieve myself, the pot was red with blood. I knew about infections of the kidney and bladder from eavesdropping in Dr. Schulte's consulting room, but this seemed different. Then I recalled my grandaunt's lesson on menstruation and momentarily panicked. The curse had arrived.

I'd been feeling moody for days, but now I felt completely out of control. I had to force myself to think clearly. When I reached between my legs, I felt the warm stickiness. I brought out my hand and saw it bright red with blood. There was a red stain on the sheets. Methodically, I poured water from the pitcher and washed. I exchanged my soiled night dress for a fresh one.

I had the presence of mind to call the maid and asked her to bring Veronika. The maid glanced into the pot and saw it filled with blood. She snatched it up and hurried off.

Veronika flew into the room and embraced me. "Dear girl. Let me help you." She opened the little embroidered bag she had brought and took out a pad of cotton batting covered with a woven mesh. "Fortunately, we now have such modern conveniences. In my youth, we used cloths. Such a messy thing!" Out of the bag she took out what looked like a garter but, as she explained, it was actually a belt to be worn around the hips.

"May I?" she asked, raising my nightdress. She demonstrated how to pull the tabs of the pad through a metal ring and secure the tails of mesh on a little spear. Then she cinched the belt securely around my hips. She pulled down my night dress. "Congratulations, Grethe. You are now a woman."

The maid returned. She ripped off the bedsheets and replaced them with fresh ones. Veronika eased me back to bed and pulled up the coverlet. When I began to sob, she said, "There, there my darling. Every woman bleeds. It's entirely natural." She stroked my hair and kissed me. "Do you have cramps?"

I nodded mournfully. She asked the maid to bring aspirin and a hot water bottle.

The next day, all I could do was lie face down on my bed with my fists balled beneath me. Finally, the aspirin helped ease the cramps. I was able to dress and join my hosts at dinner.

When Father arrived from Africa a few days later, he came to take me home.

I didn't eavesdrop on his parting conversation with Veronika, but it was obviously warm and intimate. Before we departed, Veronika handed me a little embroidered bag like the one she had brought that night. "Ring me if you need anything…anything at all." She raised my chin to study my face. "I can see a change in you. Now, you are one of us." She kissed me. "Telephone me later to tell me how you are feeling."

I promised that I would.

I dreaded the return to Edelheim. Before he'd arrived, Father had ordered the servants to move his quarters to the other side of the house. No one needed to explain to me what that meant.

～

I was happy to return to Raithschau and my grandparents. At least, they spoke to one another during meals.

One morning, the majordomo brought a folded note to Grandmother. She opened it and picked up her lorgnette to read it. "It's from Klara," she explained, "She has good news, and she would like you to call on her today." She put the note aside and began to butter her roll.

I jumped up from my seat ready to depart at once.

"Sit down, Grethe. Let me finish my breakfast, and I shall accompany you."

I didn't want to wait, but the smoked whitefish on the sideboard looked inviting. Since summer had begun, I was always ravenous, so I filled my plate again and ate a second breakfast while Grandmother finished her first.

I begged Grandfather to allow me to drive his motorcar until he finally relented. "Don't spill your grandmother on the road," he said, wagging his finger, "or that will be the last time you will drive it. Understood?"

I was still a bit shaky behind the wheel, but I succeeded in getting us to Oberroth without ejecting Grandmother from the passenger seat.

When we arrived, Sister Portress had the gate open and escorted us directly to the office of the headmistress. *Tante* tried to tempt me with sugar biscuits. I ate a few, despite having just finished my breakfast. I'd finally realized that it was my grandaunt's way of keeping me occupied while she and my grandmother exchanged news, but I was surprised when *Fräulein Doktor* joined us. Whenever this august committee met, big changes were in the offing. I suddenly lost my appetite for sugar biscuits. Once *Fräulein Doktor* was seated, Sister Scholastica turned to the real business.

"Margarethe, I am delighted to tell you that I have received a letter from Miss Emily Penrose of Somerville College. She has confirmed your acceptance for the fall term of next year. Congratulations."

Tante handed the letter across the desk for me to read. I rapidly scanned it. "But there are stipulations."

"Yes, you must be accompanied by a governess or a responsible lady's companion."

"Why?"

"My dear, you'll be only fifteen, a mere girl in their eyes."

"But they have boys my age at Oxford."

"Yes, but they are boys," Grandmother said, as if that explained everything.

"I'm too old for a governess," I protested, crossing my arms on my chest.

"Indeed, you are," my grandaunt agreed. "We must find you a lady's companion. *Fräulein Doktor* has some suggestions." *Tante* turned in my teacher's direction.

Fräulein Doktor smiled warmly. "I know a young lady, who was studying with me at university. Unfortunately, she could no longer afford the tuition and was forced to take a position as a governess. It doesn't suit her, so she is looking for other employment. When I raised the possibility of accompanying you to Oxford, she was delighted, especially when she learned she could attend lectures. She speaks English competently, not as well as you do, but well enough to be understood."

"Could she also serve as a lady's maid?" asked Grandmother, being practical, as usual.

I could see *Fräulein Doktor* was struggling not to make a face. I guessed that she was insulted by the idea that grandmother would expect an educated woman to be a maid. "I suppose she could," *Fräulein Doktor* finally said after making an obvious effort to calm herself.

"I don't need a lady's maid. I am perfectly capable of dressing myself," I declared.

"Of course, you are, dear," soothed Grandmother. "But you never know."

The "committee," as I began to call them, decided to invite Fräulein Kirchner to an interview, which I didn't attend. Grandmother and *Tante* were satisfied with her credentials and her manners. In the interim, Grandmother agreed to finance her final term at LMU, allowing her to complete her degree.

~

One day I looked in the mirror and saw that the bloom of pimples had cleared, the bones in my face had set, and my budding breasts had ripened into discernible hemispheres. There was a different look in my eye, a confidence that only comes with maturity. I had become a woman.

After my menses began, I stopped growing. I was grateful, for I was now nearly as tall as Father. When Dr. Schulte measured me against the height gauge in his surgery, he noted that I was one hundred eighty-six centimeters tall, in imperial measure: six feet, one inch and a fraction.

In early April, I was summoned from music class to the headmistress's office. This was not unusual. Sister Scholastica often held my private classes outside of her other duties, and her availability was often on the spur of the moment. When I arrived, I was surprised to find Veronika sitting there. Warm smiles from both godmothers dispelled any worry on my part, but I also sensed a plot afoot from the canny look they exchanged. My grandaunt gestured to a chair, and I sat down.

"Tea, Margarethe?" she asked, poised to lift the pot.

"No, thank you, *Tante*."

"But of course, you will have a sugar biscuit. Of course, you will." She handed me the plate with the biscuits.

"You're looking well, my darling," observed Veronika, taking me in with her green eyes.

"I am. Thank you. How nice to see you, *Tante*. What brings you to Obberoth?"

She glanced in my grandaunt's direction. "Sister Scholastica and I have been discussing ways for you to improve your French."

I raised my left brow in skepticism rather than insult. My French was excellent by any measure and in little need of improvement. "What did you have in mind?" I asked politely, playing their game.

Veronika summoned her Viennese charm. She was practically purring when she reached for my hand. "I invited you to Paris when you visited last summer. Don't you remember?"

The memory of the invitation had been nearly obliterated by the painful events that had followed. Now that I'd been reminded, I recalled the invitation.

"What does my father think of this excursion?" I asked, very curious.

"He endorsed it," said Veronika brightly. "And he has given us a small fortune to spend however we wish."

I had been watching my grandaunt's face for clues. From her slightly defective smile, I began to suspect that she was not in complete agreement with the plan.

"Will you allow me to be away from school, *Tante*?"

"Yes, of course. Your trip to Paris will be highly educational."

"How long will we be in Paris?" I asked, turning to Veronika.

"For the remainder of the term."

"What about my lessons?"

"These lessons are also important," replied Sister Scholastica, obviously making an effort to sound enthusiastic. "I shall give you books to read. You will write to me weekly and give me a full report. Now, see to packing your things as if you were going home for the summer. Your grandparents will send someone later to collect them."

When I approached my grandaunt before I left her office, she gripped my shoulders more firmly than one would expect for a brief farewell. I could see a hint of sadness in her pale eyes and finally perceived that something important was taking place. Our time as teacher and student had drawn to an end. One of my godmothers was handing me off to the other. A new phase of my education was about to begin.

After dinner, while the other girls were studying and the dormitory was vacant, Grandmother arrived. She and Veronika oversaw my packing for Paris and the items to be sent directly to Edelheim. I had outgrown some of my clothes that year, so those were put aside to give to the poor. Others still fit, but they landed on the pile as well. Nearly all of my undergarments were being evicted and a fair number of dinner and day frocks. Some of these clothes were like old friends, comfortable and soft.

"If you throw away all of my clothes, I shall have to go naked!" I protested as the pile of castoffs grew ever larger.

Grandmother laughed. Veronika sat down beside me on my cot and took my hand. "Grethe, darling, you have become a beautiful woman. It's time to put away your girl's clothes. We'll find you some pretty things in Paris. I promise."

Perhaps she hadn't intended to reveal the real purpose of the trip, but now that I understood, my enthusiasm wilted.

"I think I prefer to remain at school."

"Nonsense, darling. We shall have a marvelous time. Excellent food, theater, art exhibits. I shall take you to the Louvre, of course. And there is all that amazing music. After all, the Paris opera is without compare!"

She was very clever to dangle the promise of music, knowing I couldn't resist.

~

Veronika was good for her word. On our second night in Paris, we attended a splendid performance of Gounod's *Faust*. My heart nearly burst during the stirring finale with its feverish trio and the sight of the shining archangel banishing the evil Mephistopheles to hell. The following evening, Veronika took me to hear a Berlioz symphony at the Philharmonie. The next night, we returned to the opera. By then, I had worn all of the evening dresses Veronika had deemed fashionable enough to be retained in my wardrobe.

Now, she skillfully played her hand. "Grethe, if you wish to continue attending concerts and the opera every night, you must have some new gowns." Of course, I recognized the bribe. I also saw that Veronika was even cleverer at gamesmanship than Sister Scholastica. Veronika's strategy was to addict me to the drug, then dangle it in front of me when I was most vulnerable. She smiled her charming little smile. "We shall visit Mme. Lanvin's atelier tomorrow and see what she has to offer."

My response was to pout.

"Afterwards, I shall take you to the Louvre."

Obviously, another bribe, but I agreed.

~

My breakfasts in Paris always included several cups of chocolate as well as *pains au chocolat* because one can never have enough chocolate. I liked to tarry leisurely over my breakfast, especially after years of wolfing it down at Obberoth, but that morning Veronika hurried me along.

We arrived at Mme Lanvin's boutique at the appointed hour. We were treated to a brief show of her latest creations, modeled by mannequins who looked like they had not eaten for a month. I began to worry. Perhaps I would need to starve to wear such garments.

Veronika introduced me as her cousin and goddaughter. Mme. Lanvin's gaze fell to my feet and slowly rose to the top of my head.

"She's very tall," she observed.

"Yes," agreed Veronika, "which is precisely the reason she needs ladies' clothes. Everyone thinks she's so much older."

"How old are you, my dear?" asked Mme. Lanvin, finally addressing her remarks to me.

"Fourteen, Madame. I shall be fifteen in September."

She smiled at me and turned to Veronika. "I see she has begun to develop, but she's too young for a dress form."

"That can wait for later. We know she is a work in progress."

Madame tittered at the little joke. "What are you seeking from me, Baroness?"

"She needs everything—day dresses, dinner gowns, evening wear, suits, sportswear."

"All from me?"

"Who better? You are known to cater to young ladies."

Veronika had evidently said exactly the right thing. Mme. Lanvin gave her a satisfied smile. She escorted us to a dressing room and asked me to disrobe. She rolled her eyes when she saw my undergarments.

"I know," Veronika commiserated. "The poor girl has been in a convent. Our next visit will be the corsetière."

Madame's assistant beckoned me to follow her to a dressing room where she carefully took my measurements with a tape measure and entered them on a little drawing of a woman. I was allowed to dress while Veronika and Mme. Lanvin reviewed her sketches. Completely bored, I occupied myself with Madame's yappy, but affectionate Bichon Frisé. We became instant friends. Veronika interrupted our play with a question.

"Grethe, what do you think of this gown for our evening at the opera tonight?"

I had no opinion and only agreed to its suitability so that we could leave as soon as possible. The gown had to be lengthened considerably to adjust to my height. Madame cleverly decided to add a panel of silk below the existing hem in the same contrasting color as the bodice. Veronika pronounced the idea inspired.

Unfortunately, Veronika made good on her promise to take me to the corsetière. Again, I endured disapproving inspections and eye rolls at my undergarments. Shortly, I was introduced to my first ladies' corset. A moment later, the breath was literally yanked out of me.

"Must I really wear this…this thing?" I asked Veronika with exaggerated gasps.

She sighed. "Unfortunately, yes. If you wish your clothes to fit properly. It might not seem so, but these long-line corsets are better than what we used to wear."

We purchased four corsets, three "chest improvers" as my newly developed breasts were still lacking, and a "bum improver" because mine was completely flat. Added to the list were lace drawers and petticoats. We went to a hosier to purchase stockings for day and evening, and then on to the shoemaker. I drew the line at the milliner.

"No wagon wheels," I insisted.

"But you must have some hats."

"No, I must not. Now, we *must* go to the Louvre. You *promised*."

Veronika gave me a contrite look. "Yes, I promised. And you have been very patient." We returned to our hotel for a brief respite, and then headed out for lunch.

"Why do I need so many outfits?" I asked Veronika as we ate poached salmon at the Café de la Paix.

"Different occasions call for different costumes. You can't wear a riding habit to the opera."

"That's obvious. But why do I need a visiting dress and a day dress? Why aren't they the same?"

Veronika smiled indulgently. "Just as each character in a play wears a costume to represent the role he is playing, so do the garments we choose for certain occasions. Think of it as dressing up to play in an opera, and it will make sense."

I nodded, trying to absorb this bit of strange wisdom.

Afterwards, she accompanied me while I happily spent the afternoon browsing the collection of Greek and Roman antiquities at the Louvre.

Before we went to the opera, Veronika put powder on my face, rouged my lips and cheeks and used kohl around my eyes. When I looked in the mirror, I had a startling flashback to the hollow-headed dolls I had decapitated in my youth.

I surveyed myself curiously. My complexion had the slightly golden tone some blondes enjoy, so I had no need for powder to give it color, but the rouge enhanced my looks in interesting ways. My young face was still soft and indistinct. The makeup gave my features dimension and defined the bone structure.

"Make up is how we create the glamor that men find so irresistible," Veronika explained. "But we really make ourselves beautiful for other women, so that we can rank ourselves in female society."

I listened carefully because this was a useful perception. I put aside the image of the empty-headed dolls and studied the newly adult Margarethe in the mirror.

~

In all, we spent nearly two months in Paris. I browsed booksellers and libraries while Veronika shopped. Sometimes, she dragged me along to the salons, where we added to my wardrobe until I had all the clothes I could possibly need. The educational part of the trip, besides the museums and libraries, was taking in all the sights one usually visits in Paris.

On a carriage ride through the Jardin de Tuileries, we encountered a troop of women exercising their horses. They all rode astride, outfitted in breeches, tall boots, and top hats. They nodded as they passed, and my eyes followed them.

"Who were those women?" I asked.

Veronika looked back. "I expect that was Natalie Clifford Barney and her entourage of Sapphists."

"What are Sapphists?"

"Women who love other women instead of men," Veronika replied in a matter-of-fact tone. "They're also called lesbians after Sappho's home island of Lesbos."

I turned around in my seat to look at them again, but by then, they were out of sight.

In the last week of our visit, Father arrived. He took another hotel room for me to occupy during his stay. I took the change of accommodations as a badge of maturity rather than the practical purpose it served, namely giving him privacy with Veronika.

The night before we left, they took me to the Moulin Rouge. I would have happily remained in the hotel to read, but I was very glad I agreed to go because it opened my eyes to how adults "play."

Veronika picked out the gown I was to wear that night, something quite sophisticated. "You're a bit young to be in a nightclub," she explained. "We want to avoid questions about your age." She insisted that the maid cinch my corset very tight to push up my tiny breasts, making them look marginally more impressive. I could barely breathe. When Veronika had gone to meet father, I insisted the maid loosen the stays.

Although the wealthiest Parisians frequented the nightclub, there were also grittier elements, and despite Veronika's worries, many underage girls, some much younger than I. I stared at them, wide-eyed, until Veronika reached for my hand and said, "Look at me, Grethe. Forget them." I did, but I couldn't take my eyes off the sight of ample female breasts bursting out of their owners' dresses.

My father ordered champagne for Veronika and me. For himself, he ordered a pale-green drink.

"This is *la fée verte*, the green fairy," my father explained. "Absinthe is made from herbs including anise and green fennel. You like licorice, don't you, Grethe?"

I nodded.

"It also contains wormwood, which is mildly poisonous. Of course, that's part of its appeal."

"Yes, I remember reading about wormwood in Margarethe von Raithschau's herbal."

"Good. That means you were paying attention." Father positioned a uniquely shaped, engraved spoon with slotted holes over the glass. He carefully balanced a sugar cube on the spoon. Then he poured some ice water from a little pitcher into the green liquid, which turned it completely opaque. He tasted it and smiled. "Would you like to taste it?"

"Fritz! She's just a girl!" exclaimed Veronika, her eyes wide with disapproval.

"So? If she were my son, I would allow him to sample it." Father smiled to reassure me that we were doing nothing wrong.

He slid the glass in my direction.

"Fritz, I don't think this is a good idea."

"Never mind, Veronika. Grethe needs to experience everything of life. Better that she be wise in the ways of the world."

I took a sip of the green drink and found it horribly bitter. I screwed up my face. Father laughed and took back the glass. "Drink the champagne. You can develop the taste for the green fairy later."

We watched the stage show. Scantily clad dancers raised their legs and shook their skirts in unison to catchy tunes that played in my ear long after. It was well past midnight when we returned to the hotel. I perceived that Father and Veronika were anxious for privacy, so I went through the adjoining door and locked it on my side. I read a book, so I wouldn't imagine what they were doing on the other side of the wall.

On the train ride to Berlin we shared a large first-class compartment. Father left to have a cigarette. Veronika reached over and patted my knee.

"Did you enjoy Paris, my darling?"

"Yes. Except for the visits to the modiste. However, I am grateful that you were there to assist."

"I enjoyed helping you put together your first wardrobe."

"Now, I seem to have everything I need."

"Oh, you'll need many more clothes. Your figure will change as you grow fully into womanhood. And it will certainly change after you bear children."

I winced at this remark.

"Grethe, why does that disturb you so? Every woman wants children. I used to pray every day to bear a child, but God hasn't seen fit to give me one. For you, it is a duty. You must have heirs to your titles."

My face must have revealed my pure anguish at this idea, for Veronika suddenly looked very solicitous.

"Don't worry, darling," she soothed, putting her arm around me. "That is far in the future. For now, enjoy your time as a girl."

⁓

I never returned to Obberoth as a student. After our trip to Paris, Father opened the house in Grunewald. He would be living in Berlin now that he'd been assigned to the foreign office as an expert on England. Veronika moved into the villa with us, and our extended conversation continued.

During the day, she and I visited the zoo and took long walks in the Tiergarten. We enjoyed afternoon coffee at the Cafe Berlin or ice cream at Kranzler's. She kept off the sun with her parasol while I rowed her around the lake behind the house in our little skiff. At night, we attended operettas in the park. We managed to dislodge Father from the foreign office long enough to have picnics on the lawn abutting the Dianasee.

That summer, I had my first taste of real freedom. Father decided that if I was old enough to go up to Oxford, I could explore Berlin on my own. He gave me a purse full of coins and a map of the city. I spent many happy hours browsing the collections on Museum Island, sometimes with Veronika, but often on my own. She said she'd seen enough classical art in Paris to last a lifetime, but I couldn't get enough of the Roman and Greek collections. I briefly thought of abandoning medicine to become an archeologist. Grandfather had been filling my head with stories of intrepid treasure seekers since I was a girl. At night, I dreamed of uncovering an ancient city like the heroic Schliemann.

Unaccompanied, I took the train to Raithschau to visit my grandparents. I passed an idyllic fortnight with them. Before I left, I said my farewells to my grandaunt. She ordered me in a stern voice to write to her every week, and I agreed. Flouting her cursed Rule, she held me in her arms. For the first time, I was aware of her breasts as I returned her embrace. I'd always imagined that she was sexless under all that serge and linen, but like me, she was a woman. I was even more surprised when she began to weep. It took all the control I could muster not to join her.

Finally, she wiped away her tears and smiled. She held my face in both her hands and said, "Pride may be forbidden, but my dear girl, you make me so proud!" My eyes filled, and one impertinent tear escaped. She smiled and brushed it away with her fingertips. She kissed my forehead, lingering a moment. "Be well." She traced a cross with her thumb over the spot where she had kissed me. "God bless you and keep you, my dear."

6

Father escorted me and my companion to the Anhalter Bahnhof. Our luggage—three large steamer trunks and a fleet of suitcases—had been sent ahead. We carried only what we needed for the journey. Although Fräulein Kirchner was supposed to be in charge, Father had given me the sheaf of travel documents and tickets, which made me feel very grown-up.

"Do you remember when I would bring you to school?" he mused as we stood on the platform, waiting for our boarding call. At the memory, I was suddenly salivating for cucumber sandwiches and egg salad with sliced gherkins.

Father glanced at Fräulein Kirchner. "But now you have someone else to look after you." He raised his chin and regarded my companion from under his eyebrows. "You will look after her, won't you, *Fräulein*?"

The young woman anxiously pressed her gloved hands together. "But of course, *Gnädiger Herr*. I will execute my duties *exactly* as we agreed."

He sized her up as if he didn't entirely believe her. I wondered what he sensed that I was missing. Perhaps he worried that she'd take up with men. From her demeanor and looks, I seriously doubted it. She was not unattractive, but one had to look carefully to see her virtues. She wore her flaxen hair in two braids wound into tight buns pinned at the back of her head. The severity of the style and her plain way of dressing would make one think she wanted to escape male attention, not draw it. Veronika had a different opinion. She speculated that Fräulein Kirchner wanted to avoid outshining me, her mistress.

Although we'd spent a fortnight in the Grunewald house to get acquainted, I had yet to decide what I thought about my hired companion. From what little I knew of her, she seemed intelligent and pleasant. She kept her opinions to herself, despite my attempts to draw her out.

The locomotive suddenly ejected a blast of steam, which startled me. The scream of the whistle was earsplitting. "Boarding! Train to Hamburg! All passengers aboard!" barked the public address system.

"Well, this is goodbye for now. Be well." Father shook Fräulein Kirchner's hand. Although he wasn't given to emotional displays, he scooped me into his arms. "My dear girl, never think that you are less because you are my daughter and not my son," he whispered into my ear. "I am ever so proud of you!" He squeezed me until I could hardly breathe.

Holding back tears was difficult, but I knew Father would never forgive me for weeping in public. He gave us each a hand up into the train. We waved from the compartment window until the platform was out of sight. Once we were settled and the door shut tight, I allowed myself a few tears. Fräulein Kirchner kindly looked away.

Despite the natural selfishness of youth, I wept with gratitude that so many had conspired to make this journey possible. I could understand my grandaunt's determination to see me off to Oxford. In her day, women were banned from university. She'd shocked me by confessing that education was her motivation for entering the convent, where she was able to indulge her intellectual interests. Through her own efforts, she'd become as learned as any professor.

Fortunately, my grandmother had raised my father to believe in female education and had taught him by example that a daughter, especially an heir to a great house, must be raised to be more than attractive and biddable. Veronika has shown me how to make the most of my looks, but I was certainly never biddable. I knew from the other girls of my class how unusual my upbringing had been. No matter how many educational opportunities were placed before them, their one and only goal was winning the marriage lottery.

∼

When we disembarked in Dover, the familiar sound of English spoken all around me was thrilling. Fräulein Kirchner's German accent instantly identified her as a foreigner, so I asked for directions to the train that would take us to Oxford. The first thing I did after settling my hand baggage in our compartment was to order tea.

"What do you think?" I asked Miss Kirchner, as she was now styled.

She cautiously took another bite of the cucumber sandwich. "Bland," she pronounced.

"Most English food is tasteless, but you'll get accustomed to it. Ours isn't much better."

"You're so lucky you can speak their language. Not a trace of an accent. They must think you're one of them."

I considered her statement and decided that, no matter how well I spoke the English language, or tried to "get on" by using an anglicized name and downplaying my German connections, I was never really one of them.

After a brief ride, we finally arrived at the destination where my father and grandaunt had plotted that I would one day be. Perhaps if another patron had taken an interest in Father as a young man, he might have landed at Cambridge, and that would have been better for me. In my heart of hearts, I was a scientist, but Cambridge was never even considered. As far as Father was concerned, there was only one English university.

The very air in Oxford smelled of learning. I felt so honored to be standing in that place, on that hallowed ground, to finally be there after so many years of waiting! Perhaps that sounds odd. After all, I would one day inherit titles and command great wealth, but on that day in 1911, I was a junior scholar, who wanted nothing more than to immerse herself in the intellectual enterprise.

The house mother showed us to our apartment in the college. The pleasant sitting room had a coal fireplace. The walls were lined with shelves for books, and there was a small desk for each of us. Miss Kirchner had her own bedchamber. Mine faced the courtyard.

We spent the day unpacking our luggage. I'd brought boxes of books although I had an unlimited account at Blackwell's. After I shelved the books, I sat back, savoring being in that place, once again amazed at my good fortune.

Miss Kirchner and I reviewed my schedule of lectures and tutorials. Because I was in her charge, she would be allowed to attend all of my classes. Although she was a distinguished scholar in her own right, Miss Kirchner was officially considered my servant. She would take her meals with the university servants rather than in the college dining hall.

The next day, when I presented myself to be invested in my academic robes, I could feel her envious eyes on me. *Fräulein Doktor* had encouraged her to sit for the entrance examinations, but she was reluctant, saying she needed to better her English before she could pass.

"Examinations will be coming up in November," I reminded her as we walked back to the college after the robing ceremony.

She shook her head. "I'm not ready."

"I could help you prepare. We could practice English together."

She gave me a skeptical look. "Why would you do such a thing?"

"You'd make better company if you were more cheerful." I grinned, and a moment later, I saw my smile mirrored in her face.

"You are an imp," she pronounced. I took it as a compliment and grinned even more.

After dinner, as we sat reading in our little sitting room, Miss Kirchner asked, "Would you really help me prepare for the examinations?"

"I said so, and I always mean what I say. I think if you were attending the lectures and tutorials of your choice, instead of mine, you would be far less gloomy."

She looked thoughtful for a moment. "It's true I would rather be studying science than playing nursemaid to a child."

I raised my brows at this insolent remark. "I may be a child," I replied indignantly, "but I know many things, including Greek and classical philosophy, which *you* need to pass your examinations."

"But why would you help me? How does it benefit you?"

"My father says the highborn must be of service to others. It is our duty."

"And you are a good Prussian girl, aren't you?"

I perceived this wasn't a compliment, but I shrugged.

"Your father is paying me to be your companion, not to tutor me."

"He can't pay you to be happy, and unlike a real servant, you aren't very good at hiding your anger and self-pity. So, let me help you prepare for examinations. If you aren't able to win a scholarship, I can ask my grandmother to contribute to your tuition."

"You would really do that?"

"Yes, and I think she might agree. She is a true believer in education for women. That's why I'm here, and you too."

She frowned as she considered what I'd said. "Very well, I accept your kind offer."

I smiled my agreement. Our collaboration began the next morning. After breakfast, I quizzed her on the English names for everything in our sitting room. Every day we practiced English for at least an hour.

$$\sim$$

A second-year student had been assigned to help me find my way around the college. She introduced me to my tutors. I had elected to do a double course in preclinical medicine and *Literae Humaniores*, affectionately called "greats" by Oxonians.

"Such laziness on your part is unworthy of you," Sister Scholastica wrote in her first letter after learning I intended to read the Great Books. "You have already read nearly everything on the list!" She was right, and it was lazy to read Greats. My tutors quickly grew wise to my scheme. The fresher academic advisor suggested I take the mods examinations. My performance showed that I should really be in the upper level courses, so I was promoted.

Miss Kirchner professed disappointment at the change. She'd hoped to learn enough about the classics to pass the entrance examinations, although she'd been drowning in the texts because her Greek was so rudimentary. I quickly determined her deficits and we focused on the essential material.

Although her knowledge of the classics was lacking, she was a clever woman, a scientist like *Fräulein Doktor*. Her specialty was the biological processes driven by chemistry, and it was she who inspired me to choose physiology as my concentration. Although she'd secretly hated the Greats classes and only saw them as a means to an end, she truly enjoyed accompanying me to my first-year medical courses.

In the anatomy laboratory, we were organized into small groups to dissect a female corpse, some pitiful suicide or murder victim, occasionally a felon. We weren't given so much as a look at the body of a man. I wondered how they expected us to learn about male anatomy without first-hand inspection. The answer, when it came, was laughable. We all received a printed diagram of the male genitalia without further explanation. The drawings were so abstract that it was nearly impossible to see any resemblance to the real thing.

Anatomy became my favorite class, despite the acrid smell of formaldehyde that permanently lodged in my nostrils and clung to my hair and clothing until I could smell nothing else.

⁓

After three months of sharing quarters, Miss Kirchner and I had warmed to one another sufficiently to be on a first name basis. Marta sat for the November examinations, but when she returned from the main hall where the results had been posted, she looked grave.

"Well? Are you going to tell me?" I asked.

She smiled, her gray eyes teasing. "I passed! With first honors! And I won a scholarship!"

I threw my arms around her.

"Margarethe, you'll crush me!" she protested, laughing.

We instantly abandoned our scholarly personae. Squealing with delight, we jumped up and down like little girls.

"This calls for a celebration!" I said. "Let's go down to London."

We prowled Blackwell's for an hour, then headed to the dressmaker to buy Marta new skirts and dresses in dark colors, the *sub fusc* garments that must be worn beneath the academic robes. I dug into my allowance and gave her extra funds to buy some pretty dresses as well.

As we left the shop, Marta said, "I may be a scholar now, but I'm still in your service."

In fact, Marta never had any real duties as my servant. The university provided meals as well as housekeeping and laundry service. Certainly, I didn't require a lady's maid in order to dress. Thanks to my training with the cadets, I could even prepare a rudimentary meal outside the usual dining hours.

"Let's say you are my companion and leave it at that."

She smiled broadly. "Thank you. That sounds exactly right."

Marta's overnight transformation from my resentful servant to a happy, young woman was breathtaking. She wore her new pretty dresses, loosened the tight braids, and styled her hair in fashionable curls. She even began wearing cologne. Her scholarship meant that she could now eat in the dining hall at the college with the other students. Occasionally, she accompanied me to physiology class, but mostly, she went to lectures and tutorials of her own choosing.

By spring, Marta had made some friends her age among the senior students and dons. One day, when I came home from class, she was waiting for me in the parlor.

"Margarethe, we must speak." Her somber tone caused me some anxiety. With a sigh, I removed my coat and sat down across from her.

"Is something wrong?"

She shook her head. "Not wrong really, but it may not please you. I've been invited by one of the lecturers to room with her in town."

"Have I offended you in some way?"

"No, you've been nothing but gracious and kind."

"My father is paying you, and you know the conditions under which Somerville accepted me."

She reached out for my hand. "And I never would do anything to jeopardize your position here. I would call on you every day, and my mail would continue to come here."

"Why is being with this friend so important?"

She blushed fully crimson. "Someday, you will understand," she murmured.

I waited for her to continue, but that was all she said. I was a bit sad because now that we'd become friends, I enjoyed her company. Although I found her sudden need to leave odd, I agreed to the arrangement.

She moved out her things within the week. For the first time in my life, I was completely on my own. Marta honored her agreement. We told no one of the change and continued the pretense that she was looking after me. She checked on me most days, when she came to call for her mail or her wages. We spent time catching up, and then she returned to her mysterious friend.

I nursed hurt feelings over the abandonment, but I felt very grown-up being on my own. For most of my classmates, this was their first taste of freedom. The house mother kept a sharp eye, but some of the freshers imbibed too much. My elders had allowed me wine or beer from my earliest years, so I had no interest in inebriated debauchery. It took time to sort out the revelers from the earnest students. The girls I befriended were mostly those reading science of one stripe or another. Like me, some intended to study medicine. A few of these young ladies became rather dour in the process and were so boring I could barely stand them.

The Greats courses required little effort on my part. The medical classes were more demanding, but not excessively so. As I settled into my studies and had more time for leisure, I began to look for diversion.

At the freshers' fair, I had enrolled in the Gilbert and Sullivan society, the fencing club, the science society, and the Oxford Opera. I also arranged for private voice and music lessons now that I could no longer rely on Sister Elfriede's instruction. I had thought about joining the women's rowing club but decided that I had enough on my plate. It seemed that my every waking moment would be occupied by one pursuit or another.

The leader of the Opera Society said he was impressed by my voice, but I wasn't given any solo roles that year. Instead, I was relegated to the alto section of the chorus.

One of the lead sopranos caught my eye. Her name was Daphne Richardson. To me, she was the most beautiful woman imaginable. She was skillful with cosmetics, but her face was unremarkable. Her eyes were hazel. Her nose was small and absurdly upturned. She tended to plumpness, which she fought with great vigor. Her best quality was her pallor, which some of us considered deliciously romantic.

She was also reading Greats, but at another college—Lady Margaret Hall—which was why our paths hadn't crossed until we met through the Opera Society. She had quite a nice coloratura soprano and had won the title role in our student performance of Purcell's *Dido and Aeneas*.

Drunk with infatuation, I followed her around like a puppy. I offered to carry her books. I composed horrible poetry, creative literary pursuits not being one of my talents. Oh, I could write scannable verse, but the content and style were abysmally mediocre. I brought her little nosegays, which I sometimes found tossed in the common dust bin. She mostly ignored me, and perhaps rightly so. I was insufferably obsequious and needy.

The friendship went nowhere. When I left for Edelheim at the end of the spring term, I more or less forgot about her.

~

That summer, Grandfather had come to Edelheim to discuss plans to expand the quarry. The economy was humming and had created a building boom in Berlin. Our stone, which was easily worked, was in high demand. I rode out with Father and Grandfather to inspect the area where a new limestone pocket had been uncovered. While my elders discussed the project with the engineers, I looked for fossils of ancient ferns and giant snails in the stone.

On our ride back to the house, Grandfather tried to interest Father in talk of new ventures beyond our properties.

"Fritz, have you heard of this thing called 'Bakelite'?" asked Grandfather. He glanced in my direction. "Grethe probably knows all about it." I did know because *Fräulein Doktor* had shown me a newspaper clipping when it was discovered and encouraged me to read the scientific papers in the library. "Grethe, can you tell your father about this remarkable new material?"

"It is a moldable substance formed by the reaction of phenol and formaldehyde. It is non-conducting, which means it could be useful for electrical insulation and replace shellac and mica in electronics."

"The inventor has created a company," Grandfather said. "I think we should invest in it."

Father responded with a grunt. "I don't approve of speculating on unproven inventions."

Grandfather and I exchanged a look. "But Fritz, imagine the possibilities! We must look forward, not wallow in our past glory. Some chances are worth taking."

"You said we should invest in petroleum," my father replied. "So far, we haven't made a single *Pfennig*!"

"We will. Mark my words. It is the fuel of the future."

"I should live so long," Father scoffed.

"Never mind, I intend to buy some shares."

"What are shares?" I asked.

Grandfather raised his finger to his lips. "I'll explain later."

When we were alone, I approached him and repeated my question.

"Hah! I would have thought you'd have forgotten by now, but you are a persistent creature, aren't you?" We sat out on the terrace and Grandfather explained the basic concepts of investment.

When he finished, I said, "I have some money I've saved from my allowance. I'd like to invest in the Bakelite company too."

"Why?"

"*Fräulein Doktor* says it has many possibilities that haven't even been invented, and in the future, plastics will be an important material for all kinds of things."

"Who is this *Fräulein Doktor* who offers investment advice?"

"She's a chemist. You know. My teacher at Obberoth."

"Ah, yes. I remember now. The Wunderkind from the LMU." He gazed at me intently. "How much money have you saved, Grethe?"

I told him the sum. It was modest, but to me, it was a small fortune.

"You can probably buy a few shares with that, but you might lose it all. Can you tolerate that?"

I nodded. "Certainly. I have enough money for my needs, and there's always more where that came from."

He laughed heartily. "Spoken like a true capitalist!"

He probably regretted having mentioned capitalism, for I badgered him into explaining that too.

∽

Konrad finally arrived at Edelheim, desperate to get away from his father. Thomas von Holdenberg, Konrad's elder brother, had headed to Africa to find his fortune. After my unpleasant experiences with my uncle, I could understand why my cousin couldn't wait to get away. Father had given his nephew a generous loan to establish himself in our colony in

Rwanda. Thomas intended to farm the rich soil, with coffee as his main cash crop. Many young aristocrats were leaving home to seek their fortunes in foreign lands, whether in Africa or the Americas. It was becoming increasingly evident that the future would look nothing like the past. Yet at Edelheim, things had hardly changed. Mother was still depressed. Father was even more impatient with her. Neither was speaking to the other. The stalemate was ridiculous and boring.

My parents' foul mood became so burdensome that when Grandfather was ready to depart for Raithschau, I asked if we might accompany him. Grandfather frowned in Konrad's direction. "Is he coming along?"

"Please."

Although we were all cousins of the *Uradel*, my family had never been close to the Holdenbergs. In fact, Grandfather had unsuccessfully tried to dissuade Father from marrying his beautiful cousin, the woman who became my mother. It was easy to see why Grandfather had such disdain for them. Like most Prussians, he valued efficiency, competence, and frugality. Obviously, Konrad's father displayed none of these traits.

As Grandfather gazed at Konrad, his expression softened. Perhaps he saw what my father had once seen: a cowed second son, who desperately wanted to be liked. "Maybe it would be good for the boy to meet his southern cousins. Bring him along."

Konrad had become interested in politics, and on the train south, he and grandfather kept up a nonstop conversation about the Kaiser's punitive policies toward workers. Bored to distraction, I read about fermentation processes.

Grandmother fussed over us and mused about our likeness to one another. "You could be twins," she said. In fact, we now looked more alike than ever. Konrad had finally shot up and he was, as he had predicted, slightly taller, but we needed to stand back to back in order to see the barely perceptible difference.

"You must call on your grandaunt," Grandmother suggested the next morning at breakfast. "I'm sure she'd like to meet our cousin."

"And I would love to meet her!" declared Konrad. "Grethe speaks of her in such glowing terms. What an amazing woman she must be!"

Grandmother beamed in Konrad's direction. Obviously, he had charmed her as he did everyone. I sighed and shook my head.

I needed little encouragement to visit my grandaunt. I'd missed her while I'd been away, but I was also leery because our recent correspondence had been testy. Given the choice of where to concentrate my Greats studies, I'd elected ancient history and archaeology. Of course, she'd rather I read philosophy.

I'd tried to explain that what went by the name of philosophy at Oxford was not what she understood it to be, and most of the bright lights of the discipline—Russell, Anscombe, and Wittgenstein—were at the other place. By that, I meant Cambridge, of course. We didn't like to actually say the name of our rival unless forced to do so.

Grandfather allowed me to drive his new motorcar, a Daimler. I had already become a fervent devotee of the new mode of transportation and determined that as soon as I was able to save enough money, I would have my own motorcar.

As we drove to Obberoth, the June sun was bright overhead. The birds hurried to harvest the grass seed just ahead of the mowers bringing in the first hay. The delicious scent of newly cut grass filled the air. It felt good to be home.

"This is such a beautiful place, warm and sunny. So unlike the North," said Konrad. "I can see why you like it here. Your grandparents are delightful. You're lucky to have a family who loves you," he said in a voice devoid of envy but full of longing. I'd never thought of it that way, but he was right.

Sister Scholastica embraced me and kissed me on each cheek. "My darling child, how wonderful to see you." She gave Konrad a careful inspection before offering her hand.

"It's uncanny how much alike you look." She studied his face, and then mine. "So, Margarethe. How is it to look into the mirror of his face and see yourself reflected as a man?"

Konrad grinned charmingly to demonstrate his pleasure in this remark. "Yes, we look alike, but not only am I better looking, I'm taller," he said to rub it in.

Despite my worries, the controversial subject of my studies never came up. *Tante* spent most of the time interviewing Konrad, which she liked to do whenever she met someone. For his part, Konrad enjoyed the attention, and I happily let him have the spotlight. We spent most of the afternoon in my grandaunt's company.

As I readied myself for bed that night, I gazed into the mirror and thought about my grandaunt's question. Now that she'd put the idea in my head, I couldn't stop thinking about it. What was it like to be a man? To have a man's privileges? To bed a woman…?

What was it like, indeed?

⌇

Somerville had finally decided that, at sixteen, I was old enough to be on my own. That meant Marta could give up the pretense of looking after me. Unfortunately for her, the change also meant my father could stop paying for her services, and he did. She managed to make up for the lack of funds by working as an assistant in the college laboratories. I'd gotten accustomed to my privacy, so I used some of the profits from my investments to pay the other lodger's fees and lived alone in our apartment.

Over the summer recess, Daphne had learned through a friend, whose family had German connections, that I would come into a sizable fortune on my eighteenth birthday. From the same source, she'd heard that I would inherit noble titles. After that, she boasted about our friendship to everyone who would listen. Soon, all of Lady Margaret Hall knew about it. I tried to avoid the place when I could.

I wish I could say that I had a healthy skepticism about Daphne's sudden transformation from a bored snob to my dearest friend, but I was besotted and only saw what I wished to see.

To be fair, she wasn't simply an opportunist who wished to take advantage of a wealthy friend. Once we got to know one another, we found we had much in common. Our collaboration began with studying together. Having read most of the titles in the Great Books program, I could easily provide her with notes off the top of my head. This saved her an immense amount of time. We spent some of the free time in London, where we haunted the museums. I loved the collections of the British Museum, and I could justify these excursions because they related to my studies.

I loved to hear Daphne read classical Greek. She had a rich, melodic voice with perfect modulation and cadence. We read the poems of Sappho together. To be sure, these amazing works were not on the list of Great Books, and despite their innocuous content, were considered slightly obscene, certainly not fit for young ladies. Many people confused the extant writings of Sappho with a notorious pseudotranslation by Pierre Louÿs entitled *The Songs of Bilitis*. Those poems were truly erotic and quite scandalous. We read those too.

"Do you suppose that Sappho really had female lovers?" I asked, as I lay on the divan in Daphne's sitting room.

"Of course, she had, you goose. Hasn't every woman?"

I sat up and stared at her. "Have you?"

She smiled slyly. "I thought you'd never ask." Whereupon, she pushed me back on the divan and began to kiss my mouth. Stupidly, I lay there with my jaw locked tight.

Daphne sat up and laughed. "You are such a child, Meg. I'll wager you haven't been with a man either." Of course, I hadn't. My youth suddenly became a huge liability. "You need someone to teach you a few things," said Daphne with a sly smile as she reached under my skirts. When she began to stroke the inside of my thigh, I never thought to protest. "One thing you must learn is that a woman requires a very careful approach, very gentle, something like this." She began to stroke me through my undergarments and again tried to kiss me. This time, I closed my eyes and let the delicious stroking and kisses transport me to another place.

She rose to lock the doors. I felt a sudden chill as she moved away. When she returned, she unbuttoned her blouse and slipped out of her skirt. While she worked the buttons on my blouse, she kissed me in the strangest way. All the kissing I had ever done had been dry and contained, so when Daphne pressed her tongue against my lips, I had no idea what to do.

"Open up," she encouraged gently. I instantly obeyed, and she began to explore my mouth with her tongue. Naturally, I was quite surprised by both the nature of the activity and the sensations it was arousing in me. Her saliva had a completely neutral taste, except for a hint of lemon from the drops she liked to suck while she studied.

"Come, love, sit up and help me a little. This ought to be a mutual thing." I instantly obeyed and helped her undress me. Modestly, we retained our undergarments. She drew the coverlet over us, leaned on her elbow, and gazed into my eyes. "You are quite beautiful. Has anyone ever told you?"

I could barely think to form words. I managed to mumble, "No, never." This wasn't entirely true. Veronika often told me, I suspect, to encourage me to make more of a fuss over my appearance.

"You look so perfectly Prussian, quintessentially so," said Daphne. "So blond and blue-eyed, heroic like a Valkyrie. You should sing Wagner." She stroked my hair. "Now, my dear. I am going to touch you. Tell me if you like it."

The amazing stroking began again, but this time, Daphne reached inside my pantaloons and touched my bare sex. I thought I would leap out of my skin.

"Ah," she said, "You are quite ready. Can you feel how wet you are?"

Actually, I could also hear my slickness as her fingers tickled my sex.

"I suppose you know from your physiology studies why you are so wet." I did not, and stupidly admitted it. Daphne proceeded to explain to me the role of the moisture in easing the sexual act between a man and a woman. She described it quite clinically, yet listening to her beautiful voice tell me such things, excited me all the more.

"Now, here we go." When I felt her fingers move into my body, I thought I would faint from the pleasure. She continued in this vein, inside, then out, the stroking measured, patient, gentle. Then suddenly, there it was— the climax. I knew exactly what it was because I had learned to pleasure myself at a young age. But this was very different because someone else was controlling the pace and the rhythm. Daphne went within again, and I experienced another climax.

"Simply beautiful," she murmured and kissed me. She smiled with great satisfaction. "You have been an excellent pupil! Now let's see what you have learned." She lay down beside me, and I understood that I was to return the favor.

So, it began. Afterwards, we were inseparable. Daphne more or less moved into my apartment at Somerville because it was larger. We would spend hours in bed as she taught me everything she knew. When she described the mechanics of that most intimate kiss, I was quite sure I wouldn't like it, but again I was surprised by the neutrality of the scent and the taste of my lover. Of course, being on the receiving end was the greatest pleasure imaginable.

At term break, I went home to Edelheim. While we were apart, I simply ached for Daphne. I became so moody and introspective, that Veronika looked quite concerned and asked me what was wrong. Of course, I couldn't share anything about Daphne, so I blamed it on menstrual woes. Meanwhile, I wrote to my friend every day without fail. Daphne was an equally faithful correspondent. I poured out my heart to her and wrote detailed descriptions of everything I experienced during the day. Sensibly, I had given up writing mediocre poetry and confined myself to journalistic observations.

Our reunion after the holiday was accompanied by a joy that bordered on pain. We went to bed at once and didn't emerge for days.

The trouble began soon after. Our lives outside the bedchamber began to disintegrate. Daphne's academic performance suffered, and her tutors questioned the cause. Until then, she had been an outstanding student in line for first honors.

I'd been able to limp along in my medical studies because they required that I regularly present myself in the laboratory. But I became more neglectful of my attendance at lectures, which angered my tutors. Although I was very careful to send notes ahead when I would be late or absent, this didn't always mollify them.

There were other signs of disturbance. When I finally took my horse out for a ride, I became aware of how I had neglected her. She pulled at the bit and fought my attempts to rein her in.

Finally, something drew us back into the sunlight. The Opera Society was staging Handel's opera, *Ariodante,* and I was cast in the title role. Daphne was the female lead. Playing the role of Daphne's beloved and kissing her on stage was ironic in so many ways, but it forced us to emerge from our darkened rooms. Even so, we were always groping one another whenever we thought we couldn't be seen. Then, having been driven to a fever pitch, we would return to our rooms at the college, where we made love until we were exhausted. We would sleep a few hours, then recommence our impassioned embraces.

But now I had a new obsession. Although I had performed in public at Chilton Hall and Obberoth, I had never sung the lead role in a fully staged opera. I was very excited, so excited I could barely sleep at night. I wrote to Sister Elfriede to tell her about it, and she wrote back words of encouragement. Despite my delight, I was overwhelmingly anxious, convinced that I would step on the stage and forget it all. I scribbled detailed annotated notes all over my score and practiced incessantly. I rehearsed until I could sing every note of every bar of not only my part but all the others as well!

Despite all my careful preparation, I was a heap of nerves on opening night. Our little student theatre at Oxford was tiny, and in that last week of May before the semester recess, stifling. Behind the last traveler, a ridiculously thick and opulent velvet, the gift of a moneyed Victorian-era alumnus, it was hotter still. I was sweating profusely into my costume, as much from anxiety as the temperature.

Daphne slipped into the space beside me and put her arms around my waist. "You look so very heroic, my lord prince," she whispered, rubbing my buttocks in a most suggestive way. Her hand slipped between my legs to caress my sex. I groaned with pleasure.

I tried to kiss her, but she turned her head. "Don't ruin my makeup."

I mumbled an apology.

"Touch me instead," she said, taking my hand. Her costume for the role of Ginevra was deliciously sheer, and I could feel the nipple of her small breast pucker to my touch. Just then, the stage manager cued Daphne and she slipped away. She walked on the stage with elegant steps and began to sing in her crisp soprano.

I was counting measures when the director stepped behind the curtain. "Lord Ariodante," he said with a bow and a grand flourish. Laughing at this ridiculous display never occurred to me. At my parents' home in Prussia, everyone addressed me as, *"Gnädige,"* or occasionally, if somewhat prematurely, *"Eure Liebdenin."*

"Are you ready?" asked the director.

"Not quite," I replied.

He nodded. "You shouldn't worry. You'll be splendid. You have an excellent voice, and you are completely convincing in the role." I studied him, trying to decide what he meant by that remark.

"Are you saying I make a good man?"

"Since you are asking, yes. You have just the right swagger." If he only knew how hard I'd practiced to achieve such perfection!

He narrowed his eyes. "Is there something between you and Daphne Richardson?"

I feigned surprise. "Why do you ask?"

He leaned over to speak confidentially. "I have eyes. But have no fear. I've been known to take a boy to my bed myself."

I'd lost my count, and now the stage manager was cueing me. "Ariodante in fifteen bars!"

The director gave me an encouraging pat on the shoulder, man-to-man, and I tripped out on to the stage.

The music began to play. I stared out into the darkness and listened to the coughs and shuffles. The spotlight shone on me. Then the audience disappeared and the stage. One, two, three…I opened my mouth and entered the bar at exactly the right place.

∼

Instead of going home to Edelheim, I spent the early part of the summer with Father in Berlin. He had moved Veronika into the Grunewald house, ostensibly to look after me. I was at the point where even he admitted I could manage on my own, so the excuse for her presence was transparent.

Daphne and I wrote as feverishly as before. A letter came every day, sometimes two. Then suddenly, they stopped. There was no letter for a week. I became very anxious. I sent a wire to Daphne in Kent, but there was no response. I sent more wires. Three in all.

Finally, a letter arrived:

> Dearest Meg,
>
> Please forgive me. I cannot see you again nor receive any correspondence from you. My mother discovered your letters among my belongings and has forbidden me to speak or write to you. Neither can I return to Oxford in September. I have no idea what will become of me. This is a complete disaster! Know that I love you with all my heart, and to do this, wounds me to the core, but I have no choice.
>
> Yours ever,
> D

Staring at the letter, I tried to force the information to penetrate my mind. This could not be happening, but it was. There was no mistake. This was Daphne's handwriting, and the message was clear. I sent two more wires but never received an answer.

Grief and anger vied for precedence in my heart. I took the letter and all the others Daphne had written to me. I collected the photographs of us and all of the little gifts she had given me. Although it was July, I built a roaring fire in the library fireplace. I burned everything to ash, watching as the flames engulfed the precious mementos of my first love.

Veronika saw me leaving the library. "Grethe, what's the matter? You're pale as death. Why, you're trembling." She took my hands. "Dear girl, tell me what's wrong."

I shook my head because I couldn't speak.

Veronika pulled me by the hand to her room and sat me down. "Now, tell me what's wrong at once."

I took a deep breath. "My heart is broken," I managed to say. "I want to die."

She nodded knowingly. "Who is this boy?"

"Not a boy."

"Ah." Her face registered no surprise nor expression of shock. Again, she nodded wisely. "Don't worry, my dear. It's more common than you think. Once you're grown, you'll go on to other kinds of love."

"But you don't understand. I want to die."

"I know you do. And there will never be another heartbreak like this because it is your first." She took me in her arms and held me against her ample bosom while I cried. "Don't worry, my dear Grethe," she said with a deep sigh. "You will survive this. It may not seem like it now, but one day the pain will end."

"Please don't tell Father."

"Good heavens, no! I shall never tell a soul."

Veronika looked after me solicitously. She made excuses when I failed to appear at dinner or at breakfast the next morning. She arranged for food to be sent up to my rooms, but I was unable to swallow more than a few morsels. She sat with me, while I gazed wordlessly out the window.

Perhaps it was foolish to give up her kind attention in favor of returning to Edelheim and my mother's indifference, but I had agreed to meet Konrad there. His arrival had been delayed by family matters at home.

I had my mother's silent company, but no playmate to distract me from my misery. I rode out every day into the fields and lay on my back to stare at the sky. I simply ached. I felt torn open inside. My soul lay in tatters. Curiously, I never wept. I just hugged myself while smelling the sweet earth and the hay awaiting the mower. I was quite sure I would never be the same again. And, in fact, I never would be.

Konrad finally came to Edelheim, full of apologies for being late. He went out with me on my rides. One day, he finally asked, "When will you tell me why you're so sad?"

"It's none of your concern."

"Yes, I know, but I wish you would tell me. Perhaps telling me will make you feel better." So, I told him the entire story from beginning to end. He nodded from time to time but said nothing. Finally, he said, "Does this mean you prefer women in your bed?"

"I have no idea. I've never been with a man."

"Hmm," he intoned. "I've never been with a woman."

Suddenly, I had an idea. "Then let's find out, shall we?"

"You're not serious," he replied, looking alarmed.

"I assure you I am. Who better than the two of us? We've always loved one another."

He still looked doubtful. I saw that I would need to employ some of the techniques I'd learned from Daphne. To excite me, she would describe in her rich voice how to pleasure a man, so I knew what to do…at least in theory.

Konrad proved surprisingly easy to seduce. Although we had explored one another's bodies as children, much had changed since. I was shocked to see how everything about him had grown, even more so when he became excited.

We were fortunate to have a thick bed of bracken where we lay. I hiked up my riding skirt, and Konrad opened his trousers. Without further ado, he burst into my body. I felt like I'd been torn on jagged glass. It was such a sharp, burning pain, the likes of which I had never experienced. I gritted my teeth until the pain passed, replaced by a deep ache. Eventually, that too passed, and feeling my body filled to such depth became almost pleasant. I was beginning to enjoy it when Konrad finished and rolled off.

"You're bleeding," he said with faint disgust.

"It's nothing." I blotted the flow with my handkerchief, then left it there to absorb the rest.

He sighed. "That was interesting, but I think I like men better than women."

"I should have guessed."

"But now that I've had you, perhaps I could be otherwise persuaded."

"Don't be too hopeful," I said, attempting to put myself in order, but he eased me on my back.

"This time, I promise to do better."

7

The Great Books program required an additional term, so I reluctantly returned to Oxford, where everything reminded me of my lost love. Somehow, I had to muddle through a few more months of lectures and tutorials. At least, I would have company. At the end of the summer, Marta had written, asking me if I would like to share lodgings.

The cozy, domestic arrangement with her "friend" had ended. She never admitted it aloud, but I suspected she was also suffering from a broken heart. How frustrating to have a sympathetic ear so near, and yet fear the consequences of bending it! Walled off in our separate agonies, we moped and made a pretense of being lost in our studies. Marta reverted to her severe dress. I became a bit unkempt. I wore the same skirt and blouse for days at a time. We both left our unwashed teacups and plates around the place, earning complaints from the student maids.

It didn't help that most of my time was spent in solitary research while I wrote my thesis, which argued that the spread of Christianity into the provinces ultimately caused the downfall of the Roman Empire. Finding a don to oversee this scandalous idea was something of a miracle, but the college had quite a few radicals on the faculty. Meanwhile, I tried to use the forced hiatus in my medical studies profitably by enrolling in the pharmacology and histology courses that were technically part of advanced study.

In an act of revenge, because I had met Daphne in the opera society, I resigned. The fact is, the idea of singing in grand tragedies was too depressing. When I ran into the director on campus, I turned to head the other way, but he'd already noticed me.

"I hear you've left us," he called from five paces behind, hurrying to catch up. "This has nothing to do with Richardson leaving the college, does it?" he added when he was close enough to speak more confidentially.

"No, no. I'm simply in the mood for lighter fare. I've renewed my membership in the Gilbert and Sullivan Society. I joined at the freshers' fair, but I rarely attended the meetings."

He cocked his head and gave me a skeptical look. "A shame to waste a voice like yours on such silliness. Gilbert and Sullivan indeed!" he sniffed.

His arrogance irritated me. "Is it really any of your business?"

He shook his head. "No. Not a bit. But you have talent, Stahle, don't waste it on operetta." I liked the man, and I knew he meant well, but I was not about to admit why I couldn't return, even knowing his own secret. "If you have a mind to return, we'd welcome you. We can always use a good mezzo voice like yours." I thanked him for his interest and headed to my lecture.

Despite my untidy habits, I bathed and dressed more carefully before taking myself to the first meeting of the Gilbert and Sullivan Society. My expectation was only an opportunity to sing, but I wanted to make a good impression. Singing, especially in the company of others, had always raised my spirits.

The group had a tradition of launching its meetings with a rousing chorus from one of the more popular operettas, usually from *Pirates* or *Pinafore* or *Mikado*. It was always a men's chorus. Given the composition of the colleges, males greatly outnumbered the females. The men would sometimes dress in female costumes and sing falsetto with comic results. Real women with good voices were highly valued and warmly welcomed into the club.

The exuberance of the group was a startling antidote to my gloomy mood. Everyone seemed to know all the lyrics to the famous choruses, trios and duets. The members would spontaneously break into song at the least provocation. Their enthusiasm was contagious.

At first, I failed to notice an extraordinarily tall, blond man who had slipped in after I'd arrived. He had a high, noble forehead and a beautifully shaped mouth. Because my lips are thin, almost bitter, I have always admired a sensual mouth. His eyes were the exact color of a perfect autumn sky, and he had a head of blond, curly hair that he wore on the long side.

His arrival instantly attracted a knot of well-wishers. As he chatted with his fellows, I observed him from afar. I noted that he gave one of the tenors a positively smoldering look and began to suspect that we had more in common than a love of music. Certainly, such a person was worth cultivating, if for no other reason than having a beau to squire me around.

I located the secretary of the society and asked to be introduced to the handsome giant. The secretary mischievously tapped the man on the opposite shoulder, forcing him to turn around the wrong way. Their easy laughter made me smile.

"Lytton, dear, this lady would like to meet you."

When the tall man turned to face me, his full lips curved into a broad smile. "Well, hello," he said, "What a pleasure to look a woman right in the eye!" To be sure, this was an exaggeration. He was a few inches taller. "What is your name, my dear?" he asked, reaching for my hand and holding it warmly.

"Meg Stahle, Somerville."

"Ah," he said, raising one brow. We even had that trait in common! "I bet you're German."

"Yes, how can you tell?" I asked, anxiously wondering if he could somehow hear an accent.

"How can I tell? Simple. That's a German name. Any relation to the Stahles of Langenberg-Edelheim?"

Now, I began to wonder if in addition to his other remarkable traits, he was a mind-reader. "Yes, as a matter of fact."

"Hah! My father went to school with the count. Sandhurst, then Balliol."

"That would be my father, Friedrich von Stahle."

"Oh, what wonderful luck to meet you! And how do you do, Count Stahle's daughter?" he said, raising my hand to his lips. His eyes smiled mischievously over my knuckles.

Amidst all the boisterous singing and laughing, we were having this amazing sidebar conversation. We gazed into one another's eyes for a long moment. Finally, he introduced himself. "Lytton Compton-Wickes, Balliol College." He bowed with great flair. "At your service, Countess Stahle." I was positively charmed.

"A pleasure to meet you, Mr. Compton-Wickes. May I invite you to tea in my rooms at Somerville?" I asked, completely ignoring the fact that the invitation was outrageously forward.

His eyes twinkled with amusement. "Tell me the day and time, and I shall be there." Again, he bowed with flourishes. His penchant for theatricality reminded me of someone else…Konrad.

The head of the society clapped his hands for the meeting to come to order. I found a seat. I was pleased to see Mr. Compton-Wickes choose the chair next to mine.

∼

"How was your meeting?" asked Marta when I returned that evening.

I explained that it had been quite profitable. I had been identified for contralto roles, and, after a brief audition, assigned to play Lady Blanche in the fall production of *Princess Ida*.

"Splendid indeed," Marta agreed. "I look forward to it." She studied me. "That club is definitely for you. Your mood has changed completely…much for the better, I would say."

I beckoned to her to sit beside me on the sofa. "I met the most extraordinary gentleman."

Marta eyed me curiously, perhaps wondering as I often did, if the time had come to reveal our shared secret. "Is that good?" she asked in a hesitant voice.

"Well, yes, it's good. Eventually, I must marry and produce heirs, and if I don't choose a husband, someone else will."

I described Compton-Wickes' virtues in the broadest terms.

"He's a baritone. Quite a good one."

"Delightful," opined Marta. "He sounds perfect."

"Yes, perfect." I smiled, remembering the flirtatious look Compton-Wickes had given the handsome, young tenor.

∼

Before my new interest came to tea, I made inquiries about him. He was actually Lord Compton-Wickes, second son of the Marquess of Bromsley. Like Lytton Strachey, the literary critic, he was a descendant of the Earl of Lytton. Despite their noble lineage, the Bromsleys had fallen on hard times. The family's estate, Larkhurst, was highly leveraged. A blight and subsequent crop failure had recently driven the estate even deeper into debt. In short, they were aristocratic paupers. A wealthy daughter-in-law would certainly be advantageous, and all the better that she be of the German aristocracy rather than an arriviste. Some of England's most noble lines had been forced to overlook the dilution of their blood merely to save themselves from ruin. They even reduced themselves to marrying nouveau riche Americans!

I wired my father to ask his opinion of Lord Bromsley. Father replied in a long letter, which glowingly recommended Lytton's father as generous, kind, and dutiful. The operative word was "dutiful." There can be no higher praise from a Prussian military officer.

I traced the Bromsleys' heritage in Burke's and wrote to the editors of the *Handbuch des Adels* to confirm that young Lytton qualified as sufficiently noble to ensure the inheritance of any offspring he might sire. The answer was affirmative. Next, I made inquiries regarding his schooling. He was reading ancient history and archaeology at Balliol. Prior to enrolling at Oxford, he had attended Eton College. His mother was a prominent suffragist, and his father was notorious in the House of Lords for his liberal views, especially regarding rights for women.

Like a gumshoe, I investigated young Lord Compton-Wickes, coldly plotting his future and mine. The poor man had no idea what he had gotten himself into when he appeared at my apartment at Somerville College that splendid autumn afternoon.

Hours before, Marta and I had flown into a frenzy, like two birds tidying a dirty nest. Our clothing finally found its way into drawers and closets. The stacks of books returned to their shelves. I sent Marta with the used plates and teacups to the college dining room and asked her to order a plate of tea sandwiches.

Before the arrival of our guest, we lit a candle to freshen the stale air and set out a vase of fresh flowers. Marta opened the drapes on the courtyard window to let in the best of the evening light. She kindly volunteered to act as chaperone.

Lytton arrived, fashionably late, with a volume of Seneca the Younger's collected works under his arm and a bottle of fine sherry in hand. He was dapper in a white, linen suit. When he smiled, I noticed that he had perfect teeth.

I scarcely remember our conversation because I was so busy scrutinizing the poor man. I did manage to extract some additional points of information. Philosophically, Lytton was a stoic as the book he'd brought as a gift portended. He adored classical art and travel to the very places where it had originated, which was why he spent his summers in Greece or Italy. He liked sport. He was a champion rower and avid Alpinist. He enjoyed hunting, but not especially.

"Do you fence?" I asked hopefully.

"A bit. Do you?"

"I adore it."

Before he left, we agreed to meet in the sports palace for a match.

∾

On the appointed day, I donned my fencing attire, white pantaloons and matching vest with a short skirt. When I arrived at the sports palace, Lytton was already there, keeping our piste open for us with warning stares to any encroachers. He looked splendidly heroic in his white fencing uniform.

"What's your pleasure?" he asked, gesturing to the racks on the wall. "Foil? Epee?"

"I favor the sabre," I said, opening my sword case. I took a few practice swipes in the air.

Lytton watched, looking slightly worried, but he took down a sabre from the wall.

After I won three brief matches, I asked, "Would you like another?"

He laughed. "No, thank you. You are deadly. Where did you learn to fence like that?"

I told him about the cadet summer camp. He smiled. "It's not often one finds a woman interested in sport. Do you play tennis?"

"I do."

I expected him to invite me to a tennis match. Instead, he said, "Perhaps you would consider joining me for dinner tomorrow. I know a fine tavern offering the best mutton anywhere."

I was no great fan of mutton, but I agreed to join him for dinner.

Thereafter, Lytton and I spent most of our free time in one another's company. We played tennis, which he preferred to fencing, and rode our mounts through the countryside. We often joined the other cast members for dinner after rehearsals. He was singing the part of Florian, and his rich, lyric baritone was perfect for the role. Occasionally, I joined him and his friends in taverns that were not quite the place for a lady of my station. One of the gentlemen would inevitably forget my presence and make an off-color remark. Despite my protests that I didn't care, he would apologize.

Although Lytton and I were inseparable, it was by no means the kind of obsessive friendship I'd had with Daphne. There was no physical component, not even a kiss. For the physical part, we had other partners. Lytton sought the company of his male friends, while I had feverish trysts in a supply closet with one of the laboratory assistants. Unfortunately, she wanted more than a casual affair and made a scene when I ended the liaison, which taught me a valuable lesson. One must be tidy when it comes to affairs.

In late October, Lytton invited me to Larkhurst to meet his parents. Lord Bromsley spoke warmly of my father. Lady Bromsley sparked with intelligence and spoke passionately of rights for women. Unlike my own mother, she freely expressed her opinions in the company of men, and they in turn listened politely. I found the atmosphere at Larkhurst refreshing.

At the height of the season, Lytton and I went down to London. Lytton's aunt was kind enough to host us in her townhouse and act as chaperone. Aunt Elizabeth was an ardent suffragette and bluestocking like her sister. She had attended Lady Margaret Hall, and the Oxford connection created an instant bond between us.

"My nephew tells me that you intend to study medicine, Lady Margaret," she said one evening over sherry. "What made you choose that profession?"

"I adore science and see medicine as my way to be of service."

"I admire you, dear, for taking your *noblesse oblige* so seriously, but it's not the easiest path for a woman. Medical men are often at their most hostile where female physicians are concerned."

"Well, we'll simply have to change that, won't we?"

She smiled broadly. "Exactly." She turned to Lytton. "I like this one. You may bring her around more often."

Lytton had been invited to several balls that season, and I accompanied him. People were beginning to speak of us as a couple. The papers took note in the society pages. We did nothing to disabuse anyone of the idea that we were destined to marry.

~

In December, I passed my examinations with a double first. Unfortunately, that meant little. Women were still not permitted to matriculate at Oxford, otherwise I would have qualified for the degrees of Bachelor of Medicine and Master of Arts.

I'd concluded my education with the Michaelmas term, an odd time to begin medical studies. A less ambitious person might have gone on the grand tour or some other holiday before embarking on another arduous course of study, but I couldn't wait to begin medical school. Because of my sex and age, finding a hospital to accept me was a challenge. I wrote to my grandaunt in a cloud of discouragement. Once again, *Fräulein Doktor* came to my rescue. She contacted a friend on the faculty of medicine at Ludwig Maximilians, and I was granted admission to the winter term.

Although Lytton was three years older, he was not due to sit for his examinations until May. The impending separation forced us to make some decisions. We finally had a frank talk about our future.

"It's certainly no love match," I observed without emotion.

"I disagree," said Lytton, looking injured by the suggestion. "I have grown very fond of you, Meg. I've never met a woman like you. You are handsome, brilliant, accomplished at sport and a marvelous singer. And you will inherit three noble titles and boatloads of money. What more can a man want?"

"So, your motive is practical."

Lytton screwed his beautiful mouth into a pout. "Now you're insulting me. I'm not ticking off a list to see if you're a suitable mate."

"I am."

He laughed. "Of course, you are, but noble marriages have always been contracted for the purpose of exchanging assets and forming alliances. At least, we are making the choice, not our parents. And I think you do like me…at least a little…don't you?" he added in an uncertain tone.

"In fact, I like you very much."

He pursed his lips and let out a long sigh. "That's all?"

"All right, if you must know. I am very fond of you and have come to care for you," I admitted. "But there is one thing you must know."

He raised his brow. "I think I know, but if you feel you must say it, then do."

I was intrigued. How could he know what I was about to say? The silence grew ever longer until he leaned forward and spoke in a confidential voice. "I also prefer the company of my own sex, at least in bed, and otherwise too. What makes you so appealing is that I genuinely enjoy your company. A marriage to you would be no hardship."

"But I need heirs to my titles."

He raised his chin. "I assure you when my duty is required, I can and will do it!"

I reached over and covered his enormous hand with mine. "Then we have a bargain!" To seal our pact, he raised my hand to his lips and kissed it. Then he took his signet off his smallest finger and gave it to me to wear.

We decided to formally announce our engagement and plans for a wedding to take place the following year when I would be eighteen and come into an income.

∼

I left Marta with my schoolbooks and enough money to pay for the next term's lodging and departed for Berlin. I had reluctantly agreed to attend the Kaiser's annual presentation ball, a formality signaling my availability for marriage. The grand affair required a white dress specially made for the occasion. Circumstances being what they were, it seemed a complete waste of time, but Father insisted it would be good for his career. He was in line for promotion to general, and he thought the exposure would do him good.

I was surprised to hear him say such a thing. He had a warm relationship with the Kaiser, who enjoyed stag hunting, and was a frequent guest at Edelheim. To accommodate his withered arm, Father had commissioned a set of decorated shooting sticks and rifle props. I once found myself sitting beside His Imperial Majesty at dinner and discovered that he was an intelligent man, who enjoyed talking about science and technology. It was hard to understand why everyone complained about him.

At the ball, I endeavored to smile graciously and danced with a dozen young men. Then I found Father on my dance card. "You're doing splendidly, my darling. Clever, charming, and beautiful. Were any of the young men you met to your liking?"

I mentally reviewed my dancing partners. Most of them were shorter than I. Some had bad skin. One had horrible breath from a bad tooth. A few were handsome with the brief beauty of young men. None of them could hold a candle to Lytton.

"I think I've found someone, but not here at the ball."

Father cocked his head to one side. "That Englishman you wrote me about?"

"Yes."

"When will we meet him?"

"Soon. I mean to invite him for Christmas."

Father smiled. "I look forward to it. Tell me about him."

I shook my head. "I don't want to prejudice you. I want an unvarnished opinion from your observations."

"You know I shall give it to you, whether you want it or not."

"I am counting on it."

~

We returned to Edelheim in time for the winter solstice. The days were short, and the nights, cold and dark, but as soon as Lytton arrived, things warmed and brightened. He was a sparkling conversationalist and could talk about anything. I often envied him this knack. I hated small talk because it bored me.

My father said he favorably reminded him of Lord Bromsley. Mother, however, was appalled that I should even consider marrying an Englishman, even worse, an Anglican. We had a huge row, the likes of which I had not seen since I had announced my intention to study medicine. Fortunately, my grandaunt had smoothed over that one. Father made attempts to mollify my mother by speaking generously about his old friend, Lytton's father.

"The English aristocracy are mostly arrivistes," my mother said dismissively. "I'm not impressed." It was true that our bloodline was far older and bluer, despite being of lesser rank than my fiancé's.

At dinner, my father carried the conversation, politely asking Lytton about his plans following his term at Oxford. As far as I knew, Lytton had no plans, so I was curious myself.

Lytton began to speak of an archeological expedition in Rome that his friend was organizing. "Simon already has the necessary permits. All we lack is funds," he explained. He had that earnest look that made him even more handsome.

"So that explains your interest in my daughter," Mother concluded bluntly. While this was true, it was shocking to hear it spoken aloud, especially at the dinner table. "Otherwise, I cannot imagine why you would find her attractive."

Her remark stabbed me like a knife. For a moment, I felt so nauseous I thought I might need to excuse myself. My father looked aghast that Mother could say something so obviously cruel. Lytton stared but returned to the subject of his friend's expedition without missing a beat.

Stunned, I was silent for the rest of the meal. Finally, I reminded myself that I was known to turn a few heads, especially when I made some fuss over my appearance. While I might not be a great beauty, I was not unattractive. I mentally thanked both Lytton and my father for being sensitive enough to ignore the remark. Addressing it would only have given it power.

After entertaining us with some Beethoven piano sonatas, Mother retired for the night. I finally breathed a sigh of relief.

Father reached across the coffee table and took my hand. "Dear Grethe, please overlook your mother's harsh remark. It's unforgivable, but you know how she is." He turned to Lytton. "Pay no mind to what my wife says. She has no say in this matter. Grethe's choice of a husband is hers to make, not her mother's." His distaste when he referred to his wife was abundantly apparent in his tone.

"Perhaps Lady Stahle should meet my parents," Lytton suggested anxiously. "Maybe then she'll see I come from worthy stock."

"There's nothing wrong with you, boy. You are fine the way you are. And your family is more noble than ours. We shall deal with it," Father said in a voice that left no room for discussion. "Don't let my wife dissuade you from courting my daughter. I think it's a brilliant match."

Lytton didn't look persuaded by this hearty endorsement, but he was superb at affecting a "stiff upper lip." After Father went up to bed, I could see that all the discord had left Lytton anxious. I invited him to play a game of billiards, not the best choice because I beat him handily and crowed about it.

"Meg, are you sure this marriage is a good idea?" he asked, hanging up his cue. "Your mother hates me."

"Oh, no, you're wrong, Lytton. She hates me." It was the first time I had admitted it, even to myself.

His eyes widened. "You can't really mean that."

"I assure you I do."

He saw that I was quite beside myself and tenderly took me in his arms to comfort me. That was the precise moment when I began to love him.

～

The highlight of our *Silvesterabend* ball was always a grand fireworks display. Bundled in fur coats, we stood on the veranda to watch multicolored sparks light up the sky as we rang in the new year of 1914. The thunderous explosions, like cannon fire, reverberated against my chest. The loud volume of the brilliant finale made me want to plug my ears with my fingers.

After the pyrotechnics, we gratefully returned to the warmth of the ballroom. The orchestra struck up the "*Fledermaus* Waltz," and I danced in Lytton's arms. He was a superb dancer, so I never minded when he led. He was subtle about it, never dragging me along if I didn't instantly take his direction.

I'd had a new ball gown made especially for the occasion. Lytton looked dapper in white tie and tails. He'd had a handkerchief made from the blue silk of my dress, and it rakishly dangled from his pocket. Guests remarked as we left the dance floor that we made such a handsome couple.

But it was to be our last night together for some time. When I'd confided my plan to leave early for Munich, Lytton had feigned elaborate disappointment at the idea that we would be parted so soon. He'd pouted like an enormous, charming child, but I knew that he couldn't wait to get back to Oxford and his friends.

He left the next morning on the first train to Hamburg. I rose early to see him off. Huddling in my fur coat, my breath coming as vapor, I watched the carriage drive away against a ghostly sunrise. I reflected that I was now betrothed to this man. One day, I would marry him. I turned this over in mind, understanding the words, but not the implications.

We always had special treats on New Year's Day—blini with smoked fish, my favorite, as well as *Speck* to bring good luck in the new year. Beside my plate, I found a marzipan chimney swift with a coin protruding from his bottom as well as a fat, rosy pig with a paper coin in its mouth. Grandmother knew how I loved marzipan, so it was easy to guess the origin of these little tokens of good luck. When I glanced at her for confirmation, she winked. "Happy New Year, my darling." She spread some crème fraîche on her blini and added a sprinkle of gray caviar with a horn spoon. "I hear you're leaving today." She gazed at me with an expectant look.

"Yes, on the afternoon train. I'll spend the night in Berlin and then head to Munich."

"So soon? Your term doesn't begin for another week."

"Yes, but I need to find somewhere to live. All the rooms in the medical student residence are already occupied. As it is, only five rooms are set aside for females."

My grandmother added a sugar cube to her coffee with tiny, silver tongs. "A lady of the *Uradel* shouldn't be living in an old storehouse. Your grandfather and I will accompany you to Munich to make sure you find *suitable* quarters."

I drew breath to object, but Grandfather gave me a stern look and a little wag of the head. Roughly translated, this meant: "Don't argue with her. It's pointless." Of course, he was not telling me anything I didn't already know.

My grandmother's casual promises did little to reassure me. Although I remained at Edelheim, I secretly continued making inquiries about suitable flats near the *Klinikum* of the Ludwig Maximilians University. Now that I was beginning the clinical phase of my studies, I would be spending the majority of my time in a hospital rather than in lecture halls.

We departed the next day at first light. The winter sky was ablaze with color, but it was bitterly cold. Two motorcars conveyed our considerable luggage to the train station. I had nearly everything I owned with me, for wherever I landed would be my new home for at least the next two years.

I passed the long hours on the train catching up on correspondence. I wrote to my grandaunt and composed thank you notes for my Christmas gifts. The gift with the most significance had come from *Fräulein Doktor*: a state-of-the-art combination binaural bell and diaphragm stethoscope. Although I eventually came to own more modern instruments, I always treasured it because it was my first.

My teacher's chatty and encouraging letters had grown warmer and less formal as time passed. She'd kept me apprised of all the activities of my successors in her laboratory. She lamented that none of them approached my intellectual gifts, which I dismissed as mere flattery, but I enjoyed her tales of student mischief. In this one aspect, I was willing to allow that I had no peer.

While I was scribbling my note to *Fräulein Doktor*, my grandmother reached over and patted my knee. "I am very proud of you, Margarethe."

"Thank you, Grandmother," I said, looking up. I wondered what had inspired this sudden declaration and scrutinized her for clues.

"I want you to know I appreciate how hard it was to give up the notion of becoming a singer. Choosing medicine wasn't what I expected, but it is a noble endeavor, and I approve."

I gave her a long, cool look because I wasn't sure where this conversation was heading. "I haven't given up singing if that's what you mean. As soon as I am settled in Munich, I mean to engage a voice teacher."

"Yes, I'm sure you will. You never allow anything to get in your way, do you?"

"No. I fear that's a family trait."

"It is. But you make good plans and stick to them," said Grandmother. "I'm not worried."

"So, you think my plan to marry Lytton is a good one?"

"Yes, I like your Lytton. I think he is a fine young gentleman and very handsome. He will make more tall, blond Stahles."

I rolled my eyes. "I mean, do you like him other than as a stud horse?"

She laughed. "Margarethe, you say the most amazing things. Yes, I like him very much. I can see how he suits you perfectly. But I have eyes, you know. He's a very practical choice. Intelligent, sufficiently noble. Your interests overlap. He respects you. With you holding the purse strings, which you will, and very adeptly, you can manage him rather well."

My mouth gaped a little at her blunt assessment, but it was completely accurate.

~

Naturally, I was very curious about the arrangements when we arrived in Munich, but Grandfather grinned mischievously when I asked. "Be patient, Grethe. You'll see soon enough." Grandfather and I shared a penchant for practical jokes, so I always expected surprises from him, not all of them as humorous as he liked to think.

Grandfather engaged two taxis to convey us to our destination. I had expected that we would head to a hotel near the old city, but Grandfather directed the driver to Lehel, the fashionable district where some of Munich's oldest and wealthiest families had their homes. I hadn't been in Munich for years, so I took in the sights along the way. The great domes of the Frauenkirche dominated the landscape as we passed through the embassy district. Finally, the taxi drove into the circular drive of a magnificent townhouse enclosed all around by walls.

"What's this?" I asked, surveying the impressive structure from the taxi window.

"Your new home," Grandfather explained.

"This?" I asked incredulously. "This enormous house for one person?"

"You'll need room for your staff," said Grandmother with a shrug.

Two men I recognized from Raithschau came out of the house. One opened the door for me. He bowed to my grandparents, then offered his hand. "Welcome to your new home, *Gnädige*," he said with a deep, formal bow.

"You remember Schmidt?" Grandmother said, gesturing to the man, who had been her head footman at Raithschau. "He will be your majordomo."

Surprised, I turned to Grandmother, who smiled and shrugged. "We intended to give you a house as a wedding present, but you need it now, so now you will have it," Grandmother explained. "The title will be turned over to you when you reach your majority."

"I got it for a good price," Grandfather confided near my ear. "One of my cousins owned this house. He was your cousin too, of course." In the extended family of the *Uradel*, he was yet another cousinly relation whom I'd never met. "When I'd heard he'd died without leaving an heir, I was able to purchase the house with all the contents, a very good investment." He winked at me. I gazed up at the massive structure, taking in its elegant baroque lines. "We'll have a look inside in a moment, but first you must see the best part of the deal!" Grandfather pulled me along by the hand to the rear of the house where a garage stood. The footman strained to pull back the door. The rollers screeched as he did. "Needs some oil," Grandfather explained unnecessarily.

Inside, stood a shiny, new motorcar painted grasshopper green.

"This came with the property. It's hardly been driven. Roland purchased it barely a month before he died."

"How did he die?" I asked.

"Bad ticker," said Grandfather, tapping his chest. "They found him dead in the bathtub."

Grandfather raised the hood. "This Adler has eighty horsepower. It cost a pretty penny, you can be sure. But now, it's yours." While he gave me a tour of the engine, Grandmother stood by patiently. Eventually, she complained of the cold, so we gave up the engineering talk and reluctantly followed her into the house.

The entrance hall was decorated with some of the most beautiful Rococo detail I had ever seen—ornate gilt carvings and murals of exquisitely rendered, nude women in positions certain to raise a few brows. There was a ballroom with painted mirrors that rivaled those in the Würzburg Residenz. When I mentioned this, Grandfather proudly told me the house had been designed by the same architects.

Schmidt showed us to a large library with floor-to-ceiling bookshelves and a clever circular ladder to ascend to the uppermost levels. All of my cousin's books were now mine. Like me, he was interested in science and nature, so I was delighted to own those volumes, including a splendid edition of the paintings of Marianne North. However, our tastes in literature could not be more different. He had an extensive collection of graphically illustrated, erotic novels, which I resolved to sell at the first opportunity.

Adjoining the library was a generously sized study with plenty of space to house my medical books. A large dining room, down the hall, was suitable for entertaining a large number of guests. There was a music room with a grand piano, and a drawing room with good light. That was the first floor. Above, there were five large bedrooms, including a master suite with its own toilet and bath. Despite the eighteenth-century appearance of the house, it had been outfitted with modern plumbing and central heating.

The servants' quarters, kitchen, and storage cellars were in the sub-level. There, I was introduced to the household staff, which included the second assistant cook from Raithschau and a scullery maid to assist her. There was a chambermaid in addition to a lady's maid. The majordomo and the footman, who would double as a chauffeur, completed the staff.

I had expected to live the life of an ordinary student, finding my meals as I could, so I was overwhelmed by the opulent circumstances in which I now found myself. I was but a few months past seventeen, yet in charge of an enormous house and a household staff. I realized that, in handpicking my servants, Grandmother was ensuring my domestic success.

My grandparents said they were weary from the journey and retired to their room to rest. While my new lady's maid unpacked my luggage, I treated myself to a hot bath. Reclining in the deliciously hot water, I noticed the provocative mural on the bathroom ceiling. It featured a satyr with an enormous member ravishing a comely nymph. I didn't need to wonder what my cousin had been doing in the bath when he'd brought on his fatal heart attack.

After dinner, we sat in the music room for coffee and cognac. I played the piano, delighted to find it perfectly tuned, and sang some *Lieder*. I was tired from travel, so I kept the recital short.

"Does the house please you, Grethe?" my grandfather asked, pouring me another glass of brandy as I took a seat beside him. "I think it was a wonderful acquisition."

"It's not a house. It's a palace. Don't you think it's a bit lavish for a student?"

"Not for a student who will one day be twice a countess and inherit significant wealth," said my grandmother. "You'll soon be a wife and need to learn how to manage a household. Might as well start now, don't you think?"

What could I do but agree?

8

O n my first day at the *Klinikum* of the Ludwig Maximilians Unversity, I was greeted by the stench that would stick in my nostrils and cling to my clothes and hair for the rest of my medical career: strong antiseptic and stale urine. Armed with my new stethoscope and other instruments a physician usually carries in a medical bag, I presented myself for duty. Only credentialed physicians were entitled to wear full-length clinician's coats. Like the other students, I wore a short, white smock made stiff with an over-abundance of starch. It made an irritating swishing sound as I proceeded down the hall.

My first rotation would be internal medicine. Dr. Tobias Geisler, a pale man with sandy hair and glacially pale-blue eyes, was the senior physician in charge of the medical students. He was tall and seemed rather annoyed when I looked him in the eye. Later, I learned he liked to use his height to intimidate the students and staff. Obviously, that trick wasn't going to work with me.

"So, you are the countess," he said, looking me over from head to toe. Of all the things he could hold against me—my height, my sex, or my youth—he had chosen my title. He spat it out like an epithet. No one could criticize him because it was entirely correct to address me in that manner. However, his tone and the challenging look in his eyes told me it had nothing to do with respect.

No matter how fashionable it had become for young aristocrats to enter the profession, some medical men still took a dim view of us. Unfortunately, like the smell of antiseptic and urine, this mockery of my social rank would stick, and there was nothing I could do about it. As a medical student beginning my clinical rotations, I was at the bottom of the professional heap. Only nurses and their assistants were lower.

Geisler grumbled and introduced me to the other students in the group. They were all looking smart in their short clinical coats. I was the youngest by four years, so it was fortunate that I had height in my favor.

Somehow, that always made me look older and more confident. Some of the men in the group regarded me with suspicion, others with obvious contempt. It was clear that I was not welcome.

"All right, then, gentlemen…and Countess," Geisler said with a deep bow in my direction. The others chuckled. "Now that everyone's here, let us proceed on our rounds."

Our first patient was a middle-aged man whose pock-marked skin had a distinctively yellow cast. As we approached, the poor man turned his eyes in our direction. The whites were also yellow.

"Kurtz!" barked Geisler at one of the students, who'd been gaping at the patient.

The man snapped to attention, reminding me of the Groß-Lichterfelde cadets from those summer camps long ago.

"What is this patient's most obvious symptom?" Geisler demanded.

"*Herr Doktor*, his skin is yellow," replied Kurtz.

"Good. At least, you noticed that obvious sign. Wake up! All of you!" At that ridiculous hour, still dark outside, some fogginess was to be expected. Apparently, not where Geisler was concerned.

He invited us all to step forward and have a closer look. Only I was curious enough to pull down the patient's lower lids and have a look at his eyes. I could feel Geisler regarding me with a little frown as I did.

"Countess, what do we call the yellowing of the whites in his eyes?"

"Scleral icterus."

"And what is the proximate cause? Who knows?" He glanced around the group, snapping his fingers. "Keller?"

Keller looked alarmed to be put on the spot, but he answered correctly. "It is caused by the release of bilirubin into the bloodstream."

"Very good," said Geisler, nodding. "Who knows the source of the bilirubin?"

Every hand shot up.

"Winter," said Geisler, pointing to a small, thin man.

"The liver releases this form of bile when it is in distress."

"Etiology? One at a time, thank you." He pointed at each of us in turn, and we answered accordingly.

"Gallstones."

"Fatty liver."

"Tumor."

"Infection."

"Cirrhosis."

"Cancer."

"Absorption of a large hematoma."

"Hemolytic Anemia." My answer.

Geisler narrowed his eyes. "They evidently taught you something at that English college, Countess." In fact, I hadn't learned it at Somerville, but from the medical books I'd read in Dr. Schulte's office at Raithschau. Geisler leaned against the wall and folded his arms on his chest. "Countess, tell us more about hemolytic anemia."

I began to recite the article on hemolytic anemia from memory until Geisler's eyes began to glaze over.

"That's enough, thank you!" A furrow formed between his blond brows, and I perceived that the thoroughness of my response had surprised him.

The others gazed anxiously in my direction as he quizzed me on the techniques used to diagnose anemia. The furrow between his brows grew deeper.

Rounds continued in this manner. Geisler persisted in giving me frowns and finally, filthy looks. I began to worry. I needed this man to teach me everything he knew, so for practical reasons, I had no wish to get on his bad side. I debated whether to abbreviate my answers to his questions, but I just couldn't help myself. Whatever he asked, I answered as thoroughly as I could.

At the conclusion of our tour of the ward, Geisler signaled that he wished to speak to me privately. For a long moment, he drummed his fingers on his desk and gazed out the window. "Countess, I'm going to give you some advice."

"Thank you, *Herr Doktor*. I appreciate your interest."

He stared at me. "You will find in most professional situations, there's no need to say everything you know," he finally said. "Sometimes, it's good to reserve something for later. Do you take my meaning?"

I thought about this for a long moment before I understood what he was trying to say.

"That is wise advice, *Herr Doktor*. I shall follow it."

"Good," he said.

I rose to leave.

"Stahle, you are intelligent and exceptionally knowledgeable, but there is more to medicine than brilliance."

I nodded to indicate that I'd understood.

He waved to dismiss me. "That is all. Get out."

❦

I thought I'd learned how to get on when I was in England, but closer to home, it was far more difficult to hide the salient facts. My grandparents had unintentionally made my life harder with their gifts, which I hadn't realized until I was invited to the students' residence by my study partner.

Christina Voight was anxious, as we all were, to build friendships with other women in our class. It was critical to our survival to connect with one another and form our own self-protective group. Medical school was a cut-throat affair, and some students would do anything to knock the others, particularly the female students, down a few rungs. We were often victims of harassment or practical jokes. The humor was nearly always sexual. Posing corpses in obscene positions was popular.

The places where we women could gather to study were limited. The men had first option on the study areas in the library and by the time I had arrived in January, all the rooms had been reserved. Women were banned from the student eating clubs. Taverns were too loud. Restaurants shooed us out when we finished eating. The cramped common room in the women's residence was often so crowded one couldn't find a space to sit down.

Absent other possibilities, Christina graciously invited me to her room. Female students had finally been admitted to study medicine less than a decade earlier. They were housed in an old building that had once served as a storehouse for hospital supplies. The halls were dark. The hastily applied wall plaster was already crumbling. The clothes of the women who lived there always smelled musty.

Christina's tiny room, like the others', was barely large enough for a bed, a table, a chair, and a small armoire to hold dresses and clinicians' smocks. Had my grandparents not intervened, I might have been consigned to a cramped space such as that. Instead, I lived in a spacious townhouse in a posh district, and a chauffeur drove me to my hospital duties.

My hostess heated water for the tea on an electric coil heater. She explained that spirit heaters were forbidden because of the fire hazard. She brewed the tea in a pot stained black inside, but her tea was as good as any I'd had in England. We took a few moments for conversation before we got down to our task: reviewing the etiology of lung infections.

"I'm glad I drew you as my study partner," she said. "I'm sure the others are jealous. You're so smart."

I shrugged. "I have a good memory. It helps."

"You know all the right prescriptions."

"I took pharmacology up at Oxford."

"I knew it! Those English schools are so forward-thinking."

"They've been educating women longer. Here, we're an afterthought."

"Yes, it certainly seems so," she agreed with a sigh. She finished preparing her tea, adding a bit of condensed milk from a tin and adding some coarse sugar. The room had only one chair in the room, so she moved aside the duvet and sat down on the bed.

"What do you do when you're not studying?" she asked.

"I ride or take long walks in the English garden. I sing…"

"You sing?" she asked in an excited voice. "I sing in the church choir. You must come with me one Sunday and hear. What part do you sing?"

"Alto to mezzo."

"Perfect!"

Her church choir was fine indeed. After the Mass, Christina introduced me to the choirmaster. A spontaneous audition led to an assignment to shore up the altos. I happily wrote to my grandaunt that I was singing again. She replied that she was pleased to hear it, but I'm sure she was even happier to know that I'd found my way into a church.

Usually, we parted company after Mass, but one Sunday, I felt bold and invited Christina to lunch in the Lehel villa.

"You really live here?" she said under her breath as she took in the atrium ceiling.

"Yes."

"Alone?"

"Only me…and the servants."

At the mention, she finally remembered to hand off her hat and coat to my majordomo. Her eyes were everywhere as she accompanied me into the dining room.

"You really are a countess," she finally said, staring at me down the long table.

"Yes, I am. Does it matter?"

"Not to me. I think it's wonderful, but maybe the others won't."

I signaled to Schmidt to serve the meal, an English cooked breakfast of fried eggs and rashers, accompanied by roast tomatoes. Her eyes grew large.

"Tomatoes? At this time of year?"

"They're from my hothouse," I explained, "…in the garden." She continued to stare at them. I cleared my throat to get her attention. "Do you think the others would be put off if they knew?"

"I don't know. Maybe."

"Then it must be our secret. All right?"

She nodded her agreement.

"Would it be better if I were more like the others?"

She thought for a moment. "You can't help being a countess. You were born that way."

I chuckled. "Yes, that's certainly true. But all of you had to work hard to gain a university education. I more or less breezed in the door."

"I'm sure that's not true."

It was, but I didn't argue.

"Promise me you'll keep this to yourself."

She promised with great fervor, stopping just short of swearing an oath.

After she left, I reflected on our conversation and began to make a plan. The next day, I left the chauffeur at home and drove myself. In nice weather,

I took the trolley. I purchased some pedestrian dresses and suits from a local seamstress. Like the other women, I repeated wearing the same dress or suit. They did it because that was all they had. I did it to demonstrate I didn't consider myself above the others.

Despite my new efforts to blend in, the prejudice persisted. Geisler or one of my other teachers would interrupt a lecture and say, "Perhaps the countess would like to say a few words on this subject." Or one of the senior attendings would say something during rounds like, "Countess, would you deign to present the patient?"

The male students found my title a ready insult. Finally, I found a solution. I simply stopped answering to it.

After rounds one morning, someone in the hall hissed, "Countess!"

I ignored it.

"Countess!" called the male voice, a bit louder this time. I finally turned and saw a gangly, dark haired man. "Stop that!" I snapped. "I'm tired of hearing it."

He came closer and said, "I was only being polite. You are a countess, aren't you?"

"Yes, but what does that have to do with anything?"

He shrugged. "Nothing, I suppose."

"Good, so let's dispense with it! Call me by my surname like the others."

He frowned but nodded his agreement.

"What do you want?" I demanded impatiently.

"Would you like to form a study group with me?" he asked.

"Aren't you already in a group?"

"I am in a group," he admitted, "but everyone in it is an idiot. I want to study with someone smarter than I am, so I can learn more."

"And you think I'm such a person?"

He hesitated for a moment. In the strong light from the window, I noticed that he had bad skin, pock-marked from adolescent acne or perhaps the pox. "You've proven that with Geisler."

"Who else are you inviting into your group?" I asked, narrowing my eyes. I suspected his interest could be some sort of prank the male medical students were trying to play. I eyed him for a long moment, trying to decide if his offer was sincere.

"So far, just you," he said.

"I'm in the ladies' group, which suits me fine."

"We could invite them too," he said slowly. "As long as we keep it small. I have to do well in school, or my father won't pay my fees."

"With you that makes seven. Small enough?"

"Yes," he agreed. He extended his hand. "Peter Harke."

"Margarethe von Stahle."

Seven made us one too many to make an even number for quizzes. It was awkward at first. One pair always needed to invite a third. Then a woman in the class dropped out of school to take care of her tubercular mother. This left an empty room in the student residence. The other women asked if I would move into it. I finally explained that my quarters were under an unbreakable lease, which prevented me from moving. It was not a complete lie. I paid rent of one Mark per month to my grandparents until I reached my majority.

❧

As medical students, we were marginally supervised by the senior physicians. Some patients came to an untimely end because we really had no idea what we were doing. The first-year students were studying pharmacology at the same time they were writing prescriptions. Thanks to the course I'd taken during my extra term at Somerville, I knew a little more than my fellow students.

In fact, there were few efficacious treatments, apart from miracle drugs like aspirin or Ehrlich's magic bullet. We were thankfully beyond bloodletting, but many of the popular remedies, like mustard poultices for chest congestion, were little more than witchcraft. The damage we could do with prepared drugs was limited, although some treatments involved heavy metals like arsenic to treat syphilis, or mercury as an antiseptic and could be quite dangerous.

Most of the time, the nurses rescued us before we could do too much harm. I needed to feign disdain for the nursing staff because my role in the pecking order demanded it, but I learned to pay attention to what they said. They saved me and my patients from more than a few disasters.

The first time I needed to examine a male patient for a urinary tract infection, I stared at the patient's chart long after I'd finished reading it. A senior nurse noticed. "May I be of assistance, Miss?" she asked with a warm smile. I handed her the chart. "Ah, yes. Herr Bauer. Perhaps catheterization might help him void?" That was how the nurses communicated what we ought to do, in carefully worded hints and suggestions, never outright statements.

"Thank you, Nurse. A good idea. Please fetch the apparatus."

While I awkwardly examined the patient, an older man, he somehow forgot his pain, which from the angry look of his genitals must have been substantial. I dared not meet his eyes, although I could certainly feel him leering at me. Predictably, his organ became erect in my hands. I desperately tried not to blush, but his snicker told me I had not succeeded. After I drew a blood sample, I palpated his abdomen and discovered that his bladder was distended.

"Are you able to urinate?" I asked the patient.

"Say again?" I knew I'd spoken loudly and clearly. His smirk told me he was toying with me.

"Can you pass water?"

"No, not a bit. Quite stopped," he replied with a grunt. "The little bit I can squeeze out comes out as a dribble. It's painful."

I could see from his grimace that he was in pain. I was now more sympathetic. The nurse returned with the catheter apparatus.

"Would you like me to do it?" she asked, unwinding the rubber hose.

"I should try, so I learn the technique." She nodded and stood back, but she watched carefully as I fitted the rounded silver tube into the end of the hose. I put my hand around the man's member, which instantly wilted as I began to thread the tube into his urethra.

"For God's sake, woman! That hurts like the devil!"

"Forgive me, but it will relieve the pressure."

Undaunted, I forced the tube into the man's bladder. A gusher of urine blasted into the glass bottle on the other end of the tube. The nurse, watching, said, "I'll fetch another bottle." The urine was dark and murky, which did not bode well for the patient. Unless his body could fight the infection, he wouldn't last long. It was probably even too late for Salvarsan.

"Should I reserve this for your inspection, Miss?" asked the nurse after I'd replaced the bottle with the empty one.

"Please," I said, handing it to her. When she reached over for the full bottle, her breast grazed my shoulder. I glanced up in surprise.

"Pardon," she said, blushing.

I shook my head, but I'd felt a flutter of arousal. When I met her eyes, I realized she had too. She hurried away with the bottles of urine. I covered up the man's naked genitals with the sheet.

"That's so much better. Thank you, Nurse," said the patient with a sigh of relief.

"I'm a medical student, not a nurse," I corrected testily, although it was common for the female students to be mistaken for nurses, despite the clinical coats we wore. The nurses wore caps or little veils to show their credentials. We were forbidden to wear hats of any kind while on duty.

I took the chart to the nurse's desk to write my notes. The senior nurse, who'd assisted me, approached. "You have good hands," she said. "Illegible handwriting, but good hands." I could hear the smile in her voice. I glanced up, my eyes resting momentarily on the rise of her breasts under the apron.

"Thank you," I murmured and returned to my notes.

"Don't ever be too proud to ask for our help. That's why we're here."

I stopped writing for a moment to look up into her face and saw how kind it was, but I also saw something else, a spark of interest. For months, I'd been so lost in my studies and working the ward at all hours that I'd completely neglected my sexual appetites. Like my long-lost cousin, whose house I now inhabited, I found my pleasure in the bath.

The woman looked momentarily puzzled, but she returned my gaze with equal intensity.

"Is there something else I can do for you, Miss?"

"Yes, in fact. Can you meet me in the supply room? I want to see where they hide the catheter apparatus." I grinned.

"Of course," she said, blinking. For a moment I feared that I'd misinterpreted her response. Then she smiled in a way that told me she understood the subtext of my request.

She told me her name was Anneliese. Not that we spoke much. She hiked up her skirts, and I found my way to her sex. I brought her to climax with my fingers, and she returned the favor.

After that, we met regularly in the supply room for feverish assignations, groping under one another's skirts and coming to orgasm in minutes. When someone nearly discovered us, flush-faced and panting, we agreed to end the liaison. Not long after, Anneliese transferred to another department. Although I was glad to have temptation out of view, when I saw her in the lift or the corridors of the hospital, we exchanged wistful looks.

◠◡

"You're becoming a dour, old woman, Margarethe, and you're not even eighteen!" accused Konrad, slouching in the chair in my study. "You're burrowed in here with your books like a hibernating animal."

"If you need money, Konrad, I'll give you money, but I must study."

"You'll become even more boring than you are if you don't have company. You need to hear other points of view."

"No, I don't."

"But since you asked, I could use some money," he said, giving me a sheepish look. "I have none until my brother sends my allowance next week."

Reluctantly, I got up from my seat. I didn't know why Konrad couldn't understand why, after working a double shift at the hospital, I might not want to swill bad wine and watery beer in a student tavern.

I took the petty cash box out of the desk drawer and counted out some notes. "Here. Now, leave me alone."

"Not until you agree to come out with me."

I sighed and glanced at the clock on the wall. "Only if we can be home by midnight."

"Of course," he said, reaching for my hand.

Konrad had begun his studies a term ahead of me and had already collected a wide group of friends he affectionately referred to as the "*Kreis.*" Because we had been in lockstep through our childhood, it felt odd that he was in the earliest stages of his university education, while I was already embarking on my clinical rotations.

Despite his oft-said remark that he had no useful purpose, he had honed his ability to persuade people into a valuable skill. He had elected to study law, but an idealistic streak inclined him to politics. His bonhomie attracted people like a magnet, which boded well for a future political career.

His glib tongue enabled him to strike up a conversation with anyone. His friends included a brilliant architect, an engineer, a philosopher, and a fascinating woman, Elise Seidl, who was a devotee of that latest fashion in psychology—Carl Jung. There were many others who came and went, as is usual in student circles.

I mostly enjoyed Konrad's friends and took advantage of their expertise to learn new things. Max von Ehrenbach, was solid and steady, in body as well as temperament, yet his voice would soar with idealism when he spoke of negative and positive space. Although I was never artistic, he patiently taught me how to draw plans with an architectural ruler and triangle. Peter Licht spoke of a world in which abundant petrochemicals would fuel a new golden age of industry and invention.

I got on well with everyone in the *Kreis* with the exception of Franz Borchert, a disciple of Edmund Husserl. Borchert often scoffed at my classical education, pronouncing it "absurdly out of date." Aside from these philosophical disagreements, his rabid Catholicism remained our chief bone of contention. He professed shock at the idea that I could be an atheist, and never missed an opportunity to evangelize. That was always my cue to drink more alcohol. Usually, I was able to stop myself from slicing Borchert to ribbons because it was so evident that Konrad adored him. One night, I simply ran out of patience. Borchert had been holding forth on Husserl's concept of time for nearly an hour, when I brought up Einstein's Theory of Special Relativity.

"Margarethe, your interest in science always reduces you to the basest materialist!"

"Is that so?" I answered, feeling the hair at the back of my neck bristle.

"You are so mired in the physical, you haven't the imagination to consider higher realms of thought," he said in a voice that oozed condescension.

"Maybe if you had the discipline to learn some mathematics, you could understand Einstein's theories before shooting off your stupid mouth!" I shot back. "You have a lazy mind and are stuck in an endless loop of meaningless blather!"

Everyone at the table fell silent and stared, waiting for me to say more. Instead, I got up and telephoned my chauffeur from the anteroom. As I waited for my motorcar to appear, I realized I'd had far too much cheap wine. I also felt slightly ill. Most of all, I was mortified at losing my composure.

After that episode, I was quite sure I would never again be invited to their meetings, but the very next evening, Konrad called and asked me to join them.

When I arrived, Konrad took me aside. "Grethe, I implore you. Please have patience with Franz."

"Why? The man is an insufferable bore."

"Yes, but you know he's special to me."

I could see why Konrad found him attractive with his vibrant red hair, muscular body, and long, elegant hands. "Well, he is beautiful. But I prefer to admire him rather than listen to his ridiculous theories. What is your interest in him?"

To my surprise, Konrad blushed a little. "Must I say it aloud?"

"All right. For your sake, and yours alone, I'll try to be more patient with *your friend*." The sarcastic emphasis on the last words were intentional.

Konrad seized my hand and kissed it enthusiastically. "My darling, you are such a dear and generous cousin."

Later that night, when the bill for our outing was presented, I was obliged to open my purse and prove Konrad's statement.

～

Our meetings weren't always only heady conversation. Sometimes, we sang. The old songs, some going back to medieval times, were still popular in the student taverns. The best places to hear the old songs were the student eating clubs from which women were banned, but that didn't stop me. Dressed in clothes borrowed from Konrad and hiding my hair under one of his caps, I succeeded in infiltrating one of the student clubs. Borchert professed horror, but he came along to watch the spectacle. Only fear of being expelled from medical school prevented me from repeating the masquerade.

I'd always preferred the company of males to that of my own sex. Age and experience had only increased my contempt for the women of my social class. In their company, I was often at a loss for a subject of common interest. While I adored well-made clothes, I could only bear to discuss fashion for a few minutes at a time. I loathed hats, and now that I was grown and could more or less do as I liked, I hardly ever wore them. That left cards, gambling, and the goings-on at the Kaiser's court, but I'd never had much interest in those topics either.

Elise Seidl was a different kind of female altogether. Her father was a professor of economics at LMU. He was brilliant and had made significant contributions to the discipline when it was still in its infancy. In intelligence, his daughter and I were well matched. However, our minds worked very differently. My interests ran from the brittle magic of mathematics to the earthy concerns of engineering. Mostly, I was interested in things. Elise was fascinated by the human psyche.

At first, Elise was distant. She observed me through half-closed eyes, making no attempt to hide the fact. Most people will glance away to avoid being caught staring. Not Elise. Whenever I turned and found her watching me, her dark eyes frankly met mine.

I found her unconventional beauty compelling. In looks, we were as opposite as in our interests. She was as dark as I was fair. She had mesmerizing dark eyes and black, tightly wound hair that formed natural ringlets. Her skin, however, was pale and lightly sprayed with freckles. She was petite, and I towered over her. In everything, we were mismatched and, in so being, brilliantly compatible.

As our surreptitious courtship advanced, Elise finally smiled at me. The next time we met, she chose the seat beside me. We were in a rather loud tavern, so conversation was difficult. She leaned closer and spoke directly into my ear.

"You hardly ever speak," she said, "but I know you absorb and ponder everything we say."

"Yes, I do."

She drew back and studied me. "You think we're trivial."

"No, of course not. But I think you're very self-absorbed."

"And you're not?"

"I'm studying medicine, which is quite consuming, so I don't really have time for mental masturbation."

She looked not the least bit shocked by such a direct statement. "Then why do you bother with us?"

"My cousin says I'll grow dull if I don't have other company."

"You will, but I'm sure you could find it elsewhere." She gave me a long, careful inspection. "I think you find our conversation stimulating."

"I like to listen. Sometimes, it's nonsense, of course. But I understand your need to hear yourselves talk to explain the world to yourselves."

"And you think you're so far above us?"

"I didn't say that."

"It was implied. You're very sure of yourself, aren't you, Margarethe von Stahle? But you're just a student like the rest of us and still have much to learn. Like us, you're still trying to discover who you are."

Afterwards, I considered her words. She was right of course. Although I was already making notes for what would eventually be my doctoral dissertation, and they were still bungling through their first degrees, I was equally young and inexperienced.

I could have taken offense at Elise's remark, but I didn't. Her forthright manner was refreshing. I finally dared to invite her to dine with me in Lehel. Over coffee, I gave her an intense look to signal my interest. She laughed. "You can get the moon out of your eyes, Margarethe. I know you like women, but I don't."

I was startled by her blunt dismissal. She smiled and took my hand. "Don't take offense. None was meant."

I assumed an impassive expression to hide my embarrassment, but I couldn't keep my face from flaming.

"Oh, really, Margarethe. You are quite seductive, but don't expect every woman to fall for you. Some of us still like men."

"I like men," I protested, "but not especially."

She squeezed my hand. "It's all right. I know we can be friends, despite it. And if you want to know, I'm flattered, so let's leave it at that."

~

I was pleased when Elise invited me to her home to meet her parents. Elise's mother, a warm woman, instantly invited me into her family. At first, Elise's father was skeptical. I overheard him ask, "Elise, why do you bring this Prussian Shikse into my home?" He'd spoken in Yiddish, which almost any German speaker can understand.

"That's not a compliment," I whispered to Elise.

"No. It means a detested female. In other words, a gentile woman."

"Oh! And he doesn't like Prussians either."

"He thinks they're stiff and militaristic."

"That's a stereotype."

"Yes, but there is some truth in it."

I glared at her, but she cocked her shoulder to let me know my opinion was irrelevant.

Professor Seidl persisted in his chilly attitude until I revealed my interest in financial matters. "My grandfather gives me a commission when an investment I recommend makes a profit," I told him proudly.

His dark eyes twinkled with interest. "And what do you do with your fee? Buy new dresses?" he asked in a mocking tone.

"Of course, not. I have a stipend from my father for such things. I invest it."

He leaned forward a little and stroked his dark beard. "How do you decide where to put your money?"

"I read about the company in the newspaper. I watch the prices. My grandfather taught me how to read the financial pages."

"It's always good to do research," he said dryly.

"If it's a scientific invention, I read the academic papers," I added.

At that, he looked impressed. "And how much money have you made from your investments?"

When I quoted the sum, his eyebrows shot up. "This isn't an idle diversion for you."

"Oh, it is, but I'm more serious about it than wagering on billiards."

He laughed.

Over coffee, he began to explain the economic underpinnings of the world financial markets—how commodities are priced and traded and how currency is valued. I absorbed every word like a sponge.

"Papa, that's enough!" Elise finally complained. "This is a social occasion. Not one of your university lectures!"

He reached over and took my hand. "We shall continue another time," he promised. He glanced at Elise and nodded in approval. "Elise, please invite your friend again."

After that, I was a frequent guest at the Seidl home for dinner. The Seidls' warm, tight-knit family was so different from my own. The parents adored Elise and her younger sister, Rebekah. They were as present and interested in their daughters' lives as my parents were absent. I began to wonder how my life would have been different had I been raised by such attentive parents.

Most intriguing of all was the fact that Elise was a Jew. In my circle, such people were rare. There were a few Jewish students up at Somerville. Their fathers were wealthy financiers, businessmen, or prominent in intellectual circles. Some said they'd bought their daughters' way into the college, but I had witnessed their brilliance in tutorials and knew this was a lie. Very few students in my medical class were Jews. The Ludwig-Maximilians, being in the heart of Catholic Bavaria, was less popular with Jews than the more liberal universities in the north, but there were some Jews on the faculty.

Elise's father wasn't at all religious. In fact, he was a confirmed atheist. "Religion, along with language, is what binds a culture together," he said one night. "Religious texts are one of the ways to remember a shared history and common experience. A way of saying, 'your God is my God, so you belong to my tribe.'" His dark eyes studied my face to see if I'd understood. Satisfied that I had, he added, "Next week is Passover. Please join our Seder."

The ritual was moving, especially because everyone in the family, from father to youngest child, had some part to play. Although I found the sweet, kosher wine completely unpalatable, the Passover foods were a new experience for my palate. Frau Seidl had prepared the meal herself. She had a cook and a maid, but she enjoyed cooking. She taught me how to cook the few meals I can prepare that are more than barely edible. Thanks to her, I can roast a chicken and make an omelette, but I remain far more adept at cooking over a campfire than a cook stove.

∽

My first clinical rotation was winding to a close. I focused my attention on learning practical techniques. I had never been trained to do anything useful, but living with the Groß-Lichterfelde cadets had taught me not only to demolish convent walls, but also to tie unbelievably complicated knots, skin and butcher animals for meat, and other tasks that now came in handy. In fact, I surprised myself at how well I could remove sutures, debride and irrigate wounds, and other minor surgical tasks.

Watching one day as I cleaned and bandaged a wound, Geisler observed, "You have a knack for that, Stahle. You should consider becoming a surgeon."

He was paying me a rare compliment, so I stared at him in surprise, especially because female medical students were usually encouraged to choose the "feminine" specialties: pediatrics, obstetrics or gynecology.

"A surgeon? I've never heard of a female surgeon."

"Oh, there are a few. Not many, of course. But I think you could be a good one."

When he walked away, my eyes followed him down the hall. He'd put an idea in my mind that, once planted, grew like a summer vine. When I spoke to my grandaunt by telephone that week, I mentioned it to her. She had never heard of a female surgeon either.

"But that shouldn't stop you, my dear," said my grandaunt. "Let me make some inquiries."

My grandaunt used her considerable influence to locate two of the five female surgeons in the *Reich*. She wrote to each of them and asked if I might correspond with them directly. Both of them agreed. Very excited, I dispatched letters to them at once. They replied soon after with words of encouragement.

Now, I had a plan. I would become that *rara avis*, a female surgeon. I only needed to work out a way to convince my parents that it was acceptable. I mentioned my dilemma to my grandaunt.

"Leave it to me," she said. Since she was the one who had convinced my parents I should be allowed to study medicine, I had every confidence she would take the matter in hand.

～

Elise decided she liked to study in my library, especially because it allowed her access to texts from a wide range of sources. The room had long tables on which to lay out books, comfortable leather chairs, and excellent lighting. She was conversant in several languages, but for some reason, never learned English. When we studied together, I proved helpful for translating English papers and books.

One afternoon, I was reviewing the consequences of eclampsia in pregnancy and made an idle remark: "Pregnancy sounds so dangerous it's a wonder anyone would freely choose it!"

Elise looked up from her book and studied me with her dark eyes.

"You loathe being a woman, don't you?" she asked in a matter-of-fact tone.

I was a bit stunned, but I instantly replied, "No, of course not!" Indignantly, I returned her stare.

"Don't try to fool me, Margarethe. You hate the idea that you must endure pregnancy to fulfill your duties."

My skin began to crawl as she said this because her words came too close to the truth, so I deflected by saying in a surly voice, "Excuse me, but at the moment, I am far more interested in the causes of renal failure in pregnancy. I have an examination tomorrow!"

Elise gave me a hard look. "There's no shame in how you feel, Grethe. And it doesn't matter what you admit to me, but you must always tell yourself the truth."

Her unique ability to read my emotions and explain exactly why I was thinking or feeling something was unnerving but invaluable. Like my grandaunt, Elise understood me in ways that escaped me. When I was perplexed, she could explain why. When I tied myself up into emotional knots, she could unravel them. Her ability to understand my personality felt more intimate than sex.

When I remarked on this, she said, "Each of us is born alone with a separate consciousness. No matter how closely we join our bodies, we can never be in the mind of another person. If someone can accurately intuit your most secret thoughts and desires, that is the deepest connection you can have in this life."

Her words put me off balance. While I considered them, I occupied myself with filling my fountain pen because I couldn't bear to meet her knowing eyes.

9

Whenever I thought about marrying Lytton, or any man for that matter, my throat constricted until I could barely breathe. I cared deeply for Lytton, but I did not love him as a woman loves a man. As the wedding day drew near, I often woke with a start in the middle of the night. My heart thundered in my chest as I anticipated my future with dread. Afterwards, I'd lie awake, trembling under the eiderdown although it wasn't cold.

It was completely illogical. I'd known since I was old enough to understand that I must marry and provide heirs to my titles. It was my duty, which ironically made the idea modestly palatable. In my youth, the idea of being someone's wife had only been an abstraction, one that I could choose to ignore. As the day grew closer and the preparations approached near frenzy, the reality that I would soon be chained to a man hit me with the force of a speeding train.

We had moved up the wedding date from September to June, deciding that summer would afford us more favorable weather. I would not come into my inheritance until my eighteenth birthday. In the interim, Grandmother made a generous gift of money and property as a down payment on my future income as well as a considerable sum for a dowry.

Despite my family's well-intentioned advice, I brokered my own marriage contract. Lytton would never control nor inherit my wealth, lands, or property. Our children would carry my family name, which I would continue to use legally, socially, and professionally. In exchange, my husband would be provided with a reliable source of income for life.

Before we met to sign the papers, Grandmother reviewed them. She took off her pince-nez and smiled. "Generous, but sensible. Well done, Margarethe."

Now, that I was nearly of age, everyone called me by my full name. The servants, even my dear childhood nurse, addressed me formally or called me "Lady Margarethe." While I reveled in my new adult status, the title I fervently desired was *Doktor*.

164

My work was a welcome distraction. By now, I was keeping more patients alive than I was killing, which I counted as a positive sign. Obviously, it helped that most of my patients in the obstetrics and gynecology rotation were young, relatively healthy women.

The male physicians viewed pregnancy as a disease needing treatment. Only the midwives saw it as a natural state. Unless a pregnancy had complications, I never interfered in the midwives' able care. They seemed to appreciate not having overbearing supervision by someone far less expert than they were. Their kindness to their patients impressed me. I decided that when my time came, I would be attended by a midwife.

"A wise idea," my grandmother said. "I insisted on a midwife when you were born. Your father wanted the doctor, but I banished all the useless males from the birthing room. They played cards and emptied a bottle of your birthday port until they were senseless." She rolled her eyes towards heaven and shook her head. "Men!"

For obvious reasons, this sentiment in no way improved my attitude toward my future.

Several mornings a week, I was able to escape from my waddling obstetrical patients into the operating theater. Dr. Edelmann, the department chief, was a gifted surgeon. He performed most of the Caesarians and hysterectomies as well as excising tumors affecting the female organs. Early in my rotation, he'd discovered that I had some surgical skill. He often asked me to assist, which I was delighted to do until the day he performed a pubiotomy on a poor woman whose labor had dragged on for nearly two days.

The midwife had offered other means to hasten the labor, repositioning the patient, manually stretching the vagina, but the doctor was in a hurry that day, so he went right for the saw. I'd read about the complications from cutting a woman's pubic bone to widen the birth opening—urinary incontinence, impaired mobility, difficult intercourse, or worse. When the doctor saw my wide-eyed stare, he said, "Well it's better than losing both mother and infant. Don't you agree, *Fräulein*?"

"Couldn't you do a Caesarian?"

"Eh, it is too late for that, and this is quicker."

I glanced over his shoulder at the midwife, who shook her head. I trusted her judgment more than Edelmann's, but there was nothing either of us could do. In the medical hierarchy, a nurse and a medical student occupied the lowest rung.

～

As the wedding drew closer so did the feverish pitch of the preparations. My emotions were in a similar state of agitation. Elise tried to distract me by demanding the translation of a British paper that she claimed to desperately need.

My insomnia had only gotten worse, and I'd been gobbling valerian capsules, which often left me groggy the next day.

"Margarethe! Wake up! I think you've got this phrase wrong."

I shook my head to clear it and focused where Elise was pointing. She was one of the few people who could consistently read my handwriting. In this case, it was so muddled that even I couldn't understand what I'd written. I went back to the original text and explained the meaning I'd intended.

"This wedding has put you completely off balance," Elise observed in her dry, analyst's voice, a tone that particularly annoyed me. "Most brides look forward to their wedding day. They revel in the preparations."

"As you know, I'm not 'most brides,' and all the fussing is ridiculous. This wedding is nothing more than a ceremony to celebrate that I will be given as a brood mare to Lytton, my fine prancing stud!"

Elise laughed until she was nearly doubled over. In my groggy state, I was irritable and saw no cause for amusement.

"Don't be so cynical," she finally said.

"Why not? It's true, isn't it."

"Technically, yes, but you're not a horse and neither is he. Try to enjoy it, and it will be less onerous. Sex with men can be quite pleasurable." She twitched her dark brows suggestively.

Then, if ever, was an opportunity to confess that I'd lost my virginity to Konrad, but I decided to keep it to myself. Elise already knew too much about me, and withholding information made me feel I had, at least, some modicum of privacy.

Elise patted my arm. "Enjoy the attention. It's the most you'll ever get as a woman. According to the world, marrying the right man is a woman's most significant achievement."

"Now, you're the cynic."

She shrugged and barked a laugh. "Yes, but at least I can see the bright side…unlike you, my dour friend."

〜

Mother and Veronika tried to lure me to Paris for a wedding dress. By then, Veronika's tutoring had made me quite fashion conscious, but in this one instance, I'd completely lost my taste for prowling the modiste's ateliers. I deflected with the excuse that I couldn't take time from my studies. In the end, they chose what I wore to the altar.

We had a debate about where to hold the ceremony. The church at Edelheim was Lutheran. St. Hedwig's cathedral in Berlin was small and unimpressive. We considered the chapel at Obberoth, appropriate given my rank, but too out of the way for the Kaiser and the other dignitaries invited to attend. Ultimately, we decided on the Frauenkirche, the Catholic cathedral in Munich. It was enormous, ancient, and close to home, at least, for me. If I had been more than nominally Catholic, it would have been my parish church.

As my godmother, Veronika was in charge of organizing my wedding party. She chose a half dozen of my noble cousins. Not coincidentally, most were the daughters of my father's military friends. She pressured me to select a maid of honor from among them, but I knew this was the one area in which I could exercise prerogative. Naturally, I chose my dearest female friend, Elise Seidl.

To Veronika's credit, she didn't even blink, but my mother looked perfectly aghast. When she finally closed her mouth, she said, "Margarethe, you can't have *that* girl as a witness at your *Catholic* wedding."

"And why not?" I asked in an innocent voice. I knew the reason and only wanted to force my mother to say it aloud.

Mother was practically sputtering when she said, "Because...because... she's a...Jew!"

"Yes, Mother, I know, but she's not at all religious." I smiled in an attempt to disarm her, which only resulted in her throwing up her hands in exasperation.

"You are *impossible!*" she declared. I delighted in this statement and grinned, but Veronika shook her head in my direction, trying to dissuade me from continuing the argument.

"Surely, Margarethe," said Veronika, "there is a well-born woman who can stand for you at the wedding."

"Perhaps, but I prefer Elise." I knew I was being deliberately difficult, but the very presence of my mother made me stubborn.

Veronika gave my arm a little squeeze. I interpreted the gesture as a friendly warning. "Margarethe, for the sake of peace and your mother's heart, make another choice for your witness."

The stalemate went on for some time before I thought of someone who perfectly fit everyone's requirements—a woman I had worshipped since girlhood, a person whom I greatly respected, and she was, not inconsequentially, the member of a noble family—Charlotte von Backenstoss—*Fräulein Doktor.*

Fräulein Doktor was chatty when I telephoned that afternoon. The term at Obberoth was winding down, and she was looking forward to spending the summer months with her parents. She sounded as excited as a schoolgirl as she described the pleasures of a summer holiday in the Rhineland. I reminded myself that she was little more than a decade older than I, barely twenty-seven.

When I continued to address her as *Fräulein Doktor* she suddenly interrupted me. "Margarethe, you are a grown woman, nearly a physician, and about to be married. Don't you think it's time we dispensed with the formality?"

At first, I didn't know what to make of this suggestion. To me, she had always been *Fräulein Doktor.*

"Then, what shall I call you?"

After a long pause, she said, "My given name is Charlotte, but my friends call me Lotte."

"Is that how you wish me to address you?"

"Yes, please. The time has come for us to put our past as student and teacher behind us."

I doubted that was possible, but I agreed to stop calling her *"Fräulein Doktor."*

I described in the broadest terms the plans for the wedding. When I finished, I added, "If I'd had any real say over all this I would have been married in the chapel at Oxford or eloped to some remote location to escape all this fussing and silliness!"

Lotte laughed. "Of course, you would, Margarethe. Feminine pursuits have never appealed to you, so I'm not surprised to hear your complaints. But remember, you are the heiress of a great house, twice a countess and a baroness as well. Your father is a prominent member of the Kaiser's military council. Your family must make this effort to prove your station."

"That doesn't make it the least bit more pleasant."

"I know, dear," said Lotte in the kind voice that could always soothe me. "But it is only one day in your life, and it will soon be here and gone." The unmentioned, but obvious fact was that after that one day, I would be a wife and shackled to a man.

"Please come to the wedding."

She hesitated for a moment. "Thank you for the invitation. I am honored."

"This is more than a simple invitation. I would like you to be my principal attendant, my maid of honor."

Although the telephone connection was a long distance and not the best, I could hear her gasp.

"Oh, Margarethe. But shouldn't this honor go to a member of your family?"

"Definitely not! I have no sisters and hardly know these cousins my godmother dug up from God knows where! And Frau....eh....Lotte. The honor is all mine."

Fortunately, she had already served in this capacity at her sister's wedding and knew what was required of her.

I informed Veronika and my mother that Lotte would be my primary attendant. They were, of course, delighted, especially because it put an end to the argument about Elise. Mother was sufficiently mollified to allow me to invite the entire Seidl family. If she hadn't, I would have insisted.

◇

As soon as I could, I vanished into my work. To maximize my time in surgery, I forced myself to overlook Dr. Edelmann's hasty pubiotomy. We had attempted to mobilize the severed bone with a cast, which only made the patient uncomfortable. Afterwards, she suffered from urinary incontinence. From that experience I learned that a surgeon's hasty judgment could have dire, long-term consequences.

However, Edelmann's disaster did not divert me from my chosen path. As Dr. Geisler had intuited, I was naturally suited to surgery. My fingers easily adjusted to the delicate work. The interior of the human body fascinated me. But most of all, I liked the challenge and the rush of excitement when things went awry, and swift action was needed to avert catastrophe.

Around my parents, I began to drop little hints that I intended to pursue a career as a surgeon, but my mother was so consumed in the wedding plans, she never heard a word I said. I didn't underscore my message. She would learn of my plans soon enough. When I wrote to my grandaunt, I nudged her to broach the subject with my parents as she had promised.

◇

In early May, Lytton sat for his Oxford examinations. I'd had concerns because, as the end of term approached, he'd spent more time carousing in taverns with his friends than with his books. Fortunately, he managed to pass—barely. When I scolded him for his poor showing, he laughed. As a nobleman, he would automatically be granted the academic rank of master. It especially annoyed me because I had no degree to show for my time at Oxford, despite my double first.

Lytton decided he needed a holiday after passing his examinations, which he'd evidently found trying, so he went to Italy. It was just as well because I had no time to entertain him.

When he arrived in Munich, a week before the wedding, he was tan from digging under the Roman sun. His bronzed skin made his eyes even bluer, and his blond hair had been bleached nearly to white. He looked like a mythological creature, a god who had descended to earth to wed a mortal woman. I was jealous of his healthy, golden tone, but my mother had forbidden me to take any sun, insisting I remain fashionably pale for the wedding.

At first, Lytton was jittery and distant. It was obvious he would much rather be back in Rome with his friends. I understood completely because I'd rather be in the operating theater than attending the pre-nuptial parties.

After a few days, my fiancé and I began to warm to one another again. We rode in the English Garden and took in a concert. We dined with Konrad and afterwards went to a nightclub. Lytton didn't really relax until we joined the members of the *Kreis* for a bout of drinking. In their company, Lytton became once more the amiable, young gentleman I remembered from Oxford. He became so at ease that Borchert and Konrad needed to pour my sodden fiancé into a taxi. After I deposited him at his hotel, I went home for some peace.

The next day, everyone looked shocked when I abandoned them to return to the hospital, but for me it was a workday like any other. I left Veronika in charge of the guests arriving for the rehearsal and the grand dinner afterward.

I asked Dr. Edelmann's permission to leave early so that I could be home when *Fräulein Doktor*, I mean, Lotte arrived. My grandparents were already there when I came home. As grand as my Lehel villa was, it was snug for such a large number of guests. I found the need to entertain them a burden and wished Lytton and Konrad would rescue me again, but they went off in search of their own mischief. I remained at home to entertain my elders. Only the presence of my former teacher brightened the evening.

Lotte took her role as my matron of honor with utmost seriousness and was almost unbearably attentive. Before she retired for the night, she knocked on my bedroom door to see if I needed anything. The scene she found was, no doubt, disconcerting. I had just removed my makeup after a long and rather trying day, and the sight of my wedding gown hanging on the dress form had reduced me to tears. It was a beautiful dress, to be sure—elegant, made of ivory organza, with a sheer overdress decorated with lace. Some poor seamstress had probably gone blind in the process of sewing on all the pearls, but she had certainly earned her fee.

The thought of what the next day would bring stole my breath. I panted, gulping for air. When I took my pulse, I found it racing.

"Oh, Margarethe, what's wrong?" Lotte asked anxiously. She knelt beside me and took my hand.

That shook me up. I wasn't used to people seeing me openly display emotion, especially not my former teacher. I pulled myself together by focusing on my surroundings. I fixed my gaze on the gas lamp beside the bed. I forced myself to take long, deep breaths. Gradually, my heartbeat returned to normal.

Lotte continued to hold my hand until I recovered. "What's the matter, dear?" she asked, tugging on my hand so that I would look at her. "Are you worried about tomorrow?" Her eyes earnestly searched mine.

I could only nod confirmation.

"It's a big step in any woman's life," she said, nodding. "I can understand your anxiety."

"I don't think you can," I said vaguely. As much as I loved *Fräulein Doktor*, I couldn't admit that the idea of marrying a man, any man, repulsed me.

"Are you afraid of the wedding night? Has anyone told you what will happen?"

Fortunately, I didn't laugh. "You're asking someone who will soon be a physician, if she knows the mechanics of intercourse?"

My flippant reply seemed to surprise her, but she squeezed my hand. "Yes, but some women find the first time painful, especially when the hymen breaks. There can be some bleeding." To her credit, she avoided euphemisms and used correct medical terms.

"You're assuming I'm still a virgin."

Her eyelids fluttered, and her mouth gaped open.

"You're not?"

"No. Are you?"

When her gaze dropped to the floor, I could instantly see I'd made a mistake. She nodded solemnly.

"Oh, Frau…Lotte…I'm sorry. I should never have asked that question."

"It's all right," she said. She looked forlorn. When I put my arm around her, she leaned into me and sighed.

"I'm sorry," I repeated stupidly.

"Don't be. It's not uncommon among educated women to remain unmarried. It allows us to focus on our work."

"Perhaps so, but we mustn't let work consume us." The irony of my saying such a thing completely escaped me. "Lotte, look at me." She left the comfort of my arm. With my fingertips under her chin, I lifted her face. "Have you ever been kissed?"

"You mean, by a man?"

"I mean by anyone!"

"Well, of course…my parents kiss me."

I resisted the temptation to roll my eyes. "I mean, have you been kissed with passionate intent?"

Her eyes anxiously searched mine, then looked away. She shook her head.

"What a shame! We can't allow that!" Bold thing that I was, I cradled her face gently in my hands, drew it towards mine, and kissed her on the lips. I half expected her to flinch away and run from the room in terror.

But she didn't. She remained sitting on her haunches, her eyes half closed as if she would like me to try again. So, I did. This time, her lips were soft and relaxed. When I opened them with my tongue, she made no protest. Her breath came faster as I gently explored her mouth.

I proceeded cautiously. Most of all, I didn't want to frighten her. She wasn't a nurse looking for quick relief in a supply closet. This was the woman who had taught me so much. Whenever my education needed a nudge or a solution to a dilemma, she had always been there. As I kissed her sweet mouth, and she responded in kind, I began to realize that she had always loved me, and it was my turn to teach her.

I urged her to rise, led her to my bed, and eased her down on the mattress. She began to tremble. "Don't be afraid," I whispered into her ear. "I would never hurt you."

"I know," she whispered back.

She closed her eyes and wouldn't look at me while I untied her dressing gown and opened it. I caressed her breasts. They were soft and full. The pace of her breathing increased as I circled her nipples with my fingertip. "I would like to make love to you. Will you allow it?"

Eyes still closed, she nodded. I rose and dropped my own dressing gown and pulled my night shirt over my head. I nudged her over so that I might lie down beside her and leaned up on my elbow. "Look at me," I urged in a quiet voice. "Are you afraid?"

"Yes," she murmured.

"I swear to you I would never hurt you."

"That's not why I'm afraid."

"I know. But there's nothing to fear. Loving another woman is perfectly natural, equally natural to a woman loving a man. It's a matter of taste. I actually prefer the love of women."

"But you're getting married tomorrow!" Her eyes were wide with surprise.

"Yes, because that's what everyone expects. Otherwise, I would happily remain unmarried…like you."

Her eyes traveled the length of my body. "You are beautiful," she murmured. "May I touch you?"

I took her hand and laid it on my breast. Her eyes closed as she kneaded it gently, testing its softness and its weight in her hand.

I eased the nightgown off her shoulders. As I kissed her breasts and sucked on the nipples, she moaned softly. She put her hand at the back of my neck to encourage me. I kissed her throat before returning to her mouth.

Tentatively, she explored my mouth with her tongue. Then she abruptly stopped. Was she having second thoughts? Her eyes opened, and she smiled. She pulled my face back to hers for another kiss. For a long time, we lay kissing and looking into one another's eyes. It was the sweetest moment since Daphne had first initiated me into the Sapphic mysteries, unhurried and simply beautiful.

Finally, I raised her nightgown a little. Her eyes widened, so I put it down. "We needn't go that far, unless you wish it," I whispered into her ear.

"Oh, I do. I do! I want to feel your touch."

I allowed my hand to find its way between her legs, where I found her lovely, warm, and so wet. I watched her face as I caressed her. I love to watch women's faces while I caress them. I want to see every feeling in their eyes, to watch their mouths open with a little gasp as I slip my fingers inside them, how they lick their lips as the moment of climax comes near. And then, Lotte came to orgasm, her arms clinging to my neck, her breaths came so fast that I momentarily worried. She cried out softly. Finally, she relaxed in my arms and let go of my neck. She gazed into my eyes, looking surprised and a little confused.

"Congratulations," I said. "You had a climax, and a beautiful one at that!"

She laughed softly and hugged me close again. After she recovered, she followed step by step what I had done to her and brought me to the sweetest conclusion. We repeated this several times before I put on my night shirt and got back into bed.

"I should go to my own room," she said. "People will wonder where I am."

"Nonsense," I said, pushing her back with a light hand on her shoulder. "We shall say that I was anxious about the wedding, and you slept here to comfort me. It's true, isn't it?"

Her eyes were full of love. "Yes, it's true."

I slept peacefully in Lotte's arms, breathing in her warm female scent.

Sitting in the bath in the morning, I wondered if it had been unkind to awaken feelings in Lotte that circumstances would not allow me to return.

The thought made me sad as she helped my lady's maid dress me in my bridal gown. The maid left to get my jewelry from my grandmother, a diamond necklace and matching earrings that would now be passed down to me.

"I hope you will forgive me for last night," I said as Lotte fussed with the folds of my dress.

She looked up and gazed at me with eyes full of love. "What is there to forgive?" she asked.

"We can never be together."

"Last night was so tender, the memory will last a lifetime. Because of you, I know what it is to feel loved."

Her words were so generous, they nearly broke my heart. The maid returning with my jewelry meant our conversation had to end.

I finished dressing and we went down to the carriage that conveyed us to the cathedral. There, before the Kaiser, the Kaiserin, the archbishop, and all of my friends and extended noble family, I wed my handsome, blond giant.

∽

After an evening of dancing in the grand ball room of the Hotel Vier Jahreszeiten, Lytton and I escaped to our room. Given the large number of guests at the villa, we'd decided that we would have more privacy in the hotel.

My lady's maid helped me get out of the wedding gown. I have never been so happy to be free of a garment in my life! While I was undressing, Lytton walked in without his pants. The startled maid stifled a scream. Fortunately, his shorts and socks remained, although one garter had come down. Above his naked legs, he still wore his tails, but his starched vest hung open and somewhere, he had lost his tie. Drinking champagne straight from the bottle, he walked around the suite, bellowing an air from *Pirates*.

"Take care of this," I said, handing the maid the hateful dress. She curtsied and ran from the room as if she feared for her life.

I helped my new husband out of his coat and shirt. I led him to bed, where I finished undressing him.

"But we need to consummate the marriage," he protested as I pulled up the duvet to his chin.

"Not tonight. We're both tired. It can wait until tomorrow."

"Good idea," he said. He rolled over and instantly fell into a stupor.

During the night, he took up most of the bed. In addition to being extraordinarily tall, he had massive muscles from all the shoveling on his archeological enterprises. The span of his shoulders left little room for me. I spent the night clinging to the edge of the bed. I could already see that our marital future would include separate bedrooms.

Before Lytton awoke, I took the opportunity to explore his body. He had trim hips and long legs, so the overall shape of his body was pleasing. His enormous feet were also well shaped. Although he had light tracings of blond hair on his back and chest, he was not one of those men who are apelike. Indeed, as I tried to find an animal metaphor for Lytton, the closest I could find was a Golden Retriever. His head was crowned by abundant blond curls, and like that breed, he was friendly, unquestionably loyal, and an eternal puppy.

As I inventoried my husband's physical virtues, I decided I could have done much worse. Then he did me the favor of rolling on his back, so I could have a look at his working parts. Like everything else about him, they were unusually large, and I was glad that for my first good look at them, they were still asleep. In all, he was a healthy specimen of the human male.

At some point, he became aware of me inspecting him and opened one bleary eye. "Meg, are you examining me?" he asked in an incredulous voice.

"Yes, but not as a physician."

"I should hope not," he said, opening the other eye. "Well then, here's the equipment," he said, grabbing his penis, which woke it up a bit. "Penis." He waved it. "Balls." He jiggled his testicles in his scrotum.

"Impressive," I said in a droll tone.

"You can see how everything works later," he said, pulling himself into a sitting position. He yawned and rubbed his eyes. "Now, I desperately need some tea."

"I shall ring for breakfast. Will a German breakfast do? Or would you prefer a cooked breakfast?"

"Oh, please! Some fried eggs would be absolutely delicious!"

"Good idea. One of the chemicals in egg yolks is apparently very good for a hangover."

"Oh, God, Meg! It's too early for medical lectures," he said, getting out of bed. He walked naked to the toilet, his organ swaying with each step. As I dialed the number for room service, I reflected that I had just been introduced to daily life with a male.

After Lytton used the toilet, he showered. His male smell had been rather pronounced when he had awakened, but I was accustomed to the aroma from having lived among the cadets. Mostly, I did not find the scent unpleasant, and Lytton's was generally mild, although a bit gamey if he went more than a day without bathing.

In anticipation of the arrival of our breakfast, I got up to brush my hair and put it up. I put on my dressing gown. Fortunately, the maid had rescued the wedding dress or it would have been in a nasty heap on the floor. I never wanted to see the hateful thing again.

My mood improved when the waiter arrived with our tea. I found the English-style breakfast of crisp rashers, fried eggs, and toast comforting. As I ate it, I thought of England and how much I missed it. Lytton devoured everything in sight, including three fried eggs, German-style black pudding, a mountain of toast and two fried tomatoes, his and mine. He was still looking for more, so I rang for another pot of tea, more toast, and soft-boiled eggs.

He ate all the eggs and had nearly demolished the mountain of toast before he said, "We should try to escape before they come looking for us." He made no move to get up. Instead, he continued to munch placidly on his toast while he surveyed the table to see what to eat next.

"Never mind. While you finish eating everything in sight, I shall bathe."

We were able to depart within the hour. Lytton drove my motorcar, packed to the gills with hiking clothes and mountaineering gear in addition to the clothing we would need for a month's stay in the mountains. We sang as we drove, mostly Gilbert and Sullivan, but I also sang arias from my repertoire. Lytton joined in on some duets. It felt so good to open my lungs and sing. I'd been neglectful of my vocal exercises and practice during my medical studies. Hopefully, with Lytton around to inspire me, that would end.

"I like this motorcar," said Lytton, thumping the steering wheel. "It has power and handles quite well."

"That's good because I intend to give it to you."

"You do? Splendid!"

"Yes, I have my eye on a new model, and you'll need something to get around town, right?"

"Right," he agreed wholeheartedly. "You are a most generous wife!"

I smiled at the idea that he thought me generous for giving him a motorcar, when my real gift lay at the end of our journey. We both enjoyed mountain sports. With my "commissions" from my grandfather, I had purchased a chalet.

It was summer and the roads were clear, so we arrived in Garmisch sooner than we expected. I had hired a young couple, who were recommended to me by the estate agent, as caretakers. The arrangement could not have been more ideal. The wife would cook and clean for us, while the husband would look after the buildings and grounds. The niece of these good people would serve as both a maid and a laundress. When we stopped for lunch, I telephoned ahead. They were waiting for us when we arrived.

After a delicious lunch of roast potatoes, field salad, and *Speck*, Lytton and I explored our Alpine nest. The chalet was set on a hillside accessible to town, but far enough away for privacy. From the patio, we had a splendid view of the surrounding mountains. A trail at the back of the house offered a challenging trek on my own property. It was large enough to entertain a dozen guests, yet small enough to feel cozy and intimate.

"My God, Meg, this place is absolutely spectacular," said Lytton as he watched me prepare G&Ts. "What a perfect wedding gift!"

I handed him a drink and sat down to enjoy mine. "It's a gift we both can enjoy. I need a place to escape from time to time."

"Indeed, you do. You've been working too much!" He gave me a critical inspection. "You're far too pale. I'm glad you'll be getting some sun."

"I have a long way to go to catch up to you. We appear to be of different races."

Lytton held his deeply tanned arm against mine. "Yes, I suppose we do."

We hiked part of the way up the hill for exercise after our long drive. After a delicious meal of rabbit stew, and not a few glasses of brandy, my husband and I repaired to our bedchamber to consummate the marriage.

I wish I could report that the lusty exuberance of our healthy, young bodies took over from there. Indeed, when I looked into my husband's blue eyes, I felt a faint stirring of desire. For one thing, he was a superb specimen of maleness. And for another, I truly cared for him. He evidently had similar feelings because he rose to the occasion. Unfortunately, that did not lead to the successful conclusion we desired.

This is how it really went: my husband, lying between my legs, laboring to penetrate me, said, "Meg, why are you so *tight*?"

"Well, Lytton, because you're so *big*."

"And you're a virgin!"

"Whatever made you think so?"

"You're not?" he asked incredulously.

"No."

"Oh, well, that's good, I suppose, but why are you so tight?"

"Because you're so big!"

Meanwhile, his enormous shoulders were blocking the light. I felt not only crushed under his weight but blinded. I punched him lightly on the back. "Get off me, you, big oaf!"

He rolled off and sat up, his penis standing at attention. When I gazed at his member with a frown, it resumed its usual size and resembled a large, friendly worm.

"This isn't working," he observed, stating the obvious.

"Oh, no?" I replied in my most sarcastic voice. "Whatever made you think so?"

He threw himself back on the pillows and sighed in exasperation. "What are we going to do?"

"Unless you plan to rape me, I suggest we give it up for now."

"That's not even remotely funny."

"No, sorry, it's not. But we're both anxious. Stress makes intercourse more difficult. The woman tightens and dries up."

"What a joy to be living with a physician-to-be."

"Someday, you will be grateful. Now, I suggest we try again tomorrow when we are more relaxed and well-rested."

"I thought we were going on a trek tomorrow."

"We are. Just as I said, 'more relaxed and well-rested.' Exercise will do us good."

Lytton got up and put on his dressing gown. He went to the drinks stand and poured himself a glass of brandy and one for me. "Now that I don't have to worry about getting Peter to rise again, we can have a drink."

"Hear. Hear," I agreed.

We each took our books from our respective bed stands and settled down to read.

~

We set out on our trek, wearing matching leather breeches from the Lodenfrey, long, thick socks and boiled-wool jackets. Although it was June, it was still cool in that mountainous region. We'd packed a lunch of wurst sandwiches and a thermos of coffee in addition to the water in our canteens. We made a good ascent to a grassy area above the treeline, where we stopped for lunch.

"This is a beautiful spot," Lytton observed, taking off his cap and running his fingers through his hair, which glistened with perspiration. "We should camp here for a few nights."

"What a splendid idea! Of course, we should. Let's plan it."

He opened his pack and produced two sandwiches wrapped in paper. He handed me one, and then hungrily bit into his own. I poured coffee into our little tin cups.

"I've decided to become a surgeon," I said, apropos of nothing.

"You have?" he said, staring at me with surprise. "Isn't that a little unusual for a woman?"

"It is, but apparently there are a few. *Tante* located two of them, and we've been corresponding."

"And what do they say about it?" Lytton had already demolished half of his sandwich.

"They are encouraging me, of course. But they haven't been sparing in describing the challenges I shall face."

"Apart from the obvious?"

"The training is severe and demanding with no accommodations for the so-called fairer sex. The certification panels are conservative. Some of them have failed women who were perfectly qualified to practice."

"That is so unfair," said Lytton with a sigh. "Are you sure you want to do this?"

"Quite sure. You know I never shy away from a challenge."

Lytton chuckled. "Unfortunately, I do."

"They suggested I find a powerful surgeon to mentor me and become my champion."

"And have you identified this person?"

"Not yet. None of the surgeons at the *Klinkum* is that remarkable, unfortunately."

"Keep looking."

"I intend to." By now, Lytton had consumed his entire sandwich and was looking enviously at the portion I had started. I cut it with my folding knife and gave him half. "Next time, I'll ask Frau Weiss to pack double for you. Beast!"

Lytton gave me a sheepish look.

"I don't intend to tell my parents of my plan to become a surgeon," I said, picking up the thread of the earlier conversation.

"Won't they find out sooner or later?"

"Oh, they never care what I do as long as I behave properly in public and can produce some heirs." I finished my sandwich and wiped away the spicy mustard in the corner of my mouth with my thumb. "That's not entirely true. My father cares, but I don't expect any trouble from him. Only my mother."

Lytton adjusted his pack so that he could stretch out and lay his head on it. "Your mother is so conventional. I'm not used to it after being raised by Lady Bromsley, suffragette and blue stocking extraordinaire!"

"Your mother is quite remarkable. And I feel very lucky because she raised a remarkable son."

"Thank you, Meg. That's the nicest thing you've said to me since we arrived."

"Don't let it go to your head."

"I know you won't ever let that happen."

I punched his shoulder, and he laughed. He gazed at the clouds overhead for a long moment. "I understand why you kept your plans to yourself until they are well underway. You'll have the element of surprise in your favor."

"I plan to enlist my grandaunt in my defense. She succeeded in convincing them that I should go to medical school."

"That's right, Meg. Sic *Tante* on them."

I laughed. That's what I loved most about Lytton. In the darkest hour, he could always make me laugh.

⌇

That night we dressed for dinner. Lytton looked suave in a dinner jacket and black tie. Frau Weiss, when she put her mind to it, could turn out elegant fare from her kitchen. In that rugged part of the Alps, we had created a small oasis of civilization. After dinner, Lytton and I sang together, switching off turns at the piano to play the accompaniment. We went more lightly on the alcohol than on the previous night.

Eventually, it was time to put frivolity behind us and get to work. With some misgivings, I undressed for bed and wondered how to approach our dilemma. I came out to find Lytton looking equally grim.

"I have an idea," I said.

He raised his eyes to me, looking as earnest as a schoolboy.

"Perhaps I should take a superior position and guide the missile, as it were."

His blond brows rose abruptly. "Now, I've heard Peter called many things, but never a missile!"

"All penetrating things are essentially missiles."

I began to see other points of comparison, such as the likeness of ejaculation to the explosion of ordinance, but I decided to keep those thoughts to myself.

"You could try touching me," I said. "I might not be so dry." To prepare for this adventure, I had spent a few minutes alone, stimulating myself to the memory of my prenuptial night with Lotte.

The sour look on Lytton's face told me that he did not consider touching me a good idea.

"Then let me touch you," I suggested. "Maybe that will stimulate us both."

"All right!" he agreed enthusiastically and rolled on his side.

We gazed into one another's eyes while I stroked him. In my hand, I could feel him growing harder, and yes, it was stimulating to feel his penis throb in my hand. I held on while I climbed up his body and positioned myself on his hips. So far, so good, I thought, as I visualized relaxing. Visualization had always proven to be beneficial whenever I was faced with a difficult physical task. After a few fumbles, I was able to insert his member and then gingerly lower myself as far as I could.

"It worked!" I exclaimed, which instantly caused him to wilt. Suddenly, the proud missile was as flaccid as a slug.

I rolled off of him in disgust.

"I'm sorry," he said with a little puppy dog face that made me want to kiss him, so I did.

He held me in his arms, as we considered our situation in moody silence.

"Now what?" I asked as if he had an answer I hadn't yet considered.

"I do have a suggestion, but I dared not share it as I thought you might be repulsed." My mind instantly recalled Daphne's descriptions of the many ways to stimulate a man. I dearly hoped that Lytton didn't expect me to take that enormous penis into my mouth.

The scientist in me was curious, however. "What do you suggest?"

He sat up and began to talk very rapidly. "I often remark on your likeness to a boy." I already didn't like where this was going, but I resolved to hear him out. "You have the hindquarters of a boy. What if we were to pretend…"

"Let me understand, Lytton. You want to take me from behind like an animal…to mount me like a beast."

"Well, I wouldn't put it quite that way…but yes."

Sighing, I got up on my hands and knees, "Anything to get this done. Go on, then. Let's do it."

He stuck his head under my face and grinned. "You won't regret it. I promise." He moved into position.

"Mind you get into the correct opening!"

"Meg, give me some credit. I'm not an idiot!"

He fumbled for only a moment and then he burst into me. The moment was shocking but not unpleasant. As he moved inside me, it gradually became less shocking and more pleasurable. I was just beginning to like it a bit when he groaned and gripped my hips fiercely.

The primary mission had been accomplished. He flopped onto his pillow and grinned, looking quite proud of himself.

～

Over the next weeks, Lytton and I divided our time between trekking and reprising our initial success in the bedroom. Eventually, we felt comfortable enough to go back to where we started. I no longer found his enormous shoulders oppressive, and I began to prize his powerful body and his strength. I taught him how to use his hands and mouth to pleasure me and bring me to climax, and he convinced me to attempt the thing that had horrified me. I cannot say that I ever found sex with a man as satisfying as with a woman, but I learned to enjoy it for what it was.

Eventually, we tired of seeing the bedroom walls and the trails near our chalet. We went into the village below our mountain retreat to seek gifts for our friends and to taste food other than what Frau Weiss could prepare. Her food was more than edible, but her repertoire was limited.

We happened into a woodcarver's shop. There were many, for that region was known for its woodcarvings. From the unfinished work in the studio, his commissions seemed destined for churches or monasteries. Most of the life-sized carvings in various stages of completion depicted saints and biblical personalities.

"Lytton! I think I shall give this gentleman a commission."

He flexed his blond brows in surprise. "I never imagined religious art to be one of your tastes."

"Oh, don't be silly, not for us, for Obberoth…something for the nun's chapel. My grandaunt's jubilee is approaching."

Lytton looked even more skeptical when I tried to explain what I had in mind—a pregnant version of the Madonna. When I first proposed it, the carver looked plainly horrified.

"Only you would think of something like that!" said Lytton to me in English while the carver recovered from his shock.

"Well, Mary must have been pregnant. The virgin birth wasn't completely mystical." I attempted to create a sketch of my idea. Finally, Lytton took the pencil and paper out of my hands. At least, he had some artistic talent. He drew while I listed the details that I expected the carver to depict: a young woman in late pregnancy, wearing a white robe with yellow trim, and a black cloak. Around her head she was to have a half moon and a circlet of stars.

"I'm no churchgoer," Lytton muttered under his breath, "but even I know that's no holy madonna. You're describing the goddess of *The Golden Ass*!"

"Clever boy! Right you are. At least, you remember that much from your studies."

The carver demonstrated his reluctance to execute my design by naming a ridiculous price. He protested that he already had too much work, and the commission couldn't be ready for more than a year, perhaps even two.

"Money is no object," I told him, smiling. "And I am certainly willing to wait." I wrote a large bank draft as a down payment to let him know that I meant business.

~

Before we left Garmisch, Lytton invited some of his friends from the excavation in Italy. Five magnificent, young men arrived by train. When we met them at the station, Lytton instantly transformed from my attentive husband into the hail-fellow-well-met man I'd known up at Oxford. Each of his friends was beautiful in his own way, three dark and two as fair as Lytton. They were all golden brown from the Italian sun and well-muscled from digging for antiquities.

From the looks of them, I was glad I had insisted my husband-to-be use a condom when we were apart. Of course, I had no way of knowing whether or not he kept this agreement, but a prenuptial blood test, which I'd performed myself, confirmed that he was free of infection when we'd married. I worried on behalf of both of us. Apart from Neosalvarsan, there were few efficacious treatments for venereal disease.

The men who came to the chalet were not merely diggers in the ancient dust, but well-heeled men from high society—three Englishmen, a Frenchman, and an Italian, all from noble families. Not surprisingly, given Lytton's love of singing, they were also musical and had good voices. This provided us with opportunities for duets, trios, even choruses. The Italian had a very good falsetto alto, so the treble parts were marginally represented.

Despite their boisterous company and probably much temptation, Lytton came to me every night. Now, that we had achieved some compatibility, he sweetly made love to me. I began to think there was some hope for the marriage.

Two days before we were to depart, we returned our gentlemen friends to the train station in Garmisch. By then I was sorry to see them go because I had truly enjoyed their company. It was the most light-hearted time I had enjoyed in years.

As I was packing to return home and was about to stow the pads that I used to absorb menstrual blood, I realized that I was late. The honeymoon had been a success.

10

"Now, this is bloody interesting," said Lytton, his toast suspended in the air as he stared at the newspaper.

"What?"

"A Serbian radical has shot the grand duke of Austria."

"Really? Let me see." I reached for the paper, but Lytton snatched it back.

"Never mind. I shall read it to you."

He read the description of how a Serbian member of the Black Hand had approached the heir to the Austrian throne while he rode in his carriage and shot him. "Both he and his wife are dead." Lytton's brows arched toward his hairline as he regarded me over the top of the *Times*. "Good God!" he exclaimed. "That's horrible!"

"What does it mean?" I asked, filching a piece of his toast, while he was otherwise occupied.

He shrugged. "I have no idea, do you?"

"No, but it doesn't sound good."

"It doesn't," agreed Lytton with a frown, putting aside the newspaper. "I hope we don't get involved."

"Which 'we'? Germany or England?"

"Neither one. The Balkans are a sewer. No one belongs there. Not even the locals."

I regarded him with a frown. Obviously, he knew more about politics than I did.

We alternated driving on the way home to Munich. As I gazed at the passing scenery, I was reluctant to leave the mountains and the wonderful spell of leisure behind, but I was happy to be returning to my studies. I couldn't imagine my life without my profession or being idle as so many women of my class were. They had servants to deal with housekeeping and child rearing, so what did they do all day? The boredom would have driven me mad. Small wonder so many women experienced fits of "hysteria" as a way to entertain themselves.

Schmidt greeted us at the door with an announcement. "You have a house guest, *Gnädige*."

"Who?" I asked with surprise.

"Your father, the Lord Count."

Last I'd heard my father had been in Potsdam meeting with the Kaiser's council, so I never expected to see him in my Lehel villa. Lytton and I exchanged a look, evidently sharing the same worried thought. "I hope nothing's wrong," Lytton whispered.

"So, do I." I handed off my wrap to the majordomo and asked my Father's location. I found him reading a book in my drawing room.

"Father, how good to see you," I said, embracing him over the rear of the sofa. I glanced at his book and saw it was a western by Karl May. I was surprised he hadn't read them all by now. He reached up and pressed my cheek to his.

He rose and extended his hand to Lytton. "Hello, boy. Welcome home. Did you enjoy the mountains?"

"Yes, sir. Very much."

"And your honeymoon?" asked my father with a salacious leer.

Lytton chuckled. "Yes, that part too."

The suggestive "man talk" irritated me, but instead of scolding them, I rolled my eyes.

"I'm very surprised to see you," I said. "What brings you to Munich?"

"A very important mission, my dear."

"Here? In Munich?"

"Not exactly. But it involves you."

"Me?"

He reached for my hand. "Grethe, darling, I need your help. Your country needs you."

"My country!" I repeated incredulously. "What a dramatic statement! I'm just a medical student. What can I do?"

"I'll explain later, but I've already booked us on the night train. Send your maid to pack for you. And bring some of your best dresses."

Lytton and I looked at one another in shock. "But sir, we've only just returned," my husband protested in a righteous voice.

"I'm sorry, son, but you're not coming along. Only Margarethe."

"What!" Lytton exclaimed.

My father raised his hand. "Calm yourself, boy. I'll bring her back soon. At the moment, this is more important than anything, and we have no time to lose."

Now, he had me both intrigued and puzzled. "Is this an espionage mission?"

"Not exactly, but there may be some spying involved…and duplicity." He glanced at my hand. "Margarethe, you must pretend you're not married. Take off your wedding ring."

"Father…"

"I mean it. I shall explain everything later."

I had never disobeyed my father, so I instantly took off my wedding ring and handed it to Lytton. With some difficulty, my husband squeezed it on his pinky finger for safekeeping.

"Father, I hope this is not a dangerous mission. You should know…that I'm pregnant."

Father smiled and his mustaches twitched up, coming along for the ride. He clapped Lytton on the back. "Well done, boy!" he said, as if my husband had done all the work, and I had merely lain there, a vessel waiting to receive his glorious seed. But that was all the acknowledgement either of us got for accomplishing the first step in our duty to the line. Father's mind was obviously elsewhere.

"Can you, at least, tell me where we are going?" I prodded.

"Yes, but you must both keep it to yourselves. We are going to Russia."

"Russia?" Lytton and I both said at once.

"Yes. I only hope we get there in time. I can't tell you more than that. Now, let's have a quick lunch and off we go."

My father briefly outlined our travel plans. Getting to St. Petersburg by train would take almost two days, even with no stops along the way. "But you've only just arrived. It will take time for your maid to pack your things, and we should have a good meal for the long journey. I've taken the liberty of asking your cook to prepare hearty fare, roast hare and leeks." Of course, he had. It was one of his favorite dishes.

While we ate. Father and Lytton talked of ancient Rome and the collapse of the Republic under the caesars. I was fascinated to hear how my husband's perceptions of the ancient Romans had been changed by his tactile perceptions of seeing and touching things from the time in which they lived. He said it gave him a connection with those long-dead people that he had never imagined possible.

"You know, Lytton, I have an old army friend whose brother is the director of the Staatliche Antikensammlungen. It's quite a fine museum. The classical collection is impressive. Would you be interested in a position there? I could make an inquiry with my friend."

"Would I be interested? Oh, yes!" A light shone in Lytton's eyes when he spoke about his research and excavations. The passion in his voice made me love him all the more.

I wanted to ask more questions about our trip to Russia, but my father gave me a sharp look. "I shall tell you everything on the train. For now, suffice it to say it is a diplomatic matter of vital importance."

I knew better than to badger him on this subject. He wouldn't budge. Lytton was obviously equally curious, but he couldn't get any more out of Father than I could.

My husband accompanied us to the train station. The stationmaster called our train. Before we boarded, Lytton caught me in a crushing hug. "Please be safe, Meg. I shall miss you!"

I didn't want to let him go, but my father tugged at my arm. "Margarethe, we must board. *Now.*"

Lytton waved enthusiastically as the puffing locomotive pulled out of the station. Even from a distance, I could still identify the tall figure who towered above all the others on the platform. When the train rounded a curve, and Lytton was out of sight, I finally settled into my seat.

Father ordered tea, and while he waited for the porter to return, he smiled like the Cheshire cat.

"Are you surprised that I'm allowing you to whisk me away from my new husband?" I asked, returning the smile. Father and I usually spoke English when we were alone, but in this case, it also provided a greater level of privacy for our conversation. "I've even restrained myself from demanding to know exactly where we're going and why."

"I'm not a bit surprised. I expect nothing less. We've trained you to always do your duty."

"But you will eventually tell me where we're going and why?"

"Of course, I shall tell you. After the tea arrives, and we are completely alone."

I gazed out the window as we waited. The tea eventually arrived in a Meissen service on a silver tray. When the porter closed the door, my father went into the hall and looked both ways to make sure it was clear. Then he locked the door to the compartment.

I poured the tea as if nothing could be more usual. I handed my father a cup and he prepared it in the correct English manner with a bit of cream and a little sugar. "Cups, thank God! None of that barbaric Russian thing until we get there!" he sighed. "Tea in a glass! Indeed!"

"So, we really are going to Russia?"

"Yes."

I drank my tea and took in the scene out the window.

"Very good, Grethe. Perhaps singing in operettas has taught you something about acting. You play the ingénue very well."

I sat back and affected mock innocence.

He chuckled. "Excellent."

"The truth is, I never sang ingénue roles. I'm too tall, and my voice is too dark."

"Of course, I was only joking, and you are exactly right for this role."

"Tell me more," I said and sipped my tea.

"We are on a secret mission," he finally said. "Only a few in the Kaiser's cabinet know about it. Not even the Kaiser himself. If we succeed, it could prevent a disaster of enormous proportions. If we fail, there will be hell to pay." He studied me with his pale eyes. "I am counting on you, Margarethe. Your country is counting on you. We are all counting on you!" As if the burden he was placing on my shoulders could be heavier!

"Dear God, Father! What is this all about?"

"You read in the paper about the assassination of the Archduke?"

"Yes, of course. It was the headline in all the papers."

"Good. Then I don't need to explain that part."

"Yes, you do because I don't know what it means."

"You know that the Empire is Austria's ally?"

I nodded.

"Austria will feel obligated to punish the Serbs. Not that the Grand Duke was beloved. In fact, he was despised, but he was the heir to the Austrian throne and that is like attacking the country itself. The Serbs have never been anything but trouble. The government does little to control the radical elements in their society. They deserve to be punished."

I raised my shoulders. I still couldn't see how this turn of events in a remote part of the world had anything to do with us.

"Russia is not formally Serbia's ally," my father continued to explain. "But if Austria punishes the Serbs, Russia may consider defending them."

All this foreign intrigue meant nothing to me and I was growing impatient, so I cut to the chase. "You still haven't said what this has to do with me."

Father looked sheepish. "Promise you won't be angry with me."

"Angry? Why should I be angry?"

"In order to get an audience with an important person in the Czar's circle, I dangled you as a possible match for his son."

"But I'm already married."

"Our society news never gets as far as Russia, so he won't know."

"What!"

Father raised his hands to urge me to adopt a quieter tone.

"Father! How dare you! You set me like bait in a snare!" I observed coldly.

"Yes, I did," he admitted, looking contrite. "But I only did it because the matter is so urgent."

"Oh, for Christ's sake, Father. Now, you've gone too far."

"No, Margarethe, listen to me. When you do, you will understand why."

I rolled my eyes. "Go on. I'm listening."

"I've tried so many times to set a meeting with Prince Oblensky to discuss diplomatic matters critical to the future of our countries. Nothing worked. Then I sent him your photograph. He showed it to his son, and the boy was smitten."

I compressed my lips to express skepticism. "Smitten? Why? I'm no great beauty."

He sat up straight and looked indignant. "You're beautiful and never think otherwise!"

"I look how I look. What I want to know is why it's so important to meet this prince."

"Oblensky is a distant cousin of the Czar, a member of the cadet branch of the imperial family. They were childhood friends. The Czar listens to him."

"And…?"

"He's a pacifist. He is desperately afraid of war because he knows the political situation in Russia is unstable. With the exception of Oblensky, no senior member of the imperial family seems to have any idea of what's really going on among the lower orders."

"So? What has that to do with us?"

"If Austria threatens Serbia over the assassination, and Russia comes to Serbia's defense, we would join with Austria, which means we would be at war with Russia. Our mission is to convince Russia not to respond to the situation in Serbia."

As I connected the dots, I was gobsmacked. How could I have come home from my honeymoon to find myself a lynch pin in an international crisis?

"Understand, Margarethe, it's not altruism toward Russia. It's pure self-interest on our part. As a member of the general staff, I can tell you, we cannot fight a war on two fronts. We must prevent Russia from getting involved."

"What do you want me to do?" I asked.

"Look beautiful and smile seductively at the prince's son. Keep him occupied. I shall do the rest."

"Really, Father, seducing men is not my forte."

"Maybe not any man, but a certain kind of man…" He gave me a canny look. "You seem to be fairly good at that, I think."

"If you weren't my father, I would challenge you for that asinine remark."

"And I would cower because I know you are a formidable opponent," he replied with a grin. "A thousand pardons."

～

When I alighted from the train in St. Petersburg, a tall, elegant man with a pencil mustache, his black hair carefully slicked into a fashionable style, reached for my hand. "Lady Margarethe von Stahle, it is an honor to meet you," he said in perfect French. He made a deep formal bow and kissed my hand. "I am Gegor Ivanovich Oblensky," he explained, "son of Prince Oblensky." He smiled, revealing perfect teeth. My breath caught because he was so unspeakably handsome he could have been a movie star. He turned to my father. "General von Stahle," he said with a crisp military bow, complete with heel clicks. "It is my most pleasant duty to conduct you and the Lady Margarethe to my father's house."

"Thank you, Prince Oblensky," I replied in Russian.

His blue eyes brightened. "You speak our language. I did not know."

"Not very well."

"Yes, well!" he said enthusiastically. "Delightful!" He offered me his arm. "Please call me Gregor. I insist!"

Such informality on first meeting was highly irregular. I glanced over my shoulder and saw my father nod in approval. "Then you must call me by my given name as well."

"Margarethe," he said with a broad smile. "Yes, I shall, and with pleasure!"

Gregor led us to a large Daimler and stood by while the chauffeur opened the door. I slid across the leather seat, followed by Father. Gegor sat in front with the chauffeur.

"Margarethe, I have taken the liberty of planning some sightseeing while you are in St. Petersburg. You must be tired, so first you may refresh at our villa and enjoy luncheon. Afterwards, we will take in the art at the Hermitage. Tomorrow evening, we are dining with His Imperial Majesty, the Czar, and his family."

Father looked surprised. "I would have thought the warm weather would find them at the summer palace in the Crimea."

"I'm sure he would rather be there," said Gregor, "but the unrest in Serbia has kept him close to home. We shall dine at the Peterhof." He turned around to look at me. "I understand that you are a singer, Margarethe. Our box at the Mirinsky is reserved for us. The opera tonight is *Eugene Onegin*."

"That sounds like an excellent plan, Your Highness," my father said, "but I would like to have time to speak to your father."

Our host's pencil mustache turned up at each end as he smiled. "Of course. I understand that he has set aside time in his schedule for you this afternoon. Please, may I accompany your daughter to the Hermitage, while you are occupied with my father?"

"If my daughter would like to see the art, which I'm sure she will, most certainly."

"I had so many things planned to show you," Gregor said with a deep sigh, "but your visit is so short. Perhaps next time."

The pleasant smile on my face felt frozen. Although I had, as my father had hoped, learned some skills as an actress, three days was a long time to maintain this charade. I gazed out the window for a mental respite. In St. Petersburg, the passersby still wore warm clothes even though it was summer. The multicolored onion domes on the buildings recalled my temporary home province of Bavaria.

All of my etiquette lessons came into full play when I met Gregor's parents. Of course, being part of the extended imperial family, they outranked us, and as I came to observe, the Russian nobility clung tightly to the old formalities. I made a deep, respectful curtsy to the elder prince and his wife. My Grandmother would have been proud.

After a luncheon of smoked salmon and poached fowl stuffed with greens, Gregor and I headed to the Hermitage. He drove his own motorcar, which I found delightfully modern. As he navigated the St. Petersburg streets, I admired his perfect profile. He was as classically handsome as a god in mortal form.

We browsed the map of the museum and he asked what I would like to see first. "Oh, the Roman and Greek statuary. I've heard the collection is amazing."

"Really? Who told you?"

It was on the tip of my tongue to say, "my husband." Luckily, I caught myself before it slipped out.

After hours of browsing the collections, Gregor suggested we take respite in his favorite tea house. Since my feet were aching in the shoes I'd worn, I gratefully agreed.

"I am so glad you like the classical statuary," said my host after we ordered tea and savory accompaniments. "I have been studying art and archaeology at university. It is my passion."

"Is it really?" I remarked and thought how much Gregor and Lytton would enjoy one another's company. "I read Greats at Oxford. I briefly thought I would like nothing more than to become an archaeologist. Someday, you must visit Berlin and see the collections of the Altes Museum."

His little mustache twitched into a cautious smile. "But you are studying medicine."

"Yes, it is the way I can be of service."

He chuckled. "I understand that the Prussian nobility highly values service. Is medicine your passion now?"

I thought for a moment. "Music is my passion. Medicine is my profession."

He nodded, evidently understanding. He sighed. "My father would have preferred I read law."

"But he allowed you to study art because you have no need to practice a profession."

"Nor do you."

"No, but I want to become a physician more than anything else. And more…I mean to earn my habilitation."

He sat back and regarded me with a little frown. "Our society is not so advanced as yours, Lady Margarethe. Would you be content living the life of a Russian Princess?"

"Not if it meant being idle."

"You mean you intend to practice medicine?" he asked incredulously.

"Yes, as a surgeon."

At that, his eyes widened dramatically, and he said something in Russian that I didn't understand. "Excuse me," he said. "That was not polite."

I wanted him to repeat it so I could learn what I presumed was some new Russian profanity, but the waiters arrived with our samovar. They poured the tea into glass cups, then set out plates for us to share a platter of cheese and cured meats. I could feel the Prince watching me carefully.

I removed a tiny sugar cube from the bowl with the silver tongs and placed it on my plate. I saw his look of approval when I put it in between my teeth to strain my tea over it.

"You know how to drink Russian tea," he said with satisfaction and evident relief. "I was delighted to learn you speak Russian. Our language is not the easiest to learn. Your accent is quite good."

"Our kitchen maid taught me when I was very young," I explained, swallowing the remnants of the sugar cube. "And I had a Russian friend when I was at my English school. I speak it better than I read it."

"You make yourself understood perfectly well." He reached for the handle of the *podstakannik* more delicately than I would have expected from a man, and I perceived that my father's instincts about Gregor's proclivities had been correct. "If we were to be married," he said, offering the platter of cured meat, "you must convert to the true faith."

"You mean to orthodoxy?" I laughed. "It wouldn't matter. I'm only marginally Catholic." While I told him about my cultural Anglicanism, he listened thoughtfully. "But aren't we getting ahead of ourselves?" I asked.

"Unfortunately, we don't have much time to become acquainted. Forgive me if I'm being too forward." He rearranged the table silver in his anxiety. "I meant no offense."

"None taken."

The conversation turned to less serious matters. I told him about the many happy afternoons I'd spent in the British Museum and about the collections of the Altes Museum in Berlin.

By then, it was dinner time. We returned to his father's house for a light supper. At the other end of the table, my father and the elder prince were laughing and talking like old friends. Evidently, the afternoon's discussions had gone well. Our host informed us of a plan to visit the prince's manor on the outside of St. Petersburg.

"It is just one of many estates," he said to my father, obviously trying to impress him, "but it is less than an hour by motorcar, so we can be there and back in time for dinner with their Imperial Majesties."

We readied ourselves to head to the Mirinsky. Tickets for the summer festival had been sold out for weeks, and for good reason. The cast was superb. Father was given the honor of escorting Oblensky's widowed sister to the performance. The elder prince graciously allowed his son and me to sit in the front seats. When Gregor allowed his long, elegant fingers to rest lightly on my arm as he passed me his opera glasses, I momentarily felt like a cheap courtesan. I clenched my teeth and reminded myself that this elaborate hoax was for the noble cause of avoiding war.

The next morning, we headed to the prince's estate in a pair of large Daimlers. We were offered fine Arabians to ride. The one thing I hadn't thought to pack was a riding habit and had to borrow one from the prince's sister. Riding sidesaddle, after so many years out of practice, left me feeling precarious.

Gregor noticed my discomfort as I tried to settle in my seat. "Is your mount not to your liking?" he asked with concern.

I patted the horse's neck. "No, she's a splendid animal. It's that I'm more comfortable riding astride."

At that, he visibly shuddered. "Ladies here do not do such things!"

He rode off, leaving a chill in his wake. I almost dismounted to head back to the house, but Father gave me a stern look and said one word, "Duty." Annoyed, I followed him, still feeling uncertain of my seat on the horse.

We rode out to see how the peasants worked the land. The elder

Oblensky proudly explained that he had freed his serfs, unlike the many landowners in other parts of the country. We watched the women harvest the hay with hand sickles, binding it with a bit of straw into sheaves. I wondered why they still used such primitive methods. Our tenants had combines and tractors to bring in the hay.

Father asked if we might sit with the peasants for lunch. The elder Oblensky looked flustered. No doubt, a sumptuous lunch awaited us at the manor house, but I could see what father was trying to do.

The peasants shared their meal of coarse, black bread and cheese with us. I ate sparingly because they had obviously had little and were only sharing out of courtesy to the prince's guests.

After their simple meal, the men took out their pipes and told stories while they rested for a moment before returning to their backbreaking work. I lay on the hay, looking up at the blue sky. The peasants were speaking the simple Russian I'd learned as a child from our kitchen maid, and I liked the sound of it.

One of the men took a harmonica out of his pocket, and the women began to sing a folk song the maid had taught me, so I joined in. The others stopped singing. Wide-eyed, the men let their pipes go out. Gaping, the women stared. I couldn't tell if I'd impressed them with my voice or the fact that I spoke Russian.

Gregor reached for my hand. "I'd heard you could sing, but I had no idea. For that alone, I would marry you."

I smiled my pleasure at the compliment and glanced at my father. His subtle nod commended my performance.

After the respite with the peasants, we returned to the villa in the city. The preparations to attend dinner with the imperial family were an extended affair. I had brought along my best Paris gowns. The household maids fussed over me until I could no longer stand it and dismissed them. Father came in while I was applying my makeup.

"Hopefully, tonight, all of our efforts will come to fruition," he said, speaking to my image in the mirror.

"Do you have a plan?"

"Yes, it's quite simple. Your young admirer has been going on about your singing. I shall encourage him to suggest you sing after dinner. Do you have anything prepared?"

I had learned so many compositions under Sister Elfriede, I was always prepared for an impromptu recital. "What do you suggest?"

"Something familiar. Brahms? Schubert?"

"As you wish, Father, but this charade is wearing thin."

"Your performance is splendid. Be patient. Tomorrow, we leave, and it will be over."

I slicked on some lipstick. He remained, studying my reflection. "You look just like your mother when she was your age."

"No wonder she hates me."

"She doesn't hate you. She hates herself."

He turned and left, leaving me to wonder what he meant by that remark.

Although the gathering numbered less than a dozen, it was a grand affair, even more formal than I'd attended at the Kaiser's court.

The Czarina was German, but like all the others, she spoke French in our presence. The young grand duchesses studied me curiously. My Paris gown was *très chic*, and I wondered if they were envious. Theirs were well-made but uninspired and at least five years behind the current style. I'd heard that their parents raised them strictly in almost Spartan circumstances, apparently based on some peculiar Russian ethic.

The Czarina watched me curiously. "I hear that you studied in England…at Oxford, but now you are in Munich."

"Yes, Your Grace. I am studying medicine."

The Czarina's eyebrows rose slightly, but she was too practiced at court etiquette to look more than mildly surprised.

"I understand that some women prefer to be attended by a female physician," said the Czarina. "Do you also have male patients?"

"I do indeed."

"And you consider that proper?" she asked, arching a brow.

I could see the question put my father on edge. He subtly nodded.

"Of course, Your Grace. Aren't women usually attended by male physicians?"

The Czarina registered slight shock at this impertinence, but it was eclipsed by my suitor proudly announcing, "Lady Margarethe intends to become a surgeon!"

All conversation at the table abruptly stopped. My father seemingly forgot the other improprieties and stared at me outright. I realized this was the first he'd heard of it. My grandaunt had failed me!

The Czarina regarded each of her daughters with a little frown, as if fearing I might spread some feminist infection to them. They seemed like nothing but spoiled girls, so influencing them with anything so intellectual would likely be difficult.

After a brief pause, the conversation changed to the previous night's performance of *Onegin*.

After dinner, we headed to the music room. Grand Duchess Titiana fell into step beside me. "You speak so boldly in front of men," she said. I studied her to see if this was criticism, but her eyes were bright with admiration. "You German women are so lucky to be able to speak your minds. We'd never dare." She smiled warmly and headed toward her seat beside her mother, the Czarina.

Grand Duchess Olga took a seat at the piano. I prepared to mentally stop my ears, having been in the audience for too many bad after-dinner recitals, but she played competently. Polite applause followed.

Gregor rose and said, "I have had the honor to hear Countess Stahle sing this afternoon. She has a voice like an angel. Perhaps it would please Your Imperial Majesties to allow her to favor us with a song."

"Yes, Countess, please sing for us," said the Czarina, evidently pleased that I was not a complete barbarian.

I'd planned to sing Schuman's sweet love song, *Dein Angesicht*, because the accompaniment was simple and easy for an amateur musician to play. I certainly didn't want to risk embarrassing our host's daughter, but then the Romanov's official accompanist stepped forward and bowed. Olga surrendered the piano bench. He flipped up his tails and sat down.

I conferred with him about the program. His eyes smiled when I asked if he knew the accompaniment for the famous aria from Tchaikovsky's opera, *The Maid of Orleans*, which I'd learned as part of my *Fach* training under Sister Elfriede. Perhaps it was bold, but I sang it, as it was written, in Russian. My voice swelled to embrace the heroic declaration. Gregor closed his eyes in ecstasy, and I saw I had made a conquest.

The last notes of the accompaniment faded away. There was silence. Complete, absolute, and utter silence. I glanced anxiously at my father. Perhaps my Russian was flawed, and I had unwittingly offended the imperial family. But the Czar rose to his feet and began to clap enthusiastically. Gregor quite forgot himself and shouted, "Brava!" Everyone began clapping enthusiastically. When the applause died, Olga asked if I knew Marina's aria from *Boris Godunov*.

After I sang it, the Czar suddenly rose. "You must excuse us for a moment," he said. "Please continue the recital in my absence." He gestured to my father and they both got up to leave. This was the moment we had been scheming to create. Now, my role was to keep the others occupied.

When my father and the Czar returned to their seats, there was a smile on my father's face that indicated the mission had been accomplished.

~

The next day, after breakfast with our hosts, Gregor drove us to the train station. While my father was occupied with arranging for the transport of our luggage, my suitor and I said our good-byes. He held my hand and looked into my eyes with great ardor.

"This visit has been a delight," he said. "May I write to you?"

I didn't know what to say. Encouraging him would be cruel. "Yes, but I don't think there is much hope for our future. I can never live in Russia."

"Why not?" he asked indignantly. "Is it not as beautiful as your homeland?"

"Yes, but I am a countess in my own right. I can't abandon my holdings."

"Of course, not. Perhaps I can come to Germany."

"You're the heir. You can't leave Russia."

"That is true," he conceded. "Why didn't I think of this before?" He seized my hand. "But I have never met a woman like you. I think we make a wonderful pair. I cannot accept that this is goodbye." To my surprise, his beautiful eyes filled with tears. I knew I had to tell him the truth.

"Yes, of course, you may write to me, but there is something you must know."

"Yes?" he asked expectantly, holding my hand more tightly. I returned the pressure almost to the point of causing pain.

"We can never marry," I finally admitted.

"Why not?"

"Because I am already married."

"This cannot be true!"

"Yes, it is. I am married to Lord Compton-Wickes, son of the Marquess of Bromsley. The wedding was last month. I had just returned from my honeymoon, when my father whisked me off on this journey."

He flung away my hand and stood back. "You lied to me!"

"My father sent my photograph before I was married. However, he knew that I was engaged to be married to Lord Compton-Wickes."

"You lied to me!" he repeated angrily. I could see my father approaching. I shook my head to warn him away.

"It was a lie of omission," I said, reaching for his hand. "It was for a good cause."

Gregor snatched his hand away and turned his back on me. I realized the gesture meant more than anger. When I touched his shoulder, he was shaking. "Please try to understand. I *never* meant to hurt you."

"Then why did you do it?" he demanded, turning to face me.

"My father needed to speak to your father about the situation in Serbia."

"And I was the pretext."

"Yes."

I watched a series of emotions pass in his face while we stared at one another. Out of the corner of my eye, I noticed my father pointing to his watch. Finally, Gregor said, "I should hate you, but I don't. Let's part as friends." He stiffly stuck out his hand, and I took it.

"I'd like that. Come to Germany and meet Lytton. Like you, he adores antiquities. He has digging projects in Italy and has made some fine discoveries. You have so much in common."

The little pencil mustache went up on one side in an ironic smirk. "Perhaps someday we shall meet again."

11

On the first day of my new rotation, Lytton demonstrated his devotion by rising before dawn to see me off. Because we slept separately, I had no idea he was awake until he helped himself to breakfast from the sideboard. No one had expected him to rise so early, so only my breakfast had been prepared. After Lytton emptied all the serving dishes filling his plate, I asked the footman to bring more food from the kitchen.

"Apparently, you missed me while I was in Russia," I observed dryly as Lytton dug into his breakfast.

"Apparently, I did." Lytton tossed three cubes of sugar into his coffee. When I frowned in disapproval, he offered an excuse. "It's hard enough to be awake at this ungodly hour! I need fortification."

"Hopefully, Father will help you get a position at the museum. Coming home every day to find you lounging around while I work long hours will not do us any good. I know your aristocracy thinks it's fine to be a layabout, but we don't."

"Even at home, I'd be expected to do something useful…some foreign service role or maybe a clerk in a bank. Something I'd hate!"

"Working as a curator in the museum might be exactly the right thing for you."

"Maybe they'll send me on an excavation," he said brightening.

"I just arrived, and you want to leave already."

"No, I don't. I rather like it here." He folded the newspaper neatly so he could read the lead story. "Bloody nonsense. All this sabre rattling and war talk."

"Let's hope it's only talk."

"Well, you should know. You and your secret missions." He scowled at me.

"Unfortunately, I don't know any more than what the papers say."

"Why don't I believe you?"

Schmidt, the majordomo, stood in the doorway. "*Gnädige*, please pardon the interruption, but this arrived from the Russian Embassy by special courier." He proffered a silver tray bearing a small package.

I inspected the return address, written in Russian. "It appears to be from Prince Oblensky."

"Your new beau?" asked Lytton, wiggling his blond brows suggestively.

"Stop it. You know that's not true."

"How do I know what you got up to when you were there?"

"For God's sake, Lytton. I was being chaperoned by my Father!"

Schmidt handed me his folding knife to cut the twine around the box. I opened it to find a pile of photographs taken during my time at the Oblensky estate and some postcards of the statuary I had admired in the hermitage. Carefully wrapped in tissue paper was a pair of Russian tea glasses with beautiful silver holders. At the bottom of the box was a note that said, "Remember me when you drink your tea." I read it aloud for Lytton's benefit. I flipped through the photographs, smiling as I remembered the scenes, especially of our lunch with the peasants.

Schmidt, who had been standing by, asked, "Will that be all, *Gnädige*?"

I handed the stack of photographs to him and gestured toward Lytton. My husband carefully wiped his hands on his napkin before accepting them. He nodded approvingly as he studied the photos. "Your Gregor is rather handsome. Are you sure you want to turn him away?"

"It's a bit late for that. Besides, you're just as handsome and more to my taste."

"You like blonds with broad shoulders?"

"It's more than physical."

Lytton held a photo at arm's length. "No doubt, but I could fancy him."

"I'm sure you could. I've invited him to visit."

"Good!" declared Lytton. "I can't wait!"

After breakfast, I donned my clinician's smock for the first time since the wedding. The crispness from the starch irritated my wrists. I'd noticed that my tolerance for small annoyances had diminished since my pregnancy, which did not bode well for the months ahead.

I was never more grateful to have Christina as my study partner. At first, she was the only person at the hospital who knew I was pregnant.

She understood when the characteristic fatigue defeated me, and I fell asleep in a lecture. Sleeping in lectures was not uncommon, given our grueling schedule. But fatigue was not the only problem. Hospitals are full of unpleasant smells from human excrement and vomit. Prior to my pregnancy, I had a cast-iron stomach, but suddenly, ordinary filth, even the stench from sweaty armpits or foul breath could make me nauseous. At such times, Christina would fill in for me while I threw cold water on my face in the lavatory.

～

After Father's army friend secured a position for Lytton in the antiquities-preparation department at the museum, he rose to eat breakfast with me almost every morning, even though he could have slept an hour or two longer. As he headed off to the museum on his workdays, I envied him his long, white coat. I consoled myself with the knowledge that soon I would be entitled to wear one of my own.

Now that we were a married couple, our life became more conventional. At dinner, Lytton delighted in sharing stories from the museum laboratory. Instead of carousing in the student taverns, we invited our friends to join us for proper dinner parties, although it seemed strange to see Max in a black tie and dinner coat and Elise in an elegant gown instead of our bohemian student clothes. After dinner, we enjoyed impromptu musicales or played ridiculous games of charades. Konrad frequently brought Borchert, and the fellows, including my husband, went off to smoke cigars, which I find repellent. Although I preferred the company of the gentlemen, when cigars were involved, I took coffee with the females.

On the nights when Lytton and I were alone, we often read together in amiable silence. I treasured such moments of domestic bliss. It was on one of these perfect evenings, that Schmidt interrupted my reading to announce a telephone call from my father.

"Father, to what do I owe the pleasure?"

There was a moment of uncertain silence, and I worried that we had lost the connection. The Munich telephone lines were mostly reliable, but occasionally, a call failed. Then my father returned to the line.

"I wanted to make certain I had privacy before I spoke," he explained.

I glanced at Lytton through the open library door and wondered if I should close it, but he was happily lost in his book.

"Why? What's the matter?"

Father's loud sigh was audible through the wires. "I regret to say that our hasty mission has come to naught."

"What's happened, Father?" I asked anxiously.

"I can't say exactly, but expect some unpleasant news over the next few days. Because you played a role in this and allowed me to whisk you away from your new husband, I wanted to thank you for your efforts."

Although Father's grave tone gave me pause, I smiled. "It was an adventure, to be sure, and I met the handsome Prince Oblensky."

"You fancied him, did you?"

"Not as much as Lytton, and it would have never worked. They treat their women differently. He expected me to move to Russia."

"No, that would never do," Father agreed.

"What is this unpleasant thing that you speak of? Come now, you must tell me now that you've brought it up. You know I won't say a word to anyone."

"No, but we have no idea who might be listening in on the line. Suffice it to say that you may have to say goodbye to some of your friends soon."

That was clue enough for me to understand what he was trying to say. "Oh, dear."

"Yes, I should have known it was a runaway train that couldn't be stopped, but I had to try. God keep you, Grethe, and your little family. It may be some time before I see you again."

"My love to you, Father," I said, trying to keep the strong emotion out of my voice. "Be safe."

I hung up the handpiece, but before I returned to the library, I allowed myself a few moments to absorb the news.

"How is your father, dear?" asked Lytton as I sat in my favorite chair.

"He's well, thank you. He asked me to convey his greetings."

"Fine man, your father," opined Lytton and returned to his book.

The next day, I stood with the other medical students on the steps of the *Klinikum* and watched the columns of soldiers march by in their fierce-looking spiked helmets. Their shiny, new bayonets reflected in the afternoon sun. Their steps pounded on the cobblestones. The cheering from the crowd lining the street was nearly deafening. Small children, perched on their elders' shoulders, waved miniature red, white, and black imperial flags. Beside me, one of the students put his fingers in his mouth and emitted an ear-splitting whistle.

"What do you think?" I asked Harke, leaning nearer to be heard over the din.

He shook his head. "The newspaper says it will be a short war, that it will all be over in six weeks."

"Do you believe it?"

He turned and shrugged. "Do you?"

"Of course not."

The dean came out and called us all back to work.

～

At first, the war was tolerable, at least for those of us on the home front. My pediatric rotation was going better than I expected, despite the fact that children were something of a mystery to me. Our courses at the medical school went on as before. I listened to dry lectures on blood gases and renal calculi.

The men in our class and junior faculty began to disappear, conscripted by the army to work in field hospitals or as medics on the battlefield. They left barely enough faculty to keep the medical school functioning. With the young men at war, we women and elderly doctors called out of retirement took up the slack in the civilian hospitals. The war had instantly catapulted those of us who had once been marginal in the medical profession into a role of importance.

Peter Licht volunteered on the first day. Max was called up within a month of the declaration. Elise was beside herself with worry. The army refused Konrad, who had once declared he would never be a soldier. They identified him as a homosexual, but he was highborn, so the official diagnosis in his military records was "fallen arches," which supposedly made his feet unsuitable for marching. Borchert, on the eve of his conscription, entered the Jesuit order. To be fair, he joined out of religious conviction rather than a desire to avoid the draft.

Of course, Lytton, being an Englishman, could not join the German army. When he met people on the street, they stared at the sight of a young, able-bodied man who was not in the army. Because he shared this unique status with Konrad, they became the best of friends.

In September, we celebrated my majority with a dinner party. My grandparents came down from Raithschau. We invited Konrad, of course, and Elise. Borchert got a dispensation to leave his Jesuit house, where he was now a postulant. I could have done without him.

I asked Christina to attend, but she shook her head and said, "Your birthday is a family affair."

"I'm inviting some of my university friends."

She stared at her feet for a long moment before she admitted, "I have nothing suitable to wear."

"Is that all? I can lend you a dress."

She glanced up, measuring the difference in our height with her eyes, and laughed.

"My maid is very good with a needle."

"Thank you, Margarethe, but your shoulders are too broad. The dress would need to be taken in everywhere. Another time, perhaps."

I was disappointed, and yes, a bit hurt too.

To mark the occasion, my father sent two wooden crates containing dusty bottles of port of a very special vintage. At my birth, my father had purchased crates of it from a Portuguese wine merchant recommended by an Oxford friend. The port had been cellared at Edelheim with the idea that I could enjoy the 1896 vintage over my lifetime. My father's note indicated that it should only improve with age and cautioned me not to drink it all at once.

The dinner party and the festivities that followed went on well into the night. My grandmother gave me a disapproving look when she and my grandfather retired for the night. By the time the party ended, Borchert had taken off his clerical collar and was singing as loudly as the rest of us. I'm surprised the neighbors never called the police.

While we were celebrating, the first battle of the Marne began.

⟿

Although I'd remained slim through my early pregnancy, the waistbands of my skirts finally grew snug, so I increased my usual exercise. I had a full complement of hand weights and a motorized treadmill in the basement, but I found fencing especially good for my reflexes and agility.

When I'd moved to Munich, I'd discovered that, unlike in London, there was no place for women to fence. We were banned from the male fencing clubs. I wanted to practice, so I had included a piste in my basement gymnasium. When Grandfather heard of my plan to install a fencing room, he offered me a collection of antique fencing swords rescued from his student club before it closed. The weapons had sharp edges and points from a time when duels were real, and a *Schmiss* was a badge of honor.

Fencing is a sport for two. Occasionally, I sparred with Konrad or Lytton, when he was in the mood, but neither of them shared my devotion to the art of the blade. I posted a notice in the main hall at the university, inviting other women to join me in sparring. The response was overwhelming. Suddenly, I had the makings of an informal club. I managed to find a fencing master, who didn't mind teaching females. Some of the ladies became quite good. Our intramural matches were spirited but limited. One of the ladies wrote to invite one of the men's clubs to a competition, but we never received a response. I suspect that, after some laughter, the letter ended up in a dustbin.

Konrad moved in with us to save on lodgings. A crop failure on his coffee plantation forced Konrad's brother to reduce his stipend. He provided witty conversation at dinner and company for Lytton, so I didn't mind at first, but by November, the two of them had become quite morose. All their friends were off at war, and they were social pariahs because they weren't at the front. They hardly needed my sympathy because they excelled at feeling sorry for themselves and often commiserated with alcohol. My liquor stores began to disappear, so I had Schmidt lock up my special birthday port before they drank it all.

When Konrad and Lytton headed to the fencing room with a bottle of whiskey, I should have known to worry. The mischief began with Lytton taking a practice foil down from the rack. After a few practice lunges, he decided that his dress coat restricted his motion, so he took it off, followed by his tie, then his shirt. In his dress pants and a singlet, Lytton fought vigorously with the air like a lunatic. Konrad and I sat on the sidelines, laughing ourselves silly. I admit that I had imbibed and was not completely sober myself.

"Oh, Lytton, your lunge needs work," I said, stepping out of my shoes and rolling off my hose to join him on the *piste*. I was wearing a dinner dress, which lent more comedy to the scene. My pregnancy had made the dress snugger than it was intended to be. As I demonstrated the correct stance for a long lunge, a seam split with a loud ripping noise that sent Konrad into peals of laughter.

"How dare you insult my wife!" Lytton cried, waving the tip of his foil in Konrad's direction. Both he and my cousin were given to theatrics. Predictably, Konrad rose and stared at my husband.

"How dare you insult *me* for insulting your *wife*!" It was incredibly funny until Konrad took one of the antique sabres down from the wall. "I challenge you, sir!"

Not to be outdone, Lytton threw aside the practice foil and also took a live sabre from the wall. I watched them circle one another. Although my judgment was dulled, I was not so inebriated that I failed to recognize the potential danger.

"Stand down, gentlemen. Stand down!" I called, but they ignored me and engaged. The intensity of the match increased until I began to worry someone might be hurt. "Stop this nonsense at once!" I ordered, wading into the fray. Lytton evidently heard that I was serious. He abruptly turned, whereupon Konrad's sabre bounced off his opponent's and embedded itself just above my left breast. Everyone froze and stared at the sword sticking out of my flesh.

"Good God!" Lytton exclaimed.

"Stop! Don't pull it out," I ordered. "Lytton, is your handkerchief still clean?" I asked.

"Yes."

"Give it to me!" He stared at me. "At once!"

I wrapped the handkerchief around the blade where it exited my skin. Konrad's hand began to tremble. "Stop shaking, you bloody fool!" Unfortunately, that caused him to shake even more. "All right now, slowly, pull it out." I lightly held the blade to guide the speed of the withdrawal. Finally free to flow, the blood stained the immaculate, white cloth and my dress.

"I'll call a doctor," offered Lytton, turning to leave.

"You'll do no such thing! Do you want everyone to know what idiots we are?" I flashed the handkerchief away to evaluate the wound, which instantly filled with blood, but the quick look was enough to evaluate the situation. "Three sutures, maybe four." I clamped the cloth back down and pressed hard. "My bag's on the sideboard. Someone get it, please."

Konrad and Lytton exchanged a look of confusion, but Lytton ran to fetch my medical bag. Konrad stared at the makeshift bloody bandage I held against the wound. "Well, don't just stand there, you fool. Ask Schmidt for a basin of hot water and some towels." He turned to leave. "But don't you dare say what happened. I don't want *him* calling the doctor."

When Lytton returned, I searched in my medical bag for the supplies—an atomizer of antiseptic, a bottle of Novocaine, a syringe, light sutures, and rolled bandages in sterile paper.

"Unfortunately, I shall need you buffoons to assist me," I growled. Indeed, the two of them looked like refugees from a comedy act: Lytton was still in his dress pants, singlet and stocking feet; Konrad had lost his tie and jacket. "Keep up the pressure while I wash my hands." After washing, I disinfected my hands with phenol.

Lytton stared while I threaded the suture needle. "You don't mean to do it yourself?" he asked, aghast.

"What do you think?" I said with an impatient look, filling a syringe with novocaine. "All right, then! Lytton, you hold the mirror so I can see what I'm doing." I pointed to the silver-handled hand mirror from the vanity top. "Konrad, you will pass the instruments when I request them." Konrad looked queasy. "Get hold of yourself!" I snapped.

He nodded, but his face was as white as his dress shirt.

Fortunately, the wound was in the left breast. Although I am somewhat ambidextrous, I favor my right hand. The awkward approach required that I wield the suture needle by hand rather than with needle forceps, but that was the least of my troubles. The idea of piercing one's flesh is repellent, and obviously, I needed to see what I was doing, so I couldn't avert my eyes.

I took a deep breath and willed myself to block the pain, but despite my mental exercise, the sensation of the suture needle penetrating my skin was stunning.

Konrad fainted. His body hitting the floor made a loud thud. Lytton's mouth gaped open and he stared.

"Ignore him!" I ordered. "Hold the mirror steady!"

I gritted my teeth each time the needle entered my flesh, but I succeeded in placing four fairly neat sutures. Lytton held the wad of gauze while I taped it. By that time, Konrad had revived. He sat up looking sheepish.

"I'm so sorry," he said.

"You should be. What a bloody excuse for an assistant you are!"

I rang the maid to help me out of the bloody dress and threw them out of my room. Several days passed before I could speak to them civilly. I also arranged for all the antique swords to be raised on the wall, far out of anyone's reach. Despite all the drama, the blood, and the ruined dress, which had to be discarded, I was very proud of my *Schmiss*.

My pregnancy progressed, but the loose clinician's smock hid my condition. I continued to perform my duties at the hospital with no one being the wiser. As Christmas approached, the bulge under my breasts suddenly expanded, becoming obvious to everyone.

I was in the last week of my surgical rotation when the head of the department pulled me aside and said, "After this rotation, you must take leave. We can't have you fainting in the operating theater." Usually, such remarks were accompanied by complaints about the weakness of females or trotting out the old saw about women not being serious about medicine. According to the myth, we would eventually drop out of the profession to marry men and birth babies. Being already married and stubbornly soldiering on despite my pregnancy, I was a living contradiction of those assumptions. However, Dr. Vogel was correct. Fainting in the operating room would do no one any favors.

I had planned to do a second term in surgery to confirm that the discipline was truly my calling. Instead, I followed Elise's suggestion and enrolled in a psychiatry rotation. "At least, you'll be able to sit down if the need arises," she wisely said. "You can go back to surgery after the birth."

As my belly grew, so did my loathing for my physical state. To my complete horror, I began waddling like a goose. I couldn't see my feet. It became difficult to put on my stockings or tie my shoes.

When I tried to go up the narrow, spiral stairs and found it impossible, I pounded on the iron railing. "I hate this! I bloody hate it!"

Elise looked up from her book with a sympathetic frown. Although I'd been swearing in English, the meaning was clear. She quickly perceived the reason for my tantrum. "Tell me what you're looking for and I'll get it for you." I told her the title of the book and pointed in its general direction. She hurried up the spiral ladder to get it. I envied her quick and easy descent.

"Margarethe, I know you hate being forced to bear children," said Elise, handing me the book, "but you are making it so much harder for yourself by fighting it. It is the state of affairs now. Your anger won't change it."

I covered my face with my hands and began to weep, an unforgivable indulgence. Of course, I knew that pregnancy with its ebb and flow of hormonal tides can make almost any woman moody, but in my mind, that was no excuse.

Elise solicitously rubbed my back. "Oh, Grethe. Think of it as another fact of nature…such as being born with blue eyes and blond hair."

"It's not the same! I'm nothing but a prancing broodmare! Everything else about me is meaningless! My personality. My likes and dislikes. My intelligence. The fact that I am talented in my profession. None of it means anything! I am nothing more than a uterus!"

Elise sat down and regarded me with her dark eyes. At such moments, I always felt she was reading my mind. "There is something more to this than resentment of your duty. What is it?"

"Everything about pregnancy is repellent to me. I feel like something has taken possession of my body, causing it to swell like a balloon, feeding off me."

"That's a rather extreme view, don't you think?"

"Why? It's the truth. Pregnancy is a parasitic relationship. A creature takes up residence in another body. It feeds on its host until it grows self-sufficient enough for the host to expel it. All the poetry about welcoming a new life is pure claptrap, romanticizing a biological event."

Her eyes grew wide. "You can't be serious."

"I am."

She sat back and nodded, but she had on her analyst's face. "Most women look forward to having children."

"As you well know by now, I am not 'most women.' Oh, I know from my obstetrical rotation that most women cannot wait to become mothers. They long for it, hearing the maternal siren even from earliest girlhood, which is why they treasure their dolls. I don't mean to sound critical of them for wanting children, but I never, ever felt that longing. Can you understand?"

Elise shook her head. "No, I can't." I could see from the look in her eyes that she was genuinely worried about my mental state. "And no matter what you think, childbearing is necessary to the continuance of the race."

"I understand that, of course," I said, assuming a more rational tone. "I'm sure some may see my views as selfish. And they would be right. To be a mother, a woman must be willing to suffer pain, disfigurement, even death for the sake of the next generation. Many women are permanently damaged by giving birth and bear the scars and dysfunction even into old age."

"Is it fear of injury that makes you loathe pregnancy?" Elise asked gently.

"No. I can't explain it. I can only tell you what is natural for other women is not natural for me. I find the whole idea of it absolutely disgusting!" I screwed up my face to emphasize the point.

Elise sighed and put her arm around me. "Oh, Grethe. I'm sorry you're so miserable. I wish I could say something to help you feel better."

I was so moved by her compassion that I put my head on her shoulder and cried.

~

Not long after making a fool of myself in front of Elise, Christina stopped me after class and led me to a storeroom to speak privately. "Margarethe, you must think about who will attend you when the time comes." The reminder made me wince, but she was offering kind and wise advice. I am sometimes stubborn enough to treat myself, but in this case, even I knew I needed help.

"You can do it!"

She looked flattered. "I would be happy to help, but I'm not qualified. I haven't even done my obstetrical rotation yet. You need someone who knows what she's doing."

As a medical student, I would be expected to choose one of the attending doctors. They were all men, arrogant and condescending. Some continued to call me "countess" long after the others had stopped. I could have chosen a private physician or given birth in another hospital, but that would be almost as scandalous as rooting for the Cambridge rowing team.

Grandmother, who famously evicted my father and the doctor from the room when I was born, confirmed the wisdom of choosing a midwife. "Only a woman can truly understand how to help a woman give birth." As a physician, I regarded this as an excessively narrow point of view, but I took her point.

None of the hospital midwives could attend me for fear of offending Edelmann, the department chief, but one of them recommended a private clinic. The place had a dodgy reputation because it was rumored to advise women on family planning. Birth control of any kind was illegal in Catholic Bavaria, as in many states in the *Reich*. Condoms were only allowed for the purpose of preventing venereal disease. Of course, if they were employed for other purposes, who would know? But that was never discussed. The clinic in question flouted the law and discreetly dispensed pessaries in addition to condoms. I admired anyone brave enough to defy the prohibition, which made me all the more determined to find my midwife among the clinic staff.

I put off making an appointment because it emphasized the fact of my pregnancy, which I was desperately trying to ignore. Finally, I stifled my reluctance and arranged to meet with one of the senior nurses.

Nurse Alder was an attractive woman, in her late twenties with dark blond hair and calm, gray eyes. Her full lips when she smiled instantly drew my gaze. They were sensual and beautifully formed. I allowed my gaze to linger on them.

"*Frau Doktor*, thank you for choosing me!" she said, taking my hand. "I am so honored."

"I'm not yet a doctor," I scoffed.

Nurse Alder was unruffled by my harsh tone and replied mildly, "But you will be in a matter of course, won't you?" She opened a folder and took as careful a history as any physician would. "Let's have a look."

Despite my profession, I loathe pelvic examinations as much as any woman, but Nurse Alder's hands, although purposeful, were extraordinarily gentle. Some practitioners ram their fingers into the vagina and rout around like a burrowing animal. Nurse Alder explored the interior of my body with a delicate touch. She warmed the metal speculum in her hand before inserting it. She palpated my convex abdomen with care and listened to the fetal heartbeat, all the while maintaining a completely neutral but pleasant expression.

"Mother and child are completely healthy," she pronounced. She gave my arm a reassuring pat. "You may dress now, *Frau Doktor*."

Once again, I protested that I was not yet a doctor. She smiled indulgently. "But you are well on your way, and I am truly honored that you've chosen me to attend you." Only a woman who valued the achievements of women would say such a thing, which favorably impressed me.

I have always felt completely comfortable being nude in front of others, but in Nurse Alder's presence, I felt unaccountably shy. I couldn't wait to dress myself and regain the upper hand in the situation. By the time I returned to her tiny office, she had written out a schedule of visits. She explained that I would not be required to come to the clinic for future examinations. Instead, she would come to me.

"But I don't mind coming to your clinic."

"This is a rough part of town," she said, "best I see you in your home to avoid exposing you to danger."

The blatant illogic of this statement made no sense. She herself daily exposed herself to this danger, whereas I knew how to defend myself from my training with the cadets. I carried a revolver wherever I went. Of course, she had no way of knowing this, and I wondered if the real reason was fear for my reputation. That led me to wonder if in addition to advice on birth control, they performed abortions in her clinic. Because her intentions seemed kind, I agreed that future visits would take place in my home.

That night, Lytton decided to visit my bedchamber. He wanted nothing more than to inquire how I was faring and how the appointment had gone. He patted my swelling belly and lay his ear against it. "How goes it in there, sailor?"

I nudged him away. "You are such a bloody fool sometimes."

"I am not!" he protested righteously. "I merely want to visit my son."

"You're so sure it will be a boy?"

"Of course!"

"Oh, I dearly hope not, for then we will have to reprise this folly."

He shrugged. "I'm finally getting the hang of it, and you want to stop?"

"Easy for you to say. Plant your seed and run."

He patted my belly again. "That's because I know you have everything under control."

I was feeling particularly surly that night and in no mood for his witty remarks. "Get out of here, you big lout."

He leaned up on his elbow. "Oh, I thought I'd stay the night. Sometimes, it feels good to sleep with you. You keep me warm."

"You're supposed to be keeping me warm."

"Oh, don't be so conventional."

He got into bed beside me and curled his body around me. Although I felt him grow erect against my thigh, he made no move to press further. A short while later, I heard him snoring softly.

⌇

The next week, Nurse Alder arrived early for our appointment. My majordomo brought her into the library, where I was working on my dissertation. "Please have a seat. I shall be with you directly," I said, not looking up.

My visitor took off her bonnet and gazed around the room. "What an amazing library," she said. "How many volumes do you house here?"

I looked up and considered her question. "A thousand perhaps? I have no idea."

"May I look around?"

"Suit yourself."

She spent a few minutes browsing the volumes on the ground level.

"This is quite a collection, *Frau Doktor*," she said, turning to me. "Not only medical books."

"Of course not. At some point, there's not much to say about medicine, although there is certainly much to say about everything else." I finally remembered my manners and gave her my attention. "Sit down, please, Nurse Alder, I'll be with you as soon as I finish this paragraph."

She pulled out a chair and sat across from me. I pushed the books and stack of foolscap out of her way.

"Is that your doctor's paper?"

I was surprised at the acuity of her observations. "It is."

"May I ask the subject?"

I raised my head and studied her for signs of impertinence, but I perceived that she was merely curious. "You really wish to know?"

"Yes, please," she said in an enthusiastic voice.

I capped my fountain pen and set it aside. "It's a bit arcane, I will admit. I started out to write a treatise on wound care. Then I realized that the topic was too broad, so I focused on the many conditions under which wounds fail to heal normally. I think the most original aspect is the section on amputation stumps."

She blinked. After a moment, she said, "With the war going on, that is certainly an apt topic."

"Indeed, it is," I said, smiling with satisfaction that she'd had recognized its value. "You are a most remarkable person, Nurse Alder."

"Thank you, *Frau Doktor*." Her little smile let on that she was teasing me. My eyes were again drawn to her sensual lips, but remembering that our relationship was professional, I quickly averted my gaze. When I looked up, I saw my admiration had not gone unnoticed. There was a flicker of interest in her gray eyes.

"I suppose we should get on with it," I said, capping my pen. "You need to get back to work, and so do I."

I led her to my bedchamber. She gazed up at the randy murals on the ceiling. "The paintings in this house are stunning."

"Are you an appreciator of rococo art?" I asked casually.

She gave me a quick, shy look. "Only that I know good work when I see it."

"Most of the paintings in the house are the work of Matthäus Günther. Do you like them?"

She glanced at the ceiling again. "They are beautiful."

"Rather suggestive, I would say, but fine indeed." I smiled. "To what extent would you like me to disrobe," I asked, assuming a clinical tone.

"Everything below the waist, please."

"Will my bed suffice as an examination table?"

She nodded.

I undressed as she requested and lay there, gritting my teeth, as I always do during a pelvic examination. She was quick this time, but equally gentle. "All is well," she said with a smile. Again, my eyes fell on her lips, but I didn't look away quickly enough this time. She blushed a little. I found it charming.

She turned her back while I dressed. "Will you stay for a coffee?" I asked.

She checked the watch hanging from her blouse. "I have a few minutes, so yes, thank you."

I asked my majordomo to serve the coffee and cakes in my sitting room. The cakes were lovely fruit tarts made with raspberry jam and lemon curd. Fortunately, the privations of war and the rationing had not yet affected us because we could source treats like jam, fresh vegetables, and meat from the farm at Raithschau.

We sat in the drawing room, two proper ladies enjoying afternoon coffee and cake, except our conversation was not about the latest fashion nor the season's repertoire at the Staatstheater. We spoke of bacterial sepsis. I was delighted to have the company of another medical woman. Over an hour passed without either of us noticing.

Finally, Nurse Alder looked at the watch pinned to her blouse, drawing my eyes to her handsome bosom. "I fear I must leave, *Frau Doktor*," she said. I opened my mouth to protest, but she raised her finger to her lips. "Yes, I know…technically you aren't a doctor yet, but you will be soon. Meanwhile, it's good to accustom your ear to it." She tapped her earlobe. "When the time comes, it will sound more natural."

What an intriguing observation, I thought. She smiled. Again, my gaze lingered on those beautiful lips.

"I must go," she said, rising.

At the door, she gave me her hand. "Until next week," she said.

"I can hardly wait!" I blurted out.

She looked surprised, but her beautiful lips curved into a smile. "It will come soon enough," she said, patting my arm.

12

That night, I lay in bed revisiting my folly. I couldn't believe I had blurted out my interest so obviously. The scene replayed again and again, and each time, I died a little death from embarrassment. Although I was exhausted, sleep simply wouldn't come. I finally rose and took a valerian capsule. It made me drowsy, but I continued to lie awake, listening to the sounds of the house while everyone else slept.

It was one of those nights when Lytton was "out." I wasn't interested or, in my state, able to attend to his needs, so we had agreed that he should find solace elsewhere. I opened an unlimited account for him at the Hotel Vier Jahreszeiten. He agreed to use condoms during his assignations. Having seen the ravages of venereal disease firsthand, I was adamant about this point. Of course, I had no way of knowing what he did out of my sight, but I knew him to be an honorable man, so I trusted him. He was scrupulously discreet about his trysts and always arrived home by breakfast.

I hadn't even considered exercising my prerogative to indulge my own appetites, probably because I was so occupied with my studies. Nurse Alder was the first person in months to have caught my fancy. I gave myself lectures on why nothing could come of it. She was my midwife, and I was her patient. Besides, who would find me attractive in such a loathsome state, a waddling goose with an enormous belly?

Despite my firm resolution to the contrary, I counted the days until Nurse Alder returned. I gazed at the diary entry noting the appointment as if it were a beloved proverb, or a scripture verse worthy of reflection.

On the appointed afternoon, I was beside myself with anticipation. Although it was my free day, when I usually dressed more casually, I put on one of my best suits. I occupied myself with vocal practice to avoid pacing while I waited.

I was quite taken up in a Brahm's song when Schmidt appeared at the door. He usually didn't interrupt me during music practice, knowing that I didn't take kindly to it. He waited politely until I finished the passage before speaking. "Nurse Alder is here," he announced with a little bow.

I glanced at the standing clock on the other side of the room. She was early by nearly half an hour. I closed the keyboard cover with shaking fingers and smoothed down my skirt.

"Show her in, Schmidt."

Nurse Alder cautiously entered the room. "I've interrupted your practice. I'm sorry."

I extended my hand to her. "No matter. I was only passing time until you arrived."

"I heard you in the hall while I was waiting. Your voice is so beautiful I nearly wept."

Knowing my singing had moved her made my heart hammer in my chest, but I affected modesty. "Thank you, but I don't practice enough. My schedule is so burdened."

"Then please don't let me keep you from it," she said. She smiled and my eyes went to her beautiful mouth.

Somehow, I managed to shake myself out of staring at it and said, "I don't want to take up your time unnecessarily."

This time her eyes smiled instead of her mouth. "It doesn't matter. I'm very early for our appointment. Please continue your practice."

I gestured to a chair near the piano.

"You really don't mind that I listen?" she asked, taking a seat.

"Not at all, but I don't want to presume on your time."

"It's my free day," she explained. "I can spend my time as I wish."

I was intrigued. We had both arranged our appointment on our free days, which made sense from a practical point of view. My duty at the hospital often ran long, which risked the possibility of a last-minute cancellation. Nurse Alder's clinic was a good distance from my villa and required a twenty-minute trolley ride. But her smile told me that practicality was not her only motive. She wanted to be in my music room as much as I wanted her to be there.

She removed the pins from her hat and set it aside. With an expectant smile, she folded her hands in her lap to demonstrate her enthusiasm for more music. I sang another Brahm's song. At the end, she clapped. "You should sing professionally."

I shook my head. "My voice teacher, a former opera singer, thought so too, but a woman of my class can never sing on the stage. It's unthinkable."

"Why?" she asked. "You are training to be a surgeon. Isn't that also unthinkable?" The remark sounded impertinent, but I realized that Nurse Alder was merely stating a fact.

"A female surgeon isn't considered as shady as a lady of the stage. Most people think singers and actresses are practically prostitutes!" I smiled to convey that I didn't share this opinion.

Nurse Adler didn't return the smile. "Unfortunately, women sometimes need to give their favors to achieve their goals."

I wondered if she spoke from personal experience. Then I remembered that her practice gave her a view into an unsavory world.

"Please sing one more song," she said, leaning forward in her seat. "I think we have time for that."

I glanced at the clock and saw that she was right. This time I dared to sing something a bit more passionate. One of Richard Strauss's early songs.

When I finished singing, she sighed. "Such a shame you can't share your musical talents with the world."

"Then I would have to choose between music and medicine. One cannot do everything in this life."

"True," she said with a sigh. She reached for her hat. "Shall we get on with it?"

In my bedchamber, I disrobed as before and she examined me with the same gentleness. She turned her back while I dressed. Evidently, she'd perceived my discomfort. I appreciated her sensitivity.

"Can I interest you in a glass of sherry, Nurse Alder?" I asked, buttoning the side of my skirt.

"No alcohol, thank you. I'm always on call for my patients."

"Coffee, then?"

"Perfect."

We headed to the drawing room for coffee. "You mentioned being on call. Does that mean you attend the births of all your patients?"

"If I can. Sometimes, one of the other midwives covers for me.

Obviously, I cannot be in two places at once. Or, if I am in a different part of town, it may be difficult to get to that patient."

"Like me, you even work on your free days."

"It's the lot of a medical professional, I'm afraid. No rest for the weary." Schmidt handed her a cup of coffee, and she thanked him. "How is your doctor's paper coming along?"

"Well enough. I work on it when I have time or a new idea. Not enough."

"Like your music practice."

I nodded in agreement. "As I said, one cannot do everything, although I certainly try."

"If I can be of help to you, let me know. I'm not a physician, but I have years of experience in women's illnesses and childbirth."

"More than the senior doctors at the *Klinikum*, I'd wager."

"I didn't mean to suggest that." When she blushed, the little display of modesty charmed me. She suddenly brightened. "Maybe I could help you study for your examinations."

"I have a study partner. Quite a good one."

"Of course, you do," she said with faint disappointment.

"But I'd welcome your help to prepare for examinations. They always ask questions about exotic situations. I'm sure you've seen your fair share of them."

She laughed a soft, musical laugh. "You cannot imagine!"

In the next hour, she regaled me with stories of absurd obstetrical situations. Finally, the standing clock in the hall chimed the hour. "I really should go," she said. When our eyes met again, our mutual disappointment was abundantly clear.

Thereafter, Nurse Alder nearly always arrived early for our appointments. She would sit quietly and listen to me practice the piano or sing. Her examinations were as careful as before, but now, she described her observations in detail. "I'm sure you know all this in theory, but I am trying to reinforce the lesson."

"Thank you," I said, "there is nothing like experience to reinforce a lesson."

If our visits ran late, I often sent her home with my chauffeur, but one afternoon, I had time on my hands and decided to drive her myself.

She directed me to an old building near her clinic. The surrounding neighborhood was dingy and in disrepair. She explained that most of the inhabitants worked in the machine-parts factory nearby.

As usual, neither of us wanted to end our time together. We sat in the front seat of my motorcar as I inspected the miserable building where she lived.

"Is there running water in this place?"

She laughed. "Of course. Even hot water in the bathroom, but it costs two *Pfennig* for the heater."

"And a toilet?"

"Down the hall. We share it."

I shook my head.

"It's not as bad as it looks. I enjoy the company of the other tenants, mostly women. And the rent is cheap. It leaves me some money for other things, like concerts and the opera." She patted my arm. "Now I'm sorry I let you drive me home. Don't worry, *Frau Doktor*. It's a place to lay my head and good enough for that."

∾

When my psychiatry rotation ended in February, Nurse Alder recommended I take a hiatus from clinical work. "You're perfectly healthy," she assured me, "but I'm sure you must be uncomfortable."

I admitted that my feet ached if I had to stand on them for long periods. Sometimes, the pelvic pressure made me fear an early birth despite knowing it was a common symptom of late pregnancy. Worst of all, I had become a bear, growling at everyone, including my patients. At home, my household staff scurried away when they saw me approach. The maids ducked into empty rooms. Lytton suddenly found the need to spend long hours in research at the museum. Christina contrived excuses to avoid our study dates. Only Nurse Alder tolerated my irritability.

"You must hate me," I said glumly after she examined me.

She laughed. "It's so common for pregnant women to become unpleasant at the end. I'm used to it."

"Thank you for your patience," I replied, struggling to get up. She reached out to help me, but I shrugged her off. "I can do it!" I snarled.

"As you wish," she said, stepping aside.

"Forgive me. How can you be so kind when I am so intolerable?"

"Because I know it isn't your usual personality." She reached out and brushed the hair away from my eyes. "I know this is impertinent, but will you call me by my given name?"

It was more than impertinent. Between a medical professional and her patient, it was highly irregular.

She saw my disapproving expression and quickly glanced away. "I'm sorry. I only thought that since we've spent so much time together, you wouldn't mind."

"Of course, I don't mind." She didn't look convinced. I patted her arm to reassure her.

"I'm Johanna, but everyone calls me Hanna."

"I'm Margarethe. My family used to call me, Grethe, but not any more."

"May I?" she asked, searching my face. I began to feel faint as I returned her gaze. I told myself the dizziness was some new pregnancy antic, although I knew it wasn't.

"Yes, I would like that," I finally said.

"Good!" Her enthusiastic response broke the spell, and I woke from my reverie of admiration.

Using our given names seemed to open a door. Before, our conversation had focused on medicine or music, but now, it turned to personal matters. Hanna told me that she'd been orphaned in adolescence when her parents had died in a diphtheria outbreak. "My grandmother raised me. She was a strict Lutheran. I couldn't wait to get away to nursing school."

"Is she still living?"

Hanna shook her head. "No, I have no family now."

"I'm sorry," I said to be polite.

She shrugged. "It's how it is." Despite the stoic words, I could see a sad, faraway look in her eyes.

I told her about my schooling in England and my grandaunt, but I held back telling her about Edelheim or Raithschau, sensing that knowing so much about my aristocratic background might frighten her away, especially after hearing her disparaging remarks about "rich capitalists." I knew she was an ardent socialist, so I always tried to steer the conversation away from politics, partly because it didn't interest me, but also because I knew little about it.

~

As the birth approached, my misery increased, and Hanna visited more often to massage my back and legs. To distract me, she let me talk for hours about everything from stoic philosophy to the geology of Prussia. She probably had little or no interest in these subjects, but she knew that keeping me occupied and distracted was the best medicine of all.

Towards the end of my pregnancy, she came so often that it sometimes seemed as if she lived with us, which gave me an idea. Konrad had moved out as soon as improvements on Thomas' plantation enabled him to restore his brother's stipend. Konrad often complained that living with us had put a damper on his personal life. Finally, I gave him money for an estate agent, and he found a flat.

"Would you consider living here?" I asked Hanna when she appeared for her next visit.

Her eyes flew open. "You can't be serious."

"I am, I assure you. It has to be better than living in that awful boarding house of yours. Plus, you'll get good meals, and I won't charge you rent."

"What if you have guests?"

"With the war on, there are no guests coming, and we have plenty of guest rooms.

"Grethe, your offer is both kind and generous, but what will your husband say?"

I shrugged. "Who cares? It's my house."

Hanna's puzzled expression indicated my response had baffled her, but I decided that a full explanation, namely a selfish desire to have more of her company, was unnecessary. Instead, I said, "Lord Compton-Wickes will welcome the fact that I have other companionship, especially now that I have become an ogre."

She smiled, but I doubt she was taken in by my explanation.

Hanna gave the landlady at her boarding house notice and moved her belongings into the room Konrad had vacated. It was the largest of the guest rooms and had a pleasant view of the garden. While she was unpacking her things, I came in to see how she was getting settled and caught her gazing out the window.

"Will you be comfortable here?" I asked hopefully.

Her response was to stand on her toes and kiss me on the cheek. "Will I be comfortable here? I have never lived in such a beautiful place. Thank you so much!"

My hateful belly kept us apart. I would have so much liked to embrace her, even more, to return her kiss, but I couldn't.

Lytton only expressed how relieved he was that someone could soothe the savage beast. Wearing his male blinders, he saw Hanna merely as another servant. He never questioned why she was moving into the family section of the house rather than the servants' quarters. He adjusted without complaint to sharing our dining table with our permanent house guest. He was surprised, however, when I continued to interview applicants for the child's nurse because he assumed that Hanna would assume that role.

"She's a credentialed midwife. Of course, she will continue her profession," I explained indignantly. "As a professional woman myself, I have no wish to deprive her of her career or her income".

Lytton merely shrugged. "It's your household," he said indifferently. "Carry on."

I gave him a sharp look because I certainly didn't need his permission to do so.

⁓

Finally, the day of reckoning arrived. The labor pains woke me from a sound sleep around four in the morning. Lytton was "out," and, in a way, I was grateful that he wasn't hovering about anxiously. I timed the contractions and waited a while before I rang Hanna's room. She came at once, still wearing her nightdress. As a medical student, I knew better than most women that the early signs of labor were no real emergency, but even so, I was frightened. Hanna soothed me by stroking my hair and kissing me on the forehead. "Don't worry, Grethe. It's going perfectly. I'll be right back."

She left to dress, and I rose to relieve myself. By the time I returned to my bedchamber, Hanna was there, all efficiency itself. She was wearing a dress with sleeves that could be unbuttoned and rolled up almost to the shoulders. She wore a pristine, white apron with her watch pinned to it, ready to time the contractions.

After she counted the interval, she sighed. "We have quite a wait ahead of us. Would you like some tea? I recommend it over coffee."

"Tea would be nice," I agreed.

Rather than wake the servants, she went down to the kitchen to prepare it herself.

We chatted about inconsequential matters for a few hours as the labor pains grew stronger. Then the dreaded "back labor" began. I had read about it and heard women describe this awful pain while I was on my obstetrical rotation, but nothing that I had read nor heard could have prepared me. During the contraction, I felt like I was giving birth through my spine. Hanna massaged my back and applied warm compresses, which helped a little.

Fortunately, I was not one of those prima paras who take days to deliver their first child. My body worked efficiently toward its goal. Finally, my body began to push out the unwelcome guest. Although the fetus was unusually large, it required only a few forceful efforts to expel it.

Panting, I sighed with relief as the newest member of our family gave an ear-piercing scream. I was vaguely aware that Hanna was clamping and cutting the cord. Then she lay my child glistening with amniotic fluids on my belly. She took a moment to wipe the meconium from the face and nose and held the infant up for my inspection. When I saw the tiny, perfectly formed penis and proud, little scrotum between its legs, I began to weep.

"Yes, Grethe, you have a beautiful boy," agreed Hanna with a smile. She had completely mistaken the reason for my tears. "Congratulations!" she added brightly. "He's perfect!"

My weeping only increased. Hanna looked at me in consternation. She tried to place the infant in my arms, but I shook my head and turned away. Her eyes clouded with sadness, although I doubt I was the first woman she'd encountered to look upon the child she'd borne with unhappiness. I rolled away to avoid the sight.

She gave the infant to his nurse to bathe while she dealt with me. Sitting behind me on the bed, she stroked my back. "It's all right, Grethe," she said in a soothing voice, "it's been an ordeal for you. You're tired."

"You don't understand! It's male!"

"Yes, a beautiful and healthy boy."

"I must have a female heir for Raithschau. That means I must reprise this misery!"

"I don't understand."

"The title to Raithschau can only pass through the female line. I could take my chances like my grandmother and hope for a female heir in the next generation, but she made me swear an oath not to cause my family such anxiety."

I cursed my fate with a string of filthy invectives I'd learned in the operating theater. I couldn't see Hanna's face, but I'm sure she was shocked. They were pretty foul.

"Calm yourself, Grethe. Relax or you'll just make it harder for yourself.

While we awaited the placental birth, Hanna brought a basin of warm water and washed my face. "Sh," she soothed when I tried to speak. "Let's talk about it tomorrow."

Once Hanna had determined the placenta was intact, she took it away. She returned with the infant swaddled in a blanket and placed him in my arms. At least, I had the maternal instinct to cradle the tiny thing and gaze into its face. I must admit the sight moved me…a bit.

"Take him away. I don't have the patience for this now," I said, handing him back.

When Hanna returned, she found me in a cloud of despair. She sighed. "Oh, Grethe, let me help you wash. Everything will look better after some rest."

She bathed me with warm water, arranged a pad between my legs to absorb the bloody discharge and helped me into a clean nightdress. After she changed all the fouled linens, she lay down beside me. Eventually, I fell asleep with her arm around my waist.

⌇

We named the boy Wilhelm after my mother's father and the Kaiser. Hanna and my son's nurse tried to interest me in the child, but when I held him, he screamed as if I were trying to kill him. Usually, a child will quiet when placed in his mother's arms, but Willi, as he became known in the family, only wailed louder until I thought I would go mad. Amazingly, Lytton could always soothe him. When I placed the howling infant on his chest, he flopped about like a baby seal on a giant ice floe, but the screeching would stop. Lytton cooed to him or sang in his elegant baritone. Eventually, Willi fell asleep.

"See? He's a smart one," said Lytton cradling the peaceful child against his bare chest. "He knows who his Papa is. Don't you, my handsome lad?"

"Ugh! You can have him."

"Meg, why don't you like him? Because he looks like me?"

"No, because he looks like me!"

I outright refused to feed the little beast from the breast, although Hanna tried to encourage it, saying it would help my uterus return to normal size more quickly.

"Breast fed babies are healthier," she added. "They resist diseases and grow faster."

"Don't you think I know all that!" I snapped. "I'm not interested. Can you understand?"

She looked at me with a perplexed expression but didn't argue.

The milk continued to leak, spoiling some of my best clothes, and my breasts ached. Hanna was opposed to binding, although it was a common practice at the time. In fact, it leads to engorgement and sometimes mastitis. Instead, she brewed sage tea and offered cool compresses. She suggested cabbage leaves, but I drew the line at that. Eventually, the milk stopped and the pain, and my breasts returned to normal.

Hanna encouraged me to hold the child while he drank from the bottle. For the span of the feeding, he would lie contentedly in my arms and suck placidly. Eventually, he became accustomed to me and became a relatively calm and cooperative infant. Hanna smiled and nodded as if to say, "I told you so."

I couldn't wait to get back to work, but Hanna cautioned against racing headlong into a surgical rotation. Although she seldom argued with me directly, using gentle persuasion instead, she was adamant on this point. Even I knew that standing on my feet for hours would be difficult so soon after giving birth, so I enrolled in a pathology clerkship instead. It was no hardship. I'd been fascinated by the unseen world since I'd received my first microscope from my grandaunt. The preparation of slides, making thin sections and applying stains was quiet, exacting work, which appealed to me, especially with all the howling at home. The autopsies fascinated me and provided me with a harmless way to practice my surgical techniques.

You needn't be so tidy about sewing up the body cavity," said the head pathologist, raising a brow. "Big stitches will pull him back together just as well as fine ones, and it's much faster."

"I'm practicing," I explained.

"Of course, you are. All the best ones go into surgery if they can. It's so heroic! But here, we don't have time for finesse. Use big stitches and get it done!"

"Yes, *Herr Doktor*."

I enjoyed my time among the dead, and when it came to an end, Hanna gave her blessing for me to return to surgery.

The surgical department was overwhelmed by all the war wounded sent to our hospital. Many doctors had been called to the front, which left us shorthanded. My first solo surgery came even before I achieved my degree. The long hours of bending over the operating table took its toll. If Hanna caught me twisting and flexing my neck to ease the pain, she insisted on giving me a massage. Sometimes, the promise of her gentle hands working out the knots was enough to get me through a long procedure.

∼

In July 1915, I received my diploma in medicine. The following week, I sat for the panel examinations. I was finally an *Ärztin,* licensed to practice medicine. Hanna insisted that we mark the occasion with some festivity and planned a dinner party with my study group. Two of the women, anticipating the end of term, had married, so we invited their husbands. Otherwise, Lytton and Konrad would have been the only males in attendance. Even Peter Harke had been conscripted.

My grandaunt acknowledged the milestone by sending me a rare, medieval copy of Galen's works. Lotte helped Grandmother select a fine gladstone in which to carry my instruments and sent a new otoscope to carry in it. Father had a case of French claret shipped from his wine merchant. My mother never mentioned the occasion, which I could have predicted. Even so, I was disappointed.

With that hurdle behind me, I wanted to get on with making my next and hopefully, final, heir. Not that I wanted to be pregnant again. Nothing could be further from the truth. I simply wanted the messy business behind me. I discussed the idea with my husband, and he was agreeable, but Hanna was beside herself when she heard about it.

"Grethe, it's too soon," she said, her eyes wide with worry. "You should wait at least a year to be pregnant again."

"I want it over and done, so I can get on with my life." I folded my arms on my chest to demonstrate that I would not be dissuaded.

"But you could damage your body. You might not be able to have more children afterwards."

"I don't want more children!" I snarled. "That's the point!"

Lytton and I made plans to head to the chalet. Hanna continued to plead with me to wait, but her arguments fell on deaf ears. Finally, I told her bluntly that it was a matter between husband and wife. Instantly, the subject disappeared from our conversations. She continued to give me worried looks, speaking with her eyes everything she no longer said aloud.

Before we departed for the mountains, I drew Lytton's blood to examine it for signs of venereal disease. He protested as he rolled up his sleeve, "This is really unnecessary. I swear to you I've worn my third sock every time!"

"Then you certainly won't mind my examining your blood."

"It does worry me that you don't trust me."

"I do trust you. But this has to do with the health of our future offspring." I recounted the horrors of blindness and idiocy in children born of mothers infected with syphilis or gonorrhea as I prepared the slides. When I looked up from the eyepiece of the microscope, I noted that Lytton looked slightly nauseous.

"That's quite enough," he said, "I take your point."

Before we left, Hanna offered one last warning. We were standing in the atrium while Schmidt and the footman loaded our considerable luggage into the boot of Lytton's little motorcar.

"Grethe, you know as well as I do how to prevent a pregnancy."

I drew back to look at her face, realizing that she thought Lytton shared my bed on a regular basis. Although we occasionally slept together for warmth and affection, or pleasured one another, intercourse was rare. I was tempted to explain the situation but then decided it was none of Hanna's affair.

"My opinion hasn't changed," she continued, "I still think it's too soon for you to be pregnant again, but if that is your choice, I shall support you, whatever you decide."

I was so moved by her generosity that I gave her a quick kiss on the mouth. She touched her lips and gazed at me uncertainly. I worried that I had offended her by my boldness, but then she smiled and gave me a quick kiss in return. She waved from the doorway as we drove off in our motorcar.

The rolling hills south of Munich recalled our previous trip to the mountains. Evidently, Lytton was similarly affected by the natural beauty of our surroundings. "We should do this every year," he said. "The chalet is so large. We could invite our friends."

"Our friends? Almost everyone is away at the front."

"I meant after the war."

"And when will that be?" I wondered aloud.

"It can't come soon enough," said Lytton in a sad voice.

The sentiment muted both of us, but finally, the sight of the Alps in the distance cheered us. Lytton suddenly broke into song, and I joined in.

Frau Weiss prepared omelettes for us when we arrived, and the taste of her simple food recalled our honeymoon. So far, the happy memories were serving as intended. Both Lytton and I easily fell into a happy, intimate mood. That night, we began our enterprise of making another heir.

Elise liked to say that sex is not essential to a married couple, but it is a glue that can hold it together. I remembered her words as I watched my husband walk naked around our bedchamber. He was as perfect as the ancient statuary he loved so much, and he knew it. Would that his beauty could stir my desire.

~

"Let's go into Garmisch and see your carver today," suggested Lytton the next morning as he prepared his coffee.

I'd almost forgotten about the carving, although, from time to time, I received reports about the current state of the work along with a request for another payment. As curious as I might be about the carver's progress, I was in the mood for exercise, especially after the long drive on the previous day. "I thought we could hike up the mountain."

"That can wait until tomorrow."

Usually, Lytton deferred to my wishes, but he seemed quite determined about this. "All right," I agreed, "Let's drive into town."

The little motorcar I'd given Lytton was agile and powerful enough to navigate the mountainous roads with ease. Lytton sometimes drove too fast. That I should even note this is remarkable because I love speed. However, after a heart-stopping turn in which he narrowly avoided colliding with the rock face, I temporarily banned him from driving. He sulked, but I ignored him.

The carver seemed happier to see my husband than me, his patron, which I found curious. But when I saw the statue, now in its final stages, I forgot my momentary jealousy. The wood had come alive under the carver's skilled knife. The muscles and sinews appeared to move like real flesh; the breasts looked as soft as those of a living woman. Every detail had been rendered meticulously.

"Have you ever studied anatomy?" I asked the carver.

He shook his head. "Only in books," he replied, "but I look very carefully. I study from real life the way a hand moves..." he demonstrated by bending his wrist and flexing his fingers, "...or how the muscles rise under strain. To be a sculptor, one must always be watching."

The attitude in which he had posed the life-sized statue of a young woman was striking. The expression on her face was profoundly tender. Her arms were outstretched as if to welcome a child into them.

"Who was the model for this carving?" I asked.

"My daughter," said the carver, scratching his gray beard, "she often sits for me."

"Is she a mother?"

"Yes. How did you know?"

"You have captured the maternal attitude perfectly," I said, stepping closer to inspect the other details. He had, as instructed, avoided the traditional trappings of a Madonna. There was no chaste veil covering the statue's head. Her unbound tresses fell over the shoulders. The first wash of color indicated that the hair would be red. It fascinated me that he had chosen that color because it wasn't in my specifications. At the back of the statue's head was a crescent moon. She stood on what was meant to be the firmament of the heavens, suggested by a sprinkling of stars. In every detail he had captured the goddess of Apuleius' petition in *The Golden Ass.*

"Thank you for being so faithful to my original vision," I said, "but how could you remember all the details?"

He glanced at Lytton. "Your husband sent me the book in which they are described. Not long after you commissioned the work."

"So, you know she is not actually the Christian Madonna, but a pagan goddess? Does it trouble you?"

He shrugged. "No, I receive profane commissions as well."

I chuckled at the use of the word "profane." "But you rendered it faithfully and didn't try to bend the work to fit your beliefs. Thank you."

"It does worry me that this will stand in a convent," the carver admitted.

"Never mind, the recipient of this gift will understand its meaning, and her sisters will see what they want to see, namely the Mother of God. Meanwhile, you have depicted the mother of all gods, all living things, and all creation."

He frowned as he considered my words. I turned to Lytton with a smile. "Thank you, darling, for your assistance."

Lytton reached for my hand and gave it a little squeeze.

I wrote a bank draft for the larger portion of the carver's commission and promised him more when the work was safely delivered to Obberoth.

Lytton took my arm as we left the carver's shop. "You're not angry that I wrote to him behind your back?"

"Angry? No. Not at all. I'm touched that you took an interest."

"I know it means a great deal to you and I wanted it to be perfect." He leaned closer to say, "I love you."

I stopped and looked into his blue eyes. "I know. I love you too."

The warm feeling evoked by our visit to the carver brought us back to bed on our return. We spent the rest of the afternoon making love. I whispered into Lytton's ear, "It may be an old wives' tale, but it is said that a climax while the man is deep in the vagina makes female children more likely."

"Meg, I'm enjoying myself. Why do you have to spoil it with your medical talk?"

I stroked his blond curls. "I'm sorry."

He made no reply but drove deeper into me. I suspect that was the day my second child was made.

We alternated challenging climbs with sojourns in bed. Frau Weiss cooked us traditional Bavarian meals, and we were more than content with simple food. That was, after all, why we had come to the mountains: for the peace and simplicity that would put us in the right mood for reproduction.

~

The male half of our caretaker-couple had been called up to serve in the army. The chalet and grounds had fallen into disrepair in his absence. A few roof tiles had blown off in a winter storm. My husband climbed up the ladder to replace them. I never knew he had such practical skills, but I was grateful. I watched him wield a mortar trowel for the better part of the afternoon. He accepted my kisses when he finished the task, and we went back to bed.

"I might begin fancying women after all," he observed, rolling off me.

"You only need to fancy this woman. Don't get any ideas!"

"Don't worry, Meg. I was joking."

The ease of our time together made the stress of my examinations and the last months of study melt away like the Alpine snow that receded as the month passed. Our treks were strenuous, and sometimes Lytton needed to massage my legs, and I returned the favor. Then we sat by the fire, drank wine, and discussed the next day's hike.

I purchased a few postcards in a shop in Garmisch and sent them to my Munich friends and to Christina, who was heading home to Nuremburg to do her internship. I would miss my faithful study partner and my first friend in Munich. We had promised to write to one another, but I wondered if I would ever hear from her. So often when people are thrown together for a shared purpose, they drift away once the purpose is done.

Our holiday was drawing to a close. We decided to climb the trail that ran behind the chalet and camp for the night. After dinner, we sat closer to the fire because it was chilly.

"Meg, I have something to tell you," said Lytton. An ominous note in his voice gave me pause.

"Why do I think I won't like what you have to say."

"Because you probably won't." He sighed. The orange light of the campfire flickered in this face, showing the planes in high relief. I took a moment to admire his perfection.

He cleared his throat as a preamble. "Meg, I can't sit by any longer while everyone else is fighting a war."

"I should think you'd be happy to escape that horrible duty."

"You're not a man. You couldn't possibly understand."

"Really?" I turned and gave him a sharp look. "Give me some credit, Lytton. I may not be a man, but I think I can imagine something of what you are feeling. But I never took you for a man who needs to prove his masculinity by prancing around in a uniform."

"I may be a homosexual, but there are certain things a man does. Heeding the call of duty is one of them."

"Oh, good God! Lytton, don't tell me you're as stupid as the rest of them. They're nothing but cannon fodder! From what I hear, they sit in trenches with wet feet until their officers order them to go over the top, where they are shot like dogs."

For a long moment, we were silent and gazed into the fire. "I've been in contact with your grandfather," Lytton said. "I've asked him to arrange safe passage to England."

I turned sharply. "And you were angry with me when I drew your blood for not trusting you. Here, you go behind my back to my grandfather. How dare you!"

"I'm sorry, Meg. I knew you would be furious if you knew."

"I am furious." I shrugged off his arm, but it crept back to its former position and gave me a little squeeze.

"Don't worry. I mean to volunteer for the ambulance service, not military duty. I just feel I need to DO something. All this sitting around is driving me mad."

"I thought you enjoyed your duties at the museum."

"I do, but I feel guilty with everyone else at the front."

"Guilt is a useless feeling."

"Perhaps, but I feel it nonetheless."

"Well, then do as you wish."

"I'd feel better if you gave me your blessing."

"Make me pregnant, and I don't care what you do."

"That's a lie."

"Yes, it is."

To make amends, we made love in the scratchy, wool blankets. Naked, we huddled together against the night chill.

After that, I could feel him drifting away. It had little to do with our argument, or even his need to join up with the other young men serving in the war. I'd always known Lytton was a restless soul by nature and could never stay in one place too long. By the time we returned to Munich, he had already departed in his mind.

A few days later, I accompanied him to the train station. He waved from the window of the train, and that was the last I saw of him for over two years.

13

Lytton was kind enough to send a wire informing me that he had arrived safely. From past experience, I knew that he was an unreliable correspondent, so I did not expect to hear from him often, but I hoped he would let me know where and when he was deployed.

After he left, I sensed a subtle shift in the atmosphere in the house. For one thing, Hanna and I now ate alone. It had been a bit awkward when Lytton was still there. It was even more awkward when he and I went out to a dinner party or to the opera. But she had an agreeable disposition and never complained, not even when we left her at home and headed to Raithschau for my grandmother's birthday.

Everyone in my household loved Hanna. Cook knew she liked a particular fine-grained Braunschweiger liver sausage with her breakfast and always made sure to have some in the larder. For Hanna's sake, she always chose the freshest fruit in the market—luscious, ripe peaches, crisp apples, grapes like jewels.

My son adored Hanna. Willi could shriek like a creature possessed when I held him, but Hanna was always able to settle him. He liked to drink his bottle nestled against Hanna's full breasts while she rocked him. She had a pleasant voice and often sang to him, but when I suggested she sing with me, she always declined shyly. I would have liked her to join me, especially after Lytton left, which meant I'd lost my singing partner.

One night, after I'd cajoled her into a few glasses of wine, she finally sang some popular songs with me. Afterwards, she explained why she believed in temperance. In her clinic, she'd treated scores of wives forced into intercourse by their drunk husbands.

"The women arrive with their faces covered with bruises, often bludgeoned beyond recognition by fists. Sometimes they are bitten until blood flows or are torn inside from rough handling. It breaks my heart."

Clearly, she needed to be a tough sort to put up with such sights. The more she confided, the more I realized how little I knew about her work or about her. With some prodding, she told me about her parents. They'd been nearly penniless when they died. The grandmother, who'd taken her in, had begrudged her everything. Hanna had worn her second-hand dresses until her wrists showed. The grandmother was a devout Lutheran who spent half of every Sabbath in church. She wanted to marry off Hanna as soon as possible and had promised her to a widower in the congregation.

"I take it the man wasn't to your liking."

"An old farmer twice my age with two grown daughters? No. Fortunately, I'd won a scholarship to nursing school and escaped in the nick of time."

"What if a more attractive proposal came your way? Then what?"

She glanced away. "The truth is, I've never felt any desire to marry."

Her answer gave me pause, but I decided not to probe it, sensing it was too soon for that topic.

Nevertheless, our conversations at the dinner table became more intense because, without Lytton there, we had less need to maintain idle, social chatter. Hanna began to speak more openly of her politics. When that subject arose, I usually dismissed the footman, who stood by to serve our dinner, which meant Hanna and I informally served ourselves. That suited me fine because I often found the hovering of the servants annoying.

"What do you believe, Grethe?" she asked, putting me on the spot.

I had to consider how to answer because it was not a topic to which I'd given much thought. "Of course, I support women's right to vote. My mother-in-law, Lady Bromsley, is an ardent suffragette."

"I could tell your husband was raised by an unconventional woman," observed Hanna, nodding in approval.

"Really? How?"

"He listens with respect when you speak. He seems to care about your feelings and never dismisses them out of hand. Apparently, he truly values your opinion."

What an astute observation, I thought. "Lytton is a remarkable man in many ways."

"You must miss him," she threw out casually, but I saw her carefully watching for my reaction.

I smiled. "I do miss him, but I also know he is happiest when he is off on an adventure. I would never keep him from what he loves any more than he would keep me."

"How lucky you are to have achieved such equality in your marriage."

"I am indeed. But I was raised to think women are the equals of men and would stand for nothing less."

She sighed. "In your world perhaps. Most women in a marriage are housewives and mothers. Unmarried women struggle to make a living. The opportunities for respectable female employment are few."

"Women can be nurses and midwives like you. Schoolmistresses. Governesses. There are a few."

"But most require the woman to remain unmarried. What can widows do, for example, especially if they have children?"

"A good question. I suppose they hope to remarry or have the support of their families."

"If they are lucky…"

"Yes," I agreed only to move on from that topic. "You seem well-suited to your profession. In fact, you seem to know more about obstetrics and gynecology than I ever will. Perhaps more than my teachers. Have you ever considered studying medicine? I could make inquiries on your behalf."

She narrowed her eyes. "Why? You owe me nothing. If anything, I owe you for a beautiful place to live, wonderful food to eat, and your companionship."

"You owe me nothing," I scoffed. "It's I who owe you a debt. Pregnancy makes me miserable. If not for you, I would be unbearable. Everyone else would shrink from the ogre!" I tried for a mad look in my eyes, and she laughed.

"How you exaggerate! You have your moments, but you are less of an ogre than some women I've attended."

I engaged her gaze to make sure I had her attention. "If you would like to study medicine, I am sincere in the offer of support. Not everyone has the opportunities I've had. I only had them because other women invested in me. The best way to repay them is to invest in other talented women."

"A very enlightened view for an aristocrat," observed Hanna.

"Some of us are enlightened," I replied, feeling slightly insulted. I raised a brow. "This is the first I've heard that my social rank troubles you. Why have you never said so before?"

"We've never discussed politics at length."

"No, and I have no intention of doing it now. In fact, I loathe politics."

"As you wish," she said deferentially.

"Hanna, stop that. You're not a servant. You're my friend."

"Then stop paying me to be your midwife."

"What? That is a professional fee that you legitimately earn. I will not stop paying you."

"Then we are not friends. I am merely your employee."

I had never known her to be so contrary. There was something more to this than affirmation of our friendship. "Very well. I shall open a bank account in your name and deposit your fees into it. That way, if you decide to continue your education, you'll have some money."

"Thank you for the offer of support, but I have no intention of studying medicine."

"Why not?" I asked, somewhat taken aback.

"Because my calling is to be a midwife, not a physician. Besides, everyone knows nurses do the real healing. Physicians only give orders."

I opened my mouth to protest, but she suddenly started to laugh. "Grethe, you take everything so seriously!"

❧

Despite my professed loathing for politics, Hanna kept revisiting the topic. For her, everything came down to politics. She decried how unchecked childbearing put a strain on poor families, driving them deeper into poverty. She lowered her voice when she told me how the unfortunate experience of seeing the results of a botched abortion had drawn her to the clinic in the first place.

When the discussion had begun, I had dismissed the footman as usual, but now I got up and closed the door to guard against curious ears.

"Everyone knows you offer illegal birth control at your clinic," I said, taking my seat again. I lowered my voice to a whisper. "Do they perform abortions there as well?"

Hanna gave me a sharp look, then lowered her gaze. "Sometimes."

I studied her with a frown.

Finally, she looked up. "You are shocked."

"No, not shocked. Surprised, perhaps. In Bavaria, the penalty for performing an abortion is death. Do you perform them as well?"

She shook her head. "No, but I have assisted," she admitted in a whisper.

"Hanna!" I gave her a stern look. "That makes you an accomplice. What if your clinic were raided by the police?"

"We only perform abortions under the cover of night," she said quickly, "and only when the most trustworthy staff are on hand." She eyed me, perhaps wondering if she could trust me. "Will you report me?" she asked anxiously.

"No, of course not. But I want you to stop."

For a moment, she visibly prickled. "You can't order me to stop."

"I'm not ordering you…as if I could. I'm asking you. In fact, I'm *begging* you."

My plea seemed to surprise her. She sat up straight and gazed at me with a perplexed look. "Why does it matter so much to you?"

"Because it would break my heart if any harm came to you."

She searched my face. "Why?"

"Because I love you," I blurted out. As I said it, I realized that I had loved her all along, but this was the first time I had admitted it, even to myself.

Her eyes suddenly found the table silver. "I love you too," she murmured.

After that emotional exchange, I needed to slow down my racing heart, so I picked up my fork and resumed my meal, but as I ate, I stole curious glances at Hanna. She kept her eyes firmly fixed on her plate.

After dinner, we had coffee in the music room as we did every night but we didn't linger afterward as usual for music or reading. Hanna said she was tired and went up to her room. I watched her go, but I remained to have a brandy. Finally, I went up to my room. I undressed for bed, thinking about Hanna, her calm eyes and her gentle hands. When I thought of her full lips, I felt an almost painful hunger to kiss them. I imagined how they would taste, nearly obsessed with the idea. It haunted me long after I turned out the light.

After restlessly trying for an hour to find a comfortable sleeping position, I took a valerian capsule to calm me, but after an interval for it to take effect, my nerves were as jangled as before. Finally, I flung on my dressing robe and headed to Hanna's room. I knocked very softly in case she was already asleep. All was quiet within, and I was about to return to my room when the door opened a crack.

"Yes?" asked Hanna in an innocent voice.

"May I come in?"

She opened the door wider, and I slipped into the room. She closed and locked the door behind me.

Her eyes shone expectantly. Her beautiful lips, looking lusciously dark in the half light, were slightly parted. When I touched my mouth to hers, I could feel her trembling.

She drew back and searched my face. For a moment, I worried she would ask me to leave. Then she kissed me as if my mouth were a well of sweet water in a desert. She kissed my forehead, my eyes, but her mouth couldn't get enough of mine. She led me to her bed, untied my dressing gown and pushed it off my shoulders. She lay down on the bed and opened her arms.

"You don't know how long I dreamed of this," she whispered.

I wanted to say that I had too, and when I drew breath to speak, she laid a finger on my lips to silence me and pulled me into her soft body.

Cautiously, I explored her. Her rich curves were like an uncharted land, a map I hadn't yet learned how to read. As my midwife, she knew every inch of my body, but I had never touched hers.

I fell on her like a starving beast, kissing her roughly because I wanted to devour her. My teeth bruised the skin of her neck and shoulder. I was so eager, I rent her nightgown, to get to her breasts, which were beautiful, creamy and soft. I wanted to bury my face in them, suck on her large nipples.

I wanted to squeeze them with my fingers and lips until she moaned with pleasure.

But we became tangled in the ripped fabric, laughed, and undressed to our bare skin. For a moment, we lay looking in one another's eyes. She laid a gentle hand on my cheek. "Oh, my darling girl. I'd so hoped you'd come to me tonight." She kissed me, filling my mouth with her tongue, raising my desire to a fever pitch. The moment I lay between her legs, I thought I would die. I felt her wetness against my belly as I moved against her. "Yes, please!" she said.

I used every means at my disposal to give her pleasure. I caressed her slick warmth. I probed her depths with my fingers. Inhaling her rich female scent, I realized that all my former lovers had been mere girls, whereas Hanna with her full breasts and abundant curves was a full-blooded woman. I approached her sex like a ripe fruit and took it all at once, savoring its salty taste.

When she made love to me, it was obvious that I was not her first female lover. She was skilled beyond my imagination. She found parts of my interior that I had never known existed. She gave me pleasure I had never imagined, but then she stopped. "You may be pregnant, so we'll reserve some lessons for another time." The promise of yet unknown pleasures was enough to rouse me again.

After we were finally sated, we lay in a tangle of limbs. Her braid had come undone, and her blond hair sprayed across my shoulder. As we lost ourselves in one another's eyes, there was no need to say a single word.

When I awoke the next morning, I found Hanna leaning on her elbow, watching me sleep. She regarded me with an expression I had never seen before. I knew what love looked like because I had seen it in the faces of those dear to me. I could recognize a smoldering look of desire, or the wild impulse of passion, but the expression on Hanna's face was different. It was the tender look one reserves only for a lover.

～

The rhythm of our life changed dramatically. Hanna shared my bed almost every night. Of course, my servants were well-trained and knew to look the other way. They had proven their loyalty many times over, and I never worried that they would report the goings on in my house to their former employer, my grandmother.

Hanna and I spent hour upon hour in rapt conversation as if we had never known one another before the moment we had joined our bodies. We seemed compelled to tell every detail of our lives, to report every thought we had when we were apart. She laughed merrily when I told her stories of my youthful mischief. Sometimes, I would embellish them to stoke the humor. I learned that there is a rhythm to telling a funny story, arranging the details, pausing for effect.

She told me more stories about her difficult youth, of being locked in her room for the smallest infraction, of her supper being withheld for days. When she shared her terrible memories of her upbringing, I realized the nuns of Obberoth had been nothing but kind.

"I have no family," Hanna said with a sigh of regret after one of her tales. "None at all."

"We are your family now," I said.

She kissed me and gazed into my eyes. "Yes, you are."

Hanna reintroduced me to my son. Now that he was beyond the screeching phase, I found him somewhat more agreeable. Some nights, Hanna brought him to sleep with us and he curled into her body like a puppy. The little devil nuzzled her breasts and occasionally tried to suck on them. It took time, but eventually, he cuddled with me as well. I tolerated it because Hanna set such a fine example of maternal affection.

Our personal and professional lives became a bit tangled. When she examined me, I sent my mind to the place it occupies when I am a physician. I thought of clinical rather than romantic aspects while she probed my body or touched my breasts. Mostly, this succeeded, and I learned a new level of detachment.

As my midwife, Hanna had little to do. My second pregnancy went much more smoothly. This time, there was no morning sickness. The fatigue that had nearly brought me to my knees during my first pregnancy never materialized either. Most days, I even forgot that I was pregnant, but, as my belly expanded, Hanna attempted to limit my activities, especially riding. I do not take kindly to women telling me what to do, nor anyone for that matter.

"I am a healthy woman, and I am always careful."

"Perhaps, but you are also a daredevil, by your own admission."

I didn't like being constrained. Sometimes, I would sneak off to play tennis at my club or ride and not tell her. Then the military seized my horses for the war effort, which ended that particular temptation.

I finally received a letter from Lytton, describing in the vaguest possible way because of the censors, where he had landed. I derived from what he wrote that he was somewhere in France. I noticed Hanna eyeing me as I read the letter, so I read it aloud to prove there was nothing for her to worry about: "War is a horror I never imagined, which I'm sure you as a physician most certainly can. After this bit as an ambulance driver, I shall be far better at bandaging your dueling wounds. Next time, I might not even be queasy." I looked up to make an editorial comment. "He thinks he's so clever." I scanned the rest of it to translate it for Hanna and smiled. "He's urging me to practice singing so that when he returns, we can sing duets." For Hanna's benefit, I skipped the love and kisses part.

My lighthearted approach to the letter had not had the effect on Hanna that I'd hoped. Sitting across the table, she looked grave.

"Our marriage is not what you think," I attempted to explain.

I could see that she wanted me to say more, but I would not betray Lytton in that way. I merely stared at her, hoping to make my point. Finally, she nodded, and I hoped she understood.

⁓

We spun a cocoon of happiness in my Lehel villa. We let no one in, and we rarely ventured out, except to the places where we practiced our professions. Gradually, we stepped into the light of day. Arm in arm, we took walks in the Hofgarten. Before Hanna banned riding, we exercised my horses. We met for lunch a few days a week, always at different restaurants. Finally, we went to the opera together. I treated her to a new gown for the occasion. Although the performance of *Tannhäuser* was sublime, I have little recollection of it, for I was so busy squeezing Hanna's hand and thinking of what we would do later that night.

Despite our fear that being so often in one another's company might cause a stir, no one seemed to notice. The war had taken so many men to the front that women had little choice but to socialize with other women. The sight of two women sitting together in cafés, the theater, a concert, taking in the art at the Alte Pinakothek, or casually rowing on the Starnberger See, was more and more commonplace. Granted, few of the women we saw à deux were Sapphists, although perhaps some were.

Sometimes, when we sat in a café or my box at the opera, we would try to guess which of the other female couples shared our proclivities. I learned from Hanna that it was not how they dressed or even whether they touched one another, although an idle pat on the arm or a hand laid over a companion's could be telling. "Look at how they look at one another," Hanna whispered. "Do they gaze into one another's eyes as if they are trying to see their very souls?"

Eventually, I learned to interpret the clues, but one day, while watching an attractive pair sitting on the other side of the café, I decided to test my skill. "Let me see if I'm right," I said, rising as if to head to where they sat.

Hanna caught my wrist. "Grethe! Are you mad? Sit down."

I laughed and reclaimed my seat. "Aren't you curious?"

"Yes, of course. But you don't walk up to someone in a restaurant and ask, 'Oh, by the way, are you a lesbian?'"

"Why not?" I asked, seriousness personified.

"Because it's simply not done."

I laughed.

"You imp! You had no intention of asking them, did you?"

"No, of course not."

She gave me a stern look. "Grethe, try to behave like a lady of your station."

"Oh, please! Not you too!"

"All right, then. Go make a fool of yourself. I'll watch."

"Never mind. I think I'll have another cup of coffee instead."

No matter how much we enjoyed our adventures, we were always glad to return to the safety of our Lehel nest and the pleasure we found in one another's arms. Like all new lovers, we imagined it could last forever.

∿

I had never missed Christmas at Edelheim, not even when I lived in England, but I strongly sensed Hanna's reluctance to accompany me. She protested that she didn't have clothes appropriate for such a venue, and she was right. Our extravagant holiday rites had remained unchanged despite wars and the passage of time. She would need formal dresses for evening wear and the annual servants' ball. I opened an account for her at one of the local salons, so that she might order fashionable attire, but I learned from the proprietor that she never even visited the place.

When Hanna returned that night, I challenged her.

"Grethe, I don't want you spending your money on me. I'm perfectly capable of buying my own clothes, and unless I intend to spend Christmas in your grand castle with your high-born family, I don't need such a fancy wardrobe."

"You really don't want to go," I said with disappointment.

"No," she finally admitted. "I don't. I'd rather stay here in Munich."

"But I don't want to leave you alone here at Christmas," I protested.

She shrugged. "Why not? Before I met you, I always spent Christmas alone. Usually, I volunteered for duty because I had nothing else to do. To me, it's a day like any other." Despite her stoic tone, I could tell she didn't really believe her own propaganda.

"I won't have it. I'll remain here with you."

She looked uncertain, obviously conflicted between wanting my company and depriving me of the opportunity to celebrate Christmas with my family.

"I'm staying here in Munich with you," I declared, "and that's final." However, I wondered how I would explain why to my family. I ended up using the war as an excuse. I was relieved when my grandmother said that she understood. Father was at the front, but Mother told me it didn't matter to her where I spent the holiday, which was no surprise.

In January, we celebrated Hanna's thirtieth birthday, a milestone that brought home to me the difference in our ages. I was only nineteen, over a decade younger. As I stood by to watch her open her gifts, I had the sudden memory of Daphne Richardson mocking me for my youth and insinuated myself into Hanna's embrace for reassurance.

"Are you pleased with your gifts?" I asked anxiously. I'd given her an obstetrical stethoscope, new petticoats and nightgowns, a pearl brooch, and a popular novel in which she had expressed interest.

"Yes, but there is one more gift I would like you to give me."

It was not like Hanna to ask things for herself, for the children yes, or even one of the servants, but never for herself.

"I would like you to take leave from your surgical internship for a few months."

I made a face and drew breath to speak.

"No, Grethe, hear me out. You need time to finish your doctor's paper. When you stand for long periods, you suffer from leg cramps. That's true, isn't it?"

Frowning, I confirmed with a nod. Sometimes, the knots in my legs were so painful I wept silently as she worked them out with her powerful fingers. "I know how you hate admitting weakness, but if you faint in the operating theater, it will not be good for your career." I hated to admit it, but she was right.

The next day, I set an appointment with the chief of surgery and asked permission to take leave. My dissertation made a ready excuse, but he glanced at my belly and said, "I think that's a good idea." So much for thinking I'd been hiding my pregnancy.

I was so accustomed to the grueling demands of my training, that at first, I didn't know what to do with myself. Once I began compiling my hundreds of pages of notes and refining my thesis, the enterprise consumed me. I spent long hours combing the medical journals to provide evidence for my observations. On her free days, Hanna reviewed what I'd written and proved to be a competent editor. She needed to be something of a mind reader because my handwriting was now even more illegible, and sometimes I wrote notes in the code I had devised as a child. Only I could read those.

She quizzed me on every detail to help prepare me for the examiners' questions. Everyone knew they liked to ask trick questions or poke holes in the candidate's arguments with a long needle. The only defense was to have all my evidence at my fingertips. Finally, the last draft was complete, and the paper was ready for a typist.

On the morning of my thesis defense, Hanna smoothed my hair and tidied my blouse, yanking down the starched placard so it would lie flat under my suit coat. She stood on her toes and kissed me gently on the forehead. "Don't worry, Grethe. You are prepared, and your arguments are solid."

I smiled weakly, for I was truly anxious.

"I'll be in the gallery watching…and yes, praying, even though you don't believe in God. You will be brilliant! I know it!"

The February day was overcast, dark, and chilly as my chauffeur drove us to the medical school. My steps echoed as I entered the great hall of the administration building. Seated at the long table in the front sat five dour men, all bearded except one.

As I took my seat in the lonely chair set back from the examiners' table, I noticed that the gallery was full, making me even more aware that I was the only woman to sit for habilitation that year, and at nineteen, also the youngest of either sex. To make matters worse, I was seven months pregnant, confirming every false assumption about female physicians, namely that we were all dabblers, who would drop out of the profession to marry and bear children. Although I dressed skillfully to disguise my condition, it was difficult to hide it completely.

I could tell from the set of the examiners' faces that they couldn't wait to find me unworthy of the degree, but after four hours of rapid-fire questioning, their scowls told me I had spoiled their plan. They conferred briefly, and the one without the beard stood.

"Margarethe von Stahle, the Ludwig-Maximilians University confers upon you the degree of Doctor of Medicine and habilitation, enabling you to lecture in German universities. Congratulations, *Frau Doktor*."

Hanna met me in the lobby as I left the examination hall. "You were brilliant," she said, discreetly squeezing my arm in lieu of a kiss. "You must be so relieved!"

The examiners passed and nodded in my direction. I smiled in return when I really wanted to glower at them instead.

"The professor of physiology said my thesis was unoriginal," I complained to Hanna once we were out of earshot.

"But your research was solid, and you added a whole, new perspective, which was original."

I hoped Hanna wasn't saying this merely to comfort me. She knew I could be sensitive to criticism, but the point about the solid research was accurate, and Hanna wasn't given to idle flattery.

Everyone with whom I would have celebrated the achievement had moved on. Plus, the war rationing precluded a dinner party. Nevertheless, Hanna insisted that we mark the occasion. We ate lunch in a café in the old city and watched the other women diners for clues to their inclinations.

⁓

Mercifully, my second delivery went much more smoothly than the first. The midwives liked to say that boys are more difficult to deliver than girls, but the birth of the second child is usually easier, as if the body has learned something from the previous experience. The labor lasted only a few hours before my daughter was propelled unceremoniously into the world.

Hanna swaddled the child in a towel and laid her in my arms. Lytton was hundreds of miles away, so there was no proud father to beam over the new child, but the pleasure in Hanna's face made up for it.

"Your daughter is beautiful," she said, beaming.

I unfolded the towel in which the baby lay to confirm its gender. A female child meant that I had now executed my duty to the House of Raithschau and could put the nasty business of reproduction behind me.

"Will you ask Schmidt to send a telegram to my husband?"

I could see a cloud move over Hanna's sunny pleasure in the new baby. "What is the message?" she asked, taking a pencil and notepad from her apron pocket.

"Tell him that he has a new daughter, and I shall name her Elisabeth in honor of his aunt. German spelling, of course."

Hanna nodded and replaced the notepad and pencil in her pocket. "Let me wash the baby first. Can it wait that long?" She reached for the infant.

"Of course," I said, placing my new daughter into her able hands.

She leaned down and planted a soft kiss on my forehead. "Rest now, my darling. Your work is done."

14

When I returned from leave, my male colleagues, the few who were left, addressed me as "*Frau Doktor*" instead of "Stahle" or "Countess." Even the senior doctors were more respectful. They listened attentively when I spoke instead of staring at their shoes. I might be a woman and by their definition, weaker and less serious, but now they couldn't argue with my credentials. If they did, their own would be invalidated. By then, I'd learned that hard work or greater knowledge meant less than playing men's games and winning their prizes, sometimes right out from under them.

My pleasure in their changed attitudes was brief. While I was writing my dissertation and enduring the misery of my last months of pregnancy, I had almost forgotten how brutal the pace of surgical training could be. Although I was only a junior surgeon, the war had forced all of us to take more responsibility. With the shortage of doctors, we couldn't afford to be picky about formal status.

The war made me a surgeon. Like the dirty camp doctor, who had treated Miss Westerfield, I could remove a foot in minutes. While I became extremely adept at amputations, I was also perfecting my technique at abdominal resections and picking shrapnel out of soft tissue. Soon, with the exception of neurosurgery, there were few procedures I wouldn't attempt.

Once the battle of Verdun began, even more wounded came our way. Hanna regularly needed to massage my aching shoulders and legs, and I needed to return the favor. I didn't mind because it was often a prelude to sex, but I hated to see the dear woman so exhausted.

Although pregnancies had fallen off because most of the men were in the army, Hanna and her colleagues needed to work longer hours to fill in for nurses who had volunteered for the war effort. With so many doctors away in military or field hospitals, the clinic nurses often prescribed drugs and even performed minor surgery. It was illegal, but the poor only cared that they were getting treatment and would never report them. Shortages of fuel and food had increased the cases of tuberculosis, scurvy, rickets, and other diseases of poor nutrition. Emaciated women with sickly children came to the clinic looking for help. What they needed most was food, which became scarcer by the day.

We were lucky enough to have supplies from Raithschau, but I added a vegetable plot to our garden. Schmidt, who grew up on a farm, suggested we build a chicken coop and a rabbit hutch. I readily agreed, realizing the chickens could provide eggs and the rabbits, fresh meat. It was not a large garden, so there were limits to our agricultural efforts, but I enjoyed the peppery arugula and bright lettuce we grew in our own soil. We learned to grow potatoes in barrels. Nurtured with manure from the chickens and rabbits, our cabbages were spectacular—solid, heavy heads that could feed the entire household. We now ate meat only twice a week, substituting eggs and pulses for other days. I insisted everyone be well fed because nutrition was critical to their health.

I watched Hanna wearing herself to a frazzle. She was always chiding me to pace myself, but she never listened when I advised the same. I often wished I could demand that Hanna moderate her work schedule in the same way I ordered my servants, but she had insisted that I prove she was more to me than a servant, so I dared not say a word.

Because she was the elder, I deferred to her on many things, especially regarding the children. I was glad to have her expertise because I had no idea what I was doing. Nurses had looked after me as an infant. Like my mother and so many aristocratic women before me, I left my children's care to their nurse, who went, not to me, but to Hanna about schedules, menus, nappy rashes, potty training, and other child-rearing questions, which only added to Hanna's burdens.

One night, the poor woman came home from the clinic close to midnight. I'd been reading in her bed to pass the time while I waited up for her. Wordlessly, she took off her suit coat and unbuttoned her blouse. She sat down at her vanity and removed the pins to let down her hair. Her perfect shoulders, gently sloping away from her elegant neck, looked so beautiful in the soft lamp light that my heart simply ached from the sight. I put my book aside and went to kiss them. She reached over my shoulder for my hand. She gave it a little squeeze and then, to my horror, she began to cry.

I knelt beside her. "Oh, dear Hanna. What ever is the matter?"

"I'm so tired. I'm doing all I can, but I can never do enough. So many of the men have gone off to war. The women are left alone with little money. Even if they have it, there's no food to buy. People are cold and hungry. They get sick so easily. I don't know what to do!"

"War is a horror, even for those at home." I took her hands in mine. "You must take care of yourself. If you get sick, who will take care of your patients? Come to bed. I'll rub your back."

She reached down, lifted my face to hers, and kissed me. "My darling, I'm too tired for anything but sleep."

I returned to my book while she readied herself for bed. After she settled beside me, I curled my body around her. I kissed the back of her neck and reached for her breast, but she didn't respond. I raised myself on my elbow to see her face and realized she was sound asleep.

Eventually, a competent, retired nurse was hired to manage Hanna's clinic. I was relieved and grateful because after the Battle of Sommes, I needed to spend more time at the hospital.

∽

Somehow, we muddled through that horrible summer of austerity. Then disaster hit close to home. My grandfather collapsed at Raithschau. According to the footman who had just served him tea, he dropped the cup, which shattered, spraying its contents and shards of china everywhere. His eyes rolled up in his head, and he fell to the floor, dead instantly.

I heard the news from Dr. Schulte, the town physician of Raithschau, the man who had so admirably treated the compound fracture of my femur. He telephoned me at the hospital. Fortunately, the head nurse thought the news sufficiently important to call me out of surgery.

I took the call in the tiny telephone booth at the end of the hall. Schulte gave me the particulars. He suspected either an aortic dissection or a ruptured aneurysm and assured me that the death had been quick and painless.

"Of course, without an autopsy, there is no way to know the exact cause," he said. I could hear the curiosity in Schulte's voice. I was curious myself. I also knew Schulte was shy where our family, his employers, were concerned.

"Have you asked the countess for permission?" I asked, encouraging his candor.

"Not exactly. As you might expect, she is in shock. I gave her some Chloral. She referred me to you regarding any matter of importance."

As I contemplated this responsibility, I took a deep breath to consider what to do. I now had to guess my grandmother's wishes regarding an autopsy.

"Proceed, but please be neat about it. There must be no exterior sign that would indicate we have desecrated my grandfather's remains."

"Absolutely not, *Gnädige!*" His sudden formality saddened me because I had always considered him a friend, but at that moment, it was the least of my worries.

I sat in the little telephone booth for a few minutes to formulate a plan, but when I saw the doctor in charge of the surgical residents pass in the hall, I opened the bifold door and hurried after him. Although he had once called me "countess" along with the others, he offered kind condolences and instantly granted me leave without penalty.

I returned to the booth to telephone Hanna with the news. She tried to soothe me with comforting words, but then, apparently sensing I was on a mission, she put my majordomo on the line. I gave him instructions to make travel arrangements and ask my lady's maid to organize my packing.

"Please forgive me for throwing everything in your lap," I said, accepting Hanna's embrace when I arrived home.

She laid a gentle hand on my cheek. "That's why I am here…to look after you." In her eyes was that look of tenderness I treasured, but there was no time to do anything but make ready to leave.

At the door, I attempted to apologize again to Hanna for leaving her with all my responsibilities, but she kissed me and urged, "Go! I love you. Telephone me when you arrive."

As I sat on the train to Raithschau, the loss of one of the great heroes of my youth burdened my heart. I remembered him, red-faced and flustered, trying to teach me about integrals. I could hear him cursing when his tiny ship collapsed in its equally tiny bottle, but most of all, I remembered him standing on the great hill overlooking Edelheim, sharing his thoughts on duty. His words rang in my ears, never so true, nor so apt, for I was now one step closer to my own term of duty.

When I arrived at the *Schloss*, I found my grandmother in her sitting room, browsing an album of photographs.

"Thank you for coming, my darling," she said, turning up her face for a kiss.

"Of course, I would come."

We sat hip to hip while she explained the time and setting of each photograph. I had seen many of them in my youth, but then, I'd never thought of my grandparents as anything but old. Now, as a wife and mother, I had a different perspective. I marveled over the faded print of a very young woman holding my father as an infant and suddenly saw myself.

I gave Grandmother another injection of Chloral before heading to Dr. Schulte's surgery. As curious as I was regarding the cause of my grandfather's death, I was grateful to learn that the autopsy had already been concluded and I needn't witness it. Examination of the major vessels had confirmed a ruptured aortic aneurysm. The body had already been handed off to the undertaker for embalming and preparation for transit to Edelheim.

At dinner, my grandmother said, apropos of nothing, "Your grandfather never forgave himself for beating you after the gunpowder incident. He spoke of it long afterward, how he hated himself for striking you. He loved you."

"Yes, I know."

"He was overjoyed that you understood the idea of infinity. I never understood it, but you did. That made him happy."

I smiled. "It made me happy too."

My grandfather had always been sparing in his compliments and affection, but I had known how much he loved me, his first and only living grandchild. The thought made my tasty meal stick in my throat, and I couldn't finish my dinner.

~

In accompanying my grandmother and my grandfather's body home to Edelheim, I was executing my first duty as the future Countess Raithschau. My grandmother's pale eyes were dull and distant as we rode the train north. She sighed but never complained about the long ride to Berlin. Rather than open the Grunewald house, we passed the night at the Continental, where father had an open account. The next day, we took the train to Langenberg.

My father had been granted leave and had returned from the front by the time we arrived. I watched, moved by his proud bearing in the face of his grief. My grandmother was also stoically serene as we gathered in the little chapel at Edelheim for Grandfather's funeral. We followed the casket to Langenberg in a horse-drawn carriage and stood by while my grandfather was conducted to his tomb in the crypt. As I passed the gated chamber where the four, little coffins holding my dead brothers lay, I noticed that someone had removed the dried nosegays and replaced them with fresh chrysanthemums.

Once the guests left, my grandmother retreated to her room. Standing outside her door, I could hear her sobbing within. Unlike my parents, my grandparents had truly loved one another. My impulse was to offer her comfort, but I realized she had withdrawn for privacy, so I let her be.

When I returned to the drawing room, Father surprised me by challenging me to a game of billiards. As he chalked up his cue, I said, "I am sorry for your loss, Father."

"Thank you. As am I for yours." He grimaced. "You're a physician What really happened to him?"

"A defect in an artery burst."

"Schulte told me he went quickly. That he bled to death like a soldier on the battlefield. A fitting death for the old man."

"Yes, fitting," I agreed. "You are the lord of Edelheim now."

"As you will be one day."

"May that day be long in coming."

His opening shot sank not a single ball. I could have easily taken the game, but it seemed unkind to trounce him while he was grieving. For the first time since I had been playing billiards, I deliberately threw the game. Father passed on another game. Instead, we opened a bottle of my birthday port and gazed into the fire in silent reflection.

"This war has been ugly," Father said, the sound of his voice startling me after the long period of silence. "So many have lost their lives."

"Old men send young men to die in every war."

"In other wars, it has been man against man, their beasts, and their weapons. In this war, it is man against machines. It would sicken you to see how men's bodies are blown to bits by the big mortar shells, how automatic weapons can mow them down. The men still charge with horses, and they are destroyed. They 'go over the top' and are shot instantly, then lay between the lines for days, and we hear them calling for help. Anyone who sticks his heads above the trench has a rain of bullets waiting for him." He shook his head. "This isn't war. It's slaughter."

Usually, Father avoided such talk, thinking it unfit for women's ears, but he had always spoken openly to me. He had no need to say more, for I had seen the victims in my hospital, the shattered bones, eyes torn out, holes in their bodies so deep, we could only give them morphine to ease the pain while they lay dying.

I said nothing in response to my father's remarks. He would be horrified to learn that I had already witnessed firsthand what he was describing, and he was already so sad. The last thing he needed was being pulled up short by the likes of me.

～

I accompanied Grandmother back to Raithschau. On the train, we reviewed business matters. She asked if I would take over the investments. Grandfather had been gradually turning over those responsibilities to me, so I agreed.

"The weather has been terrible this summer as you know. Almost all our wheat fields have been destroyed. The grapes are tiny and bitter. There may be no wine."

I had been reading about the impact of weather conditions on farms, but I hadn't realized until now that it had affected Raithschau. Until now, most of the food shortages had been caused by the blockade of our ports by the allies and transport being interrupted by the war. My mind began to calculate the practical implications. The wine brought in a fair amount of income, but no grain meant no bread.

"I can't ask my tenants for more when they are already hungry," Grandmother said. She looked at me and I understood that our supplies would be cut. "Of course, I would never take food out of your mouth or your children's."

I patted her hand to reassure her. "We shall manage." I described our tidy, little farm in the garden and that seemed to ease her mind.

"I knew I shouldn't be worried about you. You have always been so clever."

"Come to Munich and visit your great grandchildren."

"Perhaps in winter. After the harvest is in."

∼

But winter came and it was like nothing we could have imagined. The newspapers began calling it the "Turnip Winter" because people were so hungry that they ate the large, coarse turnips usually fed to livestock.

Grandmother wrote to tell me that she was slaughtering her dairy cattle because there wasn't enough grain or turnips to feed them. The farm manager at Edelheim killed many of the pigs and sent them to the smokehouse. He forced the pregnant sows to abort their young with ergot.

I was torn between my duties at the hospital and heading home to see to Edelheim in father's absence. At the same time, I felt pulled to be with Grandmother, who was trying to manage the estate while she was still grieving her loss. Hanna reminded me that I had duties at home to my children and my patients, so I remained in Munich.

As winter wore on, the government cut rations to half a pound of meat, three ounces of butter and four pounds of bread. The caloric value of this diet was half of what a normal adult needs to survive. Hungry people can be very uncooperative, and the street demonstrations intensified.

Hanna often came home late, despite her lighter schedule at the clinic. I had never asked her to explain her comings and goings any more than I had asked Lytton, but eventually, I became curious enough to ask where she went.

"A political meeting," she said, her eyes darting about nervously to see if anyone might be listening.

"Why didn't you tell me?"

"Because you always tell me how much you hate politics. Besides, you don't really want to know what I'm doing."

I frowned because it was true, but I said, "Be careful. The demonstrations are getting more violent. I don't want you hurt."

"Don't worry," she said and gave me a kiss to reassure me.

⌘

The battlefield provided us with an endless source of interesting cases. In war, one sees trauma to every part of the body from the digits to the deepest internal organs. With such variety, it was not surprising that war drives medical innovation more quickly than anything else.

One of these innovators was the surgeon, Ferdinand Sauerbruch. The chief of surgery was impressed by Sauerbruch's innovative prosthetics and distributed copies of an article to every surgeon on staff. When he heard Sauerbruch was to accompany a transport of wounded to Munich, he invited him to do a demonstration surgery. I remained behind after everyone else had left to pick his brain.

"You're the one they call 'the countess,' aren't you?" he asked, narrowing his eyes. They were pale like my grandaunt's and just as piercing.

I extended my hand. "Margarethe von Stahle," I said introducing myself.

He gripped my hand firmly. I returned the pressure. He gripped my hand harder, and I intensified my grip as well. This little game continued until he said, "Nothing about you is weak, Countess Stahle." This time, he said it with respect in his voice.

I nodded to acknowledge the compliment.

"Surgery requires strength," he said. "Make sure to take care of your hands."

I laughed. "Now you tell me, after you've crushed my bones! I shall try to remember that advice."

That brought a little twinkle of amusement to the pale eyes. "I read your doctor's paper. You had some original insights that I have taken to heart."

"Thank you, *Herr Doktor*. I'm flattered."

"Don't be. You have the goods." He gave me a long, measuring look. "I intend to perform surgery tomorrow morning to demonstrate how to prepare a stump for these prosthetics. Will you be there?"

"Absolutely!"

I traded places with one of the male residents for the opportunity to assist Sauerbruch during the demonstration surgery. My first-hand look at his amazing dexterity and skill made a lasting impression as did the cleverness of his prosthetics. His invention allowed the remaining muscles in the limb to direct motion of the device. Of course, the control was limited, but this was the first time anything like it had been possible.

After the procedure, the others left, but again, I remained behind to ask questions.

"Unfortunately, the preparation should begin in the field hospital," Sauerbruch said. "Otherwise, we must trim more muscle than necessary. Depending on the location of the damage, removing so much tissue can make the use of the prosthetic impossible. You should consider going to the front to see what goes on there."

"My father is stationed in the East. I could go to his camp."

He eyed me thoughtfully. "I know of your father, and you should go as soon as possible. I don't know how much longer this can go on."

"Hopefully, not much longer."

He sighed and shook his head. "It will not end well for us, I'm afraid." Saying this aloud to anyone amounted to treason. I was surprised that he would say such a thing to someone he'd only met. He gazed at me with his pale eyes. "I know you will keep this between us. I expect that Count Stahle's daughter knows how to keep a secret."

"You can be sure, *Herr Doktor*," I replied crisply, tempted to come to attention as I'd learned in the cadets' camp.

"I have asked for you to be my guide while I am here." Ordinarily, a visiting celebrity such as Sauerbruch would be accompanied by a senior doctor. Asking for me to escort him during his stay was the highest compliment I could imagine.

For several days, Sauerbruch followed me on my rounds and offered respectful comments on each of my cases. I soaked up every word that fell from his lips. He observed the surgeries of others on our staff, but he came every day to watch mine.

On his last day in Munich, I dared to invite him to Lehel for supper. I was enormously flattered when he accepted. I telephoned my majordomo to make arrangements. I called Hanna at her clinic to warn her that we would have a guest. During the war, we had relaxed the practice of dressing for dinner, but I wanted to make a good impression on my new hero. In his honor, I put on my newest Paris gown, which, because of the war, was a few years behind the fashion. Hanna looked elegant in a dinner dress from a local salon.

My household staff made the doctor welcome in the grand style to which we were accustomed before the war. Cook prepared a delicious meal of ham and root vegetables from our precious stores. Sauerbruch obviously enjoyed the meal and complimented it profusely. I'm sure that where he'd been posted, such a feast could only exist in the imagination.

Although everyone at the table was a medical professional, we spoke, not about medicine, but music. Sauerbruch had been to the Bayreuth festival several times and was a great Wagnerian.

After dinner, I offered to sing. He requested "Der Engel" from the *Wessendonck Lieder*. Hanna accompanied me on the piano. Sauerbruch's eyes never left her. I felt proud to see my lover admired. She was a beautiful woman, and fashionably dressed, she could rival any society lady.

I excused myself to kiss my children good night. When I returned, Hanna withdrew to give me privacy with Sauerbruch.

"I'm going to share some information that must remain between us," Sauerbruch said, lighting my cigarette with his spirit lighter.

"You can be sure, *Herr Doktor*, that your secret is safe with me."

He studied me for a brief moment. "As you know, your chief of surgery will be retiring in a few months. At the same time, my deployment will be coming to an end."

Obviously, I could connect the dots. "Are you his replacement?"

"It increasingly appears to be the case. Part of the reason I've come down here is to see what's what and who's who."

"And have you discovered what you'd hoped to find?"

"I found you," he said, "and a few others, who might be worth something as well. It will take time to build up the staff again. The war has taken all the good ones."

"Yes, I'm merely a leftover." I'd used the German word: *die Überreste*, meaning "kitchen scraps."

He laughed. "Hardly." Then he gave me a firm look. "I am not a fan of female surgeons, but you are better than most male surgeons I have seen. You have potential, and I mean to cultivate it."

My smile faded as I realized he was completely serious. "I am honored, *Herr Doktor,* to receive such praise from you."

"Don't be. It's not idle praise, simply a fact. I have high hopes for you, Dr. von Stahle. You are managing your career well. You've had an excellent education…despite that dalliance in England." He smiled to let me know he was speaking in jest. "You achieved habilitation, opening possibilities for teaching. Your personal life is a model for other young professionals. You married young, generated your heirs without unduly interrupting your career. And you've chosen a supportive and beautiful wife."

At this, I coughed out the cigarette smoke I'd just inhaled. "What do you mean?" I asked anxiously.

"Oh, don't worry," he said with a dismissive wave. "Your secret is safe with me."

"Is it that obvious?"

"Not in anything you do. Certainly, not in your appearance. You look like any other society lady. I only perceived the facts because I noticed how your companion looks at you. It's obvious that she adores you."

I opened my mouth to speak but found I had no words.

"And so she should," he said. "There is much to admire about you."

"And why should this be of concern to you, *Herr Doktor*?"

"When I come to Munich in a few months, I will, if you agree, make you my assistant. You may continue your residency as planned, but once you have finished, I intend to take you into my practice."

I cannot begin to describe how flattered I was by this proposal.

"Why me, *Herr Doktor*, and not one of my colleagues?"

"They can't hold a candle to you. You are the one."

After that exchange, we returned to our discussion of Wagner. Sauerbruch cajoled me into singing Brangäne's warning from *Tristan*. This time, I had to accompany myself because Hanna had already gone to bed.

"Beautiful," said Sauerbruch with a sigh. "Simply beautiful."

I nodded to acknowledge his praise and closed the keyboard.

"You are perfect," he said, smiling. "Perfect in every way."

～

I asked my father if he would allow me to visit him at the front. He agreed, but my visit was delayed. He had been summoned to the Kaiser's court to receive for the second time the Iron Cross with Gold Oak Leaves. As usual, Mother had refused to go, so I stood in her stead as I had on so many other occasions. Afterwards, I danced in my father's arms, enormously proud to be his daughter as he waltzed me around the great ballroom of the Berlin palace.

The grandeur was so at odds with the hardships I found when I returned to Munich. Almost every able-bodied man had been drafted into the military. The men left behind to keep production going in the factories were overworked and underfed. They went on strike to demand shorter hours and an increase in rations.

At home, the dinner conversation became increasingly strained. Hanna was often silent and sullen, especially after one of her political meetings. I finally prodded her to speak her mind.

"You capitalists have corrupted everything. That's why we are at war. That's why we are starving. You and that idiot Kaiser!"

I patted the air to urge her to keep her voice down. Fortunately, there was no one nearby to hear. The army had conscripted my footmen, so by that point, we had little choice but to serve ourselves at meals.

"I suppose you're a communist now," I said as calmly as I could. "What happened to the Social Democrats that you've felt the need to abandon them?"

I listened carefully as she explained that the Social Democrats were socialist in name only. In fact, there was open warfare within the party, pitting the party establishment against the liberal factions. Long before the war, the SPD had been keeping the capitalist economy of Germany afloat by suppressing measures that would have benefitted the working class, while paying lip service to socialist ideals.

I could have learned much more about this unholy alliance between the Social Democrats and the ruling class if I'd had more tolerance for political talk. Lumping me in with the "enemies of the people" made me even more impatient with the topic. "Don't you feel it's hypocritical to be living with a member of the *Uradel* and enjoying the benefits of her social status?"

"I haven't until now. You've always proven that nobility means more than a title. You chose a profession that serves others. You treat everyone fairly. You speak to the lowest of your servants as respectfully as to Dr. Sauerbruch."

"My father always said that the ability to communicate with everyone is essential to leadership."

"Evidently, he taught you that part well."

"Are you implying, he taught me other things less well?" I asked in a testy voice.

"That's not what I said, Grethe. Don't read into everything I say!"

"My noble birth is an accident of fate. I do the best I can," I said, throwing my napkin on the table. I got up and left the room.

A short time later, Hanna knocked on the door of the library. "I'm sorry our talk got out of hand. May I come in?"

I gestured to the sofa opposite where I sat, but she didn't sit.

"Perhaps, it's best we avoid politics," she said, "especially at dinner."

"A wise idea."

She studied my face. "You're still angry."

I shrugged. "Unlike you, I don't care enough about politics to involve myself emotionally."

Her face told me she'd recognized the criticism, but she didn't take the bait. "Will you come to bed soon?" she asked in a hopeful voice.

I sighed and followed her upstairs.

15

Sauerbruch finally arrived to become chief of surgery and quickly ascended to the status of a surgical god. He was brilliant, fearless, and had the proverbial nerves of steel that separate a good surgeon from a truly great one.

Although I was a woman, and beneath contempt in the surgical hierarchy, Sauerbruch took me under his wing. He appointed me chief resident, which caused some backlash, but he stood by me. Even when the men came back from the front to reclaim their lost years of medical training, he never cast me off in their favor.

It was from Sauerbruch that I learned to always undertake new and more complex surgeries in order both to hone my skills and to advance the profession. One particularly interesting case came my way shortly after Sauerbruch arrived. We were all under such pressure in those days to get a surgery done and move on to the next one, so experimental surgeries were rare, but this case intrigued me.

The patient, a man by the name of Jürgen Grauer, presented with extensive damage to his lower extremities from shrapnel. One leg was in relatively good condition; the other looked like raw meat. When I examined the wounds more closely, I discovered that all the basic structures were intact. It was like a jigsaw puzzle where one could only feel but not see the edges of the pieces.

The patient was an affable man with pale, yellow hair and startling blue eyes. He had been a mechanic and chauffeur before the war. He needed both legs to operate the pedals of a motorcar and make a living. He was willing to try anything to walk normally again, so I agreed to present the case to Sauerbruch. He too doubted the poor man would ever be able to walk without a crutch, but he encouraged me to give the repair a try.

Grauer endured, not one, but three surgeries during which I painstakingly extracted each bit of shrapnel and rebuilt his leg. He did walk normally again, albeit with a limp. When he fully recovered, he could drive and even ride a bicycle. The man was beside himself with gratitude.

"I will do anything for you, *Frau Doktor*. Anything!" he declared. "Let me tune up your motorcars."

My chauffeur had left because his mother was alone on the family farm after his brother had fallen in battle, so I hired Grauer even though I drove myself everywhere, when petrol was available, or took the tram. Unfortunately, that meant we now had another mouth to feed. My cook was furious when she discovered Grauer would be moving in with us.

~

It was February when Father finally wrote that I could visit him on the front. I asked Sauerbruch for a full month's leave because the travel alone would take over a week.

"Are you sure you want to go to Russia in the winter? The cold there is beyond your most horrible nightmare." Sauerbruch knew whereof he spoke, having been stationed on the eastern front for part of the war. "Take your furs with you."

On the last day before my departure, he patted my shoulder and said, "Keep your eyes open, Stahle, and you'll learn much." By that time, we were past formalities, and he called me by my surname like all the other surgeons. In private, he called me, "Margarethe," but to me, he was always, "*Herr Doktor*."

Reaching the eastern front required several changes of transportation— train, motorcar, even horseback. For one leg, I rode in a horse-drawn sleigh, which reminded me of my youth. I was very glad I had listened to Sauerbruch and worn my fur coat. I wore a scarf over my mouth to keep my breath from freezing.

When I arrived, Father enfolded me in his arms in a long, silent embrace. After the greetings were done and my luggage was dispatched to the head nurse's tent, he ordered me to report to the soldier's mess, where I was to help serve food to our troops. The meat looked stringy, the sauce gray, and the potatoes watery, but the men ate that miserable slop like it was the finest Parisian fare. They tipped their caps as I spooned their meager rations onto their tin plates. Some made a little bow after I served them, murmuring, "God bless you, *Gnädige*." Although I was still dressed in my traveling clothes and not looking particularly grand, they all seemed to know who I was. In a military camp, information spreads like fire.

Father and I ate at a private table in the officer's mess, where the food was barely a step up from what the common soldiers ate. "I would have asked them to prepare something better in honor of your arrival," Father explained, "but there wasn't time and there isn't much to be had. The shortages in Russia make our rations seem lavish. The Russian soldiers are starving. They die at their posts, and their bodies freeze to their artillery."

In the light of the kerosene lantern, I could see that the lines in my father's face had deepened into chasms. The creases around his mouth were like sabre slashes. "You look tired, Father. Are you well?"

He nodded. "As well as I can be on little sleep."

"I won't keep you long," I promised.

"No, Grethe, stay a while. Who knows when I shall have your company again?"

"You look so sad."

"The war is not going our way."

"That is obvious to everyone. What can I do to cheer you up?"

He managed another sad smile. "I would love to hear you sing."

"Tomorrow when we are both rested, I promise to sing for you."

"Perhaps you can sing for the men. Morale here is low, and I think a little music might raise their spirits. It's supposed to be warm for the next few days. Would you sing a little concert?"

I studied his pale eyes. "You're not joking."

"No, I am entirely serious."

"When?"

"Tomorrow evening?"

The idea of singing a concert with no preparation was unnerving, but I saw a little spark of hope in my father's eyes, and I couldn't bear to extinguish it.

"A program of student songs and *Lieder*?" I suggested. "Will that do?"

"Perfect," he replied. He reached out and covered my hand with his. "You are a good daughter."

278   The Imperative of Desire

The next day, a decent piano was found in a nearby school. A professional pianist among the officers volunteered to accompany me. The soldiers constructed a make-shift stage of planks and tent cloth.

As I sang, I ignored the sound of mortar fire rumbling in the distance and the flashes lighting up the night sky. Instead, I focused on the faces of those weary and terrified young men bundled in their blankets against the cold. I could see how the music soothed them. After a few familiar *Lieder*, I abandoned the planned program and added some popular songs to encourage them to sing along. The lyrics were unabashedly sentimental, nearly every one a paean to home and mother. I fought to keep my voice from breaking when I saw the bright tears running down the faces of the men in the front row.

"Well done," my father said and put his arm around my shoulders as he walked me to my tent.

～

My main purpose in coming to the front was not to entertain the troops nor make empty gestures of care by serving in the mess tent. The next day, I asked to be shown to the field hospital. Although the staff had been informed that I intended to work alongside them, they glared at me when I donned a gown and mask. Even so, none of them dared to say a word because my father was their commander.

The immediacy of seeing the wounded arrive fresh from the battlefield was nothing like I'd imagined. The scent of blood left a metallic taste in my mouth as I cut, sawed, and sutured the troops' torn and battered flesh. My colleagues seemed surprised that I didn't faint. They seemed even more surprised that I was able to keep up with the rapid flow of incoming wounded. This earned me some grudging respect from the other surgeons. Afterwards, they invited me to join them in the officer's mess for a drink.

The head nurse's tent, where I was quartered, was spacious and outfitted with every convenience including a coal stove for warmth.

"Forgive me for saying so, Countess, but I'm surprised at how well you've adapted to camp life."

I suppose she'd expected me to be merely the spoiled daughter of my aristocratic father. To dispel her assumptions, I recounted some of my adventures as a child in the cadets' summer camp.

"What an interesting upbringing you've had," she said in a formal voice. Other than that she had little to say.

Her staff remained equally distant. Unfortunately, I was accustomed to being viewed suspiciously by nurses. Despite my gender, which might incline them to solidarity, I was a physician, and above them in the medical hierarchy. As with any nurses, I had to earn their respect the hard way.

After a particularly horrific day in the hospital tent, one of them invited me to their tent for tea. It turned out the main beverage being offered was vodka. After we emptied two bottles, we were laughing together like old friends. "We're so glad you have taken an interest in what we're doing, *Frau Doktor*. Sometimes, it seemed we've been forgotten."

"You are not forgotten," I assured them. "Everyone is praying for this war to end and for you to come home."

"Will it be soon?" They all looked at me expectantly.

Obviously, I couldn't tell them what my father had shared. "We can only hope."

～

On my last night at the front, my father and I shared a private dinner in his tent. He had a special meal prepared for us. Unfortunately, it was as tasteless as all the others I'd eaten in the camp. The meager portion of meat was unidentifiable, and I wouldn't have been surprised to learn it had come from an injured horse.

We spoke of things at home, where the new farm manager seemed to have things in hand. I could tell that Father was distracted because I had to ask some questions twice. It was only when we each held a glass of brandy that he shared what was on his mind.

"The war is turning against us," he said, "and I've heard something that greatly troubles me."

Instead of asking him to explain, I allowed my silence to encourage him to say more.

He stared into the flame of the kerosene lamp. "The troops are tired.

Our reserves have all been called up. Now, we are sacrificing those who remain." He threw down the brandy in his glass. "I've heard rumors of things so despicable I can hardly bear to speak of them."

"You know I shall never tell another soul."

"Yes, Margarethe, I know I can trust you."

My father described a horrifying scheme. The senior military had already realized the war was lost and were secretly suing for peace with the Allies. Meanwhile, they continued to send the troops into hopeless skirmishes. The idea was to encourage the soldiers to fight on while the generals were preparing for surrender. On the seas, our navy, far inferior to the British Navy, had been kept in port for most of the war to prevent it from being sacrificed. Now, our vessels were suddenly sent out to sea to engage the enemy.

"We are sending our men into battle, knowing it's futile. The men aren't stupid. Sooner or later, they will catch on and there will be hell to pay."

"How can you go along with this, Father?"

He raised his shoulders. "What can I do? I've sworn an oath of loyalty to the Kaiser."

"Is there nothing you can do? The Kaiser listens to you…perhaps if you spoke to him."

Father shook his head. "This is beyond the Kaiser's control now."

After that, we drank our brandy in silence. Gazing at my father in the lamp light, I perceived that the persistent rosiness in his cheeks came from alcohol, his only solace on those long, lonely nights at the front. I could practically feel the weight of the horrible responsibility on his shoulders. I tried to think of something to cheer him, but I sensed there was nothing I could do. The knowledge made me moody on the long trip back to Munich.

I reflected that I'd learned much from my time at the front, and not only about battlefield surgery. I'd seen firsthand that the glamor of military life that I'd imagined as a child was mere window dressing for the horror of war. I was grateful that, as a woman, I could not be conscripted. After seeing the heroic parades replaced by the streams of broken men, I'd finally lost my desire to be a soldier.

〜

I debriefed Sauerbruch on my return. "Was it as cold as I'd predicted?"

"Colder."

"But you can see now why I sent you?"

"Yes. The ideal preparation for a prosthesis is in the field. Unfortunately, in the heat of battle, when lives hang in the balance, such niceties are far from anyone's mind."

"A shame because we could do so much more with the cooperation of field surgeons. There will be many who can never walk again because the surgeon couldn't be bothered to think ahead."

To my surprise, Sauerbruch took me off amputations. He said he had plenty of acolytes who could hack off a limb. He had identified me as a "belly cutter," as abdominal surgeons are irreverently called, and began to steer me in that direction. By that time, I had only a few months of my residency remaining. My mentor had already indicated that he would take me on as his assistant. My appointment to attending surgeon was a foregone conclusion.

My career was proceeding swimmingly, but I failed to notice that my home life was disintegrating. In many ways, the unraveling of my relationship with Hanna was a mirror of the chaos on the streets. As the riots grew louder and more violent, Hanna spent more time at political meetings and came home increasingly agitated. Meanwhile, my work consumed me, so I seldom saw her or my children.

In late summer, I was shocked to hear that the Czar's family had been executed. I thought back on that elegant summer evening and remembered the curious stares of the young grand duchesses at an outrageously bold German countess. Those innocent girls, whom I'd dismissed as spoiled, now lay dead at the bottom of a ditch. Gregor Oblensky had been a more faithful correspondent than my husband, but I'd not heard from him in over a year. Now, I feared for his life.

Finally, we were told how dire the situation was. From the steady flow of wounded to my operating table, I needed no official announcement to tell me how badly things were going. Yet, I was as shocked as anyone to hear on November 5 that King Ludwig of Bavaria had abdicated. This news was followed only days later by the abdication of the Kaiser. Despite the rumors of a cease fire, the trains of wounded continued to arrive from the front because the battles had raged until the final moment. I was up to my elbows in gore when the newspapers hit the streets, so I only read about the armistice much later in the day.

The war was finally over.

~

Battered men kept arriving from what used to be the front, but now, we also had the trauma from the street fighting to contend with. Kicking and slamming the soft parts with rifle butts or truncheons can cause injuries that need a surgeon's intervention.

For me, the political noise in the background was like the drone of a conversation in another room. I tried to ignore it, but I couldn't. As the stress cracks increased between the workers and their capitalist masters, they grew between Hanna and me. Our conversations became more intense, then heated, and finally, loud and angry.

After a particularly acrimonious argument, Hanna left the house. When she didn't come home that night, I called the few friends we had in common, but no one had seen her. Naturally, I was anxious. The children were inconsolable. They begged for her to kiss them and tuck them into bed. It broke my heart to tell them she wasn't there.

I could plainly see the void her absence left. It forced me to appreciate how devoted to me and my children she'd been, a partner in every way. She gave herself completely when we made love. She was an enthusiastic and generous lover in return. She always had an encouraging word when things went wrong in the surgery, or I came home grieving after losing a patient. She soothingly rubbed my back and told me it wasn't my fault, even when it was.

She was the one to whom the children went with their little hurts, who solved the household issues, who made certain my brandy decanter was always full. When I was so ill with the influenza, she had nursed me back to health, despite her own illness. Hanna took care of me so perfectly that

I never missed her until she was gone. Like so many busy professionals, I had neglected my "wife" until it was too late.

Three days passed, and I was near despair. Even Sauerbruch noticed. "What's the matter with you, Stahle?" he asked gruffly, although I could see from his expression that the question came from kindness.

"Nothing at all, *Herr Doktor*," I replied casually. His skeptical look told me he wasn't taken in.

Fortunately for all of us, Hanna came home. She was with the children when I arrived from the hospital after a long day in surgery. My son and daughter were so happy to see her they could barely spare me a glance while she read to them. When she looked up from the book and saw me, she kissed the children and sent them to find their nurse.

I took her in my arms and nearly crushed the life out of her. "Be gentle," she advised. "I can break."

I touched her face and her lips, trying to remember the wonderful feel of them with my fingertips. "I've been so worried about you! Where have you been?"

"Never mind. I've come home, and that's what is important."

I embraced her again, this time more gently.

"Margarethe, we must talk."

The salutation made me instantly alert. She never called me by my full name unless she was angry or had something important to say.

"Let's sit down." I led her to my sitting room. She gazed out the window while I poured a glass of brandy for her.

"Thank you," she murmured when I put the glass in her hand.

I took a seat opposite her and gazed at her expectantly, but it took an inordinate amount of time for her to open the conversation.

"I've missed you," she finally said. Her eyes held that tender look I treasured. "I love you with all my heart, but I fear our differences are too great."

My heart lurched with anxiety. "No, you can't mean that, Hanna. Please, no!"

"I'm afraid I do."

"Suppose we agree not to discuss politics?" I asked, trying to keep the desperation out of my voice.

"Avoiding discussion of our beliefs doesn't change them."

"No, but it will prevent arguments like the one that drove you away."

She gazed at me indulgently and sighed. "Sometimes, I forget you are so young. You've achieved so much at an early age, but really, you're no more than a girl."

I was so desperate that I disregarded what I might ordinarily have considered an insult. "Please, Hanna. I've been miserable since you left. I haven't told you enough how much I appreciate you, how I value you.… how I *need* you…"

She laughed softly. "You finally noticed?"

I knelt beside her. "Please, don't go," I begged.

She caressed my cheek with her fingertips. "All right, my darling. Let's try again, and I agree, no more talk of politics. At least not until things settle down."

I could not imagine when that would be. Every day it seemed the street fighting and riots became worse.

⌇

Through mutual effort, our domestic scene remained relatively peaceful, even as the political situation grew increasingly tense. Violent revolutions never really benefit anyone. The chaos caused by a political vacuum disrupts everything from the train schedules to the food supply. That in turn, causes even more unrest and more chaos. But this pot had been bubbling for so long that it simply had to overflow.

The Social Democrats cravenly enlisted leaders of the disbanded Imperial Army to defend the government. Especially in Prussia, where the military elite were firmly entrenched, there was long-standing loyalty to military leaders. My father was one of them. He had organized a Freikorps unit drawn from a division that included his former regiment. It had surrendered in Bavaria, so when the situation in Munich became increasingly unstable, he was ordered to relocate his troops to the outskirts of the city.

He sent a message by courier when he arrived. I invited him to dinner and asked Sauerbruch to join us. Fortunately, for the sake of my pact with Hanna, there was no political talk at the table. We spoke of music instead. Afterwards, I entertained our guests with *Lieder*. It was an entirely civilized evening such as we'd enjoyed before the war. Even Hanna seemed lighthearted.

While Freikorps were stationed outside the city, it was calm. Father came for dinner whenever he felt it was safe to leave his troops. Now that the Imperial Army had been disbanded, his only authority came from the force of his own personality and the loyalty of his men, so he felt the need to keep a close eye on them.

The brief calm made it seem that life had gone back to normal. The shops reopened. People went for walks in the Hofgarten. Nurses pushed their young charges along in prams. The theaters sold tickets to live performances. At the Bayerische Staatsoper, Lilli Lehmann sang a concert of Mozart arias.

Then someone threw a bomb through a bank window, which set off a riot. I heard from an eyewitness that the police tried to contain the violence at first, but they quickly realized they were overwhelmed. They retreated and sent for the Freikorps. According to my father, his troops had orders to shoot into the air, not the crowd, but something went wrong. A soldier fired his rifle at some men throwing rocks and Molotov cocktails. Then all the Freikorps troops began to fire into the crowd.

While all this was going on in the streets, I was in the middle of a routine hemorrhoidectomy at the *Klinikum*. Sauerbruch shouted into the theater: "Stahle! Incoming wounded from a street riot! Hurry up!" I left my assistant to close the surgical wound and headed to join Sauerbruch in the ambulance receiving area.

All the lessons from my brief stint as a field surgeon stood me in good stead. The wounded kept arriving with bullet wounds, lacerations by glass or other sharp objects, blunt force trauma, and burns. It was like the war all over again. I went from one patient to the next without so much as a moment's pause.

When I went out to find my next case in the triage area, I saw Hanna standing on the other side of the room. She glared at me. "Your father caused this!" she shouted, pointing to the dead on stretchers awaiting transport to the morgue. "Look at them! He killed them!"

The nurses and orderlies turned around to stare at me. Everyone momentarily fell silent. Hanna turned and left. The sound of the door slamming behind her reverberated in the room. For a long moment, there was a murmur of confusion. Then we all went back to work.

～

By the time I returned home, Hanna had left and taken all of her things with her. As before, her absence left the children bereft. They cried and crawled into my lap, begging me to read them a story. I recited Oscar Wilde's "The Happy Prince" from memory, but it was not the same. My stories had no pictures, and there was no lovely Hanna with her warm lap and soft breasts to comfort them. We all wept together—I silently, they, wailing and snotty.

I waited for two days before I searched for her, hoping she would learn that the disaster had not been my fault, nor even my father's. His ragtag little army had not followed his orders.

I inquired among our common friends, but none of them had any idea where Hanna had gone. I went to the police, but they had their hands full trying to keep order, and they were no help. Finally, I hired a private detective, but even he couldn't find her. She had simply vanished.

Meanwhile, my father withdrew the Freikorps. I was shocked when someone at the hospital told me. Apparently, Father had disbanded the Freikorps unit against the orders of the government. No one would dare stop the great hero of the eastern front, and he had left the city without a word. A week later, he finally telephoned me to say he had returned to Edelheim with fifty of his most loyal men.

"I couldn't do it anymore, Margarethe. Innocent people were being killed.

"But the police can't control the riots."

"They must learn. The military can't be at war with our own people."

Unfortunately, the withdrawal of the Freikorps only made matters worse. The Spartacists were emboldened by the absence of the military and knew the police weren't strong enough to put down the unrest. It wasn't long after my father left when another riot erupted. Again, Sauerbruch interrupted my surgery—something mundane, if I recall, removing a cyst from a woman's neck. I made quick work of the close, and I fear the woman ended up with a more prominent scar than she would have otherwise.

This time, we were forced to operate in the triage room, which now resembled a field hospital. There was blood everywhere, cut-off clothing and bandages up to the mid-calf. The wounded and the dead lay side-by-side on stretchers going into the hallway. The only surgical assistant available was a student nurse. Fortunately, she was exceptionally good. I went from one patient to the next without so much as a moment to catch my breath. As a patient was stabilized, he or she was carried off and the next appeared. Only a bucket of water flung on the tabletop cleared away the prior patient's blood.

I turned away to wipe the sweat from my brow and take a deep breath. When I pulled back the sheet covering my next patient, the sight that greeted me was like a blow to the chest. Lying on my table, ashen, blue-lipped, and barely breathing was my Hanna. A quick survey of her wounds revealed a bullet had ripped through her gut and exited through a kidney. Not even the most skilled surgeon under the most ideal conditions could save her. I put my ear to her chest. She was still alive, but barely. Her pulse was rapid and weak.

"Hanna, darling," I whispered near her ear.

She opened her eyes and looked into mine.

"It's Grethe."

She couldn't speak, but she closed her eyes and opened them to acknowledge that she'd heard. At least, that's what I hoped the gesture meant.

"I want you to know that I love you," I said, squeezing her hand. "I have always loved you."

For the briefest moment, I saw that look of tenderness I treasured.

While I held her hand and gazed into her eyes, all the noise and confusion around me receded. Someone shouted my name. I paid no attention, continuing to hold Hanna's hand.

First, her grip relaxed. Then, her eyes closed. A moment later, she was gone.

Although I knew there could be repercussions for leaving my post, I personally escorted the stretcher bearing Hanna's sheet-draped body to the morgue. Otherwise, it would have landed in the hallway with the unclaimed dead. I would not chance her burial in a common grave.

Once the stretcher bearers departed, the pathologist under whom I'd trained as a medical student came into the cold room to bring me a tag.

"Was she known to you?" he asked gently.

I nodded my assent because I couldn't speak. He offered me his fountain pen so that I could write her vital information on the tag. After I tied it on Hanna's still-warm toe, I admired her feet—long, elegant and beautifully shaped. It was cold in the room. Her body would cool fast. I pulled down the sheet from her face and kissed her full lips, pale but still beautiful. I went to the pathologist's office and returned his pen before heading upstairs.

∿

The next day, I arranged for the funeral in the church where I had once sung in the choir with Christina. I bought a plot in the Waldfriedhof cemetery, where Hanna was interred with great dignity. On my free days, I often walked to her grave to lay flowers, usually a single white rose.

I couldn't find words to explain Hanna's absence to the children, so I never spoke about it. Not with anyone. Sauerbruch knew what had happened because he saw the notes I made in the mortality and morbidity report. The report for that week was over thirty pages long.

He came into the scrub room where I was preparing for surgery and said, "I'm sorry." He put a fatherly hand on my shoulder and gave it a squeeze. That was all.

I couldn't weep. I couldn't scream. I was simply empty inside as if all of my vitality had been drained and gone into the grave with Hanna. For the first time in my life, I could not sing nor make music of any kind.

16

A few months after Hanna died, Lytton came home in the uniform of a lieutenant of the British medical corps. The children looked at him suspiciously, which was no surprise. Our daughter, Elisabeth, had never laid eyes on him, and Willi had been an infant when he'd left.

Lytton opened his arms, naively expecting a joyous reunion, but the children ran to hide in my skirts. Their father persisted in courting them with his brilliant smile until Willi warmed to him enough to sit on his knee for an instant. I was relieved when the children's nurse came to take them to supper.

"The children have grown so much, haven't they?" I said, taking Lytton's offered arm as we headed to the dining room.

"Yes, they are absolutely splendid. They look just like their mother."

"Oh, I don't know. I think Willi favors you. He has your lovely mouth."

Lytton smiled, but he looked pale and distracted during dinner. He toyed with the food on his plate and ate almost nothing. I watched with disapproval because wasting food while people went hungry was unconscionable. The Allies seemed determined to starve their vanquished enemies with their heavy-handed "peace" treaty, and food was still scarce. Finally, I perceived his lack of appetite came not from disdain for the food, but something burdening his mind.

"Lytton, what's wrong?"

"I was about to ask you the same. You look grim."

"It's been difficult," I replied vaguely.

"I surmised as much. I was going to ask what happened to your companion."

"She's gone."

"So, I see, but the new housekeeper you've hired seemed pleasant enough." I glowered at him across the table. How like a man to miss the obvious difference between the woman I cherished and a pleasant housekeeper! But how could I fault him for his blindness? Hadn't we agreed to overlook one another's sexual escapades?

Lytton finally pushed his plate away. "I'm sorry. I still can't quite get past all the horrors I saw in the war." I gave him a physician's critical look and saw that his face was pinched. He gave me a wan smile in return and stared at his wine glass as he swirled the claret. "The mustard gas was a horror. So many men are blind or can hardly breathe."

"At least, they are alive," I said. Unbidden, my mind revisited the bloody ruins I'd seen on my operating theater, the sight of the coffins being unloaded from the military trains, the acres of new graves in the cemetery. A whole generation of young men had been lost and for what?

"Yes, I suppose we should be grateful for that," agreed Lytton. "But who will employ them now? Some have no legs, no hands to do work. What will we do with all these shattered people?"

"That, my dear, is a very good question."

"I understand that Konrad has been active in advocating the cause of wounded veterans."

"Yes, he has. Since you left, he's been admitted to the bar, but I think a political career is in the cards for him."

"An ideal profession for him. He certainly has the gift of gab." Lytton's brief smile faded, and he looked introspective. "Meg, I'm sorry, but I came because I have something to tell you. I've hesitated because I haven't determined the best way to say it."

"Well, then spit it out. You know I'm rather the tough sort." My mind briefly entertained the possibilities. Perhaps he wanted a divorce or to remain in England permanently. More likely, he needed money.

He took a deep breath. "Meg, you must go to Edelheim to see your father. I stopped there on my way down. I fear things are not going well."

I'd heard almost nothing since Father had withdrawn to our country home except the telephone call to say that he had arrived. I'd been too taken up in my own worries to notice. Long silences between us were not unusual, especially when Father was posted overseas or, more recently, at the front, but something in Lytton's tone made me anxious. I made an effort to steady my voice. "Tell me more."

He passed me the wine decanter so that I might refill my glass. "The situation is difficult to describe. You must really see for yourself."

"Is everyone at home well?"

"In the main," he said, frowning. "You should go to Edelheim and have a look."

"Will you accompany me?"

"That's why I came down here…to go back with you…and to see the children, of course."

"Of course."

After dinner, I tried to draw him out regarding the situation at Edelheim, but he stubbornly refused to produce additional details. When it came time for bed, he asked if he could sleep with me.

"Only if you have condoms. God knows with whom you've shared your bed since we've been apart. Never mind that I have no intention of ever being pregnant again!"

He chuckled. "I have them, but I only want to hold you in my arms so I can remember that there is still some beauty in the world."

We ended up making love because we both needed to feel close to someone. It felt so strange to be with a man after the tender lovemaking I'd shared with Hanna. Not that Lytton wasn't tender. For a man of his size, he could be exquisitely gentle, but in order to arouse myself enough to take Lytton into my body, I needed to think of Hanna. He moved slowly and deeply inside me, kissing me, and murmuring endearments. Try as he might, he was unable to satisfy me. After his climax, he wept like a child against my breast.

"I love you, Meg. I truly love you," he murmured, wetting my skin with his tears. I stroked his blond hair to soothe him, but I couldn't return the words because I was thinking of Hanna.

∽

Sauerbruch was reluctant to give me leave because we were still short-handed. "Don't dally," he warned with a scowl. "I need you back here. Stat!"

Lytton and I reserved a berth on the night train from Munich to Berlin. We made love to the gentle rocking of the train. I hadn't realized how much I'd missed him, but afterwards, when he held me in his powerful arms, a few errant tears escaped my eyes. I was weeping for Hanna, and it was for her arms that I longed.

"It's so good to feel you close," whispered Lytton.

I wiped away my tears with my fingertips, so he wouldn't see. "What will you do now that the war is over?"

"I don't quite know," he said, sitting up carefully because the ceiling of the berth was low. "I don't think I have the patience to return to the museum. I might go to Italy. One of my friends is opening a new site for excavation."

I forced a smile to hide my disappointment. I should have known it was too much to expect that he'd want to remain and become acquainted with his children. Although the idea of being a father seemed to intrigue him, it was probably nothing more than a charming abstraction.

"How long will you stay?"

In the lights flickering by outside the train window, I could see his pensive look. "Until you sort things out," he said.

"Is it that bad at Edelheim?"

He shook his head. "You'll see when you get there." He smiled brightly. "Nothing you can't manage. Now let's get some sleep."

When we arrived at Edelheim, my father's adjutant, Hermann Klowitz, whom I remembered from my visit to the front, was at the station to meet us. He made a deep formal bow and addressed me by the old titles before explaining that he had been appointed majordomo of Edelheim. On the drive to the *Schloss*, I tried to extract a report on my parents, but Klowitz would only say that they were in good health.

Mother was quite animated, even cheerful, when she greeted us, which instantly made me wary, even more so when she carried on over Lytton. She had never made a secret of her contempt for him.

"Where's Father?" I asked, handing off my coat to Klowitz.

Mother and Lytton exchanged an anxious look which deepened my suspicion.

"He's upstairs. Why don't you have something to eat," Mother suggested. "Then you can look in on your father."

"I'll go up and give him my greetings. I'll be but a minute." I nudged Lytton to head to the dining room.

When I opened the door to Father's rooms, it was pitch black inside. Only a sharp gash of light showed through a break in the drawn curtains. Fortunately, it provided enough illumination for me to navigate.

"Hello, Margarethe," said my father, evidently recognizing my step on the floorboards. "Your mother said you were coming, but I didn't expect you so early."

"We took the night train to Berlin."

"Ah, so that explains it."

Although my eyes had adjusted to the light, I switched on a lamp on a nearby table so that I could see him better. Father put up his hand to shade his eyes. I gasped when I saw how changed he was from the man I was used to seeing. Unshaven, sitting in only his trousers and a singlet, his feet bare, he looked appalling. I struggled to avoid showing my shock. Instead, I averted my eyes, which alighted on a half-empty bottle of whiskey. An empty bottle stood beside it.

"Do you have any cigarettes?" Father asked, holding up a crumbled packet. The ashtray beside him overflowed with ash and crushed cigarette butts. The entire room stank of stale smoke.

"Perhaps you should give your lungs a rest."

"Hah, that's what I get for having a physician in the family. Unsolicited advice!" He coughed bronchially. "I suppose you're right."

"You know I'm right," I said, sitting down in a chair near his.

"What brings you to Edelheim, Margarethe? I thought you were overwhelmed by your training."

"It is demanding, to be sure, but Lytton thought I should come home."

"Did he now? I'm sure he was disturbed to see me in this state when he visited."

"Does that surprise you?"

"No." He looked away. "I would have cleaned myself up for your arrival had I known you'd be so early." He rubbed his bristly throat and managed a weak smile. "It's rather embarrassing for my daughter to see me like this."

I sighed. "I am your daughter, and I take you however you come, but you would certainly smell better if you'd bathed."

He laughed, but the laughter instantly devolved into a phlegmy cough. He spat into his handkerchief. After clearing his throat several times, he said, "I'll bathe after we talk."

"I'll ring the maid to run your bath," I volunteered, rising.

"No, sit down. We haven't talked much since I saw you in Munich," he observed, running his fingers through his greasy hair.

"Do you know what happened after you left?"

He took a deep breath and let out a long sigh reeking of stale alcohol. "The riots got worse."

"Yes, they did. Much worse. And the police couldn't control them without the support of the Freikorps. Whatever possessed you to leave?"

He sat back in his chair. It creaked a little as he leaned back. "When I called up my troops, I never expected them to shoot our own people."

"So why did you form a Freikorps?"

"My soldiers were roaming around leaderless. They were raping women and stealing from people who had nothing. I thought if I provided some leadership..."

"I'm sure your intentions were good, but how could you be so naive as to think the Social Democrats wouldn't use you to put down the revolution?"

"Of course, I knew. What I didn't expect was that the soldiers wouldn't obey my commands. They were always loyal to me."

"The old chain of command is dead. They'd had a taste of rebellion. I know next to nothing about politics, but even I could see what was coming. I'm surprised you didn't."

"Yes, it was naive, but I'd been raised to follow orders without question. And to think we went to Russia to prevent a revolution, and now it's here." He reached for the whiskey bottle, but I took it out of his hand. He reached farther, but I held my hand away. Finally, he nodded in acquiescence. "Are you sure you don't have a cigarette?"

I dug into the pocket of my skirt and took out my cigarette case and spirit lighter. He looked sublimely relieved as he inhaled the smoke.

"I heard there were many deaths in that riot."

"Yes, there were. Hanna was one of them."

"Oh no! My God, I had no idea…I know she was your friend. You were very fond of her."

My mouth twisted into a bitter smile at the euphemistic word, "fond." I suddenly couldn't bear the sight of him, so I got up to set the whiskey bottle on the drinks stand and out of reach.

"Grethe, I am truly sorry about Hanna. I know you cared for her."

"Apologies cannot bring her back."

He hung his head, staring at his bare feet and sighed. "Everything about the revolution is a disaster. We'll be lucky if they don't seize our lands."

"Konrad says the government needs our support now, so he doubts that will happen. He says that military men like you hold much sway on the new government."

"I'm done with that government. I'm done with the army. I'm done with all of it! I've brought my best men home with me. I've given those who want it land to farm. Some are serving in the household."

"Yes, Klowitz came to meet us at the station. He says he's the new majordomo."

"Yes, and he makes a good one."

"I'll call him to help you clean yourself up and dress you."

"No, I can do it myself. I don't want him to see me like this."

"I'll run your bath." I left to turn on the bath. When I returned, I said, "You should invite Veronika to visit. Perhaps that would encourage you to keep yourself tidier."

He crushed out his cigarette. "That's done now. I've made my peace with your mother. If I'm to live here, we can't be at odds all the time It's a big house, but it's not that big."

"Peace at home would be a good thing." We talked about the farm for a few minutes. "Your bath should be almost ready." He struggled to rise. I held him by the armpit to help him balance. "Would you like me to help you into the bath, Father?"

"God forbid, I should let my daughter see me naked!"

"Then let me call Klowitz or one of the footmen to help you."

"I can do it," he protested, carefully putting one foot ahead of the other.

"I'll wait outside until you're finished," I called after him, "to make sure you don't drown."

He chuckled at that, although it wasn't the least bit funny. I sat down on the sofa and picked up the newspaper to read while I waited, but I found it was a week old. There was a knock at the door, and Lytton poked his head into the room. "How goes it?"

I waved for him to come in.

"Have you had some lunch?" I asked.

"Yes, I was famished, and it hit the spot," he said, patting his belly. He sat down beside me. "Where is he?"

"Bathing."

"Thank God! He stank when I was here the last time. Now you can see why you needed to come home." He glanced around, taking in the mess. "I can wait for your father, if you want to go down to eat."

"Thank you, but I can wait. I need to make sure he gets out of the bathtub alive."

Lytton nodded and opened his cigarette case to offer me one. He lit it with his spirit lighter. "Unfortunately, I have no idea how to advise you," he said on a stream of smoke. Then he looked at me in surprise. "When did you start smoking?"

"It relieves the tension. All the surgeons smoke like chimneys."

He picked an errant piece of tobacco off his tongue. "And now my wife does too."

"Your wife does many things you don't know about. The lives of women have changed since the war. Now, we come and go as we please."

He grinned. "You always came and went as you pleased."

"Yes, I did."

"How can I help here?" he asked with a thoughtful look.

"This is not your worry. It's my burden to bear."

He smiled broadly. "That's the only reason why I offer my help, because you're perfectly capable of handling it yourself." He turned his head to exhale smoke. "Will you stay on here?"

"Not if I can avoid it. I have my own duties, and Father is the master here. It's his duty to look after Edelheim. My time will come soon enough."

Lytton regarded me curiously. "You sound angry."

"Does that surprise you? If not for the retreat of his bloody Freikorps, many people would still be alive."

"Obviously, the old man is overcome with guilt or he wouldn't be in this state."

"You mean he's wallowing in guilt."

Lytton drew back a little and regarded me with a frown. "That's a bit harsh, isn't it?"

"No. He's responsible for many deaths, including Hanna's."

I could see the exact moment when understanding dawned in Lytton's mind. He glanced away while his mind processed the information. "I see," he finally said. "It was like that, was it?"

"Yes, like that exactly."

"Oh dear." He reached over and put his arm around me. "I am so sorry, Meg. So very sorry."

"Thank you," I said, gripping his thigh to banish the insistent tears.

We sat in gloomy silence in that foul-smelling room until my father, wrapped in his dressing gown, returned.

I gave him a hard look.

"Better?" he asked, smoothing back his wet hair.

"Much."

"Now, get out, both of you and send me Klowitz. I wish to dress."

That was exactly the message I wanted to hear. "Come, Lytton. Let's give my father some privacy."

That night, Father appeared for dinner, properly groomed and attired in one of his favorite English dinner jackets. As we ate, he spoke of his plans for building a sawmill and listened intently to Lytton's report on the state of things in England, where they were also overwhelmed by the return of broken men.

After dinner, we listened to my mother play the piano. When she went up to bed, Lytton joined my father in a game of billiards. I wasn't in the mood, so I sat back and watched.

I tried to caution father away from more brandy. "Your liver won't thank you, Father."

"Oh, for God's sake, Margarethe! Can't you give up being a doctor for one blessed moment?"

"No. I won't have you wrecking your body with alcohol."

"Now that you're here to crack the whip, that's unlikely," said Father with a droll expression. Then he sighed. "Certainly, there are enough sorrows to go around." He threw down a glass of brandy. "That damned Ludendorff, I could kill him."

"I thought you were friends," I said, surprised by his adamance.

"We were…until he started spreading rumors that the pacifists and the revolutionaries at home caused our losses. That we were being stabbed in the back by our own people. According to him, that's why we lost the war. It's a bloody lie, of course. We all knew he was only trying to shift the blame away from the incompetence of the Kaiser and his faithless generals, but the rumor spread, and now everyone believes it. Most of the socialists are Jews, whom people hate anyway, so they want to believe the lie."

"Why do people hate the Jews?" I asked, speaking my thought aloud. "I never understood it."

"It makes no sense to me either. It's irrational," Father said. "Perhaps it goes back to the usury laws forbidding Christians to lend money. More likely, jealousy of their success in business and the professions. You should ask your friend, Professor Seidl, for his opinion."

"Some people claim the Jews killed Jesus," said Lytton in a scholarly tone. "That's completely false, of course. Only the Romans crucified the condemned."

"It's nothing but stupid, ignorant prejudice, ingrained for centuries," I said impatiently, "but it is a fact that Jews are prominent in the Social Democrats."

Father looked surprised. "How do you know so much about politics?"

I shrugged. "Your nephew explained it to me, and I once had a friend who was involved in politics."

With sad eyes, Father searched my face. "I am truly sorry about your Hanna. Will you ever forgive me?"

"Perhaps someday, but not soon."

I had never spoken so harshly to my father. Lytton gave me a curious look, but he said nothing.

~

We decided to stay on until the end of the week so that I could ride out with the farm manager. Not surprisingly, our tenants and the townspeople were faring better than the people in cities simply because they had a steady, local source of food. However, currency values were erratic, so barter had replaced the usual economy. Parts to repair farm equipment were hard to find. The tenants had adapted by plowing with draft horses and harvesting the hay and grain with scythes. Watching them work with such ancient implements was oddly calming.

Despite attending to business, Lytton and I found time for pleasure riding and picnics by the lake. The wonderful spell of leisure was restorative after so many years of hardship and grief. Father's mood improved with each passing day. At first, I suspected that he was merely putting on a brave face for my benefit, but as he fell into the rhythm of his normal routine, he became more like his old self.

One night at dinner, he surprised everyone announcing that he would accompany us on our return. "The Berlin police chief is an old friend from the academy. He's been begging me to provide tactical support to deal with the riots."

I gave him a disapproving look. "I hope you're not thinking of organizing a Freikorps again."

"No, no. I'm done being a soldier. I don't mind advising the police, but I shall never, *ever* put on a military uniform again."

I could see from the determined set of his jaw that he meant what he said, and it was an important statement, because he had been a soldier his entire life.

Before we boarded the train the next day, Lytton shared his plan to go on to Rome and join his friends in their new excavation. I watched his luggage being carted away to the baggage car and wondered why I hadn't noticed that he'd brought all his belongings to Edelheim. He'd never planned to come home again. I'd felt him slipping away during our last days at Edelheim. The withdrawal had been palpable, exactly as when we returned from our trip to Garmisch before the war. I knew without his saying, that, in his mind, he was already with his friends in Rome.

We said our farewells to my father in Berlin and headed south. As we awaited the train for Rome on the platform of Munich's main station, I asked Lytton when he would return.

"Soon. I hope to get in some mountain climbing before the end of the season."

∼

I was overjoyed to hear that Elise returned from Vienna, where she had spent the better part of the war. At the first opportunity, I invited her to tea.

"So, you will finally finish your doctor's paper," I scolded gently as we settled in the library. "It's about time, don't you think?"

She gave me a look halfway between a smile and a scowl. "Margarethe, I'm not lazy. You have no idea how it is! Psychoanalysis is being pulled apart by rival factions. Of course, in any new movement there are conflicts and infighting. But I'm quite done with Freud since he broke with Otto." Of course, she expected me to know she was referring to Otto Rank, which I happened to remember from her letters.

"'Otto' is it now?" I raised my brows. "Are you involved?"

"No, of course not. There are rumors about other colleagues and students. As for myself, I've nearly been a nun."

I laughed outright at what I knew was a ridiculous statement. "I don't believe you." I put a sugar cube in my mouth to strain my tea over it like a Russian.

She gave me a sly look, which confirmed what I'd suspected. "Well, as for men outside the movement…that's another story for another time. First, I want to ask if I can use your library while I write my dissertation. It's my favorite place to work. All those volumes staring down on me are hard taskmasters, but very effective."

"My library is yours to use as you like."

"Good. I was hoping you would say that. I'm going to begin work as soon as I find a place to live."

My brows rose. "You're not moving back to your parents?"

"I couldn't possibly, not after living on my own for years. Don't get me wrong. I adore my parents and Rebekah, but I need my privacy. Speaking of which, what do you hear of Max?"

"He's back from the war unharmed. But Peter died in the Battle of the Somme."

She sighed sympathetically. "Such a talented man. He had so much promise. What a pity."

"Many talented men were lost in that insane war."

"And Lytton?"

""He returned briefly, but he's in Rome, digging in the ruins before everything is rebuilt and covers up the most important sites."

"A rolling stone…"

"Or a wandering Jew," I said, intentionally needling her.

"Don't be annoying, Margarethe. You know you can't get my goat." She reached for a tea sandwich. "Do you know anyone who might have an available flat?"

"Actually, I have an empty guest room. It needs freshening, but otherwise, you could move in at once."

"Really?"

"Hanna's room is available."

"She's gone?" Else looked genuinely surprised. "I thought you might have become lovers by now. Did you tire of her already?" I tried to control my face, apparently unsuccessfully. Elise put down her sandwich she'd been nibbling and reached for my hand. "Oh, Grethe. What happened?"

"She was killed in a street riot," I said in a quiet voice.

Elise stared at me in horror for an extended moment, "Dear God, I'm so sorry. I could see how much you cared for her."

"I did care for her," I admitted, "but she's gone now, and her room is empty." I managed a weak smile. "I would be happy if you moved into it. I certainly wouldn't mind the company at dinner."

"Knowing you, you're never home, and I'll be eating alone!"

"Yes, but when I am home, it's very quiet without someone else at the table."

"All right," said Elise after giving me a skeptical look. "I'll bring my things from my parents."

I offered Grauer's services to help her move.

Over dinner, Elise explained how she had become disillusioned with the psychoanalytic movement, especially after Jung split away from Freud. She tried to explain the intricacies of the various strains of psychological thought that had caused the rift. I was too fond of Elise to say so, but psychoanalytic theory bored me to tears.

"I briefly considered going to Zurich to study with Jung, but I decided it would be too great a distraction, so I decided to come back to Munich to finish my dissertation."

"A wise decision."

"You're only saying that because you're glad I'm back."

"No, I'm only saying it because I know how you lose your head with men."

She sighed, "And when I do, I can't get any work done."

"So, now you can be a nun here. We can have our own secular convent."

"Brilliant," she said. "We shall take vows together and singularly focus on our work."

Elise briefly moved into one of the smaller guest rooms while I had Hanna's freshened. As I watched the workmen tearing off the wallpaper, I felt like they were ripping away the last vestiges of Hanna's presence. I closed the door, so I couldn't see.

My conversations with Elise were as lively as before. In the evenings, she would tell me about her most interesting patients, always scrupulously withholding the details that would violate professional ethics. Sometimes, I would fall asleep. Fortunately, Elise took no offense and wrote it off to fatigue, which it was.

Small wonder that I was glad for the respite when Lytton came to Garmisch that summer for a mountain holiday. We invited Elise and Max to come along. Unfortunately, Konrad brought the annoying Franz Borchert, but somehow, I managed to put up with him. Lytton had also invited a few of his friends from the Rome project. I remembered some of them from our honeymoon, mostly because of their fine singing voices. We often sang together after dinner.

Up to a point, our soirees were cultural and edifying, but after some alcohol, my guests grew loud, sometimes obscene, which is why I was glad to have left the children in Munich with their nurse. I always encouraged Frau Weiss to leave immediately after tidying from dinner. Of course, the next day she'd return to a disaster in the kitchen, but I paid her handsomely, so she never complained. She and her husband probably crossed themselves and considered themselves lucky to be spared our lewd shenanigans.

Fortunately, she was never there to witness Lytton's friends prancing about in their skimpy outfits boldly showing off their wares. They performed gymnastics and choreographed "modern" dances reminiscent of Nijinsky's bold moves but far more suggestive.

"Why are men obsessed with their genitals?" I wondered aloud to Elise.

Elise turned her dark eyes on me and said, "My colleagues have many theories on that subject. Would you like to hear them?"

I shook my head. "Another time, when I am completely sober."

Obviously, I knew from previous conversations that much of psychoanalytic theory had to do with sex—too much of it, not enough of it, or experienced in the wrong context. After reading Fleiss's silly theories predicated on a simple bloody nose, I'd decided the whole enterprise was ridiculous. However, I dared not insult Elise by saying so.

$$\sim$$

At the end of the holiday, I went up to Berlin to see my father. He'd been there almost six months, providing tactical advice to the Berlin police in putting down the Spartacist uprising.

When we sat over after-dinner coffee that night, he suddenly said, "I've decided to turn this house over to you."

"Why? I have enough to look after. I don't need it."

"No, not now, but you might someday."

"Why not sell it?"

"Your grandfather built this house. He put a lot of thought and care into its construction. I would never sell it."

I shrugged. "So, keep it."

"No, I don't want the temptation to stay or return. I'm done with public life."

I didn't like the fatalistic sound of that, but I had an inkling of what had brought on the remark. Konrad had been lobbying Father to stand for office. His status as a war hero would have helped him easily win a Reichstag seat, but like most military men of his generation, my father found the concept of democracy incomprehensible. When they rounded up military leaders of the Kapp Putsch, I was very glad he had turned a deaf ear to Konrad's pleas and gone home.

In some ways, it was a shame. The new government could have used his leadership and expertise in logistics. Disorder reigned in our infant republic. Rotting garbage piled up in the streets and stank. The smell was so bad, people tied their handkerchiefs over their faces as they had during the influenza epidemic.

In July 1920, I sat before the panel examination board to demonstrate that I deserved certification as a surgeon. If I passed, I would be one of seven panel-certified female surgeons in the Republic. I would also be the youngest ever to receive certification in Bavaria. The examination itself was an historic event. As if I needed a further reminder, Sauerbruch and the dean of medicine at Ludwig-Maximilians sat in the audience to listen.

The examiners, all gray-haired men, stared at me. One peered over his pince-nez glasses and frowned, reminding me of Miss Burke, my long-ago headmistress at Chilton Hall. Sauerbruch had warned me that they would attempt to trip me with trick questions, so I had spent an inordinate amount of time studying exotic cases.

The panel examination required that the candidate evaluate, diagnose, and propose a treatment plan based on a summary of the patient's characteristics and the presenting symptoms. Then the examination board could introduce all manner of scenarios, variations on the theme, or untoward consequences, depending on their whim.

The first case was an inflamed appendix. That case was easy. The next involved a tubercular lung. Also, easy. I was beginning to worry, and I was right to worry, because then they lowered the hammer.

"*Frau Doktor*, how would you address abdominal trauma involving nearly every organ?" asked the examiner with the pince-nez. The degree of involvement was explained to me in great detail.

I did not even take a moment to think but barreled directly into my strategy for managing the case and the techniques I would employ. I became anxious because the gentlemen at the table continued to stare at me with frowns, but no one interrupted me. I wondered if I were digging my own grave. When I'd finished speaking, they asked a few questions. Finally, the chief examiner said, "Thank you, *Frau Doktor*. We shall inform you of the results."

Sauerbruch's face was inscrutable when I met him in the atrium. Perhaps I should have given that last answer more thought. The dean of medicine was also circumspect. I finally began to worry.

"Do you think I passed?" I asked Sauerbruch as we headed back to the hospital.

Sauerbruch's blue eyes began to twinkle. "No," he said. "I don't think so."

"What are you saying, *Herr Doktor*?" I asked anxiously.

"It's evident you didn't merely pass. You put all those old men to shame!" He glanced at the dean of medicine, who nodded his agreement. "Brava, *Frau Doktor*," said Sauerbruch, thumping me on the back. "Well done!"

My mentor was entirely too jubilant when the results were posted. I later discovered that he had made a bet with the dean that I would not only pass, but pass with first honors, which I did.

I was now a panel-certified surgeon. I was exultant except for one thing. Hanna, who had celebrated all the previous milestones of my career, was not there to share my joy.

∽

I was reading the *Times* at breakfast as usual when an article caught my attention. The board of Oxford University had finally agreed to grant degrees to women. "Well, that's big of them," I found myself saying aloud. Now that I was living alone, I spoke to myself more frequently. For obvious reasons, I read the article with interest. Not only would women be allowed to matriculate, students who had attended in the past could claim the degrees they had duly earned. "Oh, what nonsense!" I exclaimed and put the paper aside.

I'd thought I'd long since given up my indignation over not having actual pieces of parchment from Oxford. After all, I already had a medical degree, a doctorate, and habilitation, so what need would I have for lesser degrees? So I rationalized, but it wasn't that simple. I had done the work (more or less) and earned my degrees. Why shouldn't I have them? After thinking about this subject for exactly two minutes, I told myself I had better things to do.

However, that wasn't the end of it. The next week, I received a formal letter from Emily Penrose, the principal of Somerville, inviting me to appear in person to matriculate. I wondered why I should be required to present myself for something that should have been rightfully mine seven years earlier. After uttering some choice invectives, I tossed the letter in the waste bin. Then I realized I was being churlish and pulled it out again. After all, my entire childhood had been directed toward an Oxford education. Why would I spurn the very degrees to which I had so long aspired?

At dinner, Elise listened carefully to my reasons for feeling insulted.

"That's all nonsense, Margarethe. You earned the degrees. Yes, it's after the fact, but all they are asking is that you show your face, and they will give them to you." I was annoyed that Elise was not more sympathetic. As a woman, she often experienced the same prejudice. The men in the psychoanalytic societies mostly ignored the contributions of their female colleagues. When I pointed this out, she said, "If the choice is to do something or nothing, I will always do something, just as you do, Margarethe. Now, make ready to go to England."

I decided to ask Father's advice. He listened patiently while I ranted about the injustice. Finally he said in an exasperated tone, "Margarethe, you're being childish."

"What?"

"You heard me."

"But why must I play by their unjust rules?"

"Unjust perhaps, but they write the rules, and you must play by them. Surely, you know that by now."

"Sometimes, Father, you are so…unhelpful."

"Thank you," he said, and we ended the call.

After that unsatisfying result, I sulked. I called my grandaunt in the hopes of garnering sympathy. Like Father, she listened patiently to my rant until it ran out of steam.

"Are you finished?" she asked with a slight edge in her tone.

"Yes, I suppose so."

I could imagine the pensive look in her pale eyes as she considered her response. "What they are asking seems no great burden. I'm sure you would enjoy a holiday in England."

"If I can get away. Dr. Sauerbruch is a hard taskmaster."

"Everyone is due leave, even you."

"I could take the children along," I said, warming to the idea. Their English grandparents have never met them."

"There. A perfectly good excuse," she said in a wise voice. "I envy you that you were able to go to university. In my time, it was forbidden. How lucky you are."

The deep regret in her voice shamed me into action. I wrote a letter to Emily Penrose that night and requested matriculation. Immediately after, I wrote to Lotte to ask if she and Marta would be willing to entertain a guest. Lotte was now a tutor in chemistry at Lady Margaret Hall and had moved into the same faculty residence as Marta Kirchner, who had become a don at Somerville, teaching a new discipline called biochemistry.

Within days of dispatching my letter to Lotte, I received an answer by wire.

YES! PLEASE COME. SEND DATES AT ONCE!"

～

Sauerbruch was reluctant to let me go. He had become reliant on having me as his first assistant. When I wasn't available because I had a surgery of my own, he became testy. The idea of losing me for a fortnight sent him into an absolute fury. Apparently, after his fit of pique, he realized that my Oxford degrees would only enhance his own reputation because the brilliant Dr. von Stahle, who wrote his papers, was his protégée. The more letters I had after my name, he reasoned, the more prestigious he would be. Suddenly, he was all in favor of the trip to England.

Lady Philippa wrote often how she longed to meet her grandchildren, so our first destination was Larkhurst. This served another purpose as well. I needed my academic robes for the formalities at Oxford. I located them in a closet and sent them to be carefully cleaned.

I'd missed my in-laws and their witty conversation. Despite the terrible conflict between our two countries, they seemed to harbor no animosity toward Germans. Lord Bromsley asked after my father. We had long conversations about the absurd war and the even more absurd peace. Part of me wanted to share the tragic story of the riot, but as it did not reflect well on my father, I kept it to myself.

"War never brings anything good," said Lord Bromsley, thoughtfully puffing on his pipe. "Look at what we have accomplished—four empires collapsed, and four royal dynasties deposed. The old order is dead, and the new order is in shambles."

"No more than in Germany. People are still starving, and the new government can't even collect the trash."

"I've heard things are quite desperate at the moment."

"Apparently, it's even worse in Russia. I'm sad that the Czar and his family met such a terrible end. I must write to Prince Oblensky to see if he and his family survived the war."

"You know Prince Oblensky?" asked Bromsley, his pipe stem poised in the air.

"Yes, we met before the war."

"Do tell," he said, leaning forward to encourage me.

I told the story of how father and I had gone to Russia to beg the Czar to stay out of the war. How I'd been dangled as bait to lure Oblensky into a meeting.

"What a brilliant ploy, but your father always was clever. Good heavens, Meg! In addition to being a surgeon, you are a veritable Mata Hari!"

I laughed. "I don't dance very well, and it wasn't an official mission. Apparently, the Kaiser knew nothing about it."

"Ah, Wilhelm wasn't always the sharpest knife in the drawer. Probably wise to have left him out of it."

The children adored the Bromsleys. Willi became particularly fond of his grandfather and listened with rapt attention while he told stories about his adventures in Africa on safari. Lady Philippa was the kind of grandmother who doesn't mind climbing under the dining table to hide in a child's "fortress" or play hide and seek in the garden.

The weather was nice enough for walks in the splendid formal gardens. Lady Philippa and I walked arm in arm through the boxwood hedge rows that formed a labyrinth.

"What do you hear of our favorite adventurer?" asked my mother-in-law, which told me that Lytton never wrote to her either.

"Ah, you know how Lytton is. He becomes consumed by his excavations. Nothing else matters."

She stopped and looked at me. "Meg, have you ever regretted marrying my son?"

"Marrying your son, no. Marrying at all, yes, but as you know I had no choice in the matter."

"So many women of our class don't."

"But we are fortunate to have the means to do as we wish. I had a dear friend who regularly lectured me on how difficult it is for the women of the working class to support themselves. I count myself lucky to have a fortune and a title."

"You never use your titles through Lytton," she said, peering at me inquisitively.

I shrugged. "Mine take precedence over his. Besides, the only title I really care about is 'Doctor.'"

"That's what I love about you, Meg. You have the right priorities."

"One thing I don't regret is the children. I was never enamored of the process of childbearing or rearing, but they have turned out all right."

"The children are simply beautiful. You must be so proud."

"Willi favors Lytton. He has the same beautiful mouth. Women will swoon over him one day."

"He's just a boy, but he does look like Lytton," she said wistfully.

~

I left the children in the care of the Bromsleys and headed to Oxford. What a joy to walk those hallowed halls once more, but I wasted no time on nostalgia. I headed directly to the registrar of Somerville College and signed the papers to matriculate for my degrees.

Lotte swept me into her arms when I appeared on her doorstep and nearly squeezed the breath out of me. The rooms she shared with Marta Kirchner were furnished in an old-fashioned, almost Victorian style, making them nearly indistinguishable from those I had occupied in my student days. I felt instantly at home there.

Marta came in and embraced me. We were like excited children, all talking at once. Neither woman had ever confessed anything about the nature of their friendship, but having been tutored by Hanna, I instantly recognized that my former teacher and my lady's companion were now a couple. Happily, any regret I'd nursed over initiating Lotte was now moot.

They invited me into their sitting room for a formal tea. As I sat down to cucumber and curried egg sandwiches accompanied by a fine Earl Grey, I realized how much I'd missed England.

"Margarethe, you look tired," said Lotte with a little frown after a long, critical assessment.

"As you might imagine, the practice of surgery and rest are not compatible."

"Lotte tells me that you passed your panel examinations with a first," said Marta. "Let me offer my congratulations." She leaned over to give me a kiss on the cheek. "That is a splendid achievement for a woman."

"It angers me to hear that phrase, 'for a woman.' I can't believe it's said even here, at Somerville. Isn't that the point of women's education? To achieve equality?"

Lotte sighed. "Perhaps here, in our own little world, we can pretend, but beyond, the struggle goes on."

"At least, we can vote in Germany since the revolution. Otherwise, everything is worse in every way."

"Speaking of equality," said Marta, "some fool, probably a man, has decided there should be perfunctory examinations to validate the matriculation."

I realized that I'd been misled. In order to have my degree, I would be forced to play undergraduate once more. I seethed with resentment. "Well, then they can take their bloody sheepskin and stick it where the sun never shines."

"Margarethe!" exclaimed Lotte. "Such language!"

I wanted to laugh. If she ever heard me swearing in the operating theater, she would probably faint.

"Calm yourself, Margarethe," said Marta in a soothing voice. "You came all this way for this one purpose. Go along with it. It's merely a formality."

"Listen to us," I said, "Here we are making excuses for *them*. Being grateful that *they* have *finally* allowed us to have degrees that we legitimately earned! How well we've been trained to be docile and cooperative, to be content with the crumbs they throw our way. I have a license to teach medicine in any university in the German-speaking world. I am a panel-certified surgeon, yet I must take examinations that I passed seven years ago? Absurd!"

Lotte and Marta regarded me with a worried look, and I realized I had been ranting. Lotte reached for my hand. "Margarethe, you are many things, but docile and cooperative, you are not," she said with a completely straight face. Marta chuckled behind her hand, evidently entertained. "I sympathize with your indignation," Lotte continued, "but let's not spoil our joyful reunion." She took my face in hers and squeezed my cheeks. "Oh, my dear girl, I am so happy to see you!"

"Perhaps we should skip the tea and open the sherry," suggested Marta. "It might help us all relax."

We quickly became giddy, which led to reminiscences. Despite glares from me, Lotte told the story of the gun powder incident. Marta shared her memories of the first time I entertained Lytton for tea. I was glad when they turned the conversation to the subject of how much they missed their homeland. I could hardly bear to tell them how much things had changed at home, and not necessarily for the better.

I had a pounding headache when I reported for the sham physiology examination. After practicing medicine for years, it was difficult not to be snide to the dons. Somehow, I mustered sufficient humility to make a good impression. The examination in Greats, which I sat for the next day, was ridiculously simple. However, such confidence can sometimes result in unpleasant surprises. Fortunately, my worry proved to be unfounded. In a few day's time, I received my results: confirmation of a double first.

I reported to the principal of Somerville College to pick up my degrees. Somehow, the parchments in their leather sleeves seemed enormously weighty for their size. Perhaps it was only my imagination or more likely the outsized expectations my father and my grandaunt had invested in them. With the new Leica I had purchased for the trip, I took photographs of the documents and posted prints to Father and *Tante*, so they could see for themselves that the deed was done.

Reluctantly, I said goodbye to Marta and Lotte. They extracted a promise to return soon and to bring the children. Somehow, I didn't see myself honoring that second part of the promise. The temple of learning I shared with my fellow female scholars should remain inviolate.

When I arrived in Larkhurst, Lady Philippa made a great fuss over my diplomas. The next day, she held a drinks party in my honor and invited a number of her bluestocking friends, including her sister. Lytton's Aunt Elizabeth was finally introduced to my daughter, her namesake.

17

After I returned from England, Sauerbruch promoted me to attending surgeon and took me into his practice as a junior partner. While I was arranging my new consulting room, he wandered in and looked around. Before I hung the framed documents of my credentials, I'd laid them out on my desk. He inspected each diploma and license, nodding proudly. "And make sure you hang those English degrees!" he said, waving his finger at me.

The new office, outfitted with Craftsman furniture built of fumed oak and dark leather, was intended to demonstrate that I had arrived. Outwardly, my life looked quite proper. I was a successful physician, living in a grand house in a fashionable district. I was raising two handsome, bright children. My husband was regarded as a local hero because his archaeological discoveries were reported in the newspapers. No one seemed to notice that he was mostly absent. Occasionally, he made an appearance for a few days around the children's birthdays or holidays. More often, he met us in Edelheim for Christmas or some other high feast. Otherwise, I only saw Lytton for our annual visit to the mountains.

What my colleagues and my wealthy neighbors didn't see was that nothing about my life was conventional. My husband was such in name only, and I was barely his wife. In a reversal of the traditional roles in a marriage, I held all the cards. Dear Lytton didn't mind as long as I put no constraints on him, and he had the money he needed for his adventures.

Our love life was even more unconventional. During one of our mountain holidays, Lytton had invited one of his male lovers to our bed. I experienced forms of sexual pleasure I'd only read about in books. (For educational purposes, I'd retained some of the erotic novels I'd discovered in my cousin's library.)

While we were à trois, I spent much of the time as an observer, which suited me. I knew Lytton really didn't want me there, but he was naturally kind and had included me out of generosity. Smoking Turkish cigarettes through a gold cigarette holder and sipping brandy, I learned about the vagaries of male sexuality. The men writhed like wrestlers, sweating and panting, jabbing with their penises and sucking on them as if they were breasts. I was fascinated by their raw passion, which sometimes bordered on violence. Yet they could also share sublime tenderness. I watched, feeling as detached as when I held a scalpel.

We were a trio only for the holiday, but thereafter, Lytton often invited his lovers to join us. He was never interested when I wanted to share a woman. One was enough, he said. I suppose I should be grateful.

Now that I'd performed my duties and produced heirs, pleasure was my only reason for sexual joining. Perhaps that's why I didn't follow Elise's advice when she left the following winter to move in with Max von Ehrenbach. "Take a lover," she'd recommended before she left, but I didn't.

My emotional life had been a desert since Hanna died, and I had nothing to give a lover of either sex. Instead, I satisfied my needs with women I found in the demimonde. As the decade advanced, women of my persuasion were becoming bolder. In clubs devoted to women who loved other women, they openly danced together. Some dressed like men. That sort didn't interest me. I preferred women who looked like women with abundant curves and full breasts. Occasionally, I had a feverish tryst with a nurse or a secretary, but I preferred to keep my sex life away from the hospital. More often I took solace in pleasuring myself in the bath.

After Elise left, the house felt sad and empty. Although I'd been living in Munich since I began medical school, it had never felt like home. The house now held too many memories. It was as if ghosts walked the halls at night, rattling their chains and howling in the dark. Of course, it was just the wind against the windows.

I made the children my little project, not out of great maternal affection, but as a distraction. Providing them with the best possible education was my duty, of course, and I threw myself into the enterprise with great enthusiasm. We spent hours in Munich's famous museums. I instituted a regular program of strenuous exercise, brisk walking, rowing on the lake, and chasing hoops.

Both of the children showed musical talent from an early age, so I had my miniature piano brought from Edelheim. When the time came, I sent Willi to the primary school in England my husband had attended as a boy. I knew Lytton would like that idea, but I didn't consult him before enrolling my son, because I knew he wouldn't oppose me. I had made it clear from the beginning that I would make all the decisions regarding the children's upbringing, and he'd agreed without complaint.

I contented myself with thinking I was doing all the things that others expected of me. Yet, I moved through my life like in a dream. When a year went by, then two, and another, I wondered if the wound left by Hanna's death would ever heal.

To maintain my equilibrium, I kept a rigid routine. Each day, I rose and headed to the hospital. I scrubbed for surgery, went home, ate my dinner, kissed my children, and went to bed. The next day, I did exactly the same, except Sunday, when I went to the Waldfriedhof cemetery to lay flowers on Hanna's grave.

I was like a tree that has gone dormant for winter. My roots were frozen. I took in little water or light, yet I was still alive…barely. My body functioned well, fed by nutritious food and conditioned by strenuous walks and exercise in my basement gymnasium. Music was mostly absent from my program, but I practiced the piano daily. I almost never sang for pleasure, but I dutifully sang the exercises meant to keep my voice limber.

One splendid spring day, everything changed. As usual, I went to the Waldfriedhof to lay flowers on Hanna's grave. I imagined, as I sometimes did, how she might look in her splendid mahogany coffin, the lid collapsed by the weight of the earth on it. I imagined the grimace of her bare teeth where once her full lips had been. I pictured the beautiful satin gown in which we'd buried her, now gone moldy and fallen into a pretty heap over her bones. At such times, I felt no repulsion but philosophically reflected on the oft quoted scripture passage: "dust to dust."

Then a nightingale alighted on a nearby lime tree and burst into song. She sang warbling staccato notes almost like the code of a telegraph transmitter, a sound so intrusive that it demanded my attention. I stood transfixed while the bird serenaded me. Although I have never been superstitious, I wondered if it was a sign. Could Hanna be singing through the nightingale? Indeed, the song of the little bird seemed to say, "Enough! Enough! No more brooding. The world is beautiful. The air is clear and fresh. Breathe it in!" I imagined Hanna's warm lips pressing softly on the back of my neck.

When I arrived home, I went straight to the music room, flipped up the keyboard cover, and began to sing Brahm's song, "*An die Nachtigall,*" followed by Schubert's song of the same name. I sang for the better part of the afternoon until Schmidt finally dared to knock on the door to announce my afternoon coffee.

I situated myself in the library in my favorite club chair. While waiting for the coffee to arrive, I noticed a stack of medical journals that had been set aside to be shelved. Idly, I flipped through a copy of *The Lancet*. My eye fell on an announcement set off with a thick mortise. The chief of surgery at St. Bartholomew's Hospital in London was seeking a fellow in abdominal surgery. Intrigued, I took the time to read the fine print. The description of the post sounded as if it had been written for me. I found some stationery in a drawer. As I drank my coffee, I composed a letter of inquiry to Dr. Matthew Abrams at Barts.

~

Once I knew there was an alternative, I finally allowed myself to realize how tiresome my role as Sauerbruch's protégée had become. There was no question I enjoyed prestige through our association, but there were also disadvantages. Some of the senior staff still mockingly called me "the countess"—ironic because, under the Weimar constitution, hereditary titles had been abolished and were now merely part of our names.

Sauerbruch's patronage had mostly spared me from the worst ridicule of my colleagues, at least in my presence, but I had no illusions that they weren't grousing about me behind my back. For obvious reasons, my role as the chief's favorite assistant drew their contempt, yet it was clear they considered me little more than Sauerbruch's appendage, and, in a way, I was. He left me to mop up the mess after his surgeries. He presented my important cases as if they were his own. I wrote all his papers, but it was he who delivered them at conferences.

Two weeks passed before I heard from Dr. Abrams, but finally I received a letter requesting me to elaborate on my interest. That letter led to a flurry of correspondence. Finally, Abrams wrote that he would like to meet me. Would I, by any chance, be attending the upcoming surgical conference in Paris? I sent a wire to confirm that I would not only be attending but also performing a demonstration surgery. We arranged to meet for luncheon on the first day of the conference.

⁓

Abrams was not what I expected. Most surgeons are scrupulously neat and clean, but Abrams needed a shave, and his tweeds were as rumpled as if he'd slept the night in them. He lit a cigar while we awaited our meal. I wondered if, even for the sake of professional advancement, I could get past my loathing for cigar smoke.

"So, we finally meet *Frau Doktor*," Abrams said in heavily accented German. "After reading your papers with Sauerbruch, I am honored."

"To be sure, the honor is all mine."

He sat back, looking a bit surprised. "I'm relieved to hear that you speak English. Very well, in fact. You sound like one of us."

"As you may recall, I was educated in British schools. I did my pre-clinical at Oxford, but my father spoke English to me from infancy."

"Ah, that explains it. Always best to learn a language as a young child. Unfortunately, I learned German from my grandparents. As you probably heard, some Yiddish crept in."

I smiled and said, "You make yourself understood, Dr. Abrams."

He clucked his tongue. "You realize that in England surgeons are not addressed as "doctor," despite their academic credentials. And so, *Frau Doktor*, you may have duly earned your doctorate, but here you would become Miss Stahle again."

"I'd forgotten about that odd little tradition."

"Do you know the reason for it?"

"No, I'm afraid not."

Abrams settled back in his chair and leisurely relit his cigar, obviously readying himself to tell a tale. "It goes back to the time when we were mere tradesmen overseen by educated *doctors*. Of course, the so-called doctors really knew very little. They were nothing but shamans minus the spells and incantations." He looked momentarily thoughtful. "Maybe they did use incantations, but they had few efficacious treatments—some herbal remedies, most of them harmless, but some deadly! It was the surgeons who did the real healing, cutting out tumors and infection, removing bad teeth, suturing wounds. So, we surgeons take our lack of title as an honor."

"That is a convoluted argument to be sure."

Abrams cocked a bushy brow. "Are you a philosopher, *Frau Doktor*?"

"Among other things."

"Ah yes, now I remember. You read Greats at Oxford."

I nodded to confirm his assumption.

"You've had an impressive education. Will you be troubled when no one calls you 'doctor' in England?"

Considering how diligently I'd labored to earn the title, I was understandably reluctant to take what on the surface, seemed like a demotion. In fact, I preferred my professional title to those I would inherit and even used it socially. But the opportunity to train under the most renowned abdominal surgeon in Europe inclined me to be diplomatic. "If you choose me for the position, I shall adjust," I finally said.

Abrams smiled and flicked cigar ash into a nearby spittoon. "Good. I prefer surgeons who can 'adjust.'"

We spent the rest of our lunch discussing bowel resections without the least disturbance to our appetites. When we parted, I hoped I had made a good impression.

The following day, as I scrubbed for my demonstration surgery, I found myself wishing I had scheduled an abdominal procedure to show off my skills to Abrams, but I had agreed to demonstrate a new amputation technique Sauerbruch had recently invented. Once again, it irked me to realize how often I deferred to my mentor.

While the operating theater filled, I searched the crowd for Abrams, momentarily panicking that he might not appear. Finally, I spotted him at the extreme right in the third row. Wearing a decent suit and clean shaven, I hardly recognized him.

I began to describe the procedure in French. Then I noticed Abram's busy brows rise, and I repeated what I'd said in English and continued the presentation in both languages. We had more bleeding than usual during the surgery. By the time we finished, my apron and gown were red. I feared for the skirt of my new suit beneath, but it wouldn't be the first time I'd spoiled a suit with bodily fluids. One expected that.

Some of the observers in the gallery descended to inspect the amputation stump, asking questions about why I had arranged the flaps in that manner and why the sutures needed to be so fine. I took my time answering the questions, pleased to see that Abrams politely waited in line for his turn.

"*Frau Doktor*, can you spare a moment after you dress? I shall wait for you in the lobby."

I answered a final, complicated question and greeted another well-wisher before I could take off my bloody surgical gown. I had a red stain on my blouse. Fortunately, the blood hadn't seeped through to my skirt.

Abrams was leaning against a fluted column and, of course, he was smoking a cigar. "Let's find some tea. There's a café in the hotel. Will that do?"

The offer of a meeting over tea, even in the hotel, sounded like good news could be in the offing, so I happily agreed. Abrams didn't even wait for the tea to arrive. He leaned forward and announced, "I'll have you as my fellow, *Frau Doktor*, if you'll have me." As he delivered this news, he watched my face carefully.

"Thank you, Mister Abrams. I am honored. However, it's a big step to uproot my family and move to another country. May I have a fortnight to consider your offer?"

He relit his cigar, puffing odorous smoke. "Of course. Take as long as you need, but I'd wager good money on how you'll decide."

"Really? How can you be so sure?"

"You've learned all you can from Sauerbruch. Time for a change."

❦

I decided I needed a holiday to mull over the idea. Sauerbruch grumbled at my request for yet another leave, but my success in Paris pleased him, so he let me go. I took the children along because Grandmother hadn't seen them since Christmas. Although my daughter's nurse accompanied us, the children clamored for my attention on the train. Whenever the children had me, even for a moment, they wanted *all* of me. I entertained them with fairy tales, some simple magic tricks that I had learned from one of the orderlies, and sang to them.

Willi, being older, was the more reasonable of the two. Liesel, at seven, was quite tall but still liked to climb into my lap like a baby. She squirmed, making the long train ride to Raithschau even more uncomfortable. When I undressed that night, I found she'd left me with a few bruises on my thighs.

The next day, I left Willi with Grandmother because the nuns seemed less tolerant of active children and headed to Obberoth to pay my respects. *Tante* now had a new role in the order. Reverend Mother Wilhelmina had passed, and the community had elected my grandaunt to be their leader. Reverend Mother Scholastica as she was now styled, wore a ruby pectoral cross like the abbesses of old, the gift of one of my Raithschau ancestors. I noticed that she liked to clutch it, perhaps to assure herself of its presence, but more likely for solace when she was anxious.

Fortunately, Liesel was mannerly, if a bit shy, in the presence of strangers. She'd met my grandaunt on several occasions, but the visits had been too sporadic to leave a lasting impression. When we entered the mother general's study, Liesel gripped my hand fiercely and refused to let it go even when a plate of sugar biscuits conveniently appeared.

"It appears that you frighten children, *Tante*," I observed with a sarcastic smile. "You terrified me when I first met you."

"Yes, I remember. But you weren't actually frightened, just cautious. You observed me carefully, as I'm sure your daughter is doing now."

She knelt beside Liesel and spoke to her in the same gentle tone she'd adopted with me all those years before. The change in my daughter's attitude amazed me. *Tante* had calmed her simply by giving her attention.

"Perhaps you should leave her here with us, Margarethe," Mother Scholastica said, ably getting to her feet despite her age. "I think we could manage her quite well."

"Oh, I don't think so. The poor thing needs to learn a reasonable way of thinking before being exposed to that Catholic tripe."

My grandaunt smiled shrewdly "Certainly, teaching a child reason has high value in any educational setting. At our first meeting, you had already attained the age of reason." This was an exaggeration, but she'd made her point. However, that was not the only point she wished to make. "As you know, there are many gifts of the mind: intuition, imagination, creativity, and wisdom. Perhaps when you have attained the last, you will learn to appreciate the others."

It took a moment to realize she had bested me again. I gave her my most withering look, and she chuckled.

⁓

At dinner that night, I noticed that Grandmother looked pale. She rebuffed my offer to examine her and promised to consult the town doctor soon. Pleading fatigue, she went up to bed early, which provided the opportunity to slip back to Obberoth for a visit with my grandaunt. I drove Grandfather's old Daimler with the top down and enjoyed the play of the wind in my hair. The vehicle seemed primitive and cantankerous compared to modern motorcars, but it conveyed me to Obberoth in a matter of minutes.

When I arrived, *Tante* opened her credenza and offered me a glass of cognac. The same bottle had probably been there for years. Occasionally, she had visitors "from the world" as outsiders are called in the convent and wanted to be properly prepared. It was excellent cognac, but it was high summer and something lighter would have been more refreshing.

"To what do I owe the pleasure of a visit at this hour from my *reasonable* grandniece?" *Tante* asked, her hands carefully hidden under her scapular.

It took a moment for the barb to penetrate. Finally, I chuckled. "Well played, *Tante*. Perhaps I overstated my case a tiny bit." I measured with my pinched fingers to demonstrate.

"Evidently, your training has sharpened your tongue as well as your scalpel." To my surprise, she poured a glass of cognac for herself. "I always enjoy your hyperboles, Margarethe. They are so imaginative! Catholic tripe indeed! You can be sure we won't be eating *that* for Lent." She settled back in her chair. I suddenly craved a cigarette, but *Tante* considered the habit high on her list of modern vices, so I refrained in her presence. "I have no illusion that you came for another viewing of your old grandaunt," she continued. "What is the *real* reason for your visit?"

"You're not old, *Tante*. Stop being modest. But you're quite right about the visit. I do have something on my mind."

She raised her glass to indicate I should begin.

"I've been offered a fellowship at St. Bartholomew's Hospital in London. The head of the department of surgery, Matthew Abrams, is considered the world's greatest abdominal surgeon. It is certainly an honor to be considered for the post, especially for a woman."

"So? Accept."

"It's not that simple. Father has retreated from public life. He keeps to Edelheim and seems to be growing old before his time. Mother, well, you know about Mother. I am managing all the finances for the family, which takes up an inordinate amount of my time, but I promised Grandfather that I would look after the money after he passed. Grandmother is a very competent farmer, but frankly, she doesn't look well."

"I am aware of all these things, Margarethe. Why are you telling me?"

"I'm taking an inventory of my responsibilities to assess their extent."

"It's true. You have many responsibilities, including those you take on without being asked. I often wonder why you do. Don't you have enough to do?" I was pulled up short by that remark because it poked uncomfortably close to the truth.

"My duties keep me thoroughly occupied," I replied mildly.

"I'm sure they do." My grandaunt studied me with her pale eyes. "Then why are you burdening yourself with more?"

"My father thinks it's good training for my future role. The war has taken a toll on him. Grandmother is alone since Grandfather died—"

"Your parents and your grandmother are adults and quite capable of looking after themselves."

"Yes, I know, but I feel anxious about leaving them."

Tante regarded me without speaking for a seemingly unending moment. "I think you've taken your grandfather's lectures on duty too seriously. The Prussians are such joyless people. They are totally lacking in humor. I warned Katje against marrying one of them."

"She loved my grandfather."

She smiled. "Yes, she loved him. She was lucky. The calculus of aristocratic marriage can so often result in disaster."

"Yes, it can, which is why I chose Lytton with great care."

She raised a brow. "Why isn't he with you?"

I averted my eyes to escape her shrewd gaze. "He's still in Italy. With his friends."

"I thought so."

"But if I were in England, he might visit more often. He only moved to Munich because that's where I was studying medicine."

"If you say so," replied my grandaunt with a shrug. Despite her attitude of indifference, I knew what she was trying to say. She'd previously shared her opinion of my unconventional marriage.

"Actually, Lytton has nothing to do with this decision. My reasons for considering the post are totally selfish. Sauerbruch has been an enormous boon to my career, but I feel stifled working under him. My only concern is leaving the country while things are so unsettled at home."

"Margarethe, there will never be a good time to get on with your life. Someone will always be expecting something of you. You will never be younger than you are now. This is the time to enjoy life. True responsibility will knock on your door soon enough."

"Just like that?"

She shrugged. "What are you waiting for? A formal proclamation in the refectory before my sisters?"

When I laughed, she stared at me in surprise. "I'm demonstrating my sense of humor," I explained. "Not all Prussians are joyless."

"Ah," said my grandaunt, raising a blond brow. "You have our blood in your veins as well."

~

When I returned to Munich, I rang Elise to explain that I was heading to England to begin a fellowship. "I'm reluctant to sell the Munich house because it came from someone in the family. Would you and Max be willing to live there in my absence?"

"With pleasure."

"Ought you not discuss it with Max first?"

"No need," she said breezily. "He'll agree." Although Max was like a bear and liked to growl, he was quite tame where Elise was concerned.

That night, I wrote two letters: one to Sauerbruch to advise him of my resignation, and one to Matthew Abrams to accept the fellowship at Barts.

In a few days I received a packet containing the contract and copies of some of Abrams' papers to read in preparation for joining his staff. It also included the address and telephone number of one of his fellows so that I might ask his advice regarding living quarters.

Charles Calder replied to my inquiry at once, sending carefully annotated real estate listings from the newspaper, the name of a London agent, and photographs of an available townhouse in Mayfair. Although the Mayfair location was far from ideal, I sent my new majordomo to inspect the house along with a few others Calder had listed.

Stefan Krauss had been sergeant-quartermaster under my father, who thought I could use his expertise in logistics. He also spoke passable English, which was equally useful. Krauss' report on the townhouse was favorable, so after he returned, I went up to London to see for myself.

~

Calder was kind enough to meet my train from Dover. He strode up to me on the platform and introduced himself. "Charles Calder at your service," he said, offering his hand.

"How did you know I'm the right person?" I asked, intrigued.

"I'm psychic," he said with a perfectly straight face.

"Not really," I scoffed.

He held up a medical journal and grinned. "All right, I cheated. I had your photograph for reference."

Calder was a good-looking man with straight, black hair. One lock tended to fall rakishly over his left eye. He had voltaic, blue eyes, pale skin, and ruddy cheeks. His well-worn tweeds gave him that slightly disheveled, relaxed look that simply reeks "upper class."

He gallantly looked after the fee for the porter. "I was quite surprised to hear that Abrams had engaged a woman for the fellowship," Calder candidly admitted while we waited for the taxi driver to load my luggage. "He never has anything good to say about female surgeons. But he thinks highly of your mentor, Dr. Sauerbruch."

"I hope that wasn't the only reason he brought me on."

"Oh, I rather doubt it. I've read some of your papers. They're first rate. I hear you're quite the wunderkind. A brilliant medical brain that only happens to reside in a female skull." He struck a match on the sole of his shoe and leisurely lit his pipe. He smoked a fine-cut Virginia tobacco of the most aromatic and delicious variety. I was relieved to see he hadn't adopted his mentor's liking for cigars.

"And where have you heard these rumors?" I asked.

"We have friends in common. Martin Fox was in your Gilbert and Sullivan Society at Oxford. He's over at University College Hospital these days. Once you're settled, we must dine with him. As you may remember, he's quite a pleasant chap, and he thinks you're the bee's knees."

Calder followed like an obedient hound while the estate agent gave us a tour of the townhouse down the street from his parents'. The place was more than sufficiently large for my small family, occasional house guests, and a modest household staff. In addition to the usual living areas, there were rooms suitable for a library, a large music room adequate for an intimate concert, and a pleasant study with large windows overlooking a garden. It was clean, in good repair, and had a favorable, east-facing position on a wide street.

"Well, what do you make of the place?" asked Calder in a hopeful tone after the estate agent had departed. "The price is good."

"It is indeed. Yes, I think it will do perfectly well for me and my family."

"Wonderful! This calls for a celebration. And I know just the place!"

He took me to his parents' house, identical to the one I was about to purchase. Calder, the bachelor son, lived there with his parents and his sister. He explained that everyone was out for the evening and appropriated a bottle of his father's prize scotch from the man's study.

As we got more deeply into the alcohol, I learned why Calder had warmed to me so quickly. He wanted a playmate, and I mean this in the most innocent way. By the end of the evening we were laughing hysterically at one of his plodding jokes and addressing one another by our given names. As before, I styled myself, "Margaret Stahle." My friends called me, "Meg."

~

Charles allowed me barely a week to settle in before inviting me to dine with his family. It was the usual Sunday afternoon grand event, featuring a roast joint of beef. English cuisine, if one might call it such, has never been a favorite of mine, but the Calders' cook was quite skilled. The meal was more than edible.

Afterwards, we sat enjoying more of Charles senior's prize scotch. I was developing a taste for the strong, peaty flavor of a single-malt whiskey. Like Charles, his father smoked a pipe, but the flavor he preferred was quite different from his son's. Together, they created a complex, but not unpleasant aroma redolent of burning, autumn leaves.

The elder Calder knew my grandfather, who had once been a prominent member of the Empire's foreign service. Grandfather had been posted to London for a brief time and was well thought of in British foreign-service circles.

"Thank God, the old man never lived to see that sorry war, and the even sorrier peace," opined Charles' father, puffing thoughtfully on his pipe. "If only the Kaiser had responded to Wilson's offers to broker a just peace. Nothing good ever comes of an ignominious defeat except, perhaps, another war."

"Forgive me, Mr. Calder, but can we change the subject?" I asked, which appeared to startle the man. "I try to avoid discussion of politics. For one thing, I understand next to nothing about it. And for another, being on the wrong side of an issue only makes for bad blood among friends."

Charles laughed. "She's quite right, Father. Let's table the political discussion, shall we?"

"But it's not every day that I have Henry Stahle's granddaughter sitting right here in my study."

"Well, if you want her to come back, you might want to leave off the politics as she asks."

"Of course," said Charles Sr., giving me an indulgent smile. "What do you think of our miserable weather, Miss Stahle?"

We commiserated over the week of rain, which had left us all feeling nearly moldy.

Not long after, Charles' sister, Alexandra, came looking for us, so we relocated our conversation to the parlor. According to Charles, his sister was quite the scholar and had received a spectacular first in languages at Lady Margaret Hall. She'd found employment as a schoolmistress, but apparently, her tenure had been brief, so she was living with the family.

Like her brother, Alexandra Calder had dark, nearly black hair, large, luminously blue eyes, and pale skin. She was striking and quite alluring. During a lull in the conversation, she began speaking about Tolstoy.

"Charles tells me you've read the great Russian authors," she said, now completely directing her conversation toward me. To my great surprise, I realized that she had been speaking to me in Russian. When I replied in kind, she gave me the most beguiling smile. Only later, when I lay in bed, was I able to realize that Alexandra Calder had been flirting with me.

18

In theater, Charles and I were well matched. Together, we made an amazing team, which had been Abrams' plan all along—to build an incomparable surgical department at Barts. After an extremely risky, but triumphantly successful liver surgery, Charles and I repaired to his father's study and got into the old man's scotch. Fortunately, the family was on holiday at their country house, so there were no witnesses to the sodden episode that followed.

When Charles, reeking of liquor, attempted to kiss me, I almost didn't push him away. I was lonely for sexual attention and might have been inclined to respond to the pass, but I liked Charles too much to risk our friendship. Absent alcohol, it was as straight-forward as a brilliantly shining sun on a cool, spring morning. Fortunately, I wasn't so deep into my cups as he was and gently pushed him away. "Charles, we've become such good friends. Let's not spoil it."

His cheeks flamed scarlet, helped along by the alcohol. He was obviously embarrassed and apologized over and over again until I begged him to stop.

It saddened me that he felt it necessary to attempt a seduction. Why can't people conceive of a relationship between a man and a woman without sex? Why can't friendship be enough?

And we had more than friendship. Abrams was an unbearably hard taskmaster whose demands made Sauerbruch's seem almost kind. In me, Charles found a stalwart ally. Abrams could never resist our requests when we approached him with a united front. The old man would cough up a harrumph, replace his cigar stub in his mouth, and retreat rather than argue.

By the autumn of 1924, I was comfortably settled into my new home. My new majordomo had recruited an able staff, all British with the exception of Grauer, whom I'd brought along as my chauffeur. All I lacked was a motorcar for him to drive.

Mayfair was relatively convenient for Charles' father, who worked in the Foreign Office, but I daily needed to find my way into the city proper. I headed to a showroom and bought a shiny new Bentley. A few weeks later, Charles bought one exactly like it. When our schedules allowed, we rode together, switching off the driving. Most of the time, I drove myself, which left Grauer with little to do beyond maintaining the motorcar, so I asked Krauss to teach him English and train him to be the under-butler.

I cannot begin to describe my joy and pleasure in my new-found freedom. I found a voice teacher, a choral group that would have me, and an amateur opera society. Now that I was in England, I felt less anxious about sending Liesel off to school, despite her difficult personality. Freed of my children, I could indulge my other interests, not that their presence had ever really stopped me.

Because of my duties at the hospital, my children often spent their school holidays at Larkhurst. Lytton was consumed with his excavation and did not return from his travels that year. We all missed him, of course, especially the children, although I began to sense that their memory of him was growing dim. Elisabeth, who had been nicknamed Liza by her English schoolmates, looked puzzled when we spoke of him. He still wrote to me and the children every few months, and for that I was grateful. Occasionally, he enclosed a few photographs, which I treasured.

As we sat in the garden at Larkhurst, Lady Philippa turned to me and said apropos of nothing, "I fear our Lytton is a disappointment to you."

How to respond to this? I was sad to be deprived of Lytton's company. He was witty and bright and could always lift my spirits in the darkest of times. Physically, I missed his presence. Not for sex, for I could find that anywhere, but when I was enfolded in Lytton's powerful arms, I could believe, if only for a brief moment, that I was safe, and everything would be all right.

"I do miss Lytton," I confessed with a sigh, "but I want him to be happy. Clearly, he is happiest when he is digging in the ancient dust."

His mother sighed and shook her head "I fear he is restless, seeking something he can never find. The antiquities are merely a metaphor. Of course, we all have dreams that can never be fully realized. Most of us learn to find satisfaction where we can." She gazed out into the garden with a faraway look. I wondered if she was entertaining memories of her own unrealized dreams. "I don't know whether to scold Lytton for abandoning his family, or admire him for following his heart."

"He harms none. Let him pursue his quest if it makes him happy."

"But the children…"

"Which of our class has the attention of our parents? We must be content with our assets: good blood, a good name, and a good education. With that, anyone can get on in this world."

"So, you are content?"

I took a moment to consider this. "Yes, I have my work. I indulge my interests. The children are coming along…Yes, I'm content."

Lady Philippa, who'd been watching my face, observed, "But not happy?"

"I have moments of joy…like everyone. Happiness is a feeling, not a constant state."

She nodded thoughtfully. "I should have known better than to ask that question of a stoic philosopher."

I laughed and patted her hand fondly. "Indeed. I'm sure Lytton would have replied in a similar fashion."

～

My neighbors adopted me as one of their own. We alternated Sunday dinners between our homes, followed by charades and musicales. I found the rhythm of their middle-class household comforting. The family reminded me of the Seidls. Being British, the Calders were not as demonstrative in their affection, but I sensed their shared warmth. Unlike Elise's mother, Mrs. Calder never handed me an apron and invited me into her kitchen. Mrs. Seidl always had much to say, whereas Mrs. Calder, a proper lady, seldom expressed her opinions in my presence.

Despite their middle-class sturdiness, the Calders came from noble stock. Charles senior was the second son of a viscount. Not that there was anything to show for it. The family money had been pissed away generations before, and their estate had long since crumbled into ruin. I drove up to the site with Charles to have a look, but there was nothing to see save the outline of the foundation, the heaps over the midden pits, and some stray stones.

"They took most of the stones for building the bridge over the river," Charles explained.

"Someday, Edelheim may look like this," I said moodily.

"For your sake, I hope you never live to see it."

"Indeed, for it would break my heart."

Charles and I became inseparable. We spent many happy evenings reading together. Sometimes, we would play chess or cards. I spent so much time with him that I wondered why the neighbors never buzzed with gossip. Of course, a confirmed bachelor, living at home with his parents, would hardly be considered a symbol of sexual prowess. Had he not attempted a seduction, I would never have known he even thought about sex. I began to wonder if he preferred men until I realized that romantic adventures simply didn't interest him.

At Christmas, Charles' younger brother, who'd been posted to Persia, came home on leave. His flamboyant dress left no doubt that he was a homosexual. Nigel had the same coloring as his siblings—dark, almost black hair and compelling eyes that were shockingly blue. He wore a pencil mustache that gave him a debonair, movie-star look. Among certain circles, he was considered deliciously handsome. His resemblance to Gregor Oblensky endeared him to me as well as our shared proclivity.

Once we established where one another stood, we found diversion in London's fashionable homosexual clubs. After everyone was asleep, he would knock on my door and say, "Come, Meg. The night is young!" Some of the nightclubs were mixed—male and female, and I was able to find a bed partner for the night.

Although my friendships with her brothers flourished, the youngest Calder remained a cipher. Alexandra had finally found employment in a posh girls' school in York. Before heading off, we said our goodbyes. To my great surprise, she kissed me full on the mouth, lingering for a long

The Imperative of Desire

moment. Then she shocked me by delicately licking my lips until I gave her a proper kiss. She smiled when I let her go. "Until we meet again," she promised with a smoldering look. "You will write to me, won't you, Meg?"

"If you wish."

"I do wish. I wish it fervently. Meanwhile, I shall miss the only person I know who speaks Russian. Can you also write in Russian?"

"Yes, a bit."

"Then I shall expect wonderful missives in Cyrillic. It will be good practice for you and a special joy for me." Again, she gave me a smoldering look. I had no idea what to make of it.

~

By summer, I'd finished the term of my fellowship, and Abrams made me an attending. Charles, who'd been appointed to staff three months ahead of me, took me out to the pub the doctors frequented to celebrate. I wrangled a fortnight's holiday out of Abrams, gathered my children from their respective schools, and dutifully headed to my in-laws.

Despite Lady Philippa's fervor for women's rights, she had largely withdrawn from politics once female suffrage was granted. Her retirement was not completely voluntary. On my previous visit, she'd confided that she suffered from some vague gynecological complaints. I'd offered to examine her but she'd brushed the suggestion aside. I had referred her to Lord Abbott, the head of the department at Barts. To my knowledge, she never consulted him.

Fortunately, my mother-in-law was not as resistant to my medical attention as other members of my family. Her complaints continued, and I persisted in offering my services. Finally, she allowed me to examine her. I struggled for detachment as I palpated her abdomen and discovered a sizable mass on her ovary.

"Meg, what is it? You look so grave," she said anxiously, reading the concern in my eyes.

I took her hand to reassure her. "Many women of your age develop ovarian cysts, which can cause discomfort but pose no serious threat to their health," I explained. "When I return to London, come with me. I'll set an appointment with Lord Abbott before we leave."

She took my face in her hands. "How could I be so lucky in a daughter-in-law? Yes, I shall go down to London with you." She gave me the warmest smile. While her generous response touched me, it also underscored how little my own mother appreciated me.

Later that day, I telephoned Abbott to make arrangements. He was cordial, although like the other physicians at Bart's and elsewhere, he had been known to make disparaging remarks about medical women. I described my impressions, and he agreed that the abnormal growth was likely a cyst.

When we departed for London after the holiday, Lady Philippa accompanied us. She was an extremely indulgent grandmother and kept the children occupied with stories of her youth while Victoria reigned. As I listened to these tales of the grand empire under the queen, I recalled my own youth in another time and under a very different sensibility.

George Abbott, whom we addressed as "Lord Abbott" because he had been raised to life's peer for his work on hysterectomies, was very proud of his title. He was the son of a country doctor from Kent, and the peerage meant a great deal to him. He asked why I never used my titles.

"I wish to be judged on merit alone. My earned titles mean far more to me," I explained.

"Don't be absurd, Miss Stahle. No one is *ever* judged on merit alone." Unfortunately, what he said was true. My titles and wealth had certainly smoothed my path.

Abbott allowed me the courtesy of joining the consultation as he examined my mother-in-law. While she was dressing after the examination, we withdrew to his consulting room to confer.

"It's likely, as you suspected, a large fibroid tumor," he said. "However, given its size and the discomfort it's causing Lady Bromsley, I think it should be removed. What do you think, Miss Stahle?" His tone when he asked the question reminded me too much of Sauerbruch or Abrams quizzing me for instructional purposes. I had learned to be cagey in my responses.

"Of course, I defer to your greater experience, Lord Abbott."

He looked annoyed and said impatiently, "I asked, Miss Stahle, because I am interested to hear your opinion."

I was momentarily taken aback by his tone but answered honestly. "Then, yes, I agree. On the basis of the discomfort alone, and to allay any fear of cancer or a future malignancy."

Apparently, that was exactly what he wanted to hear. "Abrams tells me that you are an excellent belly-cutter. Would you like to scrub in with me?"

What a question! Of course, I would jump at the opportunity to operate with the most celebrated gynecologic surgeon of our time! I agreed at once.

The tumor was impressive, the size of a croquet ball. Prior to the surgery, Lady Philippa looked like a woman in early pregnancy. Afterwards, with a flat belly, she looked like a normal woman in her early fifties.

After the surgery, Abbott and I dined together at Simpson's in the Strand, known for its joints of meat, swimming in bloody juices and accompanied by a proper Yorkshire pudding.

When two doctors dine together, medical conversation is inevitable. After our review of Lady Philippa's case, the conversation turned to a discussion of fibroid tumors.

"I hear you've scheduled with the pathologist to examine it yourself," said Abbott. "Is that your usual practice, Miss Stahle?"

"Not always, but in cases where I have a personal interest, I usually check the slides myself."

Abbott looked up from his bloody plate where the wreckage of a lamb shank remained. "Don't you trust the pathologists?"

"Oh, I know our department to be first-rate, but it's how I keep up my skills with the microscope and reinforce what I learn. There is so much to learn in medicine."

The waiter came, took away Abbott's plate, and brought a fresh one.

"There is, indeed, much to learn," Abbott said. "I read constantly, but I can never keep up."

"I've often thought I should get some training in gynecology," I said casually. "So many abdominal complaints in women have to do with their female organs."

"You are correct," said Abbott, helping himself to an absurdly large portion of beef from the passing cart. "I can't imagine being a competent abdominal surgeon without a basic understanding of gynecology."

"It makes sense to me."

"So why not train with me?" he asked, peering at me before sticking a forkful of beef into his mouth.

"It's a bit late now. I'm rather deep into the surgical game."

"Never too late," he said, shaking his head. "Come do a residency with me. Given your background, you'll need far less than the usual two years. Then you can sit for your certification examinations and go on your merry way."

I put down my table silver to demonstrate that he had my attention. "You're serious."

He looked indignant. "I assure you, Miss Stahle, that I am completely serious."

"But Abrams will be furious. He only recently appointed me an attending."

"Never mind Abrams. If you decide to come aboard, I shall deal with him."

∽

The night after Lady Philippa's surgery, I was surprised to find a late-night visitor in my bed. Of course, I didn't sound the alarm, instantly knowing it was Lytton. He had slipped in behind me after I'd fallen asleep. I was surprised that he could find the way to my bedchamber. He had never even seen the London house, never mind visited there before. No doubt, Krauss had directed him to the right place. As usual, Lytton slept naked except for his shorts.

"When did you arrive?" I asked, pinching his thigh,

"Oh, long after midnight. I'm surprised your man even let me in. I had to swear I was your husband."

"Krauss knows exactly who you are. He's seen you in photographs. I assume you haven't changed that much."

"Not at all."

"Well, I must have a thorough look at you in the morning. What brings you to London?"

"To see Mother. Thank you, by the way, for looking after her."

"It was my pleasure. She is dear to me."

"You are the kindest wife." He moved closer and I became aware of his erection pressing against the back of my thighs. He tugged at the trousers of my pajamas. "What's this, Meg? You've become so mannish." He kissed the back of my neck. "And you've cut off all of your beautiful hair!" I had done it in a fit of irritation. Dressing and undressing for surgery left me impatient with my long hair. The new style had ended up being the most practical of solutions, and short bobs had become all the rage.

"I thought you liked my masculinity."

"Mostly, I do, but can we get rid of these?" he asked, tugging at the trousers of my pajamas.

"Perhaps. If you have condoms."

"As a matter of fact, I do."

The next morning, while Krauss served us a formal breakfast in the dining room, he stole suspicious glances at Lytton. If I ever doubted my majordomo's loyalty, I was now doubly assured of it. If necessary, he would protect me even from my own husband.

"You may accompany me to the hospital," I said, when Lytton put down the newspaper to prepare his tea. "You'll need me in order to get into your mother's ward."

"But I am her son," he protested.

"Her surgery was quite extensive, and family members aren't usually allowed to visit unless the patient is fit."

"Tyrant!" he said, twisting his beautiful mouth to hide a smile. "But after you're done making sure I toe the line, and mother is back at home, you must join me on holiday."

"What did you have in mind? The weather isn't quite right for mountain climbing."

"No, I want you to come to Italy. I'm working on the most interesting excavation, and we've uncovered treasures that will simply dazzle you!" He drew theatrical curlicues in the air. "Promise me you'll come."

"We'll see."

Lytton continued to badger me on this subject until I weakened. When I agreed to accompany him to Italy, he was jubilant.

~

It was September before I could get away to Rome. Abrams finally noticed that he'd been working me too hard. After finding me nearly stuporous on a bench in the hall after a twelve-hour surgery, he decided I needed a holiday. Not only that, he ordered me to take a month's leave.

Lytton had remained in London to give a series of lectures at the British Museum. He'd spent extravagantly on his expeditions, and his funds were running low. I could have helped him financially, but I wanted him to learn to live within his means. Charles' father had a friend on the board of the museum, who suggested a lecture series on the Roman project. Lytton, a natural actor, could tell a dramatic tale that held listeners spellbound. The venture was successful, and soon Lytton's coffers were full. I briefly hoped that my husband might learn to earn his keep.

He persuaded me to travel to Rome by sea, convinced that a cruise was exactly what I needed to relax. Indeed, I felt young and carefree as we sailed out of Dover. The world in 1925 was a very different place from what it was when Lytton and I had first married before the Great War. Jazz had established itself as the trendy musical style. Women's clothing was more serviceable and less ornate. The garments for dancing and other entertainments were bold indeed. Skirt lengths had risen, provocatively showing legs and ankles, scandalous in another era, but now, quite the fashion.

On the boat to Spain, Lytton taught me all the latest dances: the Charleston, the Cakewalk, and the Lindy Hop. He was a natural dancer and could waltz me around a ballroom with grace, but he was insanely jubilant dancing those frantic steps, as if through all that twitching, he could express some of his restlessness.

He quickly found a male companion on the boat. After that, I hardly saw him in our stateroom except when he returned to bathe or dress. He tried to induce me to take one of his male lovers to our bed, but the intimacy I felt with Lytton was tenuous at best, and the presence of a third party diluted it, so I declined. His male lover disembarked in Gibraltar, but almost instantly, Lytton found another. I didn't mind his absence. The solitude afforded me an opportunity to read for pleasure, something I rarely had time to do.

In public, Lytton played the attentive husband, ever at my side, gallantly squiring me to formal dinners, plying me with canapés and cocktails. On that passage to Italy, I was introduced to martinis and found their intoxicating purity intriguing. Once I'd confessed I liked them, Lytton kept ordering more.

My good sense compromised, I allowed him to talk me into taking the stage. The band encouraged talent from the audience with mixed results. The applause was polite after I'd sung a few popular tunes, but when I switched to gritty Kurt Weil songs, all conversation in the room stopped. At the end of my impromptu recital, I received a standing ovation.

"Darling," said Lytton, taking my hands as I resumed my seat, "You are truly amazing."

"Keep giving me martinis and you'll see 'truly amazing.'"

We laughed, and that night, we slept together. Lytton suddenly got the idea that we should have another child. His pleas made me momentarily vulnerable, but I did not relent. He pouted. I stroked his cheek, which was growing scratchy by that time of the night.

"We already have two beautiful children."

"But how will you remember me when I'm gone?"

"You always come back from wherever you go."

"But what if I don't?" he asked, chilling me, although I am not superstitious.

Lytton had completely forgotten the idea of expanding our family by the time we neared the Italian coast. I felt him perceptibly withdraw from me. It was obvious that he was readying himself for his reunion with his friends, which made me wonder why he had invited me in the first place.

His arrival was welcomed by a gaggle of well-heeled, beautiful young men, all golden from the sun, their bodies sculpted to perfection. If blood hadn't coursed through their veins, they might have been statues from the garden of an ancient Roman villa.

They cheered when Lytton came down the ramp, joyfully greeting their boon companion, hugging him, and clapping him heartily on the back. They began to escort him away, leaving me on the pier to stare after them. Fortunately, Lytton noticed that I had been abandoned and came to reclaim me.

"So sorry, my dear. Please understand. They're just happy I've returned."

"Of course, they are."

Someone had managed to secure a veritable train of taxis, and we all set off for the Roman house Lytton had leased, courtesy of the income from our marriage settlement. After helping to unload the luggage, most of the young men melted away. Only one remained, a German called Hans Meyer. He was even taller than Lytton, who towered above most men.

In Meyer's presence, Lytton behaved in a manner I can only describe as feminine. He was deferential, nearly coy. Of course, as is often the case with homosexuals, his imitation of female behaviors was exaggerated, a parody of how real women act. Meyer, meanwhile, was quite the rugged, masculine opposite. I perceived these two were a couple, and it was obvious how the roles had been assigned. This made me wonder what Lytton had been thinking to bring me into the house, where it was obvious that a domestic arrangement was well established.

Yet, as the day wore on, neither man behaved in any way to make me uncomfortable. In fact, they were exceedingly accommodating. Meyer was the cook, and quite a good one. He invited me to accompany him while he went to the market to forage for dinner ingredients. He liked the idea that we could speak German together. Lytton spoke German very competently, but there is nothing like speaking one's own tongue with another who has spoken it since infancy.

"How do you know Lytton?" I asked Meyer in the market as he inspected the artichokes. He decided they weren't fresh and rejected them in favor of escarole.

"He's the leader of our archaeological expedition and pays for our expenses. He has a very nice income, you know."

"Yes, I know," I replied dryly, feeling it unnecessary to reveal its source. "Is yours a love match?" I asked.

He laughed heartily. "No, we merely find it convenient. You know how it is with men. We don't build love nests the way women do."

I had a rather cavalier attitude to sexual partnerships myself, so I counted myself an exception to this rule. Apart from Hanna, it had never occurred to me to install a female lover in my house. Besides, for the sake of appearances, I was still married to Lytton.

That night, after an excellent supper prepared by Meyer—sautéed chicken, with dried tomatoes, cockles, and escarole over hand-made pasta, we sat on the verandah to enjoy a Tuscan wine from a dusty bottle that Meyer had discovered in a local shop. It was excellent. I have always admired the ability of men of his persuasion to find the best food, the most elegant design, and other fine things in life.

In an effort to make me feel welcome, Lytton and Meyer invited me to share their bed. I never sleep well on boats, so I chose their guest room instead, where I slept peacefully under the finest linens on a mattress as soft as a moonbeam.

Refreshed and ready for adventure, I welcomed Lytton's suggestion that we explore the city. First, he took me to the beach near Fiumicino for the view, and not only of the Mediterranean! A colony of men lived there, and every morning they ran together along the edge of the water. After their run, they lifted weights on the beach to tone their bodies and build up their muscles. Their tight-fitting garments were obviously designed to show off their assets. I could see why Lytton found the sight so compelling. Truthfully, I found it rather compelling myself.

Lytton remarked as we returned to our hired motorcar, "I think you found that episode nearly as inspiring as I did."

"Not quite, I'm sure. But as you know, I like a bit of variety from time to time."

"Yes, your tastes are rather more catholic than mine. If it hadn't been for you, I might never have sampled the female sex and its many pleasures."

"I'm flattered, Lytton."

"And you should be. I've never taken a fancy to any other woman."

"Despite our many differences, Lytton, we are well-matched. Our marriage has suited me."

"You're not angry that I don't spend more time at home with you and the children?"

"I'm not particularly angry. You're never there, so the children don't miss you. I probably miss you more. Sometimes I'm lonely for intelligent conversation." I was angry with myself for admitting this weakness. Fortunately, Lytton didn't address it aloud. He only gave me a knowing smile and reached for my hand.

We ate a casual lunch of salad with pickled whelks before Lytton took me to the excavation site. A temporary structure had been erected to house, catalogue, and store the treasures that had been dug from the surrounding soil. There was no electricity in that remote place, so Lytton struck a match on his shoe and lit a kerosene lantern. He unlocked one of the several padlocks and led me into a storeroom. It was a virtual treasure trove of artifacts from that long-past era, everything from bits of pottery—carefully organized and numbered—to nearly intact statuary.

"Look at this," said Lytton. He found a pry bar and removed the lid from a wooden crate. He hung the lantern overhead, so we could see inside the box, where a nearly perfect, bronze statue of Mercury stood. The god gracefully balanced on one foot, ready to take flight. One hand held a caduceus, while the other delicately pointed up toward heaven.

"We must have this," Lytton breathed. "We simply must!"

"Obviously, we do."

He looked sheepish and shook his head. "Before I earned the money for my lectures, I took an American investor. Now, he insists this treasure belongs to him."

"That's rather greedy of him. Can't you bargain with him?"

"Believe me, I've tried." He took a deep breath and let it out in a long stream. "I've offered him everything else you see here, but he wasn't interested. The only way he will part with it is for an obscene amount of money, far more than he ever invested in the excavation in the first place."

"Engage a lawyer. Surely, you can come to an agreement."

"Not so surely. Italian lawyers are useless. Everything here is settled by paying off the judges." He sighed. "I fear that would be even more expensive."

I was annoyed that Lytton found himself in such a foolish business arrangement. Even more, I was growing impatient. "Lytton, how much money does this man want?"

He gulped audibly. "One-hundred-thousand American dollars."

For a moment, I was rendered speechless. "You must be joking."

"I am entirely serious. Now, he says he has a buyer in America who will pay his price."

"Obviously, you can't afford to buy it," I said, studying his face.

"No, but you can."

I gave him a sharp look. "I? Why would *I* wish to buy this?"

"Well, besides the fact that it's sublime, the caduceus is so obviously a symbol of your profession." I frowned sternly and folded my arms on my chest.

He sighed. "I never thought that argument would sway you, but someday this piece will be worth an extraordinary amount of money. Buy it as an investment." I gazed at the remarkable, little statue, everything perfectly intact, a bit of verdigris clinging to the eyes, remaining despite careful cleaning, and I realized he was right.

"Let me think about it."

"Don't think too long. I've been holding him off for weeks."

"Why did you wait until the last minute?"

"Because I was afraid to ask you."

"Am I that forbidding?"

"Yes, actually." He took me in his arms and held me against his massive chest. "Please, my darling, if you buy this, I shall be forever grateful. This is the prize of all my explorations." His beautiful mouth pouted in a most fetching way.

I rolled my eyes at this dramatic declaration. "Very well. Tell your American friend you have a buyer who will meet his ridiculous price, but see if you can bring it down a bit. Offer him seventy-five thousand and work your way up, but no more than one-hundred thousand. That is my absolute limit. Do you understand?"

He hugged me so tightly he nearly crushed my ribs. "You are my dearest, most wonderful, most perfect wife! Thank you! Thank you! You have no idea how happy you've made me."

The business with the American was concluded quickly. We settled at eighty-five thousand. I needed only to wire to our bank in Frankfurt to release the money. As I was now conducting all the family finances, there was no question, despite the fact that I was withdrawing an extraordinary sum.

After getting what he wished, I half expected Lytton to kiss me and send me home. But he didn't. He invited me to share in the celebration of his triumph. He'd arranged for a party in one of the men's clubs, and by "men's club," I don't mean the leather-furniture-and-dark-woods type of place that English gentlemen liked to frequent.

There was one small problem. Women were not welcome in such establishments, which Lytton had completely forgotten when he'd invited me. He offered to change the venue, but he'd already paid for the food and wine. I flatly told him that I would not pay for the party to be held elsewhere.

As he brooded over the dilemma, I could see an idea dawning. He brushed my short hair away from my face. "You need a little haircut," he said and called Meyer from the other room. They conferred. Meyer returned with clippers. He was a reasonably good barber. He left my hair long on top but clipped it close at the back of my neck and over my ears. He fussed a bit over what he called "the sideburns" but succeeded in achieving an acceptable look. Lytton held a hand mirror for me to see the result. "This is how you look as a man."

I stared at the image. Although the refinement of my features was feminine, the angular planes made my face strong enough to pass for a man's. Meyer handed me a towel. "Take off your makeup. That will help." They blackened a wine cork and used the smoke residue to slightly darken my lower face, suggesting the hint of a clean-shaven beard.

"Clothes," said Lytton. "Where can we get clothes?" They looked at one another, but it was obvious their clothes would simply swim on me.

"Crenshaw," they both said at once. Lytton turned to me and explained. "Tommy Crenshaw has a slight build, and he's about your height."

Meyer went off to call on one of their neighbors, while Lytton inspected me. "Meg, you must do something about your breasts." My breasts were not overly large, but they gave me a discernible female profile.

"I thought you liked my breasts."

"I do! In fact, I love them, but they will be a problem unless we can contrive a way to hide them." He went away and returned with a silk opera scarf. "Take off your blouse." I gave him a pained look. "Come, Meg. Don't be difficult. It's not as if I haven't seen it all!"

I removed my blouse and camisole. Lytton wound the scarf tightly around my chest, flattening the profile. He secured the scarf carefully with safety pins. By that time, Meyer had returned with a white linen suit and waistcoat. He'd also brought along a shirt, a collar, a handsome cravat, socks and garters, and wing-tip shoes.

I felt no qualms about being naked in front of my husband, but Meyer's presence was a bit unnerving. Fortunately, he perceived the intrusion and left when I began to remove my skirt.

Lytton gave me a pair of his undershorts to replace my knickers. The buttons and fly amused me. "Ah, the escape hatch for the birdie," I mused, sticking my finger through it. Lytton didn't even smile which told me how serious he was about this project. He tightly rolled one of his socks and placed it in the shorts. He called to Meyer in the other room. "What do you think, Hans? Should Meg hang left or right?"

"She's right-handed, so right."

Lytton reached into the shorts and adjusted the position of the rolled sock.

Amazingly, when I put on Crenshaw's clothing, I felt as if I had worn such attire forever. Nothing felt strange about it. I especially liked the trousers, which offered a wonderful sense of movement and freedom. I could see exactly why men favored them. The shirt and waistcoat hung perfectly, now that I had bound my breasts. Lytton helped me do up the tie and showed me how to button the socks to the garters. He lent me a pair of his cuff buttons and fastened them for me. Then he stood back to survey his work.

"Your hair is still a bit too long, but I'm reluctant to cut off more. People at home will wonder what you got up to while you were away." He returned with some pomade. After I slicked it on, he combed my hair, parting it carefully. "Hans! Hans!" he called to Meyer in the kitchen, "Come have a look."

I could see from the surprise and satisfaction on Meyer's face that my transformation had been successful. "My God, she could be one of us."

"But now we must think of a name for *him*," said Lytton, stroking his chin. "What shall we call you, Meg?"

I found myself remembering the time I'd boldly infiltrated the student clubs while dressed in Konrad's clothes. I extended my hand to Lytton. "Hello. May I introduce myself? Konrad, Baron von Holdenberg."

"Of course!" said Lytton with delight. "Why hadn't I thought of that?" His eyes grew large with amazement. "By Jove, you look exactly like him!"

The gentlemen dressed and we headed to the party. Even their friends were fooled by the disguise. I'd occasionally had to affect a male persona for plays at Somerville, so I knew how to lower my voice and speak with a male cadence. Lytton came up with a pet nickname for me: "Freddie." Frederika was one of my many names, so it fit perfectly. From then on, I was "Freddie" to our friends.

I so enjoyed my alter-ego as my cousin, I wanted to repeat it, but Mr. Crenshaw expected us to return his suit. Lytton and Meyer took me to the best men's tailor in Rome. The proprietor raised his brows when the need to take my measurements revealed that I was a woman, but he had no objection to my money.

After I ordered several suits for day and evening along with coordinating shirts and cravats, we headed to a corset shop to find something better than an opera scarf to flatten my breasts. The owner of this shop showed no surprise at my request. Evidently, I was not the only woman of means with such a need. There was a colony of women in Paris, who came to Italy to prolong the summer. Lytton and Meyer seemed to enjoy spending my money as we purchased all the items I needed to complete my "Freddie" disguise.

For the next week, I went everywhere as a man, which opened my eyes to how free men were. If an angry chief of surgery hadn't been awaiting me in London, I might have considered remaining with Lytton and his friends forever.

19

I remained in Rome longer than I had intended, so I needed to take the shortest route on my return. That meant traveling overland and then taking a ferry from Calais to England. Looking forward to catching up on my reading during the long train ride through Europe, I had purchased a stack of books. I was deeply involved in *Arrowsmith*, a medical drama, by the American author, Sinclair Lewis, when the conductor tapped on the window of my compartment.

"Telegram for you, *Contessa*," he said, touching the visor of his hat. "Should I wait for a reply?"

I opened the carefully folded stiff paper. The message was cruelly brief:

> Your grandmother has died. Come to Raithschau with all
> possible speed.—Father

To keep my footing, I reached out to the compartment wall for support. I reread the message again because I simply couldn't believe the meaning of the words.

The conductor cleared his throat to remind me that he was waiting.

"Reply to the sender, I shall come at once."

Again he touched the visor of his hat. Before he left, I asked his advice on the best route. He explained that, if I changed at the next station and took the night train, I could be in Raithschau by morning.

That night, as I lay in my berth, rocked gently by the motion of the train, I thought of my grandmother and the many times she had swooped in to rescue me from my parents' negligence. I remembered her promise to be there for me always, and how even as a girl, I'd realized it was a well-intended falsehood. Now, both grandparents were dead. Although my parents were still alive, I suddenly felt like an orphan.

Raithschau's majordomo met me at the train station. He waited patiently while I separated my luggage into two piles, one for necessities for my stay, the other for items to be sent to London on the next train. The trunk containing my fine new male wardrobe would be sent ahead.

In light of developments, the elegantly tailored suits, shirts, and cravats now seemed absurdly indulgent and frivolous. Fortunately, I had packed a black suit and a lace veil with the idea that Lytton and I might wish to visit the Vatican. My noble title and relationship to the mother general of Obberoth could probably have gotten us an audience with the pope. Once more enticing pursuits presented themselves, I'd abandoned that idea.

As Schloss Raithschau came into view, I saw a black banner flying from the highest tower. The Countess of Raithschau was dead. When I entered the castle, the waiting servants bowed and curtsied and addressed me by the ancient title of "*Eure Liebdenin.*" I was baffled until I realized that *I* was now Countess Raithschau.

Father rescued me, offering a quick embrace before leading me away to a room where we could speak privately.

"Were you with her when she died?" I asked.

I could see how it pained him to answer. "No."

"She died alone?"

"Her sister was by her side. Your grandmother died in the infirmary at Obberoth."

"Was she ill?"

"A female cancer. You must ask Schulte. He will explain."

"Were you aware of her illness?"

He shook his head. ""None of us knew," my father said. "She swore her doctor to secrecy."

"Where is Grandmother now?"

"At Obberoth. The sisters are preparing her body for burial."

I glanced around. "Where's Mother? Did she come with you?"

Father sighed. "She's upstairs resting. This has been a strain for her." My anger at hearing this could barely be contained. My father had lost his mother, and I, my dear grandmother, and my mother found it *a strain*?

"Poor dear," I said with contempt.

Father clucked his tongue. "Be kind," he reminded me. "You know how she is."

I finally noticed how gray and tired he looked. "Come, Father, let's find some alcohol," I said, taking his arm. As the presumed heir, I'd always had my own rooms at Raithschau, so that's where I led him. The majordomo had already set up the drinks table in my sitting room.

I handed a glass of whiskey to Father and raised mine in salute. "To a remarkable woman!" Without thought, I threw down my drink like a man. My father's jaw went slack, and he stared at me. He stared at my legs, and I realized that I was standing with them wide apart. In my distraction, I'd forgotten I wasn't wearing trousers. I quickly moved my feet together and affected a more ladylike pose.

Father looked relieved and changed the topic. "From what I understand, Schulte did all he could, but it was incurable."

"Still, he should have informed us. Keeping it from us is an unforgivable breach of trust."

"Wasn't he duty-bound to follow the patient's wishes? You, a physician, should know that."

"Yes, but wouldn't you have preferred the opportunity to say goodbye to your mother?"

My father batted away my question as if it were an annoying insect. "What difference does it make now? Drink your drink and calm yourself."

I let out my breath in a long sigh hoping to release my anger with it.

Father and I spoke briefly about the arrangements for the funeral. Apparently, my grandmother had planned every detail while she was still well enough to think about such things. She had requested that the Mozart Requiem be sung at her funeral. "The only wrinkle seems to be the lack of a mezzo-soprano on such short notice," my father explained. "Sister Elfriede is thinking of having one of her nuns sing the part."

I rose to pour us more whiskey. "I shall sing it."

"Margarethe, you can't be serious. What will people say?"

"I don't really give a damn what they say."

Father stared at me. "Good heavens! What have they done to you in London? Is it that hospital post you've taken?"

"Father, I am a surgeon. I was trained to perform under the most trying circumstances just as you were as a military officer. I shall sing the

Requiem." Once again, I threw down my liquor, and Father watched with a worried look.

"You've changed, Margarethe. It's a bit of a shock, but your new, commanding persona gives me cheer. Evidently, we've succeeded with you. Your grandmother would be proud."

"I doubt she'd approve of my singing at her funeral."

"Oh, I don't know. Your grandmother was more forward looking than you might think."

I used my firmest "doctor's voice" to order Father to get some rest. The pallor I had noticed earlier had only increased, and his mouth was pinched. I saw him to his room. Then I refreshed my makeup and headed to Obberoth in Grandfather's old motorcar. It had held up surprisingly well, despite its age. As it rambled along, I thought of the many times I had accompanied my grandmother on this short journey to visit her sister.

Sister Portress conducted me directly to my grandaunt's office. Once the door was shut, *Tante* held me fiercely, as if by this demonstration of combined strength, we could somehow fill the great void left by our mutual loss.

"Thank you for coming home so quickly, Margarethe. We need you now."

After she let me go, she scanned my face.

"You're angry because we didn't tell you."

"Yes, I'm angry. I could have arranged for her to be seen by the best medical practitioners in Europe."

Tante sighed. "The doctor tells me it was too late for that. She kept it to herself until she could no longer bear the discomfort. By that time, nothing could be done for her."

"Did she suffer?" I asked.

"She was uncomfortable, especially at the end, but Dr. Schulte was generous with the morphine, so the pain was much less than it could have been. Mostly she was tired and very weak. To hasten her own death, she stopped eating."

I sank down in a chair. "I wish I could have said my farewells."

"Margarethe, every time you parted, you said your farewells. None of us has any guarantees. 'We know not the time nor the hour...'"

"Yes, but I always expected to see her again!"

"And someday you will," she said gently.

"Oh, don't tell me your pretty fairy tales!" I replied sharply. "I don't believe in your heaven, nor the miseries of your hell. There is only this miserable, painful life!"

The outburst released my feelings, both the pain and the anger. I tried to choke back the tears, but they defeated me. My grandaunt rose, and the rosary beads at her belt clicked softly as she approached. She laid a gentle hand on my shoulder. "Have no regrets. You were always kind and attentive to your grandmother. She knew you loved her, and she loved you like life itself. She often spoke of you in her last weeks. How pleased she was that you had made a name for yourself as a physician, how well you were raising your children...."

My ability to contain myself finally collapsed. I covered my face with my hands and sobbed. *Tante* tried to soothe me by rubbing my back. "Shed your tears, my darling. I have already spent many hours weeping. But when we go before your family and my sisters, there can be no tears, only strength and composure."

I mopped my face with my handkerchief and took a deep breath. "I understand that Sister Elfriede is seeking a mezzo soloist for the Great Requiem. I shall sing."

My grandaunt mostly succeeded in hiding her surprise. "No, Margarethe. You must take your place with the family."

"No, I *must* sing. It will be my last gift to my grandmother." I took another deep breath to calm myself.

"This is such an emotional time for you. Are you sure you want to place this additional burden on yourself?"

"Yes, *Tante*. Yes! I *must* do it."

My grandaunt took a step back in order to take my full measure. My tear-stained face probably undercut my determined look, but I held her gaze until she said, "Yes, of course, you must. I can understand how singing will comfort you. It always has." She went into the hall. I heard her ask her secretary to fetch Sister Elfriede.

While we waited, my grandaunt reached for my hand. "My dear girl, I share your pain, but now, we must be strong together." She squeezed my hand on the word, "together."

My former voice teacher appeared, it seemed, within minutes. She embraced me and soothingly stroked my back. "My dear girl, I am so sorry. I know how you loved your grandmother."

Sister Elfriede studied me while Reverend Mother explained that I had volunteered to sing the mezzo solo in the Requiem.

"Margarethe, are you certain? Can you manage it on such an emotional occasion?"

"You can be sure that I can and I will," I said with great bravado.

"A very brave statement," said Sister Elfriede, patting my arm, "but this is not a concert." She gazed at me calmly for a long moment. "If you are sure you are able, but you mustn't put undue pressure on yourself at this time."

"Please, Sister, don't doubt me. I need you to believe in me now."

"Margarethe, I do believe in you." She exchanged a glance with her superior, who nodded her assent. Sister Elfriede laid a gentle hand on my cheek. "It will be good to hear you sing again. We shall rehearse after the noon meal."

Tante sent for tea. She urged me to eat a few sugar cookies to keep up my strength, but I had no appetite. After we finished our tea, she led me to the chapel to inspect my grandmother's tomb in the crypt. Staring into grandmother's grave, I envisioned my own. Tradition dictated that the Countess of Raithschau be buried at Obberoth with the order's dead.

The rough stone of the walls reflected no light, making the dark hole seem bottomless, almost as if I could see into infinity. That made me think of Grandfather buried in Edelheim, hundreds of miles away. I found myself wondering if the knowledge that my grandparents would spend eternity apart ever troubled them.

We ascended to the chapel, and *Tante* took my arm. I sensed that, rather than seeking my support, she was offering hers.

"Do you wish to see her?" she asked, as I closed the heavy door to the crypt. The sound of it closing reverberated through the chapel.

As a physician, I had seen many corpses in my day, but it is quite different to gaze upon a person one has loved in life. "Yes, please."

We headed to the infirmary. The sister in charge bowed to her superior and led us to the room where my grandmother lay. They both withdrew to give me privacy. I steeled myself before drawing back the sheet, but to my surprise, Grandmother looked peaceful. Her eyes were sunken and ringed by dark circles, but there was no pinching of the mouth nor other evidence that her end had been difficult. Apart from her extreme pallor, she could have been asleep. I touched her hand, finding it as rigid and cold as that of any cadaver.

I carefully drew up the sheet over her face. *Tante* took my arm as we walked in the direction of the chapel, where the rehearsal would soon begin. A professional orchestra and choir had come down from Würzburg for the Requiem, but I didn't like the idea of Sister Elfriede and her choir of nuns being shunted aside in their own chapel.

"But all those treble voices would throw off the harmonic balance!" the conductor explained when I questioned him.

"That is your responsibility, Maestro. The tenors can fend for themselves. Find a few more baritones and basses. I'm sure the local church choir can oblige." Out of the corner of my eye, I saw Sister Elfriede nodding in approval.

My favorite baritone arrived on the night train. I was also grateful to have Lytton at my side because his natural warmth and glib tongue enabled him to deflect people trying to offer condolences. While I appreciated all the heartfelt expressions of sympathy, they began to breach the fragile wall I'd erected around my heart. At such moments, Lytton skillfully intervened, allowing me to retreat to privacy.

"I have a vital mission for you," I told him the next morning. "Head into town and find some male voices."

"Here's a baritone," he said, raising his hand.

"I already counted you. Now, go find me more."

He grinned and saluted. "Aye, aye, Captain!" He went off singing a tune from the *Pirates of Penzance*. Lytton rounded up a sufficient number of male voices to balance out those of the nuns.

The next morning, the bishop arrived. My parents and I skipped breakfast because of the communion fast. I hadn't confessed to a priest or done anything remotely Catholic for years, but avoiding the communion rail would embarrass my family and the nuns.

Sister Elfriede and I had agreed on a musical cue to allow Lytton and me to escape from the family pew and head to the choir loft. I heard audible gasps as we walked down the aisle. When I took my place beside my fellow soloists, my grief lightened exponentially.

At the *Recordare*, I noticed a face turned toward the loft. She wore the white veil of a novice. She stared at me until the novice mistress, standing behind her, gave her a sharp jab between the shoulder blades. After that, I was aware of nothing but the music I sang. I could hear Lytton's distinctive voice shoring up the baritone section, and it comforted me to know he was near.

The sisters carried my grandmother's coffin to the new grave as they would one of their own.

"Shouldn't we help them?" Lytton whispered in my ear.

"She belongs to them now," I whispered in reply.

He gave me a horrified look.

My father gripped my hand as the casket was lowered. I was reminded of another funeral many years before when Miss Westerfield was buried in the churchyard at Edelheim. I was awakened from the memory by the horrible scraping sound as four sturdy farm hands from Raithschau slid the great stone into place.

We went to the visitors' parlor, where the novices served us tea. While everyone was busy enjoying the sisters' hospitality, I managed to slip away. I located the oil lamp near the steps and wasted a dozen matches trying to light it.

I imagined my lantern giving light to my grandmother in that terrible, dark place, where the sun never shone, and the air was so still. I touched the beautiful stone that covered the grave. Below, my grandmother lay in her bronze coffin. I selfishly wished for one more moment with her to speak to her, to hear her voice and feel her patting my head as indulgently as when she quieted her Affenpinchers, but I would never again in this life feel her touch, nor hear her voice.

The memories wrenched sobs from my chest. I sobbed like someone who could never be comforted. I yanked my handkerchief from my pocket. Within minutes, it was sodden, which also served to tell me I had been weeping long enough. I sensed that I wasn't alone, but when I glanced over my shoulder there was no one there.

I hurried to rejoin my family in the visitor's parlor. Lytton was entertaining my mother with his cheerful chatter, even though he knew that she despised him. The murmur of people around me rumbled in my ears. I suddenly felt a gentle hand on my back. A beautiful, white-veiled novice leaned forward to refill my water glass. "Countess, if you are ill, I would be glad to be of assistance," she whispered. I turned to see celestial blue eyes, tending to hazel, look earnestly into mine. The kindness in them made matters all the worse. I could feel the tears pressing against my eyes.

"Thank you, Sister," I murmured briskly, "but I can manage on my own."

She gave my shoulder a little squeeze and moved on to pour water in Lytton's glass.

◠

My anger towards Dr. Schulte had cooled by the time we met in his surgery. He wore his best Sunday suit for the interview, no doubt wanting to make a positive impression. The Countess of Raithschau always paid the salary of the town doctor, so I was now his employer.

Schulte had changed since I had broken my leg in the steeplechase. His sandy hair was rapidly thinning. He now wore an impressive mustache, perhaps to compensate for the lack of hair above.

"When did you realize it was cancer?" I asked.

"As soon as I palpated the mass, I suspected it. It lacked defined margins."

"Why didn't you call me?"

"That was my first suggestion to your grandmother. I said, 'let's call Lady Margarethe. She's a famous surgeon. She can find you the best care.' But she wasn't interested. She didn't want you to know. She knew you would try everything to save her life even though it was hopeless."

"But she allowed you to tell my grandaunt."

He shook his head. "No, my secrecy was to be absolute. Reverend Mother must have learned the awful news directly from her sister."

Before the interview, I had pored over his case files and carefully examined each and every entry. Schulte had even sketched the large mass he had removed and made other visual notes. The case had clearly been hopeless from the start.

"Sometimes, I feel so impotent!" I said, squeezing my hands together until they hurt. "I am a physician and yet, sometimes, I can do nothing, not even for members of my own family!"

He nodded in sympathy. "*Gnädige*, I understand your regret. I felt the same when I watched my mother die of breast cancer. The surgeons operated, but nothing could be done to save her."

"I've often thought I should have more training in female diseases," I said. "The chief of gynecology at my hospital has offered me a residency."

"Why would you go backwards after achieving so much?"

"Is it really going backwards?" I wondered aloud.

Schulte perceived that I had left the conversation to dialogue with myself. He asked if he could provide further information. I shook my head.

He was more obsequious in his farewells than I would have expected, but now that my role had changed, everyone at Raithschau was fumbling to adjust. Before I left, he said, "Take some comfort in the care the countess received in her final days. The infirmary sisters at Obberoth were like angels."

The remark inspired me to find a way to repay the nuns for their kindness. Because Grandfather had dissuaded his wife from taking a mortgage on Raithschau to finance the nuns' building projects, the order's hospital in Berlin remained smaller than originally planned. I liquidated some of my personal investments to fund a building campaign that would eventually double the size of St. Hilde's. The new wing was named in honor of my grandmother, Katharina, Countess of Raithschau.

~

In the short term, I was overwhelmed. Although Raithschau was considerably smaller and less complex than Edelheim, the estate had a winery and a sawmill in addition to the home farm and the tenants' plots. Grandmother had been an able farmer. Her managers used modern agricultural methods. The manor thrived and generated a handsome income from which the nuns at Obberoth also benefited. Leaving it without management was out of the question.

A Russian, who had been displaced by the Bolsheviks, offered to help. I had met Count Markovsky through a friend in the music world while still living in Munich. When Markovsky heard of my grandmother's passing, he wrote to me expressing his sympathies, but he also suggested he would like to be involved in the transition. He had administered his family's large estate in Ukraine and evidently knew something about farming. He even had some experience with vineyards. When I rang him, he said that country life was beckoning him and wondered aloud if I might lease Raithschau to him.

After we met with the count, Lytton persuaded me that I must take the burden of Raithschau off my shoulders. In his estimation, leasing to Markovsky seemed to be the best solution. My husband also agreed to stay on until the count and his family were settled.

Grandmother had stipulated in her will that I sit for a formal portrait to hang in the great hall. She had even chosen and paid for the artist in advance. I sat for him as patiently as I could for a week. Then I insisted he use photographs instead. He was incensed to have his efforts frustrated, but on the other side, I had Abrams sending daily wires demanding to know when I would return. I threw everything into Lytton's lap and dashed back to London.

~

When I reported for duty on my return, Abrams scowled and ordered me to get back to work. Charles looked enormously relieved to see his ally return. "You have no idea how unbearable the old man's been in your absence." While I'd been away, Charles had become the favored one. Unfortunately, being the object of Abrams' attention was a mixed blessing.

When Charles came for dinner, I told him about my grandmother's illness and Abbott's invitation to do a gynecology residency. He listened patiently while I argued with myself about whether or not it was a good idea.

"Meg, I understand why your grandmother's death inclines you in that direction," he said, thoughtfully puffing on his pipe. "It makes perfect sense to me, but Abrams will be furious."

I shrugged. "He's always furious over something. At least in this case, he can be furious about something real."

Charles took the pipe out of his mouth and erupted into peals of laughter.

But Abrams wasn't furious. He listened with thoughtful attention while I laid out my reasons for wanting to train in gynecology, puffing on his cigar all the while. By then, I had learned to ignore the vile smell.

"Well, Stahle, I can't argue against learning more about female surgeries. Abbott is correct. Much of what goes on below the waist in women is about their female parts." He leaned forward and frowned. "You're not going to leave us, are you? I mean, not permanently?"

"Good heavens, no!"

He sat back and breathed a sigh of relief. "Thank God. For a moment, I thought you'd lost your mind."

I laughed and soon, he did as well.

The next morning, I rang Abbott and arranged a dinner meeting at his favorite restaurant on the Strand. While we ate, I described the details of my grandmother's death and asked his opinion.

He waved to the waiter to bring along the cart of roast joints. "As you know, Stahle, cancer of the ovaries can spread very fast. One day, the patient feels perfectly healthy and the next, she's on death's door." He helped himself to slices of the bloody beef from the cart. "But your grandmother is gone. Why are you consulting me about her case after the fact?"

"I wonder if the offer of training in gynecology still stands."

He put down his knife and fork and rested his chin on his hands. "You would actually go backward into another residency?"

"If I learned to be a better surgeon, yes."

"And you wouldn't mind the demotion?"

"I didn't say that."

He smiled. "Well, at least, you'll be called 'doctor' again."

20

My surgical colleagues at Barts thought I was completely insane to detour into gynecology, and when I reported for duty, I wondered if they were right. I don't know why I hadn't thought about this before, but now, all of my patients were women. As a general surgeon, my domain had been the entire body; now all my work centered on the pelvis. It required some adjustment, but as I got more deeply into the practice of gynecology, I saw the female body in a whole new light.

My new colleagues were green residents, barely a year out of medical school, whereas I was literally a battle-hardened surgeon. My greater experience allowed me to anticipate their surgical disasters. I was always tempted to jump in to avoid the mishap before it happened, especially when an errant scalpel was in danger of nicking a bowel or other vital organ. Sometimes, I simply couldn't help myself and intervened. After a few of these altruistic rescues, the other residents began to look up to me and seek out my advice.

Abbott never seemed to mind these unplanned interventions. "I can't be everywhere, Stahle. You are a first-rate surgeon. The junior doctors can learn from you," he said. He studied me. "I think you like teaching, and you are rather good at it."

Managing my colleagues proved far easier than managing my patients. As a surgeon, I'd simply appeared masked and gowned, anonymous to the patient, who, in any case, didn't care because they were under the influence of ether. In gynecology, one needed to have at least a modicum of bedside manner.

Initially, I found basic communication frustrating. Many women of my generation had been raised with the idea that sex and reproduction were not fit topics for polite conversation. Such matters should only be spoken about in hushed tones behind closed doors, if at all. Some women, especially the older ladies, could barely speak of their sexual organs. I found it frustrating, but eventually, I learned an effective code for explaining essential matters.

I drew on my memory of how Hanna had dealt with her patients. She'd always spoken of delicate matters with warmth and candor, which seemed to put her patients at ease. A metal speculum can be shockingly cold, especially on a winter day. Hanna had always warmed the instrument in her hand for a moment before inserting it. Whenever I employed this method, I thought of her and could almost feel her near.

My first solo surgery came within the first week, which made sense because I was already certified as a surgeon. Soon I was performing complex gynecological surgery daily. Abbott thought my training was going so well he took me off gynecology early and moved me into obstetrics. I hadn't bargained for that part when I'd signed on for a new residency, but he insisted that it was an essential part of my training.

"You will be brilliant at caesareans. I simply know it!" said Abbott when I made a face.

I appreciated his confidence, but the first time I was required to cut open a woman's belly to pull out the infant, I was on tenterhooks. I had only performed the procedure once before when I was an intern. Abbott preferred caesareans to more drastic measures. I was relieved to learn that he thought pubiotomies barbaric and had banned them.

I found my obstetrics patients mystifying. Some were like Dr. Jekyll and Mr. Hyde of the eponymous tale. I never knew who would appear in my office for a prenatal appointment. These ladies were obviously at the mercy of their hormones and as tidal as the ocean.

My six-month foray into the world of childbirth left me no more enamored of the process than before. Being up to my elbows in blood, amniotic fluid, and meconium made all the talk of the "miracle of birth" even more nonsensical. Needless to say, I was more than happy to return to gynecology and active surgery.

The time went by quickly. Eighteen months after beginning my residency, Abbott pronounced me ready to sit for my examinations. I did and passed in both gynecology and obstetrics. Shortly thereafter, I went to Berlin to sit for the German panel. I was now certified in three medical specialties, but I had no clue what to do next.

When I returned to London, following my German panel examinations, Abrams called me and invited me to meet him for tea.

"So, Stahle, are you going back to Germany now?" he asked, flicking the ash from his cigar into the ashtray.

"I have no idea, Mister Abrams, but you can be sure I have no wish to make a career as a gynecologist."

"Thank God! I knew you'd come to your senses eventually!" he said, rolling his eyes toward heaven for emphasis. "It is a sad day, indeed, when we lose a good surgeon to the lower specialties."

I laughed aloud. "I very much doubt Lord Abbott or his colleagues would appreciate that comment."

"Well, it's true. Why would you waste your talent delivering babies? Anyone can do that. In fact, women can do it without us, and have for millennia! You can put your time to far better use."

"Do you have something in mind, sir?"

"Well, yes, I do." He put out the stump of his cigar, crushing it carefully in the ashtray. "I need a good belly cutter. Calder is a fine chest man. The two of you together make a spectacular team, especially in trauma cases. Come back to us, and I'll make you a senior attending."

"Thank you, sir. That's extraordinarily generous."

"Eh, I know, but you're worth it."

Before I accepted Abrams's offer, I extracted the promise of an extended holiday.

"A fortnight," he proposed.

"A month. I need a respite before I jump headlong into real surgery again."

He gave me a critical look. "You do look a bit worn around the edges. Well, all right," he grumbled.

In addition to enjoying a spell of leisure, I needed to retrieve my children, whom I'd left in the care of my mother when I'd gone down to Germany for the panel examinations. Actually, I'd left them in the care of my old nurse. Mother happened to be there, but I doubt she was much use. Father, on the other hand, was an enthusiastic grandparent and used the opportunity to teach William how to shoot. He became quite a good marksman.

I spent a week with the children and my parents at Edelheim before heading south to look in on my Russian tenants and my grandaunt. My agreement with Markovsky included the right to stay at Schloss Raithschau whenever I wished. The countess's rooms were reserved for my use. Despite this arrangement, I felt it would be an imposition.

When I spoke my thoughts aloud, my grandaunt proposed an obvious alternative. "Why not stay with us at Obberoth?"

She reminded me that there was a guest house for pious, Catholic women, mostly widows and elderly noblewomen, on the convent grounds. The cottage was large and comfortable, but to open it for one person, seemed plainly absurd.

"You could stay in the convent instead," my grandaunt suggested.

"Are you sure you want the bombardier living under your roof again?"

She laughed. "Hopefully, the bombardier has matured and seen the error of her ways."

"Ah, I wouldn't count on that, *Tante*."

"I'm more worried about the washing powder in the sugar bowls."

"If I am eating in the same refectory with you and your sisters, you certainly needn't worry about that."

"My thoughts exactly," she said. "Nevertheless, I shall keep you close, where I can watch for signs of mischief."

On my arrival at Obberoth, I was given a nun's cell with an iron cot. A thin mattress was all that covered the bare springs. Trying to fall asleep that first night, I wondered if I should drive down the road and beg Markovsky to let me in. The bed springs screeched whenever I rolled over. Only my fatigue kept this unwelcome symphony from keeping me awake, but my back ached the next morning. When I went to wash, I encountered the old-fashioned washstand and a pitcher of ice cold water. Fortunately, there were common toilets instead of a chamber pot under the bed.

After breakfast, I informed my grandaunt that I intended to install modern plumbing and central heating.

"But simplicity is an essential part of the religious life."

"Tell the truth, *Tante*. Wouldn't you much rather wash in hot water on a winter's day instead of needing to break the ice first?"

"Yes, in winter, it's hard, especially for the older sisters. The cold aggravates their rheumatism."

"And, as mother general of the order, it is your duty to look after their health. Correct?"

She gave me a wary look, perhaps recognizing that she had trained me a little too well in the arts of persuasion.

"Imagine, waking to warmth instead of seeing your breath as vapor," I continued in a tantalizing voice, "then, a hot bath, the steam rising around you…"

I could see the exact moment when *Tante* "warmed" to the idea. The next day, I telephoned an engineering firm in Frankfurt and asked them to make a survey of the project.

At first, living among the nuns reminded me uncomfortably of my school days, but I quickly adjusted to the rhythm of their life. The food in the refectory was plain. Meat was scarce, but the vegetables were grown in their own gardens and could not be fresher.

I especially enjoyed singing the Office with the nuns, not because of any religious sentiment on my part, but because the Gregorian chant was so utterly pure and, despite its apparent simplicity, quite complex. As part of my musical training, Sister Elfriede had taught me how to read and sing the square notes, but now, I heard it from a different perspective.

"The phrasing is so different from modern music," I observed.

"Yes, it is more fluid, more conducive to common singing. There is less focus on an individual voice. In a convent, we sing as one."

Sister Elfriede knew she had hooked her fish with this explanation, and we passed a pleasant hour singing Gregorian music together while she elaborated on the concept of phrasing.

"Thank you for the lesson, Sister. I've had many voice teachers, but you have always been my favorite."

She smiled at the compliment, which was sincerely meant. "Perhaps you'll sing something at Vespers tonight? Something of your choosing." We decided that I would sing *Laudate Dominum* from Mozart's *Solemn Vespers*. "Excellent choice." She touched her cheek to mine. "Oh, how I've missed you, my dear girl. Welcome back!"

Other than singing, the nuns made no demands on me. I found it hard to sit still, so I hiked the hills around the convent. I stopped in to say hello to the old librarian, who'd allowed me to read forbidden books on the Catholic Index. I visited the infirmary, to greet the Infirmarian.

"Sister, is there some way I can help here?" I asked. "I seem to have too much time on my hands."

"Yes, actually. Some of the sisters are shy about consulting a male physician about problems of a female nature. I could post a notice outside the refectory."

"That's a fine idea. Please do so."

The next day, I had a long list of patients waiting for me. Now that I was trained in gynecology, I felt more able to address their female complaints. Of course, treating nuns for such ailments requires a special kind of sensitivity. The cases were mostly routine: menstrual cramps or vaginal infections, but one of the nuns had a very large and painful ovarian cyst. Another presented with a breast lump, fortunately small. Disturbed, I went directly to my grandaunt in her role as the mother general of the order.

"*Tante*, both of these cases are serious. Had I not volunteered to see these sisters, they would not have gotten medical attention in time. I assume the cyst is benign, but what if it's not? The prognosis for a breast lump, even one that small, isn't good."

My grandaunt nodded gravely. "You are correct. We can't have modesty endangering the health of the sisters."

"So, what will you do about it?"

"I shall speak to Dr. Schulte so that he is more aware. And when you visit, you will hold your clinic."

"What?" I asked incredulously.

"Isn't your vocation to save lives?" she said with a shrewd smile.

I sighed, realizing I had been roped into another duty toward the nuns.

Before I left, I visited Markovsky. I didn't entirely approve of how he was managing the estate, but the harvests were good, and the income was steady. However, his wine was absolutely vile. I have fairly broad tastes when it comes to alcohol, but I found it undrinkable. When I complained, he swore to me that he would hire a new vintner.

On my last evening at Obberoth, it was chilly despite the season. I built a fire in the little tile oven in the mother general's study and *Tante* and I huddled close to it for warmth.

"How lovely it is to have your company, Margarethe. I confess that I am surprised at how well you've taken to convent life."

"Now that I've produced my heirs, perhaps I should become a nun," I said, trying to hide a grin.

My grandaunt ignored the irony. She sighed and reached for my hand. "Katje used to sit with me exactly like this."

I imagined my grandmother sitting in that chair. "I miss her too," I confessed. "Was it a great burden to keep her terrible secret?"

She sighed. "I very much wanted to tell you...and your father, not to ease my burden, as you call it, but because it would have been less of a shock. I knew that you, especially, would find it difficult. You are such a fine physician, yet even you could do nothing for her. However, I understood her desire to protect you from anxiety."

"I would have liked to have had the opportunity to say my farewells."

"Margarethe, you persist in this regret, but if you truly love someone, there is no need for farewells." She squeezed my hand. "Besides, you shall see her again."

I was too moody to engage in a debate about the afterlife, plus my back ached, so I got up to stretch. "Your iron cots are an abomination."

My grandaunt laughed. "No, Margarethe. You will never make a nun," she said, shaking her head. "No, never."

⟿

I was surprisingly reluctant to leave Obberoth. The week I'd spent among the nuns had been the most restorative holiday I'd spent in ages, but my next stop was Rome, where I would meet Lytton and his merry band of gentlemen. My trunk of male disguises accompanied me, and before we landed, I resumed my impersonation of my cousin. I gave my hair a trim and shaved it carefully over my ears and at the back of my head. The stubble felt strange, but the new look was perfect.

Lytton and his troupe met me at the pier as before, but this time I arrived as Baron Holdenberg. "Look there!" someone shouted. "It's Freddie!" Cheers went up as I descended the ramp to the dock, looking dapper in a white suit and two-tone brogues.

Lytton ran up the ramp. He caught me in a sturdy hug and kissed me full on the mouth, ignoring the curious stares of the onlookers. The cheers continued once I stood on the pier. The fellows thumped me on the back until I was staggering.

"You look absolutely splendid," Meyer said in my ear, nearly shouting to be heard over the din.

We quickly relocated our little party to Lytton's Roman house, where we entertained his friends on the verandah under the light of a full moon. Meyer served Roman delicacies: pickled hearts of artichokes, smoked mussels, paper-thin soppressata, and tangy, fragrant cheeses. The wine was excellent, especially after being forced to drink Markovsky's horrible swill. However, when I was presented with the bill for the festivities, I wasn't exactly pleased. Nevertheless, I paid it without complaint.

Before I'd arrived, Lytton and Meyer had been busily planning an itinerary for our holiday. First, we went up to Florence to take in the David of Michelangelo.

"His organ is rather small," I observed.

"The ancients thought an overly large penis unattractive," Lytton explained in a scholarly tone. "From an artistic point of view, they considered it lewd and fit only for base statuary such as fertility gods. A small, well-formed penis was considered the ideal."

"The Greeks evidently thought differently," I opined. "The organs on their pottery showed no such limitation."

Lytton sighed. "Perhaps their statuary didn't either. Unfortunately, so many marble penises were hacked off by the pious, we'll never know."

368 *The Imperative of Desire*

"Now, that desecration is the true obscenity."

"Quite," Lytton agreed. "Although the fig leaves weren't much better."

Our days were full of culture, but our nights were much less high brow. We visited the male clubs wherever we went. One night, Meyer dared me to pretend that I was singing falsetto, which was surprisingly hard to do. Lytton decided a mustache would improve my male disguise, so he cut off a lock of his hair and pasted it under my nose. At his instigation, I approached one of the ladies in a restaurant, but she slapped me for being fresh, which dislodged my mustache and left my cheek smarting.

Unfortunately, that was not the only violence we encountered. Men with clubs and stilettos were waiting for us when we came out of a nightclub. I was able to dodge their blows using techniques I'd learned in the cadet camp and planted a sharp kick in my assailant's scrotum. We scrambled away as quickly as we could. I couldn't afford the scandal of being unmasked, and the Carabinieri certainly wouldn't be sympathetic to homosexuals.

We helped the victims of the assault to our hotel. Fortunately, it was late and the desk clerk was dozing while we carried our wounded through the lobby. Meyer, who'd been a medical orderly during the war, assisted while I sutured the nasty wounds, some of them deep enough to kill if they'd landed more strategically. Meyer volunteered to watch over the patients for neurological changes from the head trauma. We left them in his able care, while we headed to our room for some sleep.

Lytton removed my stained waistcoat and bloody shirt. He kissed my breasts as he unbuttoned my trousers. "You are so kind, Meg, so very good. What have I ever done to deserve you?" he asked, easing me back on the bed.

I always loved the feel of his great, broad shoulders, tanned and freckled from the sun. His powerful thighs drove mine apart as he thrust himself into me. I wondered why, after I'd spent the day playing a man, he found it necessary to remind me that I am a woman. Then I realized my playing a man had excited him. After that, I forgot the question and simply enjoyed the feel of him inside me.

In the morning, we were shy with one another, as we always were after intimacy. When he awoke, I could feel his eyelashes brushing against my skin like the wings of a butterfly.

I had already been awake for some time, wondering if the yearning we both felt would ever be satisfied. "Why do we persist in joining like this?" I asked. "You like men better, and I prefer women. We've made the children we need. There's no purpose in it."

He caressed my breast and pinched the nipple gently. "Because the physical bits actually mean nothing. I love you. No matter what your body is like. And, in many ways, you are more male than any of my friends, even more than Meyer."

"And...despite your male bits, you are quite feminine."

"Our bad luck to be born into the wrong bodies?"

"No, good luck, because we have two beautiful children."

I could feel him smile. "Yes, they are fine. We are *excellent* breeders."

"Indeed, we are," I agreed, gently scratching his back with my fingernails, which he especially liked. After a bit of that, he sat up.

"I suppose we should fetch Meyer and find something to eat."

I checked on our wounded and found them well enough, so we headed to the café across the street. Lytton read the *Times*, while I read the Italian paper for a different perspective. Meyer read, or rather browsed, *Vogue* magazine. When our companion rose to use the lavatory, I saw an opportunity to speak to my husband in private.

"Lytton, will you come home for Christmas?"

He sighed, glancing in the direction that Meyer had gone. "I rather doubt it."

"Please, darling. The children miss you. Your mother misses you..."

He leaned on his elbow and looked sad. "I just can't at the moment. Please try to understand." His handsome face looked pained.

"Will you ever come home again?"

He sighed deeply. "There's talk of an alumni race after the undergraduate boat race. Perhaps I shall join the crew." He grinned. "You will come up to root on the Blues, won't you?"

"Of course, I will," I said and kissed him.

~

Lytton did not come home for Christmas. To be perfectly candid, I never really expected that he would. My holiday with him had confirmed that his life was now in Rome with his friends and not with his family.

My in-laws had become attached to the children, so when we went down to Edelheim for Christmas, I brought them along. My father and Lord Bromsley had been friends for years and occupied themselves for many hours hunting, drinking whiskey, and reminiscing about times before the Great War. I often joined them in their adventures or at the billiards table in the evening.

Occasionally, I took a hiatus from male pastimes to see how my mother and Lady Philippa were faring because the two could not be more opposite. Lady Philippa was an ardent blue stocking and suffragette, while my mother adhered to the subsidiary and submissive role women were supposed to play. I always held my breath when these two female archetypes met, expecting mortal combat, but my anxiety always turned out to be misplaced.

Mother could be charming with guests. Lady Philippa, whose many interests were driven by her natural curiosity, could certainly hold her own in any conversation. In my mother's presence, Lady Philippa always managed to find innocuous, non-controversial subjects—the horticultural demands of the tropical plants in the conservatory, the care of ancient tapestries, and the like. I often found the ladies in a tête-à-tête conversation that left little room for a third party, so I went back to the billiards table.

"Meg, how is it that you always win?" my father-in-law asked, after I'd beaten him.

I shrugged. "Physics."

21

After the successful Christmas holiday, Mother accepted Lady Philippa's invitation to come up to Larkhurst to watch the Oxford-Cambridge Boat Race. Everyone was excited because for the first time in ages, there would be an alumni race. The annual contest between the undergraduates was the main event, of course, but the enthusiastic wagering on the "old men's" race created an even larger purse. Both teams were "blues," we Oxonians wearing the darker shade, of course, and the Cambridge men in light blue.

I eagerly looked forward to the event. I'd always loved watching Lytton, the athlete, in action, almost as much as I loved hearing Lytton, the baritone, sing. Because he was so tall, his arms were very long. When he rowed, he could pull an enormous stroke with his powerful muscles.

He wired ahead with the details, and I made preparations to attend, but at the last minute, Abrams put me on the surgical roster.

"You can't do this!" I protested after seeing the post on the ward clerk's door. "I promised my husband I would go up to Putney for the boat race."

"What is more important to you, Miss Stahle? Sport or medicine?" Abrams growled back.

I fell silent. I couldn't argue with him because I'd already taken so much time away from my duties.

On the day of the race, the Bentley was packed with my baggage and standing at the ready in the car park behind the hospital, so that I might leave immediately after the bowel resection. But adhesions caused a rupture when I tried to separate the bowel from the body cavity. I was up to my elbows in gore and muck when the gun sounded to launch the race. I had gotten things under control and was ready to close the surgical wound when a nurse came into the operating room.

"A telephone message for you Miss Stahle…from Martin Fox."

"Read it, please."

"He said there's been an accident at Putney and to come at once."

"Anything more?"

"No, Miss. I'm sorry."

I turned over everything to the first assistant and hurried to change. Charles intercepted me dashing out the door. "You need to calm yourself, Meg. If you wait a moment, I'll go with you."

"Thank you, Charles. You are too kind, but I don't have time to wait."

He caught my elbow as I passed. "Promise me you'll be careful."

"I shall. Don't worry."

Frantically, I raced to Putney. After taking a few turns too fast, I reminded myself to focus on the road. The wire hadn't said Lytton was injured, only that there had been an accident.

But when I arrived, they were already dredging the river. I recognized one of the Oxford oarsmen, shivering under a blanket. "What's happened?" I asked in a desperate tone.

"Our boat overturned. The police still think Lytton is alive somewhere downstream. They only need to locate him," he said. "He's a strong swimmer and certainly would have made it to shore if he could."

I located the policeman in charge and asked for more details. He explained that not long after the gun, something had gone horribly wrong. The Oxford boat had suddenly skewed as if the coxswain had lost his sense of direction. The boat hit a rock and flipped over. The Cambridge boat, two lengths behind, ran into something in its wake and overturned as well. At that point the race was called off, and the police were summoned.

I saw Lady Philippa and my mother, standing near the police wagon. When they saw me, they both began speaking at once. Mother fell upon me, but I could barely manage my own wits, so I untangled myself from her arms.

"Meg is here," Lady Philippa said. "Everything will be all right now." As I surveyed the scene, I wondered how I could possibly be worthy of such confidence.

"You should go," I urged. "I shall remain until he is found."

Lady Bromsley was understandably reluctant to leave, but she apparently realized that my mother was an unwelcome distraction and agreed to take her to Larkhurst.

The police conducted me to the shore near where the collision had taken place. My father was there and Lord Bromsley. The rowers from both boats stood by, shaking with cold, teeth chattering despite the blankets wrapped around them. It was April, but particularly chilly that afternoon. The crewmen tried to reassure me. "He will be found. Of course, he will be found," one said, but I could see from the pinched faces of the policemen that this was wishful thinking.

Some of Lytton's friends were familiar from the Gilbert and Sullivan Society, but there were no heroic choruses that day as we all gazed helplessly into the dark, swirling water.

"You must take these men to someplace warm," I said to a policeman in a perfectly rational voice. "They will die from the cold if they aren't given dry clothes and warmth." But no one made any move to leave. They continued to shiver under their blankets as they watched the police boat trolling the water.

Then he surfaced. It was stunning to see his body rise, his arms outstretched like wings, almost as if he was about to take flight.

The crowd gasped.

I fought the temptation to dive into the water to attempt a rescue because the police launch was already in position. They had trouble holding on to him because of the strong current and caught him with the trolling rig. It raked my heart to see his flesh pierced. One of the Cambridge oarsmen saw the horror in my eyes and stepped in front of me, trying to block my view, but I pushed him aside. This was *my* Lytton, and I would witness every aspect of how he was returned to me.

As they towed him to the shore with their hooks, I hurried to the dock to meet them. A policeman began resuscitation, leaning heavily on his back and pulling on his arms. It was pointless. The police tried to lead me away while the ambulance attendants covered my husband with a sheet, but I brushed past them. "I am a physician. Let me pass." The police captain looked startled, but he instantly stepped aside. I felt the carotid artery in Lytton's neck for a pulse, knowing there would be none. I turned his head and saw that the back of his skull was missing. In the crowd, a woman began to wail.

"Take her away, please," I said. It sounded like an order, but it was actually a plea.

I announced that I would ride with Lytton's body in the ambulance. No one resisted. They shut the door behind me. Now that I was alone, I removed the sheet and gazed at Lytton's body. His skin was already gray, less from the end of the blood flow than the bitter cold of the bottom of the river. His flesh was as hard as marble. I took his still, cold hand and held it in mine.

When we arrived at the coroner's office, the officers removed the body to the morgue. The doctor in charge took one look at the back of Lytton's skull and declared that there was no need for an autopsy. He wrote out the death certificate while I watched. The cause of death: blow to the head, followed by drowning.

The coroner's assistant departed, leaving me alone with the body. The prow of the boat had raked away the back of Lytton's head and taken a sizable chunk of the brain away with it. Now that an autopsy had been ruled out, I decided to make things right. I found an apron and easily located sutures and a bottle of bone cement.

I carefully closed the gashes in Lytton's shoulder and chest. Then I turned the body over and inspected the head wound. Most of the bone fragments were still lodged in the scalp, some in the brain. Patiently, I dug them out and arranged the pieces on the coroner's tray. Reconstructing the skull made for an interesting puzzle. There were missing pieces, and I needed to stuff the cavity with some cotton wool to hold the form while the glue set. Then I carefully sutured his scalp with fine silks. When I had finished, Lytton looked almost normal.

Normal, except that he was dead.

The coroner came in and looked at what I had done. "You do fine work, Miss Stahle."

"The finest work cannot bring him back," I replied.

"No, but at least he'll go to his rest intact."

I brushed Lytton's hair away from his face and smoothed it. Then I kissed his forehead before covering him with the sheet.

"Thank you, Doctor, for allowing me to put my husband in order."

The local magistrate ordered an inquest to determine why the coxswain had lost direction. Some said it was the strong current. Others claimed they'd seen him drinking before the race. His fellow oarsmen swore it wasn't true. The coxswain had roomed with Lytton in their early days at Balliol, and I knew they'd been friends, so I doubted any criminal intent on his part. There were no charges filed. Nevertheless, the rowing association banned him for life.

Father and Lord Bromsley accompanied me to all the significant events. Mother, evidently consumed by grief, kept to her rooms, weeping incessantly. She'd barely known Lytton and had hardly given him the time of day. One would have thought *she* was the bereaved widow. I wished Father would take her home, but he was a great help to me, especially during the probate of the will.

Lytton never had any money apart from the income from our marriage settlement and his earnings from lectures. He'd spent heavily on his archaeological expeditions and providing entertainments for his friends, so there was little left of his endowment. I used some of the money to purchase the little Roman house in which he'd lived and turned it over to Meyer. The remainder I gave to the Bromsleys, whose economic fortunes hadn't improved.

Mother wanted me to ban the Cambridge oarsmen from the funeral because they had been the cause of Lytton's death, but I allowed them to attend. A small contingent from Lytton's archaeological crew pooled their resources and came up with enough money for passage to England. They clapped me on the back as if I were one of the fellows. "I'm so sorry for your loss, Freddie," they murmured. "So sorry."

We decided that Willi was old enough to attend the funeral. Dressed in his first suit of long pants, he looked older. Lytton had never converted to the Roman Church, so the service was High-Church Anglican. It comforted me to hear those sturdy Protestant hymns I loved so well. However, I was unable to sing that day, even as a member of the congregation.

In the sacristy, I had one last look at Lytton. The only person I allowed in the room was my father. The undertaker opened the lid of the coffin. Lytton lay cushioned on silk upholstery, still and hard. The extended time during which he had been kept from the grave had done him no favors. He had the blackened mottling of early decay, and oddly, that made him only look more like ancient marble. I did not touch him again. He had departed the dear body with which he had once loved me so tenderly.

I wept silently. Father passed me his handkerchief and put his arm around my shoulder.

"Now you are a widow."

"Yes. I'm told it is an honorable estate."

"Small comfort, I'm sure," said Father with a sigh. "I shall miss him. He always had something witty to say. A clever man."

"Irreplaceable," I said. "There will never be another like him."

Father nodded, evidently having understood the broader message. He signaled to the undertaker to come forward. The man took a miniature bit and brace out of his pocket and drove screws through the coffin lid.

～

St. John of the Cross' famous poem often came to mind in the weeks following Lytton's death. "Dark Night of the Soul" was indeed a fitting metaphor for what came next.

When I returned to London, I pretended to go back to my ordinary life. This had worked after Hanna's death, so I had no reason to think it wouldn't be equally effective. I kept myself overwhelmingly busy, and the routine gave me structure.

Unfortunately, I also developed an unhealthy taste for scotch whiskey and Turkish cigarettes. Often, I drank myself to sleep. The sound of the whiskey glass tipping out of my hand and falling to the floor sometimes woke me, sometimes not. I slept in a haze of smoke and woke coughing in the morning. Thankfully, I never set the bed afire.

My grandaunt was the first to notice the change. Alarmed by the dark tone of my letters, she began to ask pointed questions. My replies were evasive, so instead of writing, she telephoned in order to hear my voice and thereby better judge my mental state. Usually, I succeeded in sounding cheerful, if not jolly.

But she knew me too well to be fooled. When she called one night after I had gotten into the bottle, I tried to sound coherent, but she kept asking me to elaborate on my state. I rapidly grew impatient with her questions and rang off while she was in the middle of a sentence.

She called again the next morning. "Margarethe, please come home. Come to us. Let us look after you."

"Thank you, *Tante*. I shall manage. I always do."

"Please, child… Please!" It broke my heart to hear her pleading. After that conversation, I asked Krauss to contrive excuses whenever she telephoned.

In the beginning, I was able to hide my wretched state from the hospital staff. I reported for my surgeries on time, performing as well as ever. Then I noticed that my fingers sometimes trembled, so I cut back on the alcohol a little.

Charles, who knew me better than the others, was the first to notice something was amiss. We worked together on an emergency case after a traffic accident. To rest my eyes, I looked up and saw his worried look above the surgical mask. After we'd disposed of our surgical gowns, he took me aside. "Come, Meg, let's find a drink somewhere."

Ironically, I had stopped drinking in public. With the convoluted logic of an addict, I thought people wouldn't suspect my secret vice if I abstained. Charles took me to a pub near the hospital. He ordered a glass of scotch for himself. I asked for barley water. He offered me a cigarette. I virtuously declined that as well. After the waiter departed with our order, Charles studied me with a frown. "All right now, Meg. You're not pulling the wool over my eyes, or anyone else's for that matter. You're absolutely miserable!"

His concise assessment stunned me, but I managed to say, "It's been rather difficult."

"It's always hard to lose someone. But Meg, you and Compton-Wickes never seemed close. For heaven's sake, you've been living in separate countries for years!"

"Yes, I know, Charles, and my response surprises me as well, but it's one death too many." Unwittingly, I had spoken the truth.

"Yes, you've had quite a run of losses, but you always seem to take everything in stride. Where is that Amazon riding through the worst muck of the war, pulling people back from the very brink of death?"

"Even an Amazon must pause from time to time to consider her wounds," I said, suddenly thinking of the famous statue in the Altes Museum.

"Well, I can't have you moping about. We've been trying to be respectful while you've been in mourning, but you can't keep avoiding us. Mother says you must come to dinner this Sunday, and she will not take 'no' for an answer."

Dear Charles. He so wanted to help. And I did go to dinner at the Calders' on Sunday. Everyone heartily urged cheer upon me. After supper, I struggled to join in during the game of charades. It was pure torture.

Fortunately, the Calders didn't insist on returning to our pattern of alternating Sunday dinners between our homes. I don't think I could have managed that, but Charles often came to sit with me in the evenings, especially after I'd lost a patient on my table, and he worried I might relapse. As before, we'd play chess or read together, filling up the library with smoke.

I wish I could say that the Calders' dear attention and good will cured me, but my recovery unraveled the afternoon I received several wooden crates from Rome. Krauss set them in the drawing room, and opened them with a pry bar.

One crate, carefully packed with newspaper, contained the statue of Mercury we had purchased and other small artifacts of high value. The second held books, including the notebooks detailing Lytton's excavations, the boots he'd once used for mountain climbing, now dusty and cracked, and a leather tool roll with forceps, probes, and small brushes for fine excavation. In the third, were his personal effects. Folded neatly in paper were Lytton's day and dinner suits along with shirts and cravats, even his undergarments and socks. At the bottom was a small chest. Most of the contents were gifts I'd given Lytton during our marriage: cuff buttons and studs for dress wear, his wedding ring, which he never wore, and a silver letter opener. At the bottom of the chest, I found the gold watch I'd given him on our engagement. It was scratched from constant wearing. I sprang the catch and read the inscription: "Our love is like no other—M."

This sentiment expressing our secret truth finally defeated me. I lay on the floor of the library, weeping until I had no more tears to spend.

After that episode, the disorder of my mind became more apparent. I upset a surgical tray after the idiot nurse kept handing me the wrong instruments. On another occasion, in full control of my faculties, I would probably have affected an oh-so-patient voice and upbraided the woman in front of everyone. This time, the procedure needed to be stopped so that another set of sterile instruments could be obtained. I heard the nurses grumbling afterwards.

Abrams heard about it and summoned me to his office. "Stahle, if you can't get hold of yourself, you must take leave." He scowled at me, puffing on his cigar as he awaited my response. His fly was open. I tried not to look at it.

"I am truly sorry, Mister Abrams. It won't happen again."

"Bloody right it won't happen again. Now get out!"

After that dressing down, I reformed. For a week, I minded my manners and was especially patient in the operating theater. I left off the alcohol for the same period. It was a revelation to wake in the morning without a headache.

I was free at the end of the week for a few days, and the scotch beckoned. I drew the drapes, locked myself in my room, and drank myself silly. I indulged myself for two days. On the third day, there was a pounding on the door. I knew that Krauss would never dare disturb me, so it couldn't be that important. I decided to ignore the knocking until whoever it was went away, but then the barrels in the lock turned, evidently by means of someone using the pass key.

The light from the hall was unbearably bright. I held up my hand to shade my eyes. Two people stepped into the room. As I became accustomed to the light, I recognized them—my father and Veronika.

"I cannot believe what I see!" my father exclaimed. "This is shameful!"

He opened his mouth to draw breath to continue when Veronika put a hand on his arm.

"No, Fritz. Don't berate her. That won't solve the problem. Go now. Let me speak to her alone."

My father scowled, but then he nodded, and went out. Veronika lit a lamp on my bed stand. She removed her hat and coat and gazed around the room, which was in shambles—clothes, books, newspapers strewn everywhere. My plate and silver from a meal two days before remained on the table.

After staring at the mess, Veronika smiled at me. "Dear Grethe, how nice to see you looking so well." At first, I thought she was mocking me until I realized she meant it sincerely. Evidently, avoiding my grandaunt's frantic calls had caused everyone to fear the worst.

Veronika glanced at my soiled dressing gown. She patted my arm. "Come, dear. I'll draw you a bath." She rolled up her sleeves and went into the bathroom.

"You need to fire the heater first," I said, following her into the room and turning off the tap. I lit the gas heater with a match.

We went back into my sitting room to wait. "Let's have some tea," suggested Veronika as if this were any other social call she might have with her high-society friends. She looked around and located the servants' bell. The upstairs maid appeared shortly, and I asked her to bring tea. Veronika pushed aside the books on the sofa, removed her gloves, and sat down. Again, she gave me a calm smile. "I'm looking forward to a nice, long talk."

When the maid came with our tea, I asked her to send Krauss. He appeared moments later, and I gave him instructions regarding dinner preparations for our guests.

After he left, Veronika said, "That's better. Everything will be all right now." She proceeded to tell me about her recent travels with my father in the south of France. It seemed such an innocuous conversation, so normal that I was unnerved by its ordinariness. The tea arrived, and I did the expected thing and served my guest. Eventually, I became aware that the obligatory twenty minutes had passed, and I went in to turn on the hot water tap.

After my bath, I dressed properly in a dinner gown and put on some makeup. When I came down to dinner, Father gave me a long inspection. "Much better," he muttered. He nodded his approval when I declined wine at dinner. But it was not from virtue. After days of torturing my stomach lining with alcohol, I feared my dinner wouldn't stay down.

Father and I played a game of billiards after dinner. We chatted about things at home as if nothing had ever been amiss. After our game, we joined Veronika in the music room. Father asked me to play something. I chose Mozart because I needed his orderliness rather than the emotionality of a stormy romantic like Beethoven. My throat was raspy from the cigarettes and alcohol, so I dared not sing.

When I entered my bedchamber, I discovered that in my absence the room had been tidied, thoroughly cleaned, and all the alcohol had been confiscated. Fortunately, I still had a packet of cigarettes hidden in my bed stand.

There was a knock at the door. I opened it to find Veronika standing in the hall.

"May I come in?" I stood aside and she made her way into the room. "Much better," she said, looking around. She took a seat on the sofa and patted the place beside her. "Come. Sit here with me." I put out my cigarette and took a seat beside her. "I understand completely," she said, reaching for my hand.

"You do?"

"Yes, it is difficult, especially in the face of such grief, to maintain appearances. But I'm surprised to learn you had such strong feelings for your husband."

"Actually, I never realized it myself...until he was gone."

"My darling, I know your tastes are unconventional, as were his. I also understand how the loss of a deep friendship, such as you shared with Lytton, could shatter you."

A few tears came to my eyes. I furiously wiped them away. Veronika grasped my hand. "No, that's wrong. Here in the privacy of your room with an old friend, it's perfectly permissible to show emotion. You Prussians and your ridiculous self-control. There is a time and place for everything, including strong emotion." She passed me her handkerchief. "Go on. Spend your tears." But I had frightened them back into the place whence they came. I mechanically returned the handkerchief.

"Is there someone you can turn to in this terrible hour?" Veronika asked. "A friend who will listen without judgment?"

I thought for a moment. "Elise Seidl. You remember…from my wedding."

"The psychoanalyst?"

"Yes."

"Perfect choice. Tomorrow, when you are feeling better, call her and explain your plight." She took my hand and kissed me. "For now, we are here to help you."

∼

My father and Veronika stayed on for a few days to ensure that my recovery was well established. By then, Elise had arrived. She'd taken leave from her psychoanalytic practice, entrusting her patients to another analyst. I was concerned because I knew it would deprive her of income.

"I didn't know how long I would be here," she explained, "but I shall remain as long as necessary."

"Then I shall pay you for your time."

"Nonsense," she said in a definitive tone. "I won't hear of it."

She wasted no time in getting to work. After catching up on our friends, we settled ourselves in my library. She glanced around the room. "It's not as fine as your library in Munich, but I suppose it will have to do." She opened a leather-bound notebook I'd once given her as a Hanukkah gift and uncapped her fountain pen.

"Are you ready?"

"Surely, you don't mean to analyze me."

"No, we're too close. We'll talk only as friends, but it helps me to take notes." She offered a disarming smile. "You don't really mind, do you?"

I shook my head. "Work your alchemy. I'm too numb to resist."

"Obviously, you're not, or you wouldn't be trying to numb your pain with alcohol." Her dark eyes studied me. "I must admit I'm finding your breakdown a bit of a puzzle. You weren't that close to Lytton. Is there something I'm missing?"

"No, your observation is correct. We barely saw one another, but I did love him in my own way."

"But it was never a passionate romance."

"No."

"Have you ever had a passionate romance?"

I suddenly found myself telling her about Hanna. Elise listened for hours while I recounted how politics had ripped us apart and ultimately led to her death. "We were the most compatible friends one can imagine until the revolution."

Elise sighed. "You are not alone. For a time, my father and I weren't speaking. Surprisingly, he was a monarchist. He believed the revolution would only lead to disorder, which it has."

"How are things at home?"

"You don't want to know," she said vaguely. "But we are here to talk about you."

Over the course of a week, Elise listened to me every morning for several hours. Then she declared our "session" over, and we would do something else. We browsed the British Museum, where I pointed out the antiquities Lytton had contributed as well as my favorites from when Daphne and I haunted those hallowed halls. We visited the National Gallery, the Victoria and Albert museum, took in a ballet at the Royal Opera. Despite these diversions, we dutifully returned every day to my non-analysis analysis.

Finally, Elise said with a sigh. "There's so much you haven't told me before now."

"So what is your verdict, *Fräulein Doktor?*"

Elise capped her pen and sighed. "I think you put your finger on it when you said that Lytton's death was one too many. Steeling your heart and forcing yourself to maintain control could only work for a time. Eventually, the accumulated grief caused a break in your psyche. I fear you have no choice now but to face the pain and finally mourn."

384 The Imperative of Desire

"How?"

Elise shook her head. "Only you know how."

"Give me a hint."

"Let me think about it."

~

"Let's do something different today. I've very much enjoyed our visits to the museums and the ballet, but I hear the British Psychoanalytic Society is holding their annual meeting. We should go to see what they're plotting."

I looked up from decapitating my soft-boiled egg. "I thought they'd purged all the Jungians."

"They have."

"So how will we be admitted? Won't you be recognized?"

"Don't make me laugh. Do you think they pay attention to any of the female Jungians? No. Ernest Jones has no idea who I am. And they need money. As long as we pay the fee, they'll let us in." I glanced at the clock. It was almost seven, early for Elise to be awake. She followed the direction of my gaze. "Don't worry. The meeting doesn't begin until ten."

After breakfast, we headed to the hotel where the meeting would be held. The signs directed us to a large ballroom. Outside the door sat a woman selling tickets.

"Five shillings? That's outrageous!" I exclaimed.

"Oh, dear. I didn't know," Elise apologized as I opened my purse to pay the fee. "I know they need money, but clearly, they also want to keep the public from wandering in."

We'd been speaking in German and the ticket-taker eyed us.

"It is unconscionable to charge such a price!" I told her in English. "Your superiors will hear about it!" She watched me suspiciously as we headed to the ballroom entrance.

"You're in top form today," Elise said.

"Yes, I'm feeling rather brisk."

We found a seat at the back because Elise wanted to remain inconspicuous. While we waited for the program to begin, I watched the men greeting one another in the front of the room. They laughed loudly without humor and smiled broadly without mirth. I recognized the affirmation of an organizational pecking order because I'd witnessed it many times at medical conferences. Not coincidentally, all of the people on the dais were men.

"That's John Rickman," said Elise, bending toward me to speak confidentially. "And over there is Melanie Klein. Evidently, Jones thinks a great deal of her. I don't know why. I've read her papers. Mediocre at best."

I had no idea who any of these people were and really didn't care, but Elise's eyes were everywhere. Then a man in an elegant suit and waistcoat climbed the stairs to the stage. His distinctive, trimmed beard and the cigar instantly identified him.

"That's Freud," Elise confided.

"Yes, I recognize him from his photographs. I heard he thinks smoking is a substitute for masturbation. When he smokes that filthy cigar, is he really pleasuring himself?"

"Margarethe, your voice carries," Elise warned. "Try to speak more softly."

People began to take their seats, and the meeting was finally called to order. Listening to the participants babble on about hysteria, I wondered if idiocy, if not madness, was a prerequisite for membership in the psychoanalytic society. The meeting wore on, and I became increasingly impatient. Freud rose to speak, explaining that women desire intercourse because they really want a penis. He continued in this vein until my eyes began to cross, first with boredom, then with outrage.

"Oh, for God's sake! How can you listen to this rot?" I whispered to Elise.

I saw from Elise's wide eyes that I had again spoken too loudly. People turned in their seats to look at me. The speaker was also regarding me.

"Madame, do you have something to contribute?" Freud asked politely, although the look in his eyes was anything but polite. "May I ask you to stand and pose your question to the group?"

I rose and felt everyone's eyes on me.

Earnest Jones intervened. "Would you be kind enough to state your name and affiliation with the society."

"I am not a member of your group. My name is Margaret Stahle, senior attending physician at St. Bartholomew's, London."

"Welcome Dr. Stahle," said Jones cordially. "What is your interest in psychoanalysis?"

At my side, Elise was trying to make herself small by slouching in her chair while I tried to think of a plausible explanation for my presence. "Psychiatry is not my specialty, but I occasionally operate within the skull. I'm wondering if the esteemed Dr. Freud would elaborate on how the mind is related to the brain. It is my opinion that all mental states reside in the brain."

"That is a materialist view, Dr. Stahle," explained Jones patiently. "Few of us subscribe to it."

"So, you believe in the 'ghost in the machine'? Isn't it quite clear that all psychological states are caused by the brain, for when the brain stops functioning, there can be no thoughts, feelings, lust or otherwise."

"If you believe that, you are sorely lacking in imagination," replied Freud in a droll voice.

"All right then, let's imagine there are ghosts…in machines or not… perhaps there are goblins…or dragons! Perhaps demons!"

Jones visibly tensed. "You are mocking us."

"Absolutely! What I see here is a group of prurient men obsessed with sex, terrified of female sexuality, and tittering about it like little boys."

Freud furiously puffed on his cigar. I responded with a smile. Elise was tugging on my arm. She anxiously glanced toward the door. "Margarethe! We must go!" she said urgently.

I pulled my arm from her grasp. "Is that not so, Dr. Freud? Tell me. I'm listening."

"And what do you know about female sexuality, Dr. Stahle?" asked Freud.

"Well, I am female, so likely more than you. In addition, I am a licensed gynecologist and obstetrician."

"Margarethe!" Elise hissed. "We must GO!" By now, she was bright red with embarrassment. "Come on!" She tugged at my arm.

She got up and hurried out of the room. For a long moment, Freud and I unflinchingly glowered at one another. Finally, he realized he'd lost the match and glanced away.

"Good day, gentlemen," I said and followed Elise out the rear door.

When we reached the lobby, I began to laugh. I was nearly bent double with laughter. Elise stared at me in horror. "What's so funny? You insulted Freud in front of his followers!"

"Yes. Wasn't it wonderful?" I nudged Elise with my elbow. "You, a Jungian, should be glad I exposed Freud for the fool and pervert he is. Maybe I should go back in and say more. After all, I paid for those tickets. We should get our money's worth!" I reached for the door handle.

Elise snatched my hand away. "No, you don't. They'll have me blacklisted. Let's get out of here before someone recognizes me!"

"You're a Jungian, so you're already banned. What do you care?"

"I care, Margarethe. Now, let's go!"

While we ate lunch in Mayfair, Elise stole glances at me. "You're quite delighted with yourself for challenging Freud. I suppose I should be grateful to see you smiling."

"As you should be. It proves I'm still alive."

"What it proves is that you're angry."

"Really?"

"Only an angry person would enjoy savaging someone for mere sport."

"It's not sport," I protested. "I loathe charlatans like Freud who use their idiot theories to discredit women."

"You don't really care about Freud, his theories or the plight of women. It amused you to put him in his place. Tell the truth!"

I examined my conscience. "You are correct," I admitted, "But at least anger is better than wallowing in misery."

"It's a new stage in your misery, but perhaps it represents progress."

By evening, I'd repented of skewering Freud. It reminded me of when I'd flayed Borchert in front of our friends. I recognized the common denominator—losing patience with arrogant men pontificating for no purpose other than self-aggrandizement.

"You're brooding, Margarethe," Elise observed. "What's going on in that frighteningly brilliant mind of yours?"

"Men are pompous idiots."

"They often are, but not all of them. Look at your Lytton. He was a prince of a man."

I sighed. "Yes, he was. A true gentleman. His mother raised him well."

"I'm heartened to see you thinking of something other than your misery. What else gives you pleasure when you feel great pain?"

I thought for a moment. "Music…and sex."

Elise laughed. "Then you must throw yourself into learning a new composition. And you must take a lover."

22

I decided to take Elise's advice and learn some new music. When I explained my plan to my voice teacher, she suggested Alban Berg's "Seven Early Songs." Usually, my musical tastes inclined toward the great Neo-Romantics, but the mathematical complexity of modern music appealed to the intellectual side of my brain. Learning it requires great discipline because it is so unmelodic, and the discordant accompaniment is no help in staying on key. I relished the challenge and threw myself into it with great enthusiasm.

Krauss knew better than to interrupt my vocal practice, but one afternoon he stood by respectfully until I stopped singing. "*Gnädige*, you have a caller."

"Oh, good God, Krauss! Who is it?"

"Miss Alexandra Calder."

"Tell her I am unavailable," I snarled.

"As you wish," he said with a little bow and turned to leave.

"No, wait!" I was fond of my majordomo and instantly regretted being snappish to him. I also perceived that Krauss had been sensitive in perceiving the importance of polite attention to my neighbors, especially because they had been so instrumental in returning me to sanity. "Show her in," I said with a sigh.

Alexandra, despite her threats to call on me, had never done so until that day. I knew she was back in London. Her Yorkshire appointment had failed like all the others, but I'd heard that she'd been hired again as a school mistress in one of London's prestigious day schools for girls.

The dark-haired woman came in and gazed around the music room as if she had never seen it before, which was very strange because I often entertained the Calders with music after Sunday dinners. In fact, she'd often sat at that same piano to accompany me while I sang. Perhaps her unusual behavior that afternoon should have been a warning sign, but I was so surprised to see her that I completely disregarded the clue.

The Imperative of Desire

She took off her gloves and sat in a chair near the piano. "I've never heard Berg actually sung before. How very interesting." After a moment, I realized she'd been speaking in German.

"Why have you switched from Russian?"

"German is such a guttural language. I loathe it, but I wish to know how you think in your own tongue."

Despite this obvious insult, I forced my brows to remain where they were.

"Will you stay for tea?"

"That would be lovely."

I sent for tea. Alexandra was silent while we waited for it to arrive. She gazed out the window, and I used the opportunity to admire her. I'd always found her looks exotic. Her nearly black hair sharply set off her extreme pallor. Her enormous, blue eyes were her most compelling feature. She could speak volumes with them. She turned those luminous eyes on me and asked, "Do you have a lover?"

"Pardon?" I replied, completely flummoxed by the question.

"Come now, Meg. You cannot pretend that you haven't noticed my attention."

I hardly knew how to respond to this statement. Finally, I said, "Well, I would never dare to presume. After all, your brother is my colleague, as well as my dearest friend, and I am ever so fond of your family."

"I'm seeking a lover," she said matter-of-factly.

I put down my teacup and took a moment to study her. Of course, I'd known that she'd been subtly flirting with me since we'd met, but by that point, her behavior was so commonplace that I ignored it. I was a bit taken aback by her unconventional approach but also found it refreshing.

"Why not a man?" I challenged.

"Men are too simple. You, however, are the most complex individual I have ever met. I wish to know you better."

"We could begin by having a conversation," I suggested.

"We've had many conversations," she pointed out. "But I understand your reservations. Conversation could be useful in encouraging intimacy.

We shall begin with that. But I would also like to listen to you sing. Is this the usual time when you practice?"

"Yes."

"It's also the time I return from school. Do you mind if I come by and listen while you sing?"

"It's not always a pleasant experience," I explained. "Sometimes I sing scales and arpeggios, exercises to encourage the flexibility of my voice. Often unpleasant and rather boring."

"I don't mind," she said and took a sip of tea. "What else are you learning apart from Berg?"

"I'm learning Zemlinsky's song cycle based on the poems of Maurice Maeterlink. What a strange man! His wife, the actress, goes about dressed in the costume of an abbess!"

"Yes, I've heard those stories." She gazed at me intently. "I look forward to hearing these new additions to your repertoire." She smiled and gave me a penetrating look. "You like stormy romantics, don't you?"

"Yes," I confessed, "I suppose I do."

"That is what I find so interesting about Germans. You pretend to be so orderly, yet within, you are maelstroms of emotion, most of it dark."

We spent the next hours discussing the swings between reason and emotion in German music, eventually comparing it to French music, which, we both agreed, seemed far more self-contained and tidy. It was a heady conversation for two people considering a sexual relationship, but it was the most extended dialogue we'd had to date. Finally, it grew dark outside, and Alexandra decided to go home.

After that, Alexandra presented herself during my vocal practice at least two or three days a week. She sat quietly and listened while I sang. Occasionally, she requested a composition. We had tea and continued our intellectual discourse.

I began to understand what my grandaunt meant when she spoke of "eros of the mind." Engagement at that level of intellectual conversation can be as exciting and intimate as sex. The topics ranged widely. Our preferred language was German until the conversation began to change.

We discussed the origins of romantic love, and Alexandra recited the first part of Dante's *La Vita Nuova* in Italian. On her next visit, she continued. Then came love poems: Shakespeare, Donne, the poets of the great courtly tradition, the English romantics—Keats, Shelley, and Byron. She allowed me to recite Rilke, but mostly, she insisted I sing German poetry through the great *Lieder*.

Finally, she allowed me to kiss her, and what a kiss it was! Deeply passionate and prolonged, like careening into an abyss. After that, I began to dream of her at night, wild erotic dreams in which I ravaged her in every way possible.

Sensing a change in my level of excitement, Alexandra arrived for her next visit with a French erotic novel, which she read aloud. At the high points, she gave me suggestive looks with those enormous, blue eyes, sometimes coy, sometimes smoldering. I was nearly driven mad with desire for her, but all she allowed me to do was unbutton her blouse and caress her breasts. They were small, but perfectly formed. She had the most responsive nipples, which hardened instantly at my touch.

One day, before we launched into the poetry or erotic novels, Alexandra said to me, "Meg, the time has come."

I set down my teacup and stared at her. "You're quite serious."

"Completely." She gave me a weak smile. "I'd like a bath first." It seemed an odd but not unreasonable request. I called the upstairs maid and asked her to fire the gas burner and fetch one of the dressing gowns Veronika had left behind. Mine would swim on my petite friend.

"Are you nervous?" Alexandra asked while we waited in my sitting room for the water to heat.

I dared not laugh, lest I insult her. "No. Are you?"

"Yes," she admitted. "You will be gentle?"

"Of course."

While Alexandra bathed, I arranged the bedding. I undressed and awaited her in my bed. As she approached the bedside, she looked ridiculously shy for someone who'd been plotting this opportunity for weeks, if not years. I drew back the coverlet to invite her in.

She turned away to preserve some semblance of modesty as she shed Veronika's dressing gown and slipped under the covers without giving me so much as a glimpse of her naked body. I gathered her into my arms. Although she was slight, she was abundantly feminine.

"Why have you never taken a lover before?" I asked.

"I was waiting for the perfect one to arrive, and there you were."

I kissed her forehead. "We needn't do anything, you know. We can simply talk and grow accustomed to one another."

She drew closer and laid her cheek against my breast. "No. I've imagined every sublime moment of our joining, and I want to see if my fantasies prove true." She turned my face to her and offered me a deep and penetrating kiss. After that, I needed no further invitation, but because it was her first time, I approached her in a careful and stealthy way, caressing everywhere else before touching her sex. When I entered with my fingers, I discovered that she was a complete virgin. Perhaps if I hadn't been a physician, I wouldn't even have noticed, but my exploration revealed that she was *virgo intacta*. I withdrew and stroked her dark hair, now unbound and seemingly everywhere.

"There are other ways to make love. You should leave this particular pleasure for the first man who loves you."

She whispered into my ear, "If someone must break me, I want it to be you."

"But the idea of causing you pain is repellent."

"Please, Meg, don't think so much. Just take me."

I tried to send my mind into another place while I gritted my teeth and deliberately broke her hymen. Any man would have felt honored for the privilege. I only thought of the pain I would cause. Afterwards, she wept in my arms, and I understood that she had passed an important milestone she'd set for herself.

The water was still hot from the gas heater. I moistened a cloth with warm water and held it to her sex to allay the pain. She laid her hand against my cheek. "How kind you are, Meg. I hardly deserve you."

"You've given me the gift of your virginity. Besides, I'm a physician. It's my duty to look after you when you've been injured."

"Then heal me, Doctor, with your kiss." This thought proved to be quite stimulating. I tasted the iron and salt in her blood, and I was delighted to be able to give her a climax. After she had recovered, she kissed me as if she knew all the wiles of seduction, and then plotted an imaginative course to my pleasure, astonishing me with her creativity.

We were begun.

She came every afternoon while I practiced my singing and listened carefully. Afterwards, I took her to bed and explored her body. In the passion of a new romance, I wanted to dispense with the music part, but she wouldn't hear of it.

With Alexandra, I discovered an aggression in my personality that I had barely tapped. She liked to be overpowered and handled roughly, but I drew the line at pain. I explored every part of her body, becoming ever more adventurous as I roamed.

While we made love, she stoked a torrent of desire with poetic words. As I drove into her, she recited the erotic Latin of Catullus. Her delicate touch driving me to a fever pitch was accompanied by the elegant French of the troubadours.

∽

My passion for Alexandra was intensely physical, but the intellectual dimension was even more compelling. She was the most intellectually gifted of all my lovers. In fact, Alex—as I came to call her—and I spent less time in bed than in museums, libraries, and concerts. For the sake of propriety, we each lived a completely separate life. The emotional intensity was confined to my music room and the bedchamber. Meanwhile, the rest of my life went on more or less as before.

We reestablished our custom of gathering every Sunday for family dinners. In a fit of hospitality, Charles decided to invite our new colleague, Brian Tierney. I wasn't yet sure what I thought of him. When Abrams had first brought him on, I was in the throes of grief over Lytton and, in my mad state, wondered if Abrams were trying to replace me. For months, he had been dropping hints that I should consider opening a private practice. My disordered mind interpreted this advice as an attempt to push me out.

When my thoughts made sense again, I saw things more rationally. For one thing, our specialties were different. Tierney was an orthopedic surgeon. In hiring him, Abrams sought to add a new set of skills to round out the department.

Our new colleague could have been the inspiration for the Irish legend of the leprechaun. Charles and I literally towered over him. He had fiery red hair and merry blue eyes. His laughter was infectious. There were times in the operating theater when the three of us simply dissolved. He loved to play practical jokes, such as dressing up an anatomical skeleton in a ladies' corset or substituting apple juice for urine samples. The nurses both hated and loved him, but he was evidently quite popular with the ladies.

The afternoon Tierney came to Sunday dinner, he paid too much attention to Alexandra, which didn't sit well with Charles or me, for that matter, but I realized that Tierney's effusive compliments came from the Irish penchant for hyperbole. Charles was clearly annoyed. He was extremely protective of his sister and always the first to make excuses for her odd behavior. After dinner, Tierney was telling one of his ridiculous, convoluted stories, but when he reached the punch line, no one laughed. Alexandra stared at the man as if he were a toad. She rose and left the table. We all suffered through the remainder of the evening, which, thankfully, ended early.

Because of the animus between Charles and Tierney, I occasionally entertained our new colleague separately. In a more intimate setting, the man could have intelligent conversations about medicine. Eventually, I came to understand that his veneer of joviality was covering up some deep sorrow. After a few glasses of whiskey, he could become downright morose. He never shared the source of his woes. Out of respect for his privacy, I never asked.

Not long after Tierney arrived at Barts, his elder brother, Augustine, was elected the secretary of the Royal College of Surgeons. Charles and I organized a dinner party at Wiltons to celebrate. The elder Tierney was taller than his brother, and quite a bit older. His red hair had faded to burnished bronze tinged with gray.

Both brothers had been educated at Heidelberg. Our German medical education was the envy of the world, so it was not surprising that many from overseas came to our universities. While we waited for Charles to arrive, we spoke German together.

"Miss Stahle, you have set a fine example for other medical women," Augustine Tierney opined. "I understand that you are a widow and raising two children, yet you have accomplished so much!"

I studied the man to see if this was a variation on the theme of disparaging medical women's seriousness. However, there was no sarcasm in his voice, and the earnest look in his blue eyes seemed to indicate the compliment was sincere.

"I do have the advantage of money to hire those who can keep my domestic affairs running smoothly while I focus on medicine."

"You're educating your children here in England, I understand."

"Yes, it's a tradition in our family, rather like you Tierneys preferring a German education."

"I fear our Irish universities still leave much to be desired. In my role on the faculty at Galway, I am endeavoring to improve medical education."

"Barts is also working to improve its training programs."

"I would never send anyone to England to study medicine!" the elder Tierney declared with surprising vehemence. It was the first inkling that the Tierneys harbored animosity toward my adopted country. The wounds of the bitter war of independence were still fresh, so I wasn't surprised.

"Gus, you do remember that Miss Stahle read preclinical at Oxford?"

The elder Tierney reddened slightly. "Of course, I meant no insult to you, Miss Stahle."

"None taken, to be sure. But am I to understand that you would send your sons to Heidelberg to study medicine?"

"I have no sons," said Tierney sadly, "only one daughter who…" His voice trailed off. He gave me a sharp look. "Never mind that!"

Fortunately, Charles arrived, and we resumed the conversation in English. Although his family of diplomats all spoke several languages, Charles could barely muddle through in French.

When surgeons gather, the conversation inevitably turns gloomy. If we are not comparing operating room war stories, we are given to forced cheer to avoid referencing the one thing which we share. Fortunately, the Tierneys and I had something else in common. I mentioned my latest enterprise for the Sisters of Obberoth. My grandaunt, a great admirer of the medieval mystics, had decided to expand the collection of early manuscripts in the convent library. London being a world capital of rare goods and antiques, she had urged me to keep my ear to the ground.

"Well, then," said Brian Tierney enthusiastically, "I know just the man you should meet. My brother, Liam, is Professor of Medieval Literature at University College. Rare manuscripts are a specialty of his."

"What uncommonly good luck!" I agreed.

"I shall give you a letter of introduction," said the elder Tierney, "and when you visit Ireland, you must avail yourself of my hospitality."

∼

It was late spring before I could get away to Ireland. That winter, my daughter fell ill with a respiratory infection that refused to break, so the school had sent her home. Unfortunately, such bronchial infections could be difficult to treat. We mitigated the congestion with a vaporizer and fed her healthy foods, including a diet rich in citrus fruits. I don't know if this program actually helped her recover, but eventually, she was restored to health.

Veronika suggested it was simply a mother's attention that cured the girl. There were nights when my daughter could hardly breathe, but once she was on the mend, we enjoyed our time together. I'd suspended Alexandra's afternoon visits, and, perhaps, that was the reason she began to stray. Alexandra's mercurial temperament always compelled her to seek new forms of stimulation.

While Liesel recovered, we arranged the photographs from our holidays. "Tell me about Father," she suddenly asked as she pasted a photograph of Lytton into the album. This question, from a child who had barely spent more than a few months in her father's presence in her entire life, was particularly poignant.

In replying, I tried to emphasize Lytton's many talents. "He was devoted to the study of antiquities and made many important archaeological discoveries. He had a charming sense of humor and attracted legions of friends. He had a fine baritone. I always enjoyed singing with him."

"Do you miss him?" she asked with the candor of a nine-year-old.

I compressed my lips to avoid telegraphing my pain. "Yes, I do miss him. Very much."

"But you hardly ever saw him."

"Yes, but when we were together, it was wonderful. We talked incessantly."

She nodded, apparently satisfied that we hadn't hated one another.

~

Once Liesel was fit enough to go back to school, I made preparations for a trip to Ireland. Abrams allowed me to go because we were now fully staffed, and my absence would cause less hardship. Charles gallantly offered to look after my cases while I was away.

Unfortunately, Augustine Tierney had planned to be in Europe at the time of my visit. An alternative date could not be arranged, so I was unable to take advantage of his kind offer of hospitality. As it turned out, I hardly passed a day in Galway. Instead, Liam Tierney and I headed up to County Sligo and made the town of Drumcliffe our base of operations. We stayed in a farmstead, which had a spectacular view of Sligo's famous flat-topped mountain, Benbulben. Apparently, several old abbeys in the vicinity had ancient manuscripts they were willing to part with for the right price, so it was fertile ground for our search.

I wanted to get down to work, but Tierney laughed and said, "Ah, you Germans are so bloody serious. Will you take some time to look around you?" He insisted that I climb to the top of the Knocknarea, where legend says Queen Maeve is buried, standing upright in her cairn, ready to defend Ireland from her enemies. It had been years since Lytton and I had time for mountain climbing, and I found the ascent, especially at the pace that Tierney liked to walk, something of a challenge. This only served to remind me that I needed to spend less time in bed with Alexandra and more time at active sport.

"Quite the view, eh, Lady Margarethe?" said Tierney when we had both caught our breath.

"You could call me Meg as my English friends do."

"Nay! I hate doing what the English do. Bloody bastards." He spat to emphasize his point. "Do you know why I address you as lady?"

I shook my head.

"Because courtesy is so lacking in our modern world. The rites we once observed so carefully are passing away."

"Certainly, we are more informal since the war. I find it refreshing, especially being a woman."

He nodded thoughtfully. "I can see why you might think so."

We found a sunny spot to eat our lunch of sharp cheddar, dark soda bread, and dried apples. Tierney brought out a flask of whiskey and offered it to me. I struggled to swallow the barest sip. Tierney laughed at my exaggerated display of disgust.

"For pity's sake, what the hell is this vile drink?"

"That is the native liquor—*Poitín* or *Poteen*, as the fecken Anglos call it. Irish moonshine." He grinned. "Like it?" I took another swig and coughed. "It's an acquired taste," he said, thumping me on the back. "We'll get something more usual in town. I promise you'll like that." He took his flask back. "I hear you are the patroness of the convent that seeks the old manuscripts. How did that come about?"

I told him the story of my long-ago ancestor and her oath to her friend the prioress of Obberoth. "And it just so happens that my grandaunt is the current mother general."

He raised a bushy eyebrow. Unlike his brothers, Liam Tierney was not a redhead. He had dark hair and brows like the fat caterpillars I had collected in my youth. "I suppose you're the pious sort, then?"

"Good heavens, no! In fact, I'm an atheist."

"Clever girl. But of course, you are. I am consumed with curiosity and all ears. How did you become an atheist?"

I needed to review the past to determine the moment. "I think when my tutor injured her foot. I desperately prayed for her to get well, but she never did. Her foot blackened with gangrene, and she died. I decided then and there that God was useless, and if not useless, then highly temperamental if he would so blithely take a young woman's life."

Tierney nodded thoughtfully. "And how old were you when this happened?

"Six years old, nearly seven."

"Ah, a religious prodigy."

I laughed. "A prodigy perhaps, but not in religion. I hardly thought much about God, despite the pains my grandaunt took to educate me. I had the sense that she didn't believe the official doctrines any more than I did. They say she's a mystic."

"The vision of such people hardly ever agrees with the views of ordinary people. They see the world differently because they can look beyond what we see. Hildegard von Bingen was a mystic as well. Her *Scivias* record her great visions. Of course, the filthy church barely tolerated her because she had the misfortune of being a woman, but she cleverly manipulated the men around her, always referring to herself as humble. In fact, she had them all dancing to her tunes like puppets on a string."

"She wrote music as well and highly regarded medical texts."

"She was probably the most brilliant person of her age, a polymath. Rather like yourself, Lady Margarethe."

"I may be a polymath, but Hildegard was a creative genius, whereas I am merely a very good technician. I sing quite well, but I have never had the desire to write music."

"Fortunately, women can be educated in this day and age. For so much of history, especially the foul history of the Church, women were treated shamefully. Did you know that at one time, when a woman died in pregnancy, the child would be cut from her body? Being unbaptized, the poor creature could not be buried in hallowed ground. Stupid, barbaric customs..." He took another sip of his vile firewater. "The Church lies about its past and covers up its sins. Look at all those poor women burned at the stake as witches. Some were simply old and touched in the head. Criminal."

I was silent because I agreed.

After our lunch, we descended from Queen Maeve's cairn and found a public house where we installed ourselves for the afternoon. There, I could get a drink of ordinary Irish whiskey. As Tierney and I drained the bottle, we continued to flog the Church for its sins.

"But your grandaunt seems a most interesting sort of woman," said Tierney, "a mystic, a classical scholar, and a philosopher. I've read some of her work."

"You have?"

"Yes, of course, haven't you?"

I shrugged. "Philosophy never interested me. I'm a scientist."

"Ah," said Tierney, "philosophy, like medicine, has an abundance of drugs, few good remedies, and hardly any specific cures." He grinned. "Now, who said that?"

"I haven't a clue."

"Nicholas Chamfort. In 1796. You still have much to learn, Lady Margarethe. I wish you a long life in which to learn it." He raised his glass to me.

"And to you, Professor Tierney."

As it turned out, Tierney had known all along exactly where my precious manuscript would be found. A small Benedictine nunnery outside of Donegal had an impressive medieval library. The sisters, of course, were reluctant to part with their treasure, but they were desperately in need of a new roof, so our negotiations came to a swift conclusion. They were especially pleased to know the manuscript would be in the possession of another convent, not sent to a museum or hidden away in a private collection.

23

A prestigious girls' school in Cornwall hired Alexandra as a schoolmistress. With great emotion, she bid me farewell at the train station. "Please write to me, Meg," she said, clinging to my neck. Her slight weight hung heavily. "Please!"

"I promise to write."

"Every day!" she demanded. "Every day, or I shall die!"

I glanced around at the others waiting on the platform. Fortunately, they were occupied with their own farewells and not paying attention. Not that I really cared what anyone thought, but Alexandra was capable of unexpected outbursts, and I wasn't in the mood for a scene.

"Alex, I cannot promise to write every day," I said in a rational tone. "You know I have many responsibilities, and my time is not always my own, but I shall write as often as I can."

She reached for my cheeks and pulled me down into a prolonged kiss, which did attract some attention. I was relieved when she finally boarded the train that would take her far from home.

The intensity of our affair was draining at the very time my career demands were increasing. Abrams' subtle hints about opening a private practice had become a campaign. Finally, he sat me down in his office for what amounted to a kind of father-daughter talk.

"Stahle, you know I have nothing but the highest regard for you, but it's time you got out from under my shadow and let your own light shine."

The point of this trite metaphor was obvious, but I still wondered if he was trying to push me out in favor of Tierney. "Are you sure you don't want my office for another surgeon?"

Abrams took his cigar out of his mouth, so he could laugh. "Very funny. No, of course not. But if you open a private office, I'll give Tierney yours."

"So, you do want my office." Now that I was reassured, I was merely trying to get his goat.

"No, girl. I want you to get out of here and make a name for yourself.

This is your time. You are certified in three specialties. You will be in high demand. Think of what you could do for the ladies if you expanded your practice."

"I hadn't thought of that."

"Stahle, for a woman of considerable intelligence, you surprise me sometimes."

"But I don't really like practicing obstetrics." I made a face.

"So, don't. Practice gynecologic and abdominal surgery. You'll still have privileges here, and I'm sure other hospitals will welcome you. I have many friends who would be happy to refer patients. I'm sure Abbott would as well."

With that kind of support, I couldn't possibly fail, but the prospect of leaving Barts and the happy alliance I had formed with Charles and Tierney was uncomfortable. However, Abrams was right. A private practice would allow me to draw prominent patients beyond those I encountered as an attending, and thereby build a name for myself. As a side benefit, I could reclaim the title of "Doctor."

One of Abrams' friends referred me to an estate agent, who helped me find a spacious suite on Harley Street. It was larger than I needed, but the agent encouraged me to consider the future.

The practice grew more rapidly than I'd anticipated. Abrams and Lord Abbott sent interesting cases my way. My mother-in-law, Lady Bromsley, launched a one-woman advocacy campaign, and I became the physician of choice of the high-born women of Britain. The newspapers seized on it, calling me the "lady doctor," which brought in yet more patients. *The Daily Mirror* even published a cartoon! When I met Charles and Tierney for lunch and saw a scrap of newspaper hanging in the doctors' dining room, I instantly knew who had posted it. Tierney laughed when I threatened to run him through with a butter knife.

The cartoonist had depicted me with my trademark short hair and wearing a clinical coat as I surveyed a veritable parade of female patients. The caption listed female complaints deemed "frivolous." I frowned on such ridicule because medical men regularly dismissed women's health issues as illusory, psychosomatic, or pathetic pleas for attention. Freud, filthy, cigar-smoking bastard that he was, had only undermined women's legitimate concerns with his ridiculous theory of hysteria.

Now that I was treating more women, I witnessed how shaming female complaints led many to avoid seeking medical care. I mentioned this to Abbott when he came to dinner one evening.

He sighed. "I fear it is far easier to complain about headaches and fainting spells than to mention the lump in one's breast."

"Too often, by the time she mentions the lump, it's grown to a size that makes surgical removal less effective, and the prognosis, grim."

"Indeed, but knowing you, Dr. Stahle, you're already planning a way to remedy this problem." He grinned. "Am I correct?"

He was. I'd always included a careful breast examination in my routine, but now I showed my patients how to check for lumps. Unfortunately, most of them blushed. Some said they found touching their breasts embarrassing, and I suspect that my advice mostly went unheeded.

As more breast cancer cases came my way, I began to question the standard treatment, which entailed not only complete removal of the breast, the underlying muscle tissue, the adjacent nodes, but also the muscles in the arm and chest wall. Such drastic surgery left patients horribly disfigured. Often, their husbands rejected them, and they were abandoned when they most needed support. I began experimenting with a less aggressive approach, removing only the breast, some underlying muscle tissue, and sampling the nodes for analysis.

My colleagues were alarmed that I should depart so radically from the accepted protocol. Charles and Abrams argued that my strategy was risky because of the high rate of recurrence in breast cancer. Abbott expressed his displeasure by ignoring me. Only Tierney listened to my ideas with any sympathy, but he continued to use the standard Halstead method in his own practice. At that point, the medical journals wouldn't touch my papers, but word spread that I was trying to mitigate the horrible disfigurement, and then I had even more patients.

Because of the ridicule in the cartoon, I became fascinated by menstrual complaints and began to keep scrupulous notes to determine a pattern. As summer approached, I had so many projects underway, I scarcely knew which to give my attention. I passed on taking a holiday and foisted my children on their English grandmother. Only Alexandra, on summer holiday from her school, was able to wrest me away from my work. She demanded sexual attention and insisted that I dine in restaurants to get me out of the house.

Alexandra listened attentively when I attempted to explain that she had been the cause of all my feverish work. She would have made an ideal model for a sculptor. She had exquisite breasts, not very large, but perfectly formed. She could arouse me simply by opening her dressing gown and giving me the slightest peek. I devoted much attention to them during lovemaking, and my ability to speak poetically improved—marginally.

Alexandra's womanly perfection included her genitalia, which were demurely compact and such a delicate shade, like the first blush of a pink rose as it begins to unfurl. It was in contemplating her body that I began to worship the female form. I finally understood Lytton's adoration of the male body and his desire to perfect his own physique.

My sexual tastes had taken a decisive turn. Apart from an occasional dalliance with Konrad, I never took a man to my bed again. My evolution into a Sapphist was quiet, almost imperceptible, until it came to full flower. It was as if one morning, I awoke and saw the Eternal Feminine in an entirely new light.

$\sim$

I was at the height of my fame as London's "lady doctor" when Mrs. Nicolson appeared in my consulting room. I was instantly struck by her height. She was nearly as tall as I am. Her expressive features were large and somewhat disproportionate, particularly her nose. For an English woman, her coloring was quite dark. In all, her looks could be described as striking, but few would call her pretty. Her bearing was unmistakably aristocratic, and her strong features telegraphed ascendancy and control.

She smiled and extended her hand. "It's not every day I meet a woman taller than I. Such a pleasure to meet you, Dr. Stahle." She pronounced my name correctly, as Germans do, all syllables enunciated. "I am Vita Nicolson." I frowned because I knew this name had significance, but I couldn't quite remember why. Apparently, she intuited that I was making mental connections but needed more than a vague memory, so she provided a hint. "You may know me better by my family name: Sackville-West."

The novelist! Of all my prominent patients, she was undoubtedly the most famous.

"I've so enjoyed your books, Mrs. Nicolson," I said, offering my hand. She returned the pressure with a firm grip. "The pleasure is all mine."

I invited her to sit. With new patients, I always liked to take a comprehensive medical history. Mrs. Nicolson told me that she was thirty-six years old, and the mother of two sons. Now that I was wise to the cunning ways in which women hid their real complaints, I carefully watched their faces while they described their illnesses and conditions. Mrs. Nicolson's eyes evaded my gaze when I asked about diseases affecting the reproductive organs.

"I am normally healthy as a horse, but in 1917, I was exposed to a venereal disease."

"Can you tell me the name of it?" I asked gently, knowing this topic to be extremely sensitive.

She shook her head. "Unfortunately, I don't remember. However, I was treated for it and pronounced completely cured."

I annotated my notes accordingly, but I entertained private worries. Unfortunately, our ability to "cure" sexually transmitted diseases was limited, especially in advanced cases. The symptoms could be erased, but the disease vector could lie dormant for years, only to wreak havoc long afterwards. I did not share these concerns with Mrs. Nicolson but continued to smile pleasantly.

"And what brings you today?"

She made a face. "The monthly cramps are sometimes hard to bear."

"All right, then. Let's have a look."

Once I had examined her and assuaged any concerns about pathology, I began to wonder if she had set the appointment out of curiosity to see the famous "lady doctor." If so, she was just one of many women who have used my consulting room as a means to get my attention.

After dressing, she rejoined me. "You are very kind and gentle, Dr. Stahle," she said, taking her seat. "I can see why you are so popular with the ladies." Given this remark's double meaning, I allowed my brow to arch. She responded with a canny smile.

I maintained an impassive expression. "You'll be relieved to know I found nothing remarkable during the examination, nor evidence of any previous disease. As for the menstrual complaints, I recommend aspirin, hot compresses, bed rest, if possible. For severe cramps, I usually prescribe bicarb with codeine, but use it sparingly. Codeine can sometimes make the situation worse. I'll give you an order for the chemist."

"Thank you. It's so refreshing to speak to a sympathetic physician about these troubles," Mrs. Nicolson said. "Lady Bromsley said I simply must see you."

I glanced up from writing the prescription. "You know my mother-in-law?"

"Yes, I do. She and my mother are friends." She smiled almost seductively. "Dr. Stahle, I should like to invite you to tea."

"I generally avoid socializing with my patients."

"If you cannot allow yourself to socialize with at least some of your patients, your social life will be rather limited. Your practice includes so many of our class. Besides, through your mother-in-law and my mother, we're practically sisters!" An odd way of stating our relationship, but perhaps no odder than my many family connections.

"Yes, Lady Philippa has been rather ardent in her support."

Vita studied me. "I hear you've been quite the recluse since Lytton passed."

Uncomfortable with this topic, I cleared my throat and continued writing the prescription.

"I am very sorry for the loss of your husband," she said in a sympathetic tone. "What a tragic way to become a widow! Unless I had seen it with my own eyes, I would scarcely believe the horror of it."

"You were there?" I asked, looking up in amazement.

She sighed. "Yes, I was. Harold had a friend in the Oxford boat."

I wondered which of the shivering oarsmen had been Harold Nicolson's friend. For the sake of a future friendship with Vita, I hoped it hadn't been the dishonored coxswain who'd caused the accident.

"Since you were already on given-name-basis with my late husband, I suppose we ought to be as well. My English friends call me 'Meg.'"

"Meg. It suits you, but completely understates your social standing. After all, you are a countess in your own right. Twice, actually."

"Once, for now. My father is still alive."

"Yes, of course."

Again, the seductive smile. I wondered what she thought she was doing.

We agreed to meet for tea at Claridges on my free day. I wasn't entirely persuaded that socializing with a patient was a good idea, but Vita had a point. If I refused all such invitations, I would, indeed, be without friends except my colleagues and the Calders.

~

When we met on the appointed day, the first thing Vita noted was my lack of a hat. "Evidently, you're famous, or infamous, I should say, for going bareheaded."

"I despise hats. I only wear them for riding or when it's cold, but never for ornament."

"And I thought our women were unconventional."

"We Germans, never set the standard, not being masters of the universe ,such as the English have been for centuries."

She laughed aloud, a bold, unfeminine laugh. "B. M. is right. You are a card. But a delightful one!"

I responded to this backhanded compliment with a smile. "What inspired you to consult me, apart from your rather ordinary menstrual complaints?"

Vita leaned on her hand and gazed into my eyes. "Oh, don't you see? We are so alike. Absurdly tall, daughters of great houses. Wealthy and privileged, spoilt perhaps."

I pushed down my insult at this presumption. "Perhaps we are alike in some ways but not others. For example, I have a profession."

"I do as well. Although, perhaps, not as noble as yours. And we are different in another important way. You will inherit your ancestral home. Homes, I should say. Mine had to go to my uncle, and then to my cousin."

"Salic law always does injustice to women. Fortunately, the rules of our house allow a woman to inherit. It's not true of the German nobility in general, of course, so I am fortunate."

"But you don't even live in the house you inherited."

"No. Schloss Raithschau is cold and drafty in winter, although quite pleasant in summer. Edelheim, well, that's another matter. It's enormous and quite ugly." I shrugged. "I live where I work and where I have a comfortable bed."

"I adore your pragmatism. You Prussians are quite fond of that trait, I understand."

"We are pragmatic, yes. But our most venerated virtue is duty. I cannot tell you how many times my elders have lectured me on that subject."

"Yet you don't protest. You go along with their program. You have executed your duty and followed the injunction to be of service. *Ja! Ja! Immerzu pflichtbewusst!*"

"Yes, always dutiful." I shrugged. "But I have my diversions."

She regarded me with a shrewd smile. "I see that now. There is far more to you than meets the eye."

I was uncomfortable with the spotlight on me, so I turned it on her. "Tell me about the creative life. It's foreign to me."

She raised a brow. "Modesty doesn't become you, Lady Margarethe. I hear you have a magnificent singing voice."

"Singing the words of others is not the same as writing sonnets."

At this, she looked flattered. She began to explain her great urgency to write. "Sometimes it feels as if I'm simply writing down words dictated by a source other than my own mind. As if I am recording the words of the gods. I know that sounds grand. And there's nothing divine or magical about it, but the experience is quite extraordinary." She told me that one evening, she had written eleven sonnets in a single burst of creative energy.

"I can scarcely imagine the pleasure and satisfaction of such creativity. Eleven sonnets in a sitting!"

Her eyes narrowed, judging, I think, whether this was truly a compliment, and it was.

"Has anyone ever told you how utterly German you look?" she said, carefully studying my face. "Blond hair nearly white, piercing, blue eyes, sculpted, noble features. You are the very embodiment of a Valkyrie."

"I like Wagner," I admitted, "but I prefer not to sing his work unless absolutely necessary."

At this, she burst into peals of laughter.

We talked for the next two hours about a wide range of topics: our children, our husbands, music and poetry, the duties and follies of the aristocracy.

"You must meet Virginia," Vita declared. "She will simply adore you!"

She gazed at me through half-closed eyes, and I detected more than a hint of flirtation.

∼

Vita and I exchanged friendly notes and telephone calls for most of the summer. We met several times for lunch, but I deflected her invitations to spend a weekend at Long Barn. For one thing, my practice was keeping me overwhelmingly busy. For another, my opinion of the women of my class hadn't improved.

If anyone exhibited aristocratic hauteur, it was Vita, perhaps because her place in our world was so tenuous. Her mother was illegitimate, and Vita herself was excluded from the succession because she was female. Through her husband, she had a courtesy title, but she longed to be noble. I more or less took my place in the scheme of things for granted, so I found her posturing tiresome.

I made some inquiries regarding my new friend. It was a poorly-kept secret that she was juggling a surfeit of female lovers—Mary Campbell, Margaret Voigt, and Virginia Woolf. Small wonder I never took her flirtations seriously, and so (thankfully) never found myself in her writings.

But Vita's female lovers had made her emotional life, as her husband liked to put it, "a muddle."

I had a muddle of my own. Alexandra had recently gotten it into her head that she ought to marry. Frankly, I doubted Alexandra's ability to sustain a marriage. I found it difficult enough to endure her wild fluctuations of mood, but from dealing with my mother, I was accustomed to handling difficult personalities. I could not imagine the sort of man who would put up with Alexandra's Jekyll-and-Hyde swings. When I tried to caution her against a hasty marriage, she dismissed my advice as jealousy. She pouted for a few days, but then she returned, demanding that I squire her to a concert.

By late summer, I desperately needed a change of wallpaper, so I accepted when Vita insistently extended her fifth (and from the tone, presumably final) invitation to Long Barn. She said that her husband would be there, and I wanted to meet him. We shared much in common, including an Oxford connection. Although he was several classes ahead, he'd attended Balliol, Lytton's college. I was relieved to learn Nicolson's friend in the Oxford boat on that tragic day wasn't the coxswain.

Called "Hadji" by Vita, Harold had a diplomat's ability to manage difficult situations, which made him a perfect match for his wife. He was the ultimate English gentleman, reserved, restrained, and droll. Vita, by contrast, was a force of nature.

Observing her taught me much about myself. While B. M., Vita's mother, always bordered on the edge of a breakdown, I managed my own mother quite well. Even when my love affairs became messy, I kept them more or less contained. I indulged my sexual desires as I chose, but my passions seldom spilled over into society. In a way, I felt sorry for Vita, who desperately tried to conduct her symphony with aplomb, yet always succeeded in hitting slightly off-key notes.

Despite my attempts to disguise my irritation with the women of my class, which Vita so exemplified, there were times when it peeked through. Harold caught me rolling my eyes at the loud row that had erupted at Long Barn. He went into the house and returned with two glasses. "I think a whiskey is in order, don't you?" I liked him at once.

"Do you understand women?" he asked.

"Absolutely not."

"It doesn't help to be a woman?"

"No. In fact, it only complicates the matter because I wonder why I don't have a deeper understanding. Unfortunately, women perplex me."

"I'm disappointed. I'd hoped you'd have some insight, especially being a physician who specializes in the care of women," he said, launching puffs of smoke from his pipe. "Are you interested in Vita?"

"I find her extraordinarily interesting…but not in that way." He had given me an opening, so I took it. "I think we understand one another, Mr. Nicolson. What is your interest in women? I mean, beyond the need for propriety and your career?"

"There is continuing the family name."

"In my case as well."

"Actually, despite Vita's great emotionality, she is an anchor in my life and my dearest friend."

"I understand. Lytton was the same for me. And although he was often absent, when I was with him, it was a perfect reunion."

Harold reached over and took my hand. "Yes, you do understand. What a pleasure to make your acquaintance, Dr. Stahle. Do forgive me for attempting to force you into the role of expert, but one thing continues to trouble my mind concerning relations between women. Why is there always such a need for theatrics?"

I laughed aloud. "I have no idea. I find it quite baffling."

"As do I," he said, nodding. "Is there some remedy? Something that can hold back the tidal waves of emotion?"

"Nothing medical, I'm afraid. Be patient. Eventually, the hormonal tides recede, and the sea calms. Or so, I am told."

"It cannot come soon enough," he said and breathed a deep sigh.

"Oh, my dear. Never ask that time pass more quickly, or you might regret that it has come and gone."

"You are an intriguing woman, Dr. Stahle." He grinned. "May I call you 'Meg' as my wife does?"

"It would be my great pleasure, but only if I may call you 'Harold.'"

He nodded his agreement, and we both turned a deaf ear to the loud voices from the house. I breathed a sigh of relief when all became quiet. Then a glass hit an interior wall and shattered. The shouting resumed.

"Time to retire?" I asked, gazing in Harold's direction.

"To avoid embarrassing them further? Yes, probably."

I doubt Vita was the least bit embarrassed. She seemed to thrive on stormy seas. The sound of the argument carried to the "baby's cottage." Fortunately, my ability to fall asleep on command served me well.

Vita's female guest decided to sleep in after the emotional night, allowing the Nicolsons to sit at breakfast with me like the proper people we were raised to be.

"Meg, I've invited some guests in your honor," Vita announced. "Virginia can't wait to meet you. I've also asked Vanessa, Carrington, and Strachey to join us for dinner." Lytton Strachey was a distant relative of my husband, which is how they came to share a name. More cousinly relations! Thankfully, these connections were through marriage rather than blood. It was difficult enough to keep the genealogical calculus of my own family straight.

While the Nicolson marriage served as a mirror to my own, I also saw it mirrored, albeit "through a glass darkly," in Strachey and Carrington's relationship. Both preferred their own sex. Dora Carrington's love for Strachey was more defectively returned than in my marriage or the Nicolson's. Carrington worshipped him, yet he casually disregarded her. He was quite the egoist, and I sensed his lack of appreciation for Carrington was not deliberate, merely a feature of his self-centered personality.

I was flattered when Carrington, inspired by Vita's going on about my "Valkyrie face," asked to sketch me.

"She's right. The planes of your face are like the facets of a jewel." She touched my cheek bones to define them more clearly. "Your hair is so pale, like a winter sun."

Despite the poetic language, the portrait was forthright in a most unforgiving way. She saw how my devotion to medicine burdened me. She drew the fatigue in my eyes, the compression of my lips, and the bitter set of my mouth. Yet she also captured my hope for the future in the determined, forward look of my gaze. I shall always treasure her sketch for its raw honesty.

~

After Margaret Voight departed, decorum returned to the Nicolson household. Vita became a charming and entertaining hostess and kept up almost nonstop witty conversation. Harold looked noticeably relieved. Vita tried to make up for the lapse in hospitality by becoming almost unbearably attentive. I suggested a walk to stretch our legs and provide a much-needed breath of fresh air. Harold, who was deeply into a book, declined to come along.

Vita secretly took me to Knole. It was dusk, and there was no one about. "Let's go over the wall," she suggested with a conspiratorial look. Once we stood on what could have been her land had she not been born female, she reached for my hand and sighed.

"Will you invite me to Edelheim so that I may see where you grew up?"

"You are always welcome. Like Knole, Edelheim is ridiculously large. But come visit, and we shall play the grand aristocrats of another age."

"But you truly are one of those aristocrats. Your blood is bluer than any of ours. You are a countess of the old aristocracy. Long before the Sackvilles came to Knole, your Teutonic knights were waging their holy war."

"…and exterminating the local people so that they might seize their lands. A very ignoble thing to do."

"Unfortunately, in the brutal world of men, might does make right. Control often requires bloodshed. Gentle souls are crushed underfoot." She searched my eyes. "Despite your martial background, your soul is gentle," she said, trailing her fingers down my cheek.

She leaned closer. When I realized she was about to kiss me, I held her back by the shoulders, smiling so she wouldn't take offense. "I'm flattered, Vita, but I have my hands full at the moment. Let's not complicate our splendid friendship with a dalliance."

"I'm disappointed," she candidly admitted, turning away.

"Oh, be honest. Not really."

"Yes, because I am drawn to you romantically. You are so opposite, the clarion voice of reason and completely in control. I believe in your dispassionate strength as I know the sun will rise tomorrow. I could abandon myself to that light and rationality."

"Oh, dear Vita, then I've fooled you. It's all an act, I assure you. I'm as easily put off balance by passion as you are. I'm only less public about it."

She nodded mournfully. I put my arm around her, and she gripped my waist fiercely in return. I realized it wasn't sex she wanted from me, but reassurance. A moment later, she confirmed my intuition by saying, "Your presence comforts me. You are so single-minded and strong! I understand why your patients worship you."

I took her into my arms and held her close. "I'm sad for you, Vita, that you've lost your family home. Know that you are always welcome in mine. And please bring Harold for relief!"

At that she laughed heartily. We walked back to Long Barn, arm in arm. "I'm so glad you came," she said. "We need friends like you to provide some balance!"

24

My medical practice continued to flourish. By the end of the first year, its coffers were full. The financial success allowed me to hire a highly respected female surgeon away from the Royal London. Emmaline Grimes was an attractive woman, but still unmarried. During the interview, I casually asked why.

"My entire life has been devoted to becoming a physician. I simply didn't have the time."

"If the opportunity presented itself?" I pressed, although it was really none of my business. Dr. Grimes didn't seem to see it as an intrusion.

"It was never that important to me. My main focus in life is medicine. The world has plenty of wives and mothers, but not enough female physicians."

Her obsession with her career partly explained why she seemed much younger than thirty-two. After I brought her on, I sometimes invited her to the opera or concerts to broaden her experience. I found her company a welcome relief from the intensity of my affair with Alexandra. Emma had a sunny disposition. She laughed easily. Her humor and natural warmth quickly won over our patients. I admit to being a bit jealous of her popularity.

Our careers were inverse mirrors of one another. Emma had been a gynecologist before training in surgery. She was deeply committed to providing sympathetic healthcare to women. Until she'd joined my practice, I had continued to operate on patients of both sexes. Emma had only treated female patients. Finally, we agreed that it made sense to limit our practice to women.

Emma and I shared the patient load equitably. We covered for one another in emergencies. Meanwhile, I realized that my research interests were too broad, so I narrowed the focus to breast cancer. Alexandra was away in Cornwall, providing me with a spell of emotional peace. With more time on my hands, I pursued my other interests. I took up fencing again, which was good for both my figure and my agility. I entered the Pan-European competition in 1929 and won a second. Someone suggested that I prepare for the 1932 Olympiad, but I wasn't serious enough to engage in such intensive training. Instead, I renewed my enthusiasm for singing.

I'd sacked my voice teacher when I'd hit a wall in my progress. For a time, I limped along without one, but that wasn't getting me anywhere. I knew I needed someone to challenge me the way Sister Elfriede had. Fortunately, London, a great capital of music, had no shortage of first-class voice teachers. Graybar, a former operatic baritone-turned-impresario, was known as the best vocal instructor in the city. He had quite a clientele, so engaging him proved to be a challenge, but once I auditioned for him, he agreed to take me on. He was able to cure me of some bad habits. Within six months of training with him, my breath control improved greatly, and the transition between the registers was now seamless.

At a certain age, the voice finally settles into its natural range. The lungs and vocal cords mature, and a well-trained singer comes into her prime. One day, after my lesson concluded, Gray gazed at me intently. "Lady Margarethe," he finally said, "with a voice like yours, avoiding the stage is criminal. You must sing for others or why bother with all this training and practice?"

"I sing for myself. It makes me happy."

"That's arrogant, aristocratic privilege, and it's selfish." There were few people I would allow to speak to me in that fashion, but I respected Graybar, so I listened. "You are cheating yourself and those who could hear you sing *if* you only would allow it. You are the equal of the best mezzo-sopranos singing today. Here, in England, you have no peer."

I had good reason to be skeptical. Graybar also served as the agent for a number of prominent British singers.

"You know why I can't sing in public. Must I explain it again?"

He waved dismissively. "Yes, yes, ladies don't sing on the stage, but no one can fault you for singing for charity or appearing in amateur operas. Let me look into suitable opportunities."

I crossed my arms on my chest and frowned.

"Don't be so stubborn! They will be eminently suitable. I promise!"

The clever man succeeded in finding a charity that I couldn't possibly resist—a convalescent home for women suffering from cancer. He made arrangements for me to sing a benefit concert without saying a word. The planning went on for weeks until the day came when he simply had to admit that he had committed me. This served as a lesson. One must always be firm when dealing with impresarios. They never take "no" for an answer.

Together, we planned a program of German Neo-Romantics. Richard Strauss was a family friend as well as a favorite composer, so his music was first on the list. We added some Mahler *Lieder* and Zemlinsky's song cycle based on the poems of Maurice Maeterlinck.

"Eclectic and slightly decadent. A program to ensure a big splash on your debut. I absolutely love it!" declared Graybar.

Like any impresario worth his salt, he suggested that I sit for a glamorous publicity picture. Carefully made up, a rosebud mouth drawn with dark lipstick, my eyebrows nearly plucked out of existence and carefully redrawn, I could only think of Mother's empty-headed dolls. Vita telephoned to say she'd seen the photograph in the newspaper. "You look scrumptious, my darling. Good enough to eat!" I wondered if the double meaning was intended, but knowing Vita, I'm quite sure it was.

Graybar suggested I use my German name, insisting the "von" would give the program more credibility. Of course, it would probably ensure that news of the concert would reach my mother, which it did. I wanted to sing the concert, so I turned a deaf ear to her complaints.

At the end of the winter term, Alexandra left her school in Cornwall. She confided it was the first time she'd resigned a position instead of being sacked, but she didn't elaborate on why her employment was always so tenuous. I didn't like her reason for coming back to London, namely to renew her search for a husband.

"Why do you suddenly feel such a great need to be married?"

"For one thing, I'll soon be twenty-five and considered too old to be a bride. For another, you're not serious."

"Not serious about what?"

Elena Graf 419

"Your intentions towards me."

"What intentions?" I asked incredulously.

"You don't really love me."

"But I do!"

"If you did, you would invite me to live in your house as your lover."

Alexandra's mercurial temperament, one day up, one day down, experienced on a daily basis, would have surely driven me to distraction, so cohabitation was never even considered.

"You live a few doors from mine. You can visit whenever you like. Why do you need to live with me?"

"To show everyone that I belong to you and you belong to me."

"Oh, what rot!" I said, rolling my eyes.

That precipitated a dramatic response. "You're ashamed of me because I'm below your class!" she shrieked.

"Nonsense and you know it!" I gave her a stern look. "And lower your voice please. You're behaving like a child."

She gripped my arms. "Claim me and show me off proudly, or I shall take a husband."

"Very well," I said, throwing up my hands. "Carry on."

Despite Alexandra's continuing hunt for a husband, she was very keen on attending the concert. The thought of seeing her in the audience with one of her male suitors was unsettling.

She was pursuing a man by the name of Jonathan Stebbings-Wilder. I'd had the dubious pleasure of sitting beside the man at one of the Calders' Sunday dinners. He simply would not shut up about his cricket league. None of the Calder men were especially sports-minded, and they looked equally bored. Mrs. Calder was as attentive to their male guest as always, so he spoke mainly to her. I couldn't wait to leave.

As I walked home that evening, I wondered what Alexandra saw in this new beau. Her brilliant mind needed constant intellectual stimulation. Stebbings-Wilder was as dull as a dirty sock. I was even more puzzled when, a short time later, Alexandra appeared at my door.

"Make love to me!" she demanded, and so I did. She wanted to stay the night, but I sent her home, pleading an early surgery.

~

My preparation for the concert was excessive. Even Graybar thought so. I practiced until the early hours of the morning. I cannot imagine what my servants or the neighbors thought. Fortunately, it was winter, and all the windows were shut up to keep out the cold.

Finally, the day of the concert arrived. Shortly before the performance, Graybar knocked on the dressing room door to inquire if I needed anything. When I opened the door a bare crack, he peered in to find me a trembling heap of misery.

"I cannot do this. It's simply impossible!"

"Open the door," he ordered. I opened it just enough to allow him to enter, then shut it tightly. "Lady Margarethe, you have an audience of nearly three hundred people waiting for you," he said, pointing in the direction of the auditorium. "They have each given a substantial amount of money to hear you perform. You *must* give them what they paid for."

"I can't understand how this can be," I said, holding up my trembling hand. "I've sung in front of large audiences before. I sang for hundreds of troops during the Great War. I even sang the Mozart Requiem at my grandmother's funeral. Why should this be different?"

Grayson listened sympathetically, stroking his beard as I spoke. Finally, he said, "Then, you were merely singing. Now, you are a *singer*, and a very fine one at that. People are paying to hear you. That makes a difference."

"But what can I do? I can't stand in front of them like this—a jumble of nerves! My throat is dry. My hands are shaking. I'll make a fool of myself."

"Nonsense. You are the most disciplined singer I've had the pleasure to manage. When the moment comes, you will deliver the goods." I must have looked skeptical, for he elaborated. "Many performers experience stage fright, even seasoned professionals who have been on the stage for decades. It's actually more common than you think. When you step up to the footlights, the theater will be dark. The spotlights will practically blind you, and the audience will be nearly invisible. So, forget about them. Just sing to the poor woman who could not stay in the convalescent home without the money from your concert. Now, drink some water for your dry throat. I expect you to be on stage on time!"

I sipped some water slowly while I talked myself into coming out of the dressing room. There was enthusiastic applause when I stepped out on the stage. It was a friendly crowd, mostly people I knew, trustees of the convalescent home, and Graybar's acquaintances. When the clapping stopped, the theater was quiet, save for a few errant coughs and sneezes. As Graybar had predicted, I couldn't see the audience except for the first row, where an elderly woman about my grandmother's age sat. She gave me a radiant smile, and I imagined her to be the unknown beneficiary in the convalescent home.

The orchestra played the introduction to the first number, and the trembling returned. I wanted to dash off the stage. Instead, I focused on counting the measures to my entrance. The first stanza was a bit shaky, but I began to relax. By the next number, I felt as comfortable on that stage as when I entertained my friends after dinner.

During the brief intermission, Graybar took my hands and said, "You see, your fear was just a momentary foible. Your performance is brilliant! I can hardly wait to see what the papers have to say tomorrow."

Emboldened by my success in the first half of the recital, I allowed my gaze to depart from the smiling lady in the front row and roam the audience. Almost instantly, I spotted Alexandra with her new beau, but she had eyes only for him. However, when I began to sing the final number, her attention was suddenly riveted to my face. It was an odd song, indeed.

> She descended to the female stranger
> —Take care in the dim light—
> She descended to the female stranger
> She took her into her arms
> Neither of the two said a word
> But then went quickly away

I'd always interpreted the song to mean that a woman had come to claim the queen, her female lover, and spirit her away.

The enthusiastic applause at the end of the piece distracted me, but I noticed Alexandra's hasty departure with Stebbings-Wilder. She'd been invited to the reception that Graybar was hosting at the Savoy, so I assumed she was trying to make an escape ahead of the crowd. After the encores and curtain calls, I found people standing in line to meet me. Graybar had gone ahead to greet his guests, so I couldn't count on him to rescue me.

I arrived at the lavish reception and perceived that Graybar had more in mind for me than an occasional benefit concert, which indicated the need for a little conversation between us. I tried to find Alexandra and her escort, but they were nowhere to be seen, nor Charles, who had been sitting beside his sister in the concert hall. I couldn't believe they would even consider missing the celebration, but I was diverted from my search by the constant onslaught of well-wishers.

A few minutes later, Graybar interrupted a conversation I was having with one of my heros in the singing world, the famous soprano, Leonora Braham, who had originated many of the Gilbert and Sullian roles.

"Forgive me, Madam Braham, but I must speak with Lady Margaret." Graybar seized my hand and led me away. "Charles Calder telephoned," he explained. "You must meet him at his home at once. There's been an accident." We dashed down the steps to the Savoy lobby. At the curb, Graybar opened his wallet and paid the taxi driver. "To Mayfair with all possible speed. The lady will give you the address."

As the taxi sped through the streets of London, I tried to imagine what kind of "accident" had me heading to the Calders' residence rather than a hospital. Fortunately, the ride was brief. As we approached the house, I saw a knot of vehicles outside, including a police van.

A policeman stood guard at the door. "I'm sorry, Miss, but this is a crime scene. You cannot enter."

Luckily, Mrs. Calder came into the foyer. "It's all right. She's a member of the family," she said, vouching for me. She took me into the parlor and closed the door. Her face was ghostly white. "Oh, Meg, thank God you've come! Charles could use your help."

"Why? What's happened?"

She glanced away, evidently to hide strong emotion. "She cut herself."

"Cut herself? How? Where?"

"In the bath. Both wrists. There was so much blood!" I reached for her hand to steady her, but she brushed mine away. "Never mind me. Go upstairs and help Charles."

There was a bobby standing in the bathroom making sketches. I poked my head in the doorway to see. Despite what Mrs. Calder had said, there was no blood. None at all. Every surface of the bathroom—walls, tub, and floor—was sparkling clean.

"Good evening, Ma'am," said the bobby, touching his fingers to the brim of his hat.

"Where is Mr. Calder…the son?" I asked in a neutral voice, despite my anxiety.

"In the lady's bedroom, just down the hall," he stuck the pencil behind his ear and pointed in the direction. "I can lead you there."

"Thank you, constable. I know the way."

I hurried down the corridor to Alexandra's bedroom. Being the only daughter, she'd been assigned the largest of the secondary bedrooms. It was decorated in an overblown, Victorian-era style, which I can only describe as excessive.

Charles looked grave and was being interrogated by a middle-aged man, who I assumed to be a Scotland Yard inspector. Charles noticed me standing in the doorway and beckoned to me with a wave.

"Here is Lady Compton-Wickes now," said Charles. "I'm certain she can shed light on the situation. She is my sister's physician." In fact, Alexandra had never been my patient. Moreover, I never used my English courtesy title. I instantly perceived that Charles was alerting me to some kind of scheme.

The inspector made a little bow. "Inspector Martin Carter, at your service, my lady. I am acquainted with your father-in-law, the Marquess of Bromsley," he said. "Wonderful man. We were at Sandhurst together."

"Ah, then you may also know my father, Count Stahle von Langenberg-Edelheim?"

His face instantly brightened. "Really? Freddie is your father?"

"Indeed, he is. I am Margarethe von Stahle, Countess Raithschau," I said, overturning in an instant the years of effort I'd put into hiding my titles and noble birth. "I am also a physician. Miss Calder is my patient," I said, nodding in Charles' direction to let him know I was playing along.

Inspector Carter pursed his lips. "Perhaps we might go downstairs. We don't want to disturb the lady further. She's had quite an ordeal."

Charles shot me a look of profound relief. "Don't worry, Dr. Stahle," he said. "I shall remain to look after my sister."

Carter and I went down to the entry foyer. Despite the distance from Alexandra's bedroom, he spoke in hushed tones. "I have no idea what to make of this," he said, looking, indeed, perplexed. "The mother called us, but by the time we arrived, all the blood had been mopped up and the room wiped of any evidence. The girl's brother had already sewn up the wounds."

"Mr. Calder is a surgeon. We were colleagues at Barts."

"So he said," replied Carter, frowning.

"Inspector, you must understand that Miss Calder is extremely high-strung. She's been melancholy of late, and in fact, this terrible act does not surprise me. She's given to extremely dark moods. The family and I have been monitoring her closely."

"Then you agree that she attempted suicide?"

"Can there be any doubt?"

"What do you suggest we do?" he asked with a sidelong look.

"Mr. Carter, I so hate to invoke your friendship with my father and father-in-law, but perhaps you could respect the family's privacy and allow me to handle this?"

"There's already been a report made by the constable who took the call."

I smiled at him. "In that case, what must we do to erase the record?"

He returned my smile. "Nothing, my lady. I shall see to it. Now, let me take my troops where they are actually needed." He gazed at some imaginary point in the distance. "Good heavens, I haven't seen Freddie Stahle in forty years! Wonderful man, your father. And a delight to meet his daughter!" I silently thanked the loyalty of the British old boys' network for saving the Calders' reputation. Carter's smile gave way to a frown. "I hope you can do something for the poor girl, my lady. You know how it is with these cases. This time, she didn't succeed, but with a little knowledge and more experience, we might not be so fortunate in the future."

I sighed, fearing the same. I offered my hand and he raised it to his lips.

"Please convey my regards to Lord Bromsley, and, when you next see him, to your father."

"I most certainly shall," I promised. "Thank you for coming and the accommodation you've shown this family." I opened the front door for him.

The Bobby outside touched the brim of his hat. "G'night, Ma'am," he said and headed to the police van with Carter.

When I went upstairs, Charles met me on the landing. "Thank God you got rid of them."

"Don't worry. The police will blot the incident from the record."

"I knew you would sort it out."

"That was the best bit of playacting I've done in a while."

"What playacting?" he said. "Every word you said is true."

"I'm not her physician."

"A white lie at worst."

We heard a moan from the bedroom, and our eyes turned in that direction. "She's been asking for you, Meg. Perhaps you should go in to see her."

At the sight of me, Alexandra began to weep. I gathered her into my arms. "Oh, my darling, what have you done? Why have you hurt yourself?

"You betrayed me! In front of Jonathan. In front of everyone!"

I was puzzled, but I knew that whatever would come next required privacy.

"Charles, will you excuse us? I must be alone with your sister."

He sighed, but he left without protest.

I held Alexandra at arms' length so that I could see her face. "Alex, whatever inspired you to do something so dreadful and dangerous?"

"How could you betray me in that way?"

"What way?"

"Now, everyone will know we are lovers!"

"What do you mean?"

"You sang that wretched song about a queen throwing away her position to embrace a strange woman."

I finally understood her perception of the situation. "But I only sang the song because I wanted to promote the composer. There was no hidden message to you or anyone for that matter."

"Then, you have no objection to Jonathan?"

"That's not what I said. He's a boring man, unworthy of you, but if he's your choice, I would never stand in your way."

She began to weep. "Please stay with me tonight! I need you near."

I had never spent the night in Alexandra's bedroom, but I shed my brand-new Paris gown and slipped in beside her.

∼

In the morning, Charles woke me to say that Krauss had sent my coat so that I could walk home without drawing attention. I gratefully insinuated myself into my own bed and slept until nearly noon. Thankfully, it was Sunday, so no one was the wiser.

After my moment of compassion, I was furious with Alexandra for doing something so stupid. Over the next days, I refused to take her calls, despite my fears that she might repeat her folly to get my attention.

Then one day she showed up on my doorstep and refused to leave. Poor Krauss had no choice but to inform me that she was waiting in the foyer. "I know you aren't taking her calls, *Gnädige*, but there she was, and I had no idea what to tell her."

I drew a weary sigh. "Show her in, Krauss."

Alexandra sat quietly while I finished my piano practice. Then she asked if she could accompany me to my quarters. I consented more out of concern for her mental state than any willingness to entertain her company. She sat quietly in my sitting room and gazed out the window.

"Alex, what can I do for you?" I finally asked.

"Oh, it's quite simple. Please remove my sutures." She pulled back the sleeves of her blouse. "Charles tells me today is the day."

"Then why not ask him to remove them?"

She shook her head. "He's too busy, and I would like you to attend to it."

I unwrapped the bandage and inspected the wounds. Everything was healing beautifully, but the sutures needed to be removed. I sent the maid for my medical bag. While I snipped the silks and removed them with forceps, Alexandra watched me with dull eyes.

"You hate me now," she said while I bandaged her wrists.

"Nonsense. Why should I hate you?"

"My behavior detracted from your concert."

"You took nothing from me. All you did was hurt yourself and create an embarrassment for your family."

"You missed the lovely party." She gazed at me with a long, sad look. "According to the papers, your concert was a triumph."

I took her hand and gripped it tight. "Alex, if you ever try anything so stupid and selfish again, I shall kill you myself. If you think your trivial and useless effort was dramatic, you have no idea what I shall do to you. Is that quite clear?"

She looked at me with alarm before confirming with a nod that she had understood the message.

"Jonathan has ended our association. He says I'm mad."

I was not about to dispute Jonathan's opinion because I was beginning to see that it had merit.

"What will you do now?" I asked.

"I suppose I shall have to find someone else. Will you help me?"

Thinking back, I wonder which of us was really mad, because I agreed.

My house was better suited for large parties because I lived alone, so it became the setting for her search. Alexandra was in one of her bubbly, outgoing periods when she could engage in witty conversation and be very amusing. She filled my diary with social events, and we entertained a wide range of glittering guests—diplomatic personnel, some of Lytton's old friends, musicians I had come to know through singing, academics, Bloomsbury friends, including Vita and the Bells. The entertainment often went on well into the night. Alexandra, herself, hardly ever slept.

It was undoubtedly the most social period of my life and left me feeling overwhelmed by human company. My work became my favorite excuse to avoid a party. Sometimes, I slept in my consulting room to get away. Of course, I realized that Alexandra was using my home and capital to advertise for a new suitor, but it never troubled me because I saw her marriage as inevitable.

After all that grand effort, Jonathan crawled back to her by the end of the season. Within a month, they announced their engagement.

25

Alexandra's engagement put an end to the raucous parties and provided me with a blessed spell of peace. I reclaimed my library as a place to read and my music room as a place to play the piano and sing. The monotony was almost welcome. Then the New York Stock Market crashed, causing a tidal wave of financial calamity. Overnight, a significant portion of our wealth vanished. I scrambled to liquidate our losing investments in equities and reinvest the money in real estate, a steel plant in Bochum, and a coal mine in Silesia. It was not until late November that I got our finances in order, and I dared to breathe a sigh of relief.

I tried to eke out advice from my father, but he never had any to offer. Finally, he admitted, "Your grandfather tried to explain investment, but I've really never understood it. I'm glad you do. Carry on."

I sat brooding over this for some time, only gradually perceiving what had been true for some time—preserving our wealth was now my responsibility and mine alone.

As Christmas approached, I considered bringing the children to Edelheim, but the stock market crisis had kept me so busy, I never got around to making any specific plans. When the Bromsleys invited us to spend Christmas with them, I accepted without further thought. Through their summer holidays at Larkhurst, my children had become close to Lady Philippa. They adored her. Meanwhile, she'd become like another mother to me. She wrote and telephoned regularly merely to chat, unlike my own mother, who rarely wrote except to complain about my father or the weather.

The night before Christmas, my children and I joined the Bromsleys in town for the festivities. A choral group serenaded us with Christmas carols. On Christmas day, we attended the Eucharist in the local church. The familiarity of the service and the English hymns comforted me. Afterwards, we walked back to Larkhurst where an enormous fire blazed. The Christmas tree filled the great hall with the delicious scent of pine.

I felt so at home at Larkhurst, which confused me because it wasn't home. But where was home exactly? I knew for certain that it wasn't my London townhouse. Was it Edelheim? I imagined my parents celebrating the day and remembered Christmases past—my grandparents lifting me up to hang ornaments on the branches of the tree, Hanna simmering *Glühwein* with her own secret blend of aromatic spices, Lytton singing carols in his elegant baritone. Thinking of the people I'd lost left me moody. Lady Philippa noticed and patted my hand.

"I miss him too," she said.

I gazed sympathetically into her eyes. Of course, I missed Lytton, but how can the loss of a spouse compare to the loss of a child? I silently prayed that I would never know such pain.

~

An ice storm in January left the roads treacherous. The Bromsleys were returning from visiting neighbors when a lorry driver slid into their motorcar at a crossroads. Their butler rang me in London. My father-in-law had been catapulted from his seat and broken his neck. He was pronounced dead at the scene. Lady Philippa survived, but she was in critical condition.

I raced up to the hospital where she'd been taken, but identifying myself as her daughter-in-law wasn't enough to get me admitted to her room.

"I'm sorry, but *no one* is allowed to see her," announced the matron, crossing her arms on her chest to demonstrate that her position was immoveable.

"Please contact my colleague, Matthew Abrams at Barts, so that he might explain *why* I should be able to see Lady Bromsley. Or perhaps you could telephone Lord Abbott."

The nurse's eyes widened. Evidently, these august names had made an impression. "Your name again, please?"

"Margaret Stahle, Bachelor of Medicine, Doctor of Medicine, member of the Royal College of Surgeons, the British Society of Gynaecology, et cetera, et cetera!"

The nurse's eyes widened. "You're the 'lady doctor,'" she breathed in a tone of awe.

At that point, I was so impatient I would have admitted to being Satan! They opened the doors at once. A senior nurse escorted me to my mother-in-law's room. She gave me her chart to review, even though I wasn't technically supposed to see it because I wasn't her attending physician.

When I read the list of her symptoms—pneumothorax, ruptured spleen, blunt head trauma, broken ulna and compound fracture of the right femur—my heart sank. The prognosis for a woman of her age to recover from such trauma was poor indeed. Her injuries were so extensive that contemplating her survival was worse than anticipating her demise. My role now was to ensure that she died without pain. I rang the nurse and asked for a syringe of morphine.

Lady Philippa's eyelids fluttered. She looked at me dully. Then the light of recognition came into her eyes. "Meg?" she asked, her eyes darting around as she tried to determine where she was.

I squeezed her hand gently.

"Yes, it's Meg. There's been an accident. You're in hospital. Rest now. Save your strength."

"Oh, dear girl. You are a good daughter. The best daughter."

I fought back tears and got up to kiss her forehead. "Thank you, my dear. You are a good mother. The best mother."

She made a little sound, almost like the chirp of a small bird and closed her eyes. She was still alive. I could see the rise and fall of her chest. The fluids draining from her collapsed lung bubbled as they emptied into a glass bottle. It was difficult not to be emotional while I sat at her bedside, holding her hand until her breathing finally ceased.

⁓

The children were bereft, of course, to lose both grandparents so suddenly. Lady Philippa had been a far more attentive and loving grandmother than my own mother. Lord Bromsley always doted on the children. Willi adored him because he knew how to tell a suspenseful tale of his far-flung adventures.

My son needed a new suit for the funeral because he'd grown so much. In a sad rite of passage, Liesel was outfitted with her first black dress.

Privately, they were inconsolable, but I was proud to see that neither of them wept publicly.

After the service, I was briefly tempted to keep the children for the remainder of the term. I considered taking them to Garmisch for an extended family holiday, but the headmaster of Eton college persuaded me that school would provide structure and a beneficial routine. After I returned the children to their respective schools and headed back to London, I wondered what had possessed me to agree that discipline and order were better than a mother's attention? I was sorry I'd cancelled the family holiday, for it was a lost opportunity to reconnect with the strangers I called my children.

The Bromsleys' eldest, a brother-in-law I barely knew, returned from Africa to arrange for the sale of Larkhurst. He hadn't come home for Lytton's funeral. His parents hadn't seen him in years. The last time I'd laid eyes on him was at my wedding.

Arthur Compton-Wickes, now Lord Bromsley, being broad-shouldered, fair, and heartbreakingly handsome, closely resembled my husband. The likeness made his presence hard to bear, but the new Lord Bromsley was cordial and allowed me the opportunity to remove my possessions from the house at my own pace. He stood in the doorway while I labeled the boxes containing my belongings.

"Must it really be sold?" I asked.

"There's no money left, but you probably knew that," Arthur said, followed by a deep sigh. "Thank you for keeping them afloat. Father was a soldier. He had no head for managing money." The remark made me think of my own father.

"Perhaps you'll want to live here someday," I said. "After all, it is your ancestral home."

"My life is in Africa now. There's nothing left for me here."

"Lease it to someone in case you change your mind," I suggested.

He shook his head. "Don't you understand, Lady Margaret? The old order is dying, even as we speak. It's time to move on."

I briefly considered buying the place as a country house for Wilhelm in memory of his grandparents, but the stock market crash had depleted my funds, and I couldn't manage it.

As I drove away and saw the façade of Larkhurst House in the rear-view mirror, I realized that all my ties to Lytton and his family had been broken.

After I left Larkhurst for the last time, I found myself in a dark mood. Even music couldn't cheer me. That night, as I nursed a scotch, I wondered what additional misfortune could befall us.

~

I didn't have to wait long. A few days later, Krauss presented an envelope on the silver tray he used to deliver my mail. "A telegram, *Gnädige*," he explained, "from Herr Klowitz, the majordomo of Edelheim." I knew from my father's secretary that all communication was to come through him alone. I suspect this was to keep unpleasant information from me, but I never questioned my father's orders, and the chain of command among Edelheim's former soldiers was absolute. Only the direst circumstances could have compelled Klowitz to defy my father's orders and contact me directly. Krauss handed me my letter opener, shaped like a miniature sabre, a prize from a fencing tournament and extremely sharp. My hands shook as I sliced open the envelope.

The message was long. Such a missive must have cost dearly at the telegraph office. Did the man think he was writing a formal letter?

> My dearest Lady Margarethe
> Forgive the presumption on my part, but I must inform you of a worrisome decline in your father's health. Dr. Bultmann wished to write to you directly, but I took the responsibility on myself. Your father has suffered from a severe grippe since autumn. Dr. Bultmann has now diagnosed pneumonia. I respectfully suggest that you return home to evaluate the situation firsthand. Let me know if you would like me to make the arrangements.
> With all due honor and respect to my esteemed and gracious lady, I remain your dutiful servant,
> Hermann Klowitz

Krauss had been standing by for my orders. He clicked his heels and stood at attention as I refolded and returned the telegram to the envelope.

"Please arrange for air charter from Croydon field to Langenberg. I wish to leave on the first available flight," I said as calmly as I could manage. "Send Anna to pack my things."

"As you wish, *Gnädige*." He bowed and went off to execute my orders.

I telephoned Emma to ask if she could see my patients and perform my surgeries in my absence. Next, I rang Abbott and shared the news. He volunteered to help in any way he could. Arranging for other physicians to oversee my medical cases was the responsible thing to do, of course, for I sensed from Klowitz's telegram that my absence could be extended. I telephoned Mrs. Calder to ask if she would act in my stead regarding the children while I was away. The dear woman agreed at once. I instructed Krauss to draft notes to their schools for my signature. A few minutes later, Charles appeared at the front door and asked, "How can I help?"

"Call Emma and see if you can take some of my surgeries."

"When will you be back?"

"I have no idea."

By first light, air travel had been arranged and my luggage had been packed. Grauer had the motorcar standing at the curb ready to transport me to Croydon. Before I left, I called Sauerbruch at the Charité, where he was now chief of surgery. Fortunately, he was on rounds and not in theater when I telephoned. I apprised him of the situation, and he instantly agreed to come to Edelheim.

"When will you arrive?" he asked.

"I am flying from Croydon to Langenberg this morning. I should be there by this afternoon."

"Then I'll take the afternoon train from Berlin and meet you there."

"Thank you, *Herr Professor*. We shall wait dinner for you."

As we approached Edelheim, I watched with fascination because I had never seen my ancestral home from the air. The lake, only partially frozen, reflected the cerulean sky. At the center of the plain, surrounded by barns and servants' cottages, was the massive *Schloss*. The sight made my heart swell. I still called Edelheim "home." Despite the fact that I had only lived there for a handful of years as a child, it was the land of my ancestors. Their bones rested in the crypt of the village church; their dust lay in the churchyard.

The estate manager met me in the old Ford he used to ride around the estate. "Sorry for the informal welcome," he said. "The Daimler is being repaired."

I shrugged. "I don't care as long as this ancient wreck conveys us where we want to go."

He laughed. "It will, *Gnädige*. I promise."

Hans Bolling was a local man, who had been ambitious enough to study agriculture at university. In my memory, he'd always had a smile. Farmers must be optimistic by nature, but as he navigated the unpaved road toward the house, he looked uncharacteristically glum.

"What's on your mind, Bolling?" I finally asked.

He glanced at me, looking surprised. Evidently, I'd interrupted a deep thought. "I'm thinking about your father. I'm sorry he is ill."

"So are we all, but why do I sense you have something else on your mind?"

"I hope you will forgive me for giving you bad news."

"Of course. What good is an estate manager who can't be candid with his employer?"

Bolling inhaled a huge gulp of air. "Things have been going poorly here."

"How so?" I asked in a mild voice, trying to sound interested but not anxious.

"As you know, the weather was bad last year. It rained so much in the spring the seedlings drowned. Then we had a severe drought, which left fissures in the soil. Many tenants lost their entire harvest. They slaughtered their livestock because there was no hay." Bolling slowed the motorcar to navigate around a deep rut ahead. I had never seen the road in such bad repair. "Some tenants left their plots and went to the city looking for work."

"Where there's little work to be had," I observed.

"Yes, but they don't know it, or if they do, don't believe it. Usually, your father visits the tenants in the fall to ask about the harvest and collect their rents. Last year he asked me to go alone."

"That's odd," I said.

"I thought so too."

"Was he ill?" I found it hard to believe my father had deliberately neglected his duties.

"I don't think he was himself," said Bolling. "He seemed to have lost interest in the farm."

I nodded, absorbing his words. "What did you discover on your tour of the tenant plots?"

"It was one tale of disaster after another. The inflation has raised the bank rates. Many could not afford to take a loan to buy seed. Your father gave them seed, which bought good will, but the rents are down or delayed. Since winter began, more tenants have abandoned their land."

"That's not good news," I agreed. "I shall visit the tenants while I'm here. Will you accompany me?"

"Yes, of course, *Gnädige*."

"Have you found new tenants for the abandoned plots?"

"All but one. It abuts marshland and is not desirable for farming."

"Offer it to the neighboring tenants at one-quarter rent to keep the land worked. Let's see who's ambitious enough to take it."

"That's a fine idea. We can discuss it when we visit them." He smiled, and I saw the optimistic man I remembered.

I'd hoped when Bolling had come to meet me in his broken down Ford that I'd be spared the greeting ceremony, but as soon as we entered the courtyard, the servants came out of the house and assembled in orderly lines. There were the usual noisy orders regarding the disposition of my luggage. After accepting a string of curtsies, bows, handshakes, and a few kisses, I was escorted into the house by the majordomo.

"Thank you for coming home, Lady Margarethe," said Klowitz. "A thousand apologies for calling you back from England."

"Klowitz, you must never hesitate to ring me if you have any concerns.

My father needn't know everything." The majordomo raised a brow, but his nod told me he'd understood the message. I spoke close to his ear for discretion. "Please call Dr. Bultmann and ask him to meet me here."

"As you wish, *Gnädige*," he said, escorting me down the hall. "You'll find your mother in the music room." When I'd heard an exceptionally well-executed Schumann piano etude, I'd surmised as much. "The countess has been waiting for you. She wishes to speak to you before you see your father."

He opened the enormous mahogany door to the music room. We stood waiting until my mother looked up from the piano. After Klowitz announced me, my mother asked him to bring tea and sandwiches. I bent to kiss her, but she turned away, offering her hand instead. Obviously, she still hadn't forgiven me for the "scandal" of my concert.

"There was no need to return to Edelheim," she said coldly. "Don't you trust Bultmann to look after your father?"

"Of course, I trust him. I hired him. That's not why I came home."

"It wasn't necessary, but it's good that you're here. There are some things that need attention."

"So I've heard."

She turned and gave me a disapproving frown. "From whom?"

"Never mind. While I'm here, I shall do my best to put things in order."

"Perhaps it's time you came home and gave up your little hobby."

"If by that, you mean my singing, I admit it's a diversion, but it keeps me sane."

"You know what I mean." She gave me a contemptuous look.

Obviously, she wanted to revive the argument about my profession. I'd thought that had been long-since forgotten, but apparently not. "You can forget that idea, Mother. I have no intention of giving up medicine."

"I thought not," she said. She took a seat on the sofa and gestured to a chair opposite from where she sat. "Will you remain now that you are here?"

"We shall see."

Fortunately, Klowitz returned with a tray of sandwiches and tea, which ended that conversation. My mother had strong feelings about being decorous in the presence of the servants, so his presence noticeably lowered the temperature.

Klowitz poured the tea and handed us each a cup. "Lady Margarethe, Dr. Bultmann has arrived," he said with a little bow.

"Show him in, please."

A moment later, Klowitz brought in Langenberg's physician. Thomas Bultmann was a tall, soft-spoken man with close-cropped, brown hair and kind, blue eyes. He shook my hand warmly, and I invited him to join us for tea. He bowed to my mother, who gave him a bare nod and picked up her needlework.

"Welcome back, *Frau Doktor*," he said, giving me a warm smile. Although he was technically an employee because we paid his salary, I had tried to encourage a collegial relationship by insisting he address me by my professional title.

I gestured to the tray of sandwiches. "Please join me."

"Thank you, I shall." He served himself a plate of sandwiches while I poured him a cup of tea.

"I haven't been to my father's room yet. I was waiting for you to arrive to provide cover." I smiled so he would know I was joking. "He objects to his daughter acting as a physician."

Bultmann chuckled as he stirred sugar into his tea. "I wouldn't take it personally. As you know, he can be a grumpy patient."

"What is his current condition?"

"He seems to be on the mend. The oxygen helped him get through the worst of the crisis. When I was here this morning, his temperature was nearly normal."

"So, he will recover."

"Yes, I think so."

"That's wonderful news." I noticed out of the corner of my eye that my mother, although seemingly occupied in her needlework, was paying close attention to our conversation. I ignored her while Bultmann and I caught up on the local news.

After we finished our tea, Bultmann and I went upstairs to look in on my father. As we ascended the stairs, I asked his assessment of my father's mental state.

"Of course, the illness has depressed his mood. He seems less involved in the estate, but not entirely. He pays close attention to certain things, breeding his hounds and horses. As for the rest…"

I nodded. "So you don't think he's failing mentally?"

"No, he's far too young for that," said Bultmann emphatically. "It's lack of interest, not dementia."

I shook my head. "My father was never really interested in farming. It was my grandparents who kept things going here."

We went into Father's room. He smiled and was quite pleasant until I took out my stethoscope. "My daughter is not playing doctor with me!"

Bultmann chuckled softly. "But sir, your daughter is a respected surgeon. She is considered one of the best practitioners in London."

"I don't care," growled my father.

I allowed Bultmann to manage my recalcitrant father, while I stood back. Bultmann waited until we'd left my father's room before offering his impressions. "Your father's vitals are close to normal. He is, indeed, on the mend." At the front door, Bultmann added in a confidential tone, "You can observe, I'm sure, that the issue is more than physical. I'm glad you're here, *Frau Doktor*. We need you now."

"Next time, you mustn't hesitate to call me. I don't care what the old man says. Things here must change."

Bultmann flashed a quick grin of approval.

"Professor Sauerbruch will be here for dinner. Will you join us?"

"Sauerbruch," he repeated in a reverential tone. "Yes, of course. It would be an honor." He bowed with heel clicks. I was disappointed because it proved that, despite my efforts at collegiality, I was still his employer.

∿

Sauerbruch arrived towards sundown. When I informed my mother that we would have a dinner guest, she chose to eat alone in her rooms.

That suited me fine because I had no wish to see her bored expression while Sauerbruch and I discussed medical matters with Dr. Bultmann.

My mentor embraced me warmly when he arrived. I'd last seen him at a medical conference over a year earlier. His presence instantly made me feel better. Thinking someone older and wiser can somehow make things right is an illusion we allow ourselves, even as adults.

After examining my father and confirming Bultmann's prognosis, Sauerbruch agreed to have a cocktail with me in the music room. I anticipated the martinis with some trepidation. I had been able to teach Krauss how to make an excellent martini, but Klowitz, despite repeated instruction and all the same ingredients, never seemed to get it right. Sauerbruch and I settled into opposite sofas to catch up on the news. He had recently been appointed professor of surgery at the medical school, and I heartily congratulated him.

"You should return to Germany. The university is looking for lecturers in surgery. You have habilitation, Margarethe. They would hire you like that." He snapped his fingers to demonstrate.

"I have a very prosperous and interesting practice in London."

"Eh!" he said dismissively, "time to stop playing and get down to business."

I laughed aloud. "Tact has never been your strong suit, *Herr Professor.*"

"You expect me to be truthful, so I am." His eyes were serious. "You could work for me at the Charité. I miss our partnership."

Calling what we'd had a partnership would be extraordinarily generous. If I returned to his side, I would again be his appendage, albeit a more accomplished and skillful one. And why would I wish to return to such a subservient position after having had so much autonomy in private practice? "Thank you, *Herr Professor.* I shall consider it," I said aloud, but in my mind, I had already decided against it.

His offer did raise the question of what I would do if I returned to Germany. Langenberg already had a doctor—never mind that I would be bored to tears in general practice. A career of lancing boils and treating the grippe was not for me. At least, working for Sauerbruch at the Charité promised interesting cases. He reiterated his suggestion that I join him when he left the next morning. Again, I promised to think about it.

I telephoned my grandaunt both to inform her about her nephew's health situation and to ask her advice about returning to Germany. As always, she listened patiently while I laid out the facts. After a long silence, she said, "I completely understand your reluctance to give up your life in England, but perhaps the time has come for you to return. They truly need you now, so being closer to home makes sense."

"I was afraid you'd say that. Duty first, last, and always."

"No, dear, I'm not Prussian like your father. I am merely being practical."

I chuckled. It was refreshing to talk to my grandaunt. People might consider her a mystic, but her recommendations were always sensible.

After an extended silence, *Tante* said, "I have a counter proposal to Sauerbruch's. The chief of surgery at St. Hilde's is retiring. Few people know this, but as a member of the board, I know they are seeking a successor. It wouldn't hurt you to gain some leadership experience. It would serve you well in the future."

She was correct. In the operating theater, I might be the undisputed leader, but I had no experience in an administrative post. "What do you think my chances of being appointed are?"

She laughed aloud. "Margarethe, if I decide you will be chief of surgery in one of the order's hospitals, you will be chief of surgery."

"*Tante*! That's nepotism. I'm shocked!" I said with a heavy overtone of sarcasm.

"I assure you that I would not intervene if I didn't believe you are qualified. As a surgeon, you are more than qualified. St. Hilde's would get far better than it deserves. As a leader…well, we shall see."

We spent the remainder of the conversation catching up on the news of the family. She agreed that it was wise to leave the children in their English schools for the remainder of the term, but she asked when I would send her Liesel. I hedged on this answer, although I knew it was inevitable that my daughter would attend Obberoth. Learning about the nuns and convent life was as essential to her future as it had been to mine.

After my conversation with my grandaunt, I accompanied Bolling on a visit to the tenant farms. He seemed surprised when I suggested we make our rounds on horseback, but I wanted to connect this visit to an earlier, less complicated time. In every cottage, we heard a persistent theme. The crop failures of the previous fall had been a setback. Some of the tenants had taken loans, and now the inflation threatened them with ruin.

As we rode back to the house, I said, "We should again provide them with seed for the spring planting."

"At no cost?"

"At no cost. And we should forgive their loans." We practically owned the bank in Langenberg, so this was not as difficult as it sounded.

"Lady Margarethe, what you propose would certainly help the tenants, but it would require an extraordinary sum!"

"If the tenants abandon the land, we'll have no income for years. There are no lazy tenants on Stahle lands. They all work extremely hard. While things are so difficult, we should consider lowering the rents as well."

At first, Bolling was so surprised, he seemed unable to speak. We rode for a while before he asked, "How can Edelheim survive without the income?"

"We can develop other sources of income. My father has been talking of expanding the sawmill for years. We'll build a bigger, more efficient mill. We can reopen the lime quarries."

"That will be expensive."

I shrugged. "As they say, one needs to spend money to make money."

Bolling's look of surprise turned into a smile. "I am very glad you came home, Lady Margarethe. We need you now."

I sighed at this sentiment. It was obviously true, and it was mildly flattering to be needed. However, it would certainly mean the end of the life I'd built in London.

26

The next morning, I called Krauss to tell him that I would be extending my stay. He listened sympathetically while I described my father's health and the conditions I'd found at Edelheim. "My family needs me. I think it's time to come home." In the moment of silence that followed, I could imagine what he was thinking. If I returned to Edelheim, he would lose his position as head of my household staff and be lost in a well-established servant hierarchy.

"Don't worry, Krauss. I won't be living here permanently. Despite its size, my mother and I cannot live in the same house." His soft chuckle was audible through the wire.

"Then where, *Gnädige*?"

"Berlin. I'll reopen the Grunewald house." I had fond memories of the place from childhood. I especially liked its walled, double garden and the expansive view of the Dianasee. I wondered if the little skiff was still in the boathouse. "Perhaps you can send some staff there to freshen up the place."

"I shall go myself," he said.

"No, I need you to manage things in London. Send Grauer and one of the maids. Doesn't Anna speak German?"

"Yes, she does."

"Good. Send her with Grauer. That will be enough for now."

"As you wish," he said, but I could detect slight disappointment in his voice.

How lucky I was to have Krauss, who was ever attentive and always loyal. In giving me Krauss for my majordomo, my father had lost one of his most talented and reliable adjutants. I wondered if he would not be more useful as under-butler at Edelheim now that things there had declined, but when I suggested it to my father, he would hear none of it.

"In the coming years, you will need Krauss far more than I will," he said. "Hold on to him. He's irreplaceable."

It was easier to talk to Father about my decision to move than my plan for the tenants. I waited until his health was stable before broaching the subject. Like Bolling, he was alarmed at the potential loss of income from reducing the rents.

"How will we pay our bills?"

"We will have to infuse cash."

"From where?"

"I have some money."

My father gave me a sharp look. "You can't be doing that well as a surgeon."

"I do very well, but the money I have in mind is from my investments."

"I won't take charity from my daughter."

"It's not charity, Father. Isn't it my duty to keep Edelheim on sound footing for the next generation?"

He eyed me suspiciously. "I always told my mother it was a bad idea to send you to Obberoth. My aunt taught you not only how to argue but win!"

I laughed. "Don't blame *Tante*. It was you and grandfather who hammered the notion of duty into my brain. But you will need to ease off the reins a bit. I'll need to make some changes around here."

"I expected that," he said with a dejected expression.

I patted his shoulder. "Don't worry, Father. I won't do anything important without consulting you first."

But he did not so much as murmur in protest when I asked for power of attorney. Once he was able to leave his bed, he called our bankers, brokers, and solicitors to Edelheim to explain that he was delegating authority to me. As I listened to Father explaining my new responsibilities to the men around the dining table, I felt momentary panic, especially when all eyes turned to me. Meanwhile, Father looked overwhelmingly relieved.

In all, I was at Edelheim for a fortnight. In that time, I had managed to tidy up a bit. The tenants were given shares of seed proportional to their land to avoid hard feelings. Edelheim's mechanics and wheelwrights were put at their disposal to repair any farm equipment needing work. All the tenants' debts were restructured or forgiven. An architect drew up a plan for a new sawmill, and I hired a company to explore reopening the quarries.

My father duly noted all these changes. He wasn't completely in agreement with my plan to buy the tenants' debts, but he didn't challenge it, and it was my money, so what could he say? Before I left for Berlin, I felt I had made good progress toward putting our fortunes back on track. I had no illusions that everything was in perfect order, but I felt sure that we were now heading in the right direction. Greatly relieved, I headed to Berlin.

~

Father had suggested that I might want to refurbish the Grunewald house. It had been unoccupied for years. I didn't hesitate to take over my father's bedroom. I added a new Bechstein to the music room. Otherwise, I didn't rush to redecorate the house. For one thing, I decided I rather liked the spare military décor. The soldierly trappings—antique weapons, suits of armor, and military maps—reminded me of the time when my father was rector of Groß-Lichterfelde, and my life was simpler. With the exception of installing a gymnasium in the basement, I left everything almost exactly as it was when my father had lived there.

When I arrived, I found that my servants had done a masterful job of making the house ready. Grauer had hired another maid. All of the dust drapes had been removed, the place had been carefully aired and cleaned. My linens, when I went to bed that night, were crisp and smelled fresh.

The new maid was also quite a good cook. She prepared a tasty rabbit stew in honor of my arrival. However, I felt very strange eating alone at the head of the enormous dining table. Fortunately, the house had a smaller dining room where breakfast was usually served. Unless I had guests, I ate there.

In London, it had been "anything goes." In Berlin, the servants treated me differently. They were more formal in my presence, even Grauer, who'd known me since I was a green surgeon. It seemed that my status had changed in everyone's eyes, not unlike when I had made the transition from medical student to doctor. I considered forcing a more informal atmosphere until I realized they were honoring not me, but my place in the social order.

Grauer made a very good under-butler, but I missed Krauss, especially his martinis. He'd found a lease agent, but so far, no tenant for my London townhouse. During a telephone conversation with Emma to discuss the details of turning over the practice, I suddenly had an idea.

"My townhouse is available for lease," I casually hinted. "And it's completely furnished."

She wasn't taken in, of course, and hesitated for a moment. "I know, but I could never afford it."

"You could take on that new partner Abbott recommended. She sounds rather good. Then you could afford the rent, especially if it were lower."

"Meg, are you trying to tell me how to run the practice now that you've bowed out? And why would you reduce the rent?"

"Well, for one thing, these are hard times, and I probably need to lower rent to attract a tenant. Why not offer it to you?"

"You could sell it," she suggested.

"I'd never get the price it's worth. Besides, I'm rather fond of the place. I'd prefer to have someone I trust living there."

"Tell me your best price."

Although it went against my business instincts, I named a figure I knew she couldn't refuse. Krauss was delighted to have that chore off his hands. I ordered him to finalize the packing of my personal items and come at once.

Instead of paying to transport my motorcar, I decided to give it to Alexandra, not out of generosity but because it meant I could justify buying a new one. As I ticked off one item after another, I tried not to allow regret to creep into my thoughts. I knew I would miss life in England and especially my dear friends, the Calders, but most of all, I would miss my freedom.

༄

Before my grandaunt put my name before the board of St. Hilde's Hospital, I thought I should have a look around. I rang the superior of the convent to arrange for a visit.

Mother Agathe wore spectacles that enlarged her dark eyes making them fishlike. The dark circles under them, and the sharp planes in her face, made her look older than her years. In reality, she was probably about my age.

She declined my offered hand. Instead, she made a deep, formal curtsy as if I were the Kaiserin. "Welcome to St. Hilde's, Countess."

By sheer force of will, I avoided rolling my eyes. "Please, Mother Agathe. In a medical setting, I am known only by my professional title."

"As you wish, *Frau Doktor*," she said with another curtsy.

"And let's dispense with the gestures of obeisance, if you don't mind."

She nodded and gestured to the visitors' chair on the other side of her desk. Her hands instantly vanished under her scapula. Clearly, she observed the nuns' rule scrupulously. "Reverend Mother tells me you are a candidate for chief of surgery," she said, opening the dialogue.

"Not yet, but I am considering it," I said, taking a seat. "Before I confirm my interest, I wish to tour the facilities and observe the staff."

"I have arranged for Sister Brigitte, who is head nurse of the surgical department, to show you around. Then you will meet Dr. Ludwig, the retiring chief. He can give you his impressions of the role." Her tone was unctuous, which made me both uncomfortable and suspicious. I despise people who pander to me. I couldn't wait to be out of her presence.

She rang the surgical nurses' station to summon Sister Brigitte, who was also overly polite. When Germans show extreme courtesy, it is usually to express caution, but sometimes, it is a sign of contempt.

Sister Brigitte's running commentary as we toured the surgical department was informative, but my observations even more so. Hygiene in the theater was lax. The instruments were not kept in the order considered standard in most hospitals. When I was introduced to the nuns we encountered, it became obvious that Sister Brigitte had her favorites among them. My antennae twitched, instantly alert to a female social network with its worst characteristics, including an obvious pecking order. As the tour wound down, Sister Brigitte continued her attempts to ingratiate herself to me. Little did she know, she was doing exactly the opposite.

The last stop on the tour was Dr. Ludwig's office. To my relief, he greeted me as a colleague, without the condescension male surgeons often displayed in my presence. "I am so happy to meet you Dr. von Stahle," he said with a broad smile and a hearty handshake. "We have an acquaintance in common. My specialty is also abdominal surgery." When I looked quizzical, he explained, "I know Martin Abrams quite well."

"A happy coincidence," I agreed.

"Dr. Abrams tells me you are one of the finest surgeons he has ever seen, and we would be exceptionally fortunate to have you as our chief." This served to tell me that Ludwig had investigated my background. In fact, I approved because I believe in due diligence.

I studied Ludwig's handsome face, estimating he couldn't be more than fifty. "Forgive the impertinence, Dr. Ludwig, but you seem rather young to retire. Why are you leaving this post?"

He sighed deeply and glanced away. "I don't want to retire, but my wife is profoundly ill, and she requires more of my attention."

"I am so sorry," I said with genuine sympathy.

"A female cancer."

"As you surely know, I am a gynecologic surgeon. May I know more?"

He gestured to the visitors' chair, and I sat down.

"She suffers from uterine cancer. She wasn't yet in menopause, so the bleeding seemed usual, until it wasn't. We performed a hysterectomy, of course. Unfortunately, it was well established by the time the symptoms presented and had spread beyond the uterine wall."

"If there is anything I can do for you or your wife, medically or otherwise, please let me know."

"Thank you, *Frau Doktor*. Actually, I would be grateful if you examined my wife. Abrams tells me you trained under George Abbott."

"Yes, and I would be happy to consult on your wife's case. If you give me your address and telephone number, I shall visit her."

He took a piece of foolscap out of his desk and wrote down the information.

"I can call on your wife this afternoon."

"The sooner, the better…." His breath caught. He took a moment to compose himself, then forced a smile. "You're here to learn about the position, so let me answer your questions."

I hesitated a moment to collect my thoughts. I had no wish to offend the man by pointing out the irregularities I had observed, but in the end, I saw no alternative. He compressed his lips and nodded gravely as I itemized my concerns.

"Unfortunately, the things you mention are part of the reason I'm leaving. The frustration is more difficult to bear with my wife so ill. I have tried, and believe me when I say, I have *really* tried to address these matters."

"You are chief of surgery. Don't the sisters obey you?"

His disgusted grunt said much. "You don't really understand what it's like to work in a hospital run by nuns, do you?"

"No, of course not. I have always worked in teaching hospitals, where regulations are followed scrupulously."

He studied me, no doubt weighing my relationship to the order against his desire to tell me the truth.

"Please be candid," I encouraged. "Whatever you say will stay in this room."

"There are many lax practices here. The current head nurse, whom you've met, is the biggest impediment to making improvements. She simply doesn't agree they're necessary. It's willfulness, not laziness. She wants to have the last word on everything."

"Have you complained to her superior?"

"I wouldn't dare. That's not how it works here."

"Is that so?" I said, raising a brow. "Well, we shall see. Do you mind if I observe one of your surgeries to see how the staff performs?"

"Not in the least. Tomorrow at seven?"

"I shall be there."

As promised, I looked in on Frau Ludwig that afternoon. Clearly, she had once been an attractive woman, but now her body was gaunt, wasted by the cancer. She winced during the examination, but she said, "You have such gentle hands, *Frau Doktor.*"

Her symptoms, including pain in her back, indicated the extent of the cancer and where it had spread. We were beyond saving her life, but surgery could make her last days more comfortable. When I returned to Grunewald, I rang Ludwig and suggested we take some x-rays. "I think I can debulk the tumors to make her more comfortable."

"I would hate to cause her more pain with another surgery."

"I know, and neither do I, but the pressure is causing her more pain than necessary. I will open using the prior incision."

He agreed to the x-rays and the possibility of surgery, but I could hear the reluctance in his voice. I was still thinking of him and his wife when I rang my grandaunt at Obberoth.

Her first question was, "What did you think of the hospital you built?"

"I don't know why I never went to see it before. The plans were executed exactly as I intended. Its inner workings are what concern me."

I imagined her face, pensive, but otherwise revealing little of what she was thinking. "Tell me more, Margarethe."

I summarized my impressions, but left out Dr. Ludwig's comments as I'd promised. At the end of my recitation of St. Hilde's faults, I heard a long sigh. "Unfortunately, I cannot visit every one of our communities. I must rely on the local superiors to be frank about their needs and challenges. Mother Agathe should not tolerate such lax practices."

"Perhaps she is unaware of these problems."

"That too is unacceptable. It's her duty to be aware." Again, a long sigh through the earpiece. "I shall look into it, but would these problems prevent you from taking the post?"

"No, but Sauerbruch's offer is also attractive. As you know, the Charité is the best teaching hospital on the continent."

"Then perhaps you stake a position there," she said in a canny voice. We were playing with one another, and she knew it. She'd heard my bitter complaints when I'd worked for Sauerbruch in Munich.

"The truth is, I'm more interested in the position of St. Hilde's. You're correct. I need leadership experience."

"Then I shall lay your application before the board."

"Not so fast, *Tante*. There is one condition. You must agree to replace Sister Brigitte"

"Margarethe, that's blackmail!"

"Perhaps, but it's also smart negotiation. Put her in a second-in-command role under an able leader. Maybe she'll learn something."

There was an extended silence. "That is something only a wise leader would say. Perhaps you do have potential, Margarethe. I shall see to it."

∼

The next day, when I reported to scrub for Ludwig's bowel resection, I was disgusted to see a melting bar of yellow soap at the scrub sink. The bristles of the scrub brushes were flattened from wear. The sink was green from the dripping faucets. I cringed as I donned my gown and gloves and hoped for the best.

The operating team was bumbling and uncoordinated. The instrument trays were lacking and there were no backup trays. The nurse passing instruments seemed to be daydreaming. A few times, Ludwig looked over his mask and engaged my gaze, clearly pleading for sympathy. The fiasco in the operating theater only continued, confirming that my "blackmail," as my grandaunt called it, was entirely justified.

That afternoon, I met with Ludwig and his wife to review the x-rays. The prognosis was dismal, but draining the ascites and removing the operable tumors could provide some relief. I saw the couple struggle as they tried to put on a good face for one another. Dr. Ludwig mostly stayed out of the conversation as I attempted to convince his wife to agree to the surgery. I was completely candid about the purpose, namely to alleviate the pain. She consented to the surgery, which was scheduled for the next day.

By now, everyone knew I was a candidate for chief of surgery. One might think the staff would rise to the occasion, but it was a mistaken hope. Their performance was even sloppier than on the previous day. The nurse was slow to pass me instruments until I elbowed her aside and chose them myself.

"I could help you, *Frau Doktor,*" she said in a defensive voice.

"You can help me by getting out of here."

She stormed out. Watching her, the first assistant lost his grip on the retractor. I shouted obscenities at him. After that, everyone glared at me.

Despite the poor showing of the staff, the surgery was a success. Frau Ludwig's pain lessened and she temporarily improved. It was the best outcome we could expect. Dr. Ludwig was so grateful he decided not to retire completely but to remain on staff as an attending surgeon.

Unfortunately, my relationship with Mother Agathe did not proceed so happily. She was incensed when she discovered I had complained to the mother general, even more so to learn that her hand-picked head nurse would be replaced.

While I was eating my supper, I received a telephone call. Grauer was still new to being a butler and had no idea how to deflect an angry female. Father had often taken calls in the dining room, so the telephone apparatus had a ridiculously long cord. Grauer brought it directly to the table, leaving me no choice but to confront a snarling Mother Agathe.

Dr. Ludwig had told me the lay staff had nicknamed the nuns' superior, "the dragon." As the flames flared out of the earpiece, I perceived why. I set it down on the table and continued eating my dinner. Finally, the diatribe ceased. I picked up the handpiece and asked, "Are you quite finished?"

"Yes, but I want to know what you intend to do."

"What do you expect me to do?"

"Apologize."

"Don't be absurd."

I could hear her sigh in exasperation, which brought a smile to my lips.

"I insist!" she demanded.

"Good night, Mother Agathe," I said, hanging up the handpiece.

⁓

On my first day as the new chief of surgery, I put on my best suit and asked my lady's maid to make some fuss with my short hair. For this meeting, I wanted to appear more conventional or, at least, less odd. The maid unsuccessfully tried to soften the look of my hair with a few strategically placed curls.

Dr. Ludwig had volunteered to introduce me. "I will demonstrate that you have my full support, but it will be up to you to win them over. Try to form alliances with some of the sisters."

"Did that work for you?"

"No," he admitted with a sad look. "But you may do better, considering your relationship to the order."

"I rather doubt it."

Before I addressed the assembled surgical staff, I was seized by an unexpected case of nerves, so I stepped into the hall to have a cigarette. I watched the staff dribble into the meeting room. Mother Agathe stared at me as she passed. Her frown was always forbidding, but she gave a positively scornful look.

The surgeons on my staff, all male, glared in my direction, reminding me that I, a female surgeon, was beneath their contempt. I had almost forgotten what it was like to bear the brunt of misogyny. In England, I'd had the respect of my colleagues because Abrams and Abbott demanded it. Had I joined the Charité staff, Sauerbruch would have insisted that my authority be honored because it was an extension of his own. Even with Ludwig's endorsement, I would have no powerful male allies at St. Hilde's. I was, as he'd implied, on my own.

I stubbed out my cigarette in an ashtray on the windowsill and entered the meeting room. The assembled staff murmured as I made my way to the front. I felt a dozen pairs of eyes sizing up the new chief of surgery.

Dr. Ludwig opened the meeting. He reviewed my experience in Munich and London and reminded everyone that I was the hereditary patroness of the order. Perhaps he should have left that part out. I saw a few faces harden. Despite Ludwig's paean to my credentials, connections, and virtues, no one looked impressed. He turned the meeting over to me.

"Good morning," I said in a cordial voice. "I am Margarethe von Stahle, your new chief of surgery." I felt Mother Agathe's fish eyes on me, but the new head nurse gazed out the window as if she were insufferably bored. A few nurses in the back were having a private conversation. One of the surgeons turned to chat with his neighbor. Apparently, my pleasant tone hadn't drawn anyone's attention.

My mind journeyed back to Sister Elfriede's lessons in how to project my voice. I stood straight and sucked in my diaphragm. "Can we please begin this meeting!"

Suddenly, the eyes of everyone in that room were on me. "I am Dr. von Stahle, your new chief. I have observed that certain things here are not up to accepted standards. I can assure you that I shall enforce all sanitary and medical protocols. I shall be performing surgery as well as administering this department. I shall attend surgeries unannounced to observe how you conduct yourselves. For the time being, I shall review all medication orders. My office door is open if you have questions. Thank you."

As I walked down the hall, I could hear the buzz of confusion inside the meeting room. I heard footsteps behind me and turned around to see Dr. Ludwig hurrying to catch up to me.

"*Frau Doktor*, please…please wait!"

I slowed my pace and he fell in beside me. "Your speech wasn't very friendly."

"I began in a friendly tone. As you observed, it got me nowhere."

"*Frau Doktor*, please be patient with them. They don't realize it yet, but they *need* you."

"Well, I don't need them. I don't need any of this! I built this disgusting excuse for a hospital. I could reduce it to rubble if I wished!"

He stopped me with a hand on my arm and studied my face cautiously. His expression of forced patience told me I was behaving like the spoiled, rich girl they all assumed me to be. I took some deep breaths to calm myself. When I felt capable of speaking, I said, "Kindly overlook the outburst."

"They think it's business as usual here, but with you here, I'm sure it will never be again." I gestured for him to follow me to my office. He closed the door behind him. "*Frau Doktor*, you are a brilliant surgeon, but try to be patient with them."

"Why?"

"Because they're doing the best they can."

"Well, that's not good enough! Why not try to bring them up instead of letting them wallow in their mediocrity?"

"You can try, but there is only so much you can do. Otherwise, you will always be frustrated."

I sat down at the desk, which had formerly been Ludwig's, and took a moment to compose myself. He waited quietly in the visitors' chair.

Finally, I said, "Thank you, *Herr Doktor*. I shall take your words under advisement."

"Let me know if I can help in any way," he said, rising to leave.

No one came to my office that day except an unctuous attending surgeon, whose visit was obviously meant to curry favor. I listened to his insipid little speech and dismissed him without comment.

~

That evening I brooded over my unfortunate introduction to my new role. Sipping one of Krauss's perfect martinis, I sat in the library. I was staring into the fire when the door opened and Krauss announced Konrad. He'd said that he might stop by, but I wasn't really in the mood for company. I grunted and nodded to a chair. While we waited for Krauss to return with another pitcher of martinis, my cousin studied my face.

"Your first day did not go as planned?"

"Not exactly."

"I see. I suppose we are not going out tonight."

"Good God, no."

"What happened?"

"Despite all of Father's and *Tante's* careful training, I find myself completely unprepared for this role. I've never felt so casually disrespected in my life. They wouldn't even give me their attention when I addressed them."

Konrad nodded knowingly. "You must consider who your teachers were. Uncle Fritz was an officer in the Imperial Army. He gave a command and everyone obeyed. Your grandaunt's nuns are vowed to obedience. What you face at your hospital is the ordinary world where people obey whom they respect."

"They should respect me. I am their chief."

He smiled tolerantly. "It doesn't work that way."

"Really? How does it work."

"If you take the authoritarian approach, everyone may fear you. They may do your bidding out of fear of punishment. As soon as your back is turned, they will do as they wish. You can't compel their loyalty, and ultimately they will hate you."

"How is it that you've become such an expert on leadership?"

"I've been working for Brüning, and I see how he operates."

"That's politics," I said with a dismissive wave. "It's not the same."

"Everything is politics," said Konrad. "Wherever humans come together, there is politics—jockeying for position, negotiation, barter, currying favor. It's how the world really works."

Krauss returned with our martinis. As I sipped the icy perfection, I reflected on what Konrad had said. "How do you suggest I approach this situation?"

"First, you must cultivate alliances with your peers. Call on the chiefs of the other departments. Invite them to lunch. Get to know them."

I frowned. "And what will that accomplish?"

"If you have allies among your peers, you'll also have a sounding board to discuss strategy and people to call upon to solve common problems." I stared at my cousin, whom I often dismissed as trivial, but what he was saying made sense. "And you need to pay obeisance to the ultimate leader, whoever that is."

"That would be the chief of staff. We have a cordial relationship, I think."

"Good, but don't get too close. Don't be tempted to confide in him, only in your peers."

"Why?"

"A close relationship with the leader can cause jealousy. That's the last thing you want."

"Indeed, people are already predisposed to dislike me because of my family connections. I don't need more envy."

"Exactly!" confirmed Konrad in a triumphant voice. "Margarethe, you are a quick study. I think you may have potential."

I rolled my eyes.

"There are always hidden leaders," he continued. "You must discover who they are and cultivate a relationship with them."

I thought about it. "Probably Mother Agathe. She is a loathsome creature, cunning but not intelligent."

"It doesn't matter. You must act respectfully, no matter what your opinion of her may be. Develop an opaque persona with her. Never let your true feelings about her be known. Never share them with others. Smile and be pleasant in her presence."

"That will be exceedingly difficult."

"I know. When you dislike someone you make it abundantly evident, but you must try to hide your distaste. And the last thing you should ever do is to threaten her or flaunt your rank. She must think she holds authority in her sphere and you respect it. Overwhelm her with courtesy."

Sipping my martini, I reflected that I had probably learned more about the tactics of leadership in the last fifteen minutes than in all my years of schooling and training.

"Thank you," I said to Konrad. "Occasionally, you can be useful."

He laughed. "Some people think so. Why do you think the head of the Catholic Party relies on me?" Konrad raised his glass to me. "We shall continue our lessons another day. Now, finish your drink, and let's find some mischief!"

27

Konrad was a frequent visitor to the Grunewald villa. I was grateful, for I had no friends in Berlin, and I was holding my new colleagues at arms' length for obvious reasons. My cousin appeared at my door whether he had an invitation or not. Often, he would arrive late at night after one of the innumerable party meetings he attended.

My household staff knew that Konrad was a member of the family and indulged him. The new cook, whom Krauss had hired away from one of my Grunewald neighbors, began cooking an extra portion for dinner in case Konrad arrived unannounced. Fortunately, food was plentiful again—if one could afford it. Unemployment and the runaway inflation had put a healthy diet out of reach for many.

Konrad barged in one night while I was heading to bed. The task of bringing my staff to heel was exhausting. I had the next day free, and I was desperately looking forward to a long sleep.

"You look like you could use some cheering up," said Konrad brightly, parking himself in my sitting room. "Let's go out on the town!"

"I'm tired. Go home."

"Nonsense," he said, pulling at my arms. "You are indefatigable!" He frowned, looking down at his suit. "Unfortunately, I've just come from a meeting and don't have the proper attire for stepping out."

"Does that really matter? Aren't people more informal now?"

"Yes, they are, but I have an idea." I knew to worry when he began grinning like a fool. "You could lend me a dress, and we could both go out as ladies."

He looked disappointed when I didn't seem shocked. Ironically, I had recently wondered if I would ever again wear my male attire. Now that I had embarked on an honorable career as chief of surgery at St. Hilde's, I had expected to put my Freddie persona behind me forever. "We could impersonate one another," I wickedly suggested.

"I doubt my clothes will fit you," he said, insultingly smacking his hip.

"I don't need your clothes. I have my own."

"Show me!" urged Konrad with delight.

We went upstairs, and I unlocked my secret armoire. I took out the beautiful evening suit complete with white cravat and starched waistcoat and hung them on the door. The tailor had been clever enough to build out the shoulders of the coat because, although mine were broad, they weren't masculine enough. He'd managed to disguise my wider female hips with clever darts that allowed the trousers to drape properly. The fineness of the garments alone made me long to wear them. I opened the drawers and showed Konrad the boxer shorts, sans fly, garters, ties, special brassieres to bind my breasts, and of course, the assortment of cuff links.

"It appears you are well-prepared, indeed," he said, "but we must find a dress of yours to fit me."

We went through my evening gowns, but I despaired of finding one that would hide his chest hair. Thankfully, he didn't have very much, just a little, blond tuft.

"We'll need to shave it," I said. "Fortunately, I have a safety razor."

"What does a woman need a razor for?"

I raised my arm and pointed.

"Ah, I see."

I went into my bathroom to look for the razor along with some alcohol to sterilize it. After outfitting it with a new blade, I made a pot of soap foam.

"I feel much better with this method than a straight razor," said Konrad, cringing while I scraped the skin on his chest. "Where did you learn how to shave?"

"Be still, please."

"Apologies."

"To answer your question, I learned to shave from watching my father when I was a girl. He showed me how to sharpen the blade and strop it on the leather impregnated with emery." I rinsed off the razor in a basin of warm water. "But I much prefer this system." I handed him the razor and the mug of shaving soap to touch up his chin and cheeks. "Go sit at the vanity."

"Many men won't give up their straight razors," he said, carefully shaving his neck.

"Many men are idiots," I replied, handing him a towel to wipe up the foam remnants. "We won't bother with your legs. The long dress will cover them."

"Next time," said Konrad with a quick grin.

"Next time, bring your own razor, or better yet, prepare ahead. Have you any idea how much time we've wasted with this shaving business?"

"Ah, the night is young!" he declared with great theatricality.

I helped Konrad find a gown that flattered him and stuffed one of my brassieres with cotton wool to fill it out. I laid out my male costume while Konrad scrounged in my closet for a pair of shoes. He had long, slender feet only slightly bigger than mine, so he was able to fit them into a pair with open toes. Meanwhile, I put on my trousers and dress shirt. Konrad sat at my vanity stool, watching with a smile, as I expertly tied the cravat. Among my male clothes, I found the can of pomade I used to slick back my hair. Once I'd removed all traces of makeup, my transition to my male persona was complete.

"You look more like me than I do," Konrad opined.

"You don't look more like me than I do, but you'll pass, I suppose."

He cocked a shoulder at me in perfect imitation of a woman scorned.

I rang Grauer to bring around the car, and we headed to a club called the Dorian Gray. When we arrived, I gave Grauer money to entertain himself and told him to return at midnight. I had taken along a roll of Reichsmarks because, as Freddie, I would be paying for everything. Inside the door, I handed a heavy-set, darkly menacing man a twenty-Mark note. He grunted and looked like he expected more, so I handed over another twenty.

Once inside, I wondered why we had bothered shaving Konrad's chest. At the bar sat a pair of obvious transvestites with thatches of dark hair sprouting between their falsely plumped breasts. Their makeup barely covered their beard shadow. At least, Konrad, when he shaved, had a smooth chin and cheeks and, being blond, his incipient beard barely showed.

Our arrival created a stir among the patrons. Out of the corner of my eye, I watched people whisper to one another and point in our direction. I was used to it. Whenever we appeared together in public, we attracted attention for our likeness to one another.

We found a table and ordered martinis. Some of the "gentlemen" invited my cousin to dance. In some cases, it was difficult to discern the actual sex of the wearers of those perfectly tailored suits and dinner jackets. The ambient noise made ordinary conversation impossible. Pressing close on the dance floor and speaking directly into the ear of one's partner was the best way to be heard.

A waif-like creature, with a flapper's blond bob and hooded eyes, began to watch us carefully. My physician's eyes noticed that she was beyond fashionably thin. Her collar bones showed prominently above her dress, but there was something compelling about her. She was clearly more interested in Konrad. He was convincing in his feminine role, so I assumed she was a lesbian.

With a discreet wave, I beckoned to her to join us at the table and asked if she wanted a cocktail. She asked for champagne. While we waited for it to arrive, I noted her emaciated appearance and wondered if she might be hungry. "Would you like something to eat?"

"How kind. Yes, thank you." When the waiter returned, I requested a menu. After she'd demolished a plate of wurst, potatoes, and pickled vegetables I asked if she'd like more.

"Perhaps a sweet," she replied hopefully. The waiter recommended a multilayered chocolate torte. After clearing that away, she danced with each of us in turn.

"What is your name?" I asked as I held her close.

"Johanna," she said.

My blood froze in my veins.

"But my friends call me Hanna," she added quickly.

I bent so that I could speak directly in her ear. "I once had a dear friend named Johanna."

"It's a common name," she said casually. "Are you still friends with your Johanna?"

"She's dead," I replied bluntly.

She drew back to look at my face. "I'm so sorry." The music stopped, but she clung to me. "You're very sweet," she said, reaching for my cheek. "You're the real woman, aren't you?"

"My disguise isn't adequate?"

"Oh, you are completely convincing, but I always know the scent of a woman…and the feel of her skin. What's your name?"

"Freddie."

"No, it's not," she said with a canny look."

"Yes."

She still looked skeptical.

"One of my names is Frederika, after my father." It was no lie, but she eyed me suspiciously before saying, "It suits you. Freddie, it is."

She gripped my shoulders. "Will you take me with you?"

"For a price?"

"No charge for you. You and your friend are gentle and beautiful. This time, it's for pleasure."

Of course, Konrad agreed to take her along. He was quite taken with her as well. I pulled the gold watch I had once given to Lytton out of my waistcoat. It was near midnight, which meant Grauer would return soon.

We retrieved our wraps from the coat check. Johanna's thin winter coat was threadbare, and the February evening was chilly, so I wrapped my black opera cloak around her while we waited for Grauer to bring the motorcar. She pressed close to me and whispered, "Freddie, you are so gallant!"

Grauer averted his eyes as the three of us piled into the passenger compartment of the Horch. Like any good servant, he had learned to turn a blind eye to his employer's questionable behavior. I tapped on the window between the passenger and driver compartment and instructed him to take us to the Continental. On the ride down the Ku'damm, we were like a heap of puppies, snuggling in the rear seat to share our warmth.

My companions stumbled into the hotel entrance, while I gave Grauer instructions to return around noon with our street clothes. The clerk gave us a curious look when I arranged a suite with two bedrooms for the night, but he asked no questions. Konrad and Hanna went up to the room, while I hurried into the U-Bahn station on the corner to buy condoms from the vending machine.

Our joinings were multiple and confusing. Lytton and I had occasionally shared a man but never a woman. I watched Johanna skillfully fellate Konrad. My cousin performed his duty with both of us, but Johanna was less enthusiastic to his attentions, confirming my suspicion that she preferred women.

After rutting enthusiastically, Konrad fell asleep. He was snoring softly while I brought Johanna to orgasm with my fingers. Recovering in my arms, she whispered into my ear, "You are a wonderful lover. You touch a woman's body as if you know it inside and out!" Of course, she had no idea how apt her words were.

She wanted to return the favor, but I brushed the fine hair away from her face. "Never mind," I said, kissing her forehead. "Another time."

We left Konrad snoring while we headed to the other bedroom to sleep.

~

The next morning, I awoke to inquisitive, gray eyes peering into mine. "Good morning," I said. "Did you sleep well?"

"I did."

"Would you like to bathe?"

"May I?"

"Of course." I called the hotel maid to draw a bath for my guest. Meanwhile, I showered in the other bathroom and put on one of the terry bathrobes the hotel provided. While I awaited Johanna's return, I ordered a proper English breakfast with fried eggs, rashers, and buttered toast.

Johanna returned in one of the terry hotel robes. Her eyes glanced curiously around the luxurious sitting room.

"Feeling better?" I asked.

She nodded.

"I've ordered some breakfast for you."

"Thank you for your trouble," she murmured, suddenly shy. Without makeup she looked so young.

"How old are you?" I asked.

"Nineteen," she said to my relief. She could have been lying, of course, but I doubted it.

"Do you often go to the clubs to find bed companions?"

She nodded, looking guilty.

"Can't you find other work?"

"I'm a typist. If I can wake up early enough to get to the head of the line, I get picked for the typing pool. When I'm out late, getting up is hard. I was studying to be a nurse at the Charité, but I had to quit because my grandmother became ill and needed me to care for her."

"Do you support yourself by taking clients from the clubs?"

She shook her head. "No, that's how I eat. My wages from typing are enough to pay the rent and buy food for my grandmother, but not enough to feed both of us. Kind people like you buy me dinner in exchange for my company, or they pay me for pleasure, sometimes enough to buy food for a week."

I knew that Berlin was full of women like Johanna, struggling to find work to support themselves. Many had hungry children at home. I sighed deeply at the thought.

Our breakfast arrived on a cart with an orchid in a vase. When the waiter uncovered our plates, Johanna stared with wide eyes.

"Go on, eat, or it will get cold. Nothing worse than cold fried eggs."

We ate in silence until Johanna asked, "Are you and your friend twins?"

I laughed softly. "Everyone thinks so, but we are cousins."

"He makes a fine woman," she opined.

"You must tell him when he wakes," I said with a grin. "He'll be pleased to hear it."

"Do you visit the clubs often?"

"Not as often as my cousin would like. This is the first time we've switched."

"You are both very convincing. You put the others to shame." She eyed my stack of buttered toast hungrily. I pushed the plate in her direction. "You must look for me when you come again," she said.

I put down my fork and studied her. "How far along were you in your nurses' training?"

"Only six months remaining."

"A shame you couldn't finish." I resumed eating. "Would you like to go back to the Charité to finish your training?"

Her face instantly brightened. "Would I? I would give anything for it." The light in her face dimmed. "Why even think about it? It's impossible. I need to support my grandmother. Her illness left her weak. And who would hire an old woman like her? So many are looking for work."

"If you are willing to give me your address and your true name, I could arrange for you to return to nursing. I have some influence at the Charité."

"My name is Johanna."

She still looked hungry, so I offered her the dish of fruit on my tray. "I could pay the rent and an allowance for food and necessities while you finish your studies. But you must swear to me that you will stop visiting the clubs for your dinner. Not only is it dangerous, you could contract a venereal disease. You, as a nurse in training, should know better."

She stared at me for a long moment. "Why would you do this for me? You just met me."

"I do it because I can. I can't do it for every young woman in your situation, which is frustrating and makes me sad. You must trust me. You don't know me. We are both taking a risk."

Her face changed and her eyes softened. The next moment, they smoldered with desire. "I could become your mistress. I like you. You're beautiful and such a sensitive lover. I can tell you've had many women."

I smiled at the compliment, but I said, "I want nothing other than the knowledge that you'll continue your studies. If I discover that you've returned to the clubs seeking bed partners, our arrangement will end. Is that clear?"

She nodded. I found a pen and a block of paper on the little desk and handed them to her. I watched her write her name and address. "Is there a telephone there?"

"A common telephone in the hall."

"Write down the number," I instructed. She did, and I reached for the pad.

"Here is my private telephone number. It rings only in my quarters."

"Will you tell me your real name?"

"Frederika is my real name, one of many. For now, that's all you need to know. If there's any trouble with the rent, call me. I shall telephone when the matter with the Charité is arranged." I gave her a firm look. "You must never tell anyone that I am your benefactor, and you must keep your promise to stay away from the cabarets. That is our agreement. Swear to it."

"I swear," she said solemnly, "but I still can't believe it."

Konrad came into the room wearing only his shorts. He scratched his chest, where I had shaved it. "Good morning, ladies," he said as he headed toward the toilet. Johanna's eyes followed him.

"Do you fancy him?" I asked.

She shook her head. "No, I like women better." She trailed her fingers along the back of my hand. "I fancy you."

I smiled and sighed. "You'll find another lady, I'm sure."

A moment later, the front desk called to say Grauer was waiting downstairs.

"I think you need to leave," I said gently. "Please dress and then I'll see you out."

She wolfed down the last of the fruit and hunted for her clothes in the bedroom. I searched in my trousers for the bankroll and handed it to her. "Consider this a down payment on our agreement," I said as I slipped the notes into her hand. She reached up and drew me down into a sweet kiss.

"I will come to you whenever you wish," she said. "Only say the word."

I opened the door and watched as she headed down the hall. Then, she turned the corner and was gone. I called the front desk and told the clerk to send up Grauer.

❧

Konrad made liberal use of the room I had reserved at the Continental, but I seldom joined him or used it myself. I wondered how he could be so cavalier about tempting fate. He was now a high-level adviser to the head of the Catholic Centrist Party. It frowned on homosexuality and passionately supported Paragraph 175, which criminalized homosexual acts. When I mentioned it, Konrad shrugged and said, "All the parties hate us. What difference does it make?"

He became increasingly consumed in politics. His party meetings went on late into the night. Eventually, I recognized that I couldn't always rely on him and needed to seek companionship elsewhere.

Through music, I was able to build a social network in Berlin. The musicians, in turn, introduced me to other artists and writers. I hired a new voice teacher, Maria Ivogün, a principal at the State Opera, who had lately taken on some private pupils. Through her, I was introduced to Dieter Gürtner, the music director of the Municipal Opera and a shameless impresario in the mold of Graybar. He was an extravagant homosexual and a witty conversationalist. He and his friends made excellent dinner companions.

One of my few friends from Obberoth, Mitzi von Treppen, arrived in Berlin with her banker husband. Unlike me, she found the role of socialite agreeable, and she had surrounded herself with a coterie of society ladies more bearable than most.

Following Konrad's advice, I began to cultivate my colleagues, particularly the genial head of gynecology, Hans Becher. I also entertained Sauerbruch and his wife and some of the surgeons at the Charité, but none of these new friendships could ever replace what I'd had with Charles.

My social life gradually improved, but my relationship with the nuns on my staff continued to deteriorate. The sisters made it obvious that they loathed me. They were always courteous in my presence, but there was a palpable undercurrent of contempt.

The new head nurse proved to be even more infuriating than her predecessor. I left orders for my surgical trays to be arranged in the way they had been at Barts, allowing me to snatch an instrument without having to wait for it. I patiently explained the rationale for this organization. I even drew diagrams and hung them in the scrub room. Despite being given this instruction several times, Sister Alois disregarded it. Finally, I called her to my office to ask why.

"You must understand, *Frau Doktor*, that we cannot have one arrangement for you and one for the other surgeons."

"Then arrange all the trays as I ask. It's the acceptable organization everywhere else."

"Not here. It's always been done this way."

"I am the chief of surgery, and you, Sister, will arrange the trays as I request."

Sister Alois folded her arms on her chest and stared at me "I'll consider it." She turned and left without waiting for me to dismiss her.

That evening, when I spoke to my father, I described the scene to him. He listened carefully to my entire diatribe before speaking.

"Grethe, you cannot tolerate this kind of insubordination, especially from someone in a senior position. Get rid of her."

"Father, I already demanded the resignation of the previous head nurse as a condition of taking the post."

"It doesn't matter. Sack her before she establishes herself. You cannot tolerate such challenges to your authority. It must be absolute, and the easiest way to break insubordination is to get rid of the ringleader."

I knew that he was giving me the benefit of his long experience of military command, but my intuition told me to remain skeptical. I put up with Sister Alois' antics for another week. When she argued with me during a staff meeting, I finally lost patience and ordered her to my office.

"Thank you, Sister, for your opinion, for your *many* opinions! I've had quite enough of this. Your services are no longer required."

Her mouth gaped open for the space of a moment. "You cannot remove me from my post. Only Mother Agathe has the authority."

"I can do it, and I am doing it. Your role as head nurse is terminated. This minute! Now, go!" I pointed to the door.

When I returned to my office after observing a procedure in the operating theater, I found Mother Agathe waiting.

"You cannot dismiss a head nurse. Only I can."

"Watch me," I said in a defiant voice. I slashed the air with my hand. "There. She's gone."

"Reverend Mother will hear about this!"

"Good," I said. "Now, I'll thank you to leave my office." I held open the door for her. She wouldn't look at me as she passed.

Not an hour passed before the telephone on my desk jangled. I knew, even before I picked up the handpiece, that it would be my grandaunt calling.

"Margarethe!" she said in a voice that I had not heard since I had detonated the explosives at Obberoth. "Margarethe!" she repeated as if she couldn't find words to express her fury. "*What* were you thinking!"

"The woman was insubordinate. The only way to put down insubordination is to remove the perpetrator."

"Who told you that?" she asked in an acid tone.

"My father."

"Your father is an army general," said my grandaunt, stating the obvious. "What does he know about running a medical facility?"

"He's commanded units with field hospitals, so I imagine he knows more than you, a school teacher."

There was a brittle silence. I imagined my grandaunt's pale eyes burning with unspoken anger.

"I will support you this once. I, myself, shall appoint the next head nurse."

"Why not let me choose her?"

"Because that's not how it's done," explained my grandaunt tartly. "Margarethe, you must make this work. If you dismiss this appointment, I must rethink recommending you for your position."

"Are you threatening me, *Tante*?"

"Yes."

"Good, because I'm not backing down."

I slammed down the handpiece of the telephone. Smoldering with anger, I lit a cigarette in the hopes of calming myself.

～

A few days later, Charles called to consult me on one of his cases. Alexandra kept interrupting him and insisting that she needed to speak to me, so he put her on the line.

"Darling, I miss you so much!" she said. "Thank you for the motorcar, but I don't know how to drive it."

"Charles can teach you."

"He has no patience."

"Nonsense. He is the soul of patience."

"You're not his sister."

I realized how glad I was that Charles would be teaching her, not I.

"I want to come to Berlin," Alexandra announced.

"Impossible. I've just begun a new position. My household is barely set up…"

"But I need to talk to you about the wedding."

"Why?"

"Because you will be the matron of honor, and we must make plans."

I was momentarily speechless. Finally, I recovered my wits to ask, "When did you get that idea?"

"Oh, I've had it all along. Who else would I ask? I have no sisters. I'm not close to my cousins."

"No."

"Meg!"

"NO."

"Everyone knows we are the dearest of friends. If you refuse, how will it look?"

"I don't care."

"Then do it because you love me. You do love me, don't you?"

"Yes," I grudgingly admitted.

"So, you will be my matron of honor?"

Although she couldn't see me, I rolled my eyes.

"Good. I'm glad that's settled," she said, "Here, I'll put Charles back on the line. He's grabbing for the phone like a madman."

In fact, I couldn't wait for Charles to return to the call.

❧

The conversation about the motorcar made me think of the two Grauer had induced me to buy—a grand Horch for elegant occasions and a spirited

Alfa Romeo 1750 Gran Sport Spider for pleasure driving. I could hardly wait to take my little roadster on an extended trip. I asked Ludwig if he would look after things while I took a brief holiday.

"It might be wise to let things cool down a bit," he said, "especially after that altercation with the dragon."

"I was thinking the same."

"However, I admire you for insisting on order, especially in surgery."

"I never knew I had such a temper."

He laughed. "The nuns could try the patience of a saint. But not to worry. I shall keep them in line until you return."

The next day, I headed south. The stated intention of my trip was to look in on my tenants at Raithschau, but I also wanted to visit my grandaunt and hopefully make amends. Our notes of apology had crossed in the post shortly after our testy exchange.

I arrived in time for the evening meal. Because of my role as patroness of the order, I sat beside Tante at the high table. There was no speaking during the meal of thick vegetable soup, newly made bread, and the delectable convent cheese.

Sister Elfriede approached me to sing a Bach anthem for Vespers. She gave me a little hug in defiance of their Holy Rule. "You've been such a stranger, Margarethe. I've missed you."

"Now that I'm back, I hope to visit more often. I've learned a few things since I last sang for you. I'll show you tomorrow."

"I can hardly wait to hear."

After Vespers, the nuns filed out of the chapel. I watched from the student loft with nostalgia for my youth. The Great Silence had begun, so I expected I wouldn't speak to my grandaunt that evening. However, she surprised me by awaiting me at the entrance to the cloister.

"I've given myself a dispensation from the silence," she explained, taking my arm.

"How convenient that you are in a position to do such things," I replied with light sarcasm.

She urged me forward with a tug at my arm. "Come, let's sit together in my study. You can build up the fire."

"Oh, isn't the central boiler working?"

"Yes, it works fine…and the central plumbing."

"You enjoy a hot bath, do you?"

"You cannot imagine."

She led me to her study and closed the door. Opening her credenza, she took out the same bottle of whiskey I had brought years ago.

"I see it's still almost full."

"Only you drink it. I once offered it to the bishop, and he pronounced it the foulest stuff he ever tasted." She made a face to demonstrate. "Thank God, I had some cognac to give him instead."

I laughed. "It's an acquired taste. Next time, I'll bring some Irish whiskey."

"Thank you, but I'll pass." She poured a glass of whiskey for me and a glass of cognac for herself. We saluted one another. "How are things faring at St. Hilde's? Better, I hope."

"I'm sure Mother Agathe sends you regular reports."

"She does, but she wouldn't dare to complain to me about you."

"Really?" I said, cocking a brow. "That would surprise me."

"But I hear from others that you terrify everyone—your colleagues, the sisters…."

"Good," I said with a satisfied smile.

"Margarethe, when I recommended you for this post, I knew you were an untested leader. We have all tried to teach you leadership. Unfortunately, teaching can only go so far. Some things one must learn on one's own. One of them is patience, and the other is humility."

"So, it must be trial by fire."

"I fear that is the only way you'll learn. You never make things easy for yourself. You always have to do it *your* way, which is usually the hardest way possible. But before we have another quarrel, let's speak of something else. How are the children?"

～

Sauerbruch finally forgave me for spurning his offer, but he extracted a price—when it could be arranged, I must assist him in his experimental or particularly complicated surgeries. The truth is, the disorder in my own hospital made it almost a relief to operate at the Charité, where the surgical trays were always in order, and the hygiene and staff performance were impeccable.

My former mentor liked to brag about running a tight ship. He also liked to brag about having a chief of surgery as his first assistant. Fortunately, he was sparing in exercising that prerogative. On those occasions, the gallery of the theater would be full of students and junior doctors, eagerly hanging over their desks to see every subtle motion of Sauerbruch's scalpel and catch his every word.

Sauerbruch's operations had become legendary for their epic length. A liver resection scheduled for six hours could go on for twelve. My feet often grew numb from standing. I learned to wear comfortable shoes. Occasionally, a nurse or technician fainted. The director of nursing, who was protective of her staff, finally insisted on replacements after six hours, but we surgeons enjoyed no such luxury.

During one of these endless surgeries, the fresh nursing team arrived causing the usual, annoying disruption. When I looked up, I saw familiar gray eyes over the mask. I always remember the eyes more than any other feature. The new arrival's eyes met mine and smiled.

After the operation, someone came into the female doctors' room while I was dressing. "*Frau Doktor*, pardon the interruption." I looked up, because now I had a voice to go with the gray eyes. I finished fastening the tabs of my garters and stood straight.

"Johanna…?"

"Yes, as you can see," she said, twirling around to show off her student-nurse uniform. "I'm training to be an instrument assistant."

"And you did very well."

"Thank you, *Frau Doktor*. You see? I've kept my promise. Thank you for keeping yours."

"So, you know who I am."

"I've known all along who you are. When I saw you in the hospital, I asked who you are. They told me you are Countess Stahle, the famous lady surgeon."

I studied her to discern her intentions. The possibility of blackmail still existed. "So, what will you do now that you know?"

"Nothing. You can count on me to keep your secret…our secret."

I discreetly breathed a sigh of relief. "How is your grandmother?"

Johanna looked pained. "Not well. I don't expect her to last long. Tuberculosis."

"I'm sorry to hear it. I hope she doesn't suffer. Is there anything I can do?"

She shook her head. "I don't think so, but thank you. You are very kind, *Gnädige*."

"None of that, please. Here, I am only Dr. von Stahle."

"Then, thank you, *Frau Doktor*." She stood on tiptoes and gave me a soft kiss on the cheek. "I can still come to you, if you like," she whispered into my ear. "Say the word, and I shall be there. I really like you."

I looked into her soft, young face. It had filled out a bit from the benefit of a steady diet, making her even more fetching. I patted her arm. "Do me the honor of becoming a fine nurse…and find a lover your own age."

She looked disappointed, but she nodded.

28

B y late March, the temperature finally warmed. The trees began to bud, and crocuses bloomed along the walkways as I crossed the courtyard from the Humboldt returning from my lecture. The medical school, as Sauerbruch had predicted, was glad to have me on their faculty, especially now that he had given me the nominal role of visiting surgeon at the Charité.

The new head nurse, appointed by my grandaunt, was pleasant and cooperative, traits in her favor. Sister Ingrid was also rather attractive, which, of course, had nothing to do with her qualifications, but it improved the scenery. Her predecessors' looks could have broken a mirror, that is, if mirrors were allowed in the convent. Looking at one's image was thought to encourage vanity and therefore forbidden. Under Sister Ingrid's supervision, things in the surgical department improved somewhat.

I was becoming settled in Berlin as I never had elsewhere. I was glad that Father had given me the Grunewald house rather than selling it. More than anywhere else, it felt like home. I was so immersed in my new life that the memory of my life in England began to dim. If not for inquiring about my children at school, I hardly thought about it, save for the one thing that kept it firmly fixed in my mind.

Alexandra's wedding was fast approaching. She regularly telephoned to remind me of my obligations as her matron of honor. Mostly, I was able to avoid them, pleading my professional responsibilities. Finally, I could avoid them no longer.

I arranged with Ludwig to keep an eye on things at St. Hilde's and took a week's leave from the university. I flew from Berlin to London because I didn't want to waste the time on trains and boats. It was expensive, of course, perhaps even frivolous, but that didn't really matter. I was becoming a fervent devotee of the new mode of transportation.

Nigel, the youngest of the Calder siblings, met me at Croydon Field. "Darling! I'm so happy to see you again!" he said, kissing me on both cheeks, then fully on the mouth. "Alex is beside herself. She can hardly wait to see you. Come, let's get rid of your luggage and then head home at once!" As Nigel sped through the streets of London, I observed the familiar sights with an mixture of delight and nostalgia.

Alexandra had wanted me to stay with the family, but there was a troop of Calder relatives coming to London for the wedding, and no room for me. That suited me fine, for it gave me an excuse to avoid Alexandra. Rather than impose on Emma, I'd decided to stay at the Savoy. I registered for my room while Nigel dealt with the porters regarding the baggage.

"You're invited for dinner, of course," said Nigel, standing beside me while I waited for the clerk to locate my key.

"Oh, dear. Perhaps I should go up to my room and change for dinner."

"Nonsense. We have a houseful of people, and it's family, so it's all very informal. And if I don't bring you home straightaway, Alex will beat me."

"From what I hear, you might like that."

"Meg, you really should keep an open mind."

"Thank you, but even I have my limits."

"You never know what Alex will come up with. She is quite creative, you know."

"Now that she will be married, she can turn her creativity on her husband."

Nigel raised a brow and gave me a strange look, but I did not elaborate. It was no one's business that I considered the affair to be over. It had been going on for years, so everyone probably assumed it would simply continue.

When we arrived at the Calders', Alexandra threw herself into my arms and passionately kissed me on the mouth. Charles rolled his eyes. Nigel chuckled. "Yet another heart grown fonder," he said with a theatrical sigh. Fortunately, the senior Calders were entertaining guests in the parlor and had missed the dramatic reunion.

After supper, Alexandra informed me that her cousins would be using her bedroom, and she had no choice but to stay with me at the Savoy.

"No!"

"Would you have me sleep on the floor?"

"There's a comfortable divan in your father's study."

"Already taken."

I gave her a stern look. She responded by fluttering her eyelashes and gazing heavenward, a gesture recently made popular by cinema.

"Very well," I reluctantly agreed. "I'll ring the Savoy and arrange for another room."

She pouted, then pleaded with her luminous blue eyes until I relented. "All right, Alex. You can stay in my room."

Joyous, she threw her arms around my neck and stood on tiptoes to kiss me. "Good, then you can accompany me tomorrow to the dressmaker for the final fitting. As my matron of honor, it is your duty!"

I despise when anyone is impertinent enough to remind me of my duty, but as always, I turned a blind eye to Alexandra's offenses. Why was I not surprised that she already had her bags packed when I said it was time to leave?

As we sat in the rear of the taxi on the way to the hotel, Alexandra stroked my thigh suggestively. "You really don't mind that I stay with you, do you?"

"Yes, I mind. You are incorrigible."

"That's why you love me."

"I do love you, but that's not why."

There were two beds in my suite, but Alexandra instantly worked out which was mine and hopped on to it.

"I was about to order some whiskey," I said. "Would you like something to drink?"

"A martini would be nice."

I rang down to the front desk for a pitcher of martinis and two glasses. When I returned to the bedchamber, Alexandra had already undressed to her petticoat and was striking a most alluring pose. I turned away and lit a cigarette.

"You know you want me. Why the pretense?"

"Alex, you're to be married in a few days. Doesn't that mean anything to you?"

"You are a complete hypocrite! You told me that you had affairs during your marriage to Lytton."

"That was different. Lytton and I had an agreement before we were even engaged. Does Jonathan know that you're sleeping with a woman?"

"No, and I don't intend to tell him. He's too conventional."

"On that point, I have to agree."

She smiled slyly. "Now, let's stop talking and get on with it!" Whereupon, she opened her arms, and began to recite the sonnet from the *Vita Nuova* with which she had first seduced me. I lay beside her and eased off her petticoat and her undergarments. Her familiar scent filled my nostrils. I kissed her perfect breasts, and still she recited. I used my lips and tongue on her sex as her words filled my ears, but she waited until the poem was done before giving me her climax. She chose another sonnet to recite while she made love to me.

Gradually, I became aware of someone knocking, and realized the waiter had arrived with our martinis. I flung on a dressing gown and went to answer the door.

~

Over the next days, Alexandra kept me prisoner. I accompanied her to the dressmaker for the final fitting of her wedding gown, a sleek and very modern design that made the most of Alexandra's slender figure. We were required to attend family gatherings ahead of the ceremony, but Alexandra never let me out of her sight. She placed me at her right at the dinner before the wedding day. Unfortunately, Jonathan sat on the other side, insufferably boring as always.

In bed that night, I held Alexandra in the crook of my shoulder. "Tomorrow you'll be married. This must be our last time together."

"Oh, Meg, what nonsense you speak!"

"If you don't tell Jonathan what's going on, I refuse to continue our affair."

"Do you?" she asked and kissed me so deeply my head began to swim. That was the end of my protests.

What I couldn't tell her was that I had been looking for an excuse to end the affair. The marriage seemed the most obvious reason. I loved Alexandra. I loved her deeply and passionately, but my obsession with her was like a drug I couldn't resist. In my heart, I knew that sooner or later I must break the habit.

After we made love, Alexandra drew back to look at my face. "Take me back with you to Berlin."

I sighed. "But you've always told me how much you hate Germany. Our language is so guttural you can hardly bear to hear it. Our poetry is too romantic…our art is ugly."

She sighed dramatically. "I would turn a blind eye to all that if I could only be with you. I could organize wonderful parties for you and your friends. It would be like before."

"No, it can't. It can never be like before."

"Please, Meg," she pleaded. "Please take me with you."

"I can't, Alex. Your life is here now."

I held her while she wept in my arms.

~

I'd asked for a wake-up call from the front desk so that I could bathe and dress ahead of the arrival of the bridesmaids. As part of the festivities, I had planned a breakfast in the bride's honor to be followed by dressing the bride. Was it churlish of me to stand aside while another woman helped Alexandra into her gown? If nothing else, my sulking brought home one fact. No matter how I professed my indifference to the marriage and saw it as the path to my salvation, in my heart, I resented it.

I'd compensated by being overly generous. My gift to Alexandra, in addition to a tidy sum and my motorcar, was the lavish hotel reception following the wedding. Nigel confided that his parents were enormously grateful and could never have afforded such a grand celebration on their own.

The dean of Westminster officiated at the service. During the exchange of vows, I stiffened my face and wondered how many other women had stood, as I did at that moment, watching the woman she loved be given to a man. The pretense was an unspeakable burden, but one that we must apparently bear for the sake of the social order. After the bridal kiss, Alexandra's eyes caught mine and she nodded. I assumed that to mean she had finally accepted the end of our affair.

The reception was indeed grand. People drank excessively as is customary and danced through the night. Nigel introduced me to his friends, who helped me avoid boredom by entertaining me with their witty conversation. After midnight, Nigel whispered into my ear, "Come with us, Meg. We're heading out to find better music."

"I hired the band. You don't like it?" I asked, feigning insult.

"Oh, I like it fine. But we could find more interesting company. People more like ourselves." He wiggled his plucked brows for emphasis.

I was tempted to accompany them, but I decided that, as the matron of honor, it would be unseemly to abandon the bride. I reluctantly watched Nigel and his friends slip away one by one while Alexandra's uncle droned into my ear about the Boer War.

Despite my resolve toward propriety, I didn't wait for the festivities to end before retiring to my room. I had a full schedule planned for the following day. First, I would head up to Oxford to have lunch with Lotte and Marta, and then visit my children.

I waited for a respectable interval to elapse after Nigel and his comrades departed for their adventures. Then, I made excuses and went up to my room. As soon as my head touched the pillow, I was instantly unconscious.

The sharp ring of the telephone beside my bed tore me from sleep. Groggily, I switched on the light and saw the time on the bedside clock—quarter past two. Naturally, I had no wish to speak to anyone at the hour, but I was on record with the hotel as a physician. Anxious that my services might be required, I picked up the handpiece. "Stahle here."

"Unlock the door!" ordered an insistent female voice.

"Alex, you can't leave your husband on the bridal night!"

"He's asleep. I'm coming to your room. Let me in."

"No."

"If you do not admit me, I shall bang on the door until you do. Now unlock the door!" She hung up without giving me the opportunity to protest further. A few minutes later, she was pounding on my door. I opened it and pulled her in to avoid waking the other guests on the floor.

"What do you think you are doing?" I scolded.

She wrapped her arms around my neck. "Giving you the *droit de seigneur*. You took my virginity, so you must have me on the wedding night."

I picked her up and carried her to the bed. This sounds heroic, but in fact, Alexandra was slight and easily carried. She untied her dressing gown. Beneath, she was wearing an exquisite nightgown that strategically revealed her beautiful breasts beneath the sheer lace. I was unaccountably nervous and fumbled with the mother of pearl buttons as I freed her from the gown. She, meanwhile, was untying my pajamas. Finally, I lay between her legs while she devoured my mouth. I bit her, but not hard enough to leave marks. She must be unblemished for her husband.

"Come inside me," she begged breathlessly, "Open me!" A few moments later, she produced a shimmering orgasm.

I held her in my arms while she recovered. "This is madness, you know. What will Jonathan think?"

"He won't think anything. He's passed out from whiskey. I left him snoring like a locomotive."

"Was the marriage consummated?"

She laughed merrily. "Of course not. He couldn't rise to the occasion."

"I'm sorry," I said.

"I'm not."

"You know you can't remain here."

She sighed. "Yes, but I wanted one last time with you before you leave."

I kissed her forehead, her eyes, and then her mouth. "Alex, I shall always love you," I said, caressing her face.

"I know and that's why you'll let me stay with you tonight."

She sounded so young. In the faint light from the doorway, her eyes were wide with anxiety. "You're fearful of consummating the marriage," I guessed.

"Yes, of course. It's very large. Bigger than I expected."

"I thought you said he couldn't rise to the occasion."

"He did for a moment…but fortunately, it didn't last."

"When it comes to the bedchamber, alcoholic excess is no man's friend." She snuggled closer to me. "Men are beasts, and they smell!"

I laughed. "Yes, they do smell. But beasts can be tamed if you have the patience."

"I suppose they can. I tamed you."

She made love to me tenderly. Afterwards, I tried to send her back to her room, but she refused to leave. "All right, but you may only stay until dawn and then you must go." She nodded. I rang the desk clerk and asked him to ring me at five.

When I returned to bed, Alexandra curled into the arch of my body and pulled my arm around her waist. She fell asleep, breathing so lightly I could barely detect the rise and fall of her chest. But sleep eluded me. While I lay awake, I took in the warm fragrance of Alexandra's dark hair, hoping to inhale its scent into memory.

When the telephone rang a few hours later, I urged my sleepy companion to rise. I helped her into her dressing gown, holding the sleeves and putting her arms into them as if I were dressing a child.

"Kiss me," she begged in a whisper. I kissed her forehead and laid my open hand on her cheek. "No, kiss me!" she demanded. "I shall never know love again when you are gone."

"Oh, Alex. Don't be so dramatic!"

She pouted fetchingly, so I kissed her lips, but she clung to me and wouldn't let go. Gently, I untangled myself from her arms and escorted her down the hall.

Fortunately, the door to the bridal suite was unlocked. Loud snoring emanated from the dark room. Alexandra gave me one last, pleading look before I nudged her into the darkness.

When I returned to my room, I called for strong coffee because my head ached, not from too much alcohol, but from lack of sleep and sadness. I drank the coffee slowly, while I dully watched the maid pack my luggage.

After she left, I sat down at the vanity to put on my makeup. As I studied myself in the mirror, I noted the faint lines at the corner of my eyes and the little, permanent furrow between my brows. I felt ancient, a dusty old woman. In fact, I was only thirty-three years old. I didn't know it yet, but my life was only beginning.

A single tear ran down my cheek, leaving a glistening trail in the face powder. I searched my eyes one last time before forcibly banishing the moody thoughts from my mind. As I padded on more powder, I gave myself a stern order to embrace the day.

Books by Elena Graf

PASSING RITES SERIES

THE IMPERATIVE OF DESIRE

A coming-of-age story that takes a brilliant aristocratic woman from La Belle époque through a world war, a revolution that outlawed the German nobility, and the roaring twenties to the decadent demimonde of Weimar Berlin.

OCCASIONS OF SIN

For seven centuries, the German convent of Obberoth has been hiding the nuns' secrets—forbidden passions, scandalous manuscripts locked away, a ruined medical career, and perhaps even a murder.

LIES OF OMISSION

In 1938, the Nazis are imposing their doctrine of "racial hygiene" on hospitals and universities. Margarethe von Stahle has always avoided politics, but now she must decide whether to remain on the sidelines or act on her convictions.

ACTS OF CONTRITION

After the fall of Berlin, Margarethe is brutally assaulted by occupying Russian soldiers. Her former protégée, Sarah Weber, returns to Berlin with the American Army and tries to heal her mentor's physical and psychological wounds.

THE HOBBS SERIES

HIGH OCTOBER

Liz Stolz and Maggie Fitzgerald were college roommates until Maggie confessed their affair to her parents. When Maggie breaks her leg in a summer stock stage accident, she lands in Dr. Stolz's office. Is forty years too long to wait for the one you love?

THE MORE THE MERRIER

Maggie and Liz's plans of sitting by the fire, drinking mulled wine, and watching old Christmas movies get scuttled by surprise visits from friends and family.

THIS IS MY BODY

Professor Erika Bultmann, a confirmed agnostic, is fascinated by Mother Lucy, the new rector of the Episcopal Church, especially when she discovers Lucille Bartlett was a rising opera star before mysteriously disappearing from the stage.

LOVE IN THE TIME OF CORONA

Police Chief Brenda Harrison shows an interest in Liz's biracial PA, but first Cherie needs to get past her loathing for all law enforcement since a state trooper shot and killed her sister.

THIRSTY THURSDAYS

Liz Stolz initiates Thirsty Thursdays, a weekly cocktail party on her deck, so her friends can socialize safely during the pandemic. Pretentious, overbearing Olivia Enright pursues Liz's friend, architect Sam McKinnon, and tries to push her way into the tight-knit group.

THE DARK WINTER

Erika hires Sam to build a soundproof practice room for Lucy. Fortunately, the early Christmas gift is ready before tragedy strikes. As the women of Hobbs pull together to help a beloved friend deal with her loss, the dark winter brings tension and realignment in their small community.

SUMMER PEOPLE

Melissa Morgenstern, a high-profile lawyer from Boston, is spending the summer with her widowed mother. She's doing some trust work for Liz who introduces her to the attractive Courtney Barnes, Hobbs Elementary's new assistant principal. The arrival of Susan, Lucy's ex, complicates her deepening relationship with Liz.

STRANDS

Cherie hears her biological clock ticking and would like to start a family. When a shocking tragedy creates an opportunity for her and Brenda to become parents, their friends need to step up to make it happen.

THE RECTOR'S WEDDING

The sudden opportunity for Lucy to return to her singing career throws everything in her life into doubt—her vocation as a priest, her settled life in Hobbs, even her upcoming marriage to the woman she loves.

THE VANISHING BRIDGE

Rev. Susan Gedney tries to rebuild trust after her humiliating exit from Hobbs. Bobbie Lantry always needs to rush away to take care of a mysterious elderly woman. They need to share their secrets, but do they dare?

EXTENDED CAPACITY

A small town in Maine wakes up thinking it's just another winter day, but a tragedy has been set in motion by dark secrets from the past and an unfortunate series of recent events. The horror that every town fears is about to come to Hobbs.

About the Author

Elena Graf has published four historical novels set in twentieth-century Europe. Two of the titles in the Passing Rites series have won Golden Crown Literary Society and Rainbow awards for best historical fiction. In addition to the Passing Rites, she's written a series of contemporary novels set in a small town in Maine,

She pursued a Ph.D. in philosophy but ended up in the "accidental profession" of publishing, where she worked for almost four decades. She lives in coastal Maine.

Find out about events and new books at her website, www.elenagraf.com. You can write to Elena at elena.m.graf@gmail.com. Or find her on Facebook.

Elena is a member of iReadIndies, a collective of self-published independent authors of Sapphic literature. Please visit our website at www.iReadIndies.com for more information and to find links to the books published by our authors.

Milton Keynes UK
Ingram Content Group UK Ltd.
UKHW041410080224
437504UK00008B/18

9 781953 195005